The Critics Cheer, "Amen!"

"An important book about the kind of person who makes this country work. It is a book that should be read."
—*Boston Globe*

"The book has humor and life and death. It's a helluva book. But why shouldn't it be? It was written by a helluva writer."
—*Newsday*

"Hard-edged, unflinching, and difficult to put down . . . Breslin has brawled his way past all the barriers between journalism and a truly exceptional novel. The result is, by any standard, his sweetest victory."
—*Newsweek*

"Steamroller of a novel . . . Breslin's vignettes of blue-collar life in Queens are razor-sharp classics; and he renders old-country life with the fresh eye of a discoverer."
—*Publishers Weekly*

"WORLD WITHOUT END, AMEN is a stark, mean story, the strongest thing Jimmy Breslin has done. I wish there were something I knew as well as Breslin knows the people of Queens."
—*CBS Radio*

"Disciplined prose, rich detail, a marvelous gift for dialog, insight, decency and—because he's never without it—wild humor. It has a plot, believe it or not, and characters who interest us as people . . . Breslin should no longer be thought of as a newspaperman trying to write novels. He is a novelist, and a damn fine one."

—*Los Angeles Times*

"Powerful . . . Mr. Breslin has written a taut and gripping novel in a style that reflects the no-nonsense work he has done as a journalist."

—*Houston Chronicle*

"The achievement is large and rich and rewarding."

—*Washington Post Book World*

The Critics Cheer,

"AMEN!"

JIMMY BRESLIN
WORLD WITHOUT END, AMEN

AVON
PUBLISHERS OF BARD, CAMELOT, DISCUS, EQUINOX AND FLARE BOOKS

AVON BOOKS
A division of
The Hearst Corporation
959 Eighth Avenue
New York, New York 10019

First Avon Printing, September, 1974.

AVON TRADEMARK REG. U.S. PAT. OFF. AND
FOREIGN COUNTRIES, REGISTERED TRADEMARK—
MARCA REGISTRADA, HECHO EN CHICAGO, U.S.A.

Printed in the U.S.A.

For the former Rosemary Dattolico

prologue

You would never know you were in New York City if you stand on the beach in the late afternoon at Rockaway. It is a twenty-minute drive from the cement and El noise of 109th Place in Richmond Hill, where Dermot Davey lives. And it is only fifteen minutes from the terminal at Kennedy Airport. In actual distance, Rockaway Beach is only a couple of hundred yards from the tip of the runways at Kennedy. There are busses in Rockaway and a subway train to Brooklyn and Manhattan which comes through Rockaway on elevated tracks. Rockaway is only two blocks wide, with a bay on one side and the Atlantic Ocean on the other. If you stand on the beach by the ocean in the winter, the way Dermot did through the days of the winter in 1970, you would think you were in Montauk, never in Queens, in New York City.

Between waves, the pilings at the end of the wooden jetty rose out of the water three or four feet, three poles shining black from the ocean water, their tops coated with ice. The waves broke with a clapping sound before they reached the pilings, and the pilings were covered by tumbling white water. Far out, much farther out than where the others began, one big wave began to form. It was pulling itself together, sucking up water, swelling and rising high into the cold wind. It was the biggest wave he had seen in months. The wave was still climbing when it reached the end of the jetty. This time the pilings disappeared into a wall of green water. The wave grew faster and stronger, climbing into a threat. Dermot Davey stood on the sand, wanting to see the wave come up onto the beach and drag the rest of the ocean with it and then never stop. Come flooding across the beach where he was standing and go on through Queens, with the bottom of the water grabbing at the ground like big wet hands, pushing in foundations, tipping apartment houses, pulling up El pillars, grabbing thick trees. Then carry everything, cars from the streets, houses from the foundations, carry them all into Manhattan and break the place apart and drown it and keep going and never stop. Let me see, Dermot said to himself, how the world can stand up to one simple ocean wave that decides to keep going.

The beach was empty, not even a dog running on it, and the sun was gone for the day, leaving big streaks of pink in the winter sky. The wind was cold and heavy with moisture. It was getting ready to snow again. When the wind gusted, it came along the beach like a hand sweeping a table, throwing the sand up in swirls and blowing it in sheets into the shallow water.

The top of Dermot's wave became white and began to curl over, forming a tube of water which was too much for the body of the wave to carry. The wave collapsed, first with a clap, then with a thud which turned into a booming sound which probably could be heard for blocks. Fingers of water ran up in the sand. They were not the strong fingers Dermot wanted wrapped around the buildings, shaking them until they fell. These were just narrow little puddles of water moving towards Dermot's shoes. He turned away from the water and walked up the beach. The houses which fronted on the beach had their lights on in the late afternoon. The lights showing in the picture windows made the beach seem lonelier and colder. Bright white lights in a picture window reminded him of Christmas. He felt bad enough for Christmas.

He had to be to work at midnight. The idea made him uneasy. Everything made him uneasy. He was young and he did not like one hour of one day of one week of his life.

1:

His name was Dermot Davey and he was twenty-nine
and during this time he was a member of the Bow and
Arrow Squad of the Police Department of the City
of New York. If he was called upon to defend himself
or to apprehend a perpetrator, Dermot Davey, or any
of his fellow squad members, would have to put an
arrow in your heart. When department officials locate
a man they feel is too unstable to carry a gun, thus
dangerous to the public, they relieve him of all arma-
ments and assign him to units known, in police talk,
as Bow and Arrow Squads. Which is what Sergeant
John O'Donnell—Johno everybody calls him—kept talking about all through a gloomy Saturday night he spent
with Dermot Davey in the dormitory building on the
corner of Straight Street and Narrow Street in Paterson,
in New Jersey.

The building was once a brewery owned by Dutch
Schultz, the gangster. Now it is very important to the
New York Police Department. It is the place where
alcoholic cops—piss bums they call them in the precinct—go to dry out. The place is run by Catholic
priests. No one ever has heard of a rabbi opening a
building for alcoholics. The Paterson City Council
named the street in front of the building Straight Street
and the side street Narrow Street. This gives policemen
in New York many chances for humorous remarks. Besides piss bums, civilians use the place too. The first

13

time Johno was put into Straight and Narrow he had a man next to him who looked like a gray prune. When the gray prune woke up a day later he told Johno that he was a senior pilot for Pan American. He had identification. He told Johno about good places to get drunk all over the world. After that, Johno began taking his kids out to Kennedy Airport a lot. He told them they were going to see a lot of plane crashes.

Anybody who gets lugged over to Straight and Narrow has the guns he owns taken from him and locked up at Police Headquarters. The other police regard a man not carrying a gun as half a man. I might as well go around without a prick, Dermot Davey said to himself, after handing in his guns. He would not be around another policeman for more than five minutes when the policeman would say, "I see they took it away from you."

Straight and Narrow is part of the program run out of a building in lower Manhattan. Monsignor Carrigan, a department chaplain, is in charge. Each day he and his staff go over the sick reports watching for men with chronic absences because of gastritis or intestinal flu. Picking out Dermot was like finding Africa. The records showed he had gone sick on five occasions when he was due to return to duty after having forty-eight hours off. The Monsignor was very warm and understated when Dermot came in. A smile, a clap on the shoulder. The Monsignor had Dermot sit down with a clerk. There was a form for Dermot to fill out. The form had twelve questions to it. "You don't have to fill out the form if you don't want to," the clerk said. He looked over his shoulder toward the Monsignor as he said this.

"Oh, of course you don't have to fill it out if you don't want to," the Monsignor said.

Dermot began reading. At first he was going to put "no" after every question. The first one to catch his eye was "Do you find yourself desirous of alcoholic beverages upon arising?" That did not mean much to Dermot. A beer or something in the morning, or when

14

you get up in the middle of the day after working midnight-to-eight shift, what difference does that make? When he looked at another question, he had to think. It said, "Do you suffer blackouts from social drinking?" He was afraid not to answer it.

Dermot was sent to the department property clerk to turn in his guns. He was assigned to a group of policemen under thirty who were to meet in the Counseling Unit offices on Tuesday nights for lectures. On the job, he was reassigned from patrolman to file clerk in the office where they keep motor-vehicle records. At this time, in the spring of 1970, there were seventeen hundred New York policemen on special duty, working as elevator operators and clerks. The Monsignor said he was sure there were another seventeen hundred who had not been spotted yet and were highly eligible for special duty. Special duty means no guns. There were in New York at this time about five hundred cases of off-duty policeman discharging guns, mainly in bars. There were fifteen people killed by patrolmen in circumstances which warranted much questioning and some doubts. A policeman in the Bronx was convicted of homicide. "There should be a dozen of them convicted every year," Arnold Friedman, the Bronx District Attorney, said.

In Straight and Narrow there were five days of black coffee and B_{12} shots. And in the day room, called Duffy's Tavern, there were Alcoholics Anonymous pamphlets to read. There was no television or newspapers. The people running Straight and Narrow feel that a man coming in after a bender could spend four days drying out and attending the three lectures each day, and then he could pick up a magazine and see a four-color vodka ad and go berserk. Or he might turn on the television and see all cowboys drinking at the bar. Many times the people in Straight and Narrow are urged, which from the Monsignor is a command, to go up to a health farm at Pine Grove, New York. In precinct conversation the farm is called Piss Bum Pines. It is run by a retired detective. Board at the place is eighty-five dollars a week.

The Counseling Unit advances the money to any police-man who cannot afford to pay for Pine Grove.

When the Monsignor first started his program he had great opposition from older bosses in the department. The chief of detectives, Mike Leary, refused to allow any of his men to enter it. "We got no alcoholics in the detective division," he said. "We only got all good decent men." The Monsignor always makes a point of remarking, "Poor Michael died of cirrhosis, you know."

On the Saturday night in the dormitory, Johno was on the bed next to Dermot. Johno had his hands clasped over the front of a blue robe that would not close. The robe belonged to his wife. Johno's belly is so big that even a wife who has nine children does not wear a robe large enough to cover Johno's belly. Johno lay there and listened to the snoring and mumbling and little shouts in the night of the others in the dormitory. Finally, it became too much for Johno. He jumped out of bed.

"Freeze!" he shouted. "You there! You freeze too! Nobody take a breath. Don't move your hand any-place or you won't be alive. I am Sergeant O'Donnell of the Bow and Arrow Squad. Whoa! Stop! Oh? Try to run off on me, hah?" Johno shaded his eyes like he was the first Indian. He gave his version of a war whoop. "Woowoowoowoowoowoo." He reached over his shoulder to get an arrow out of the quiver. He squinted, bit his tongue, and drew the bow far back. He let the arrow go.

"Kachum! Another D.O.A. Lady, I'm sorry we had to kill your son. But he shouldn't have messed with the Bow and Arrow Squad!"

Once, Johno was both big and strong, but the years and his life have reduced him to a cow, a big shambling man with huge deep eyes that turn fire-red when he drinks. Johno is forty-seven now, and he is up to two hundred eighty pounds and has to be hidden in the precinct basement if somebody from borough head-quarters comes around to inspect the precinct.

The face in the bed next to him raised up from

the pillow. The face was a gray sheet dotted with little red veins snapped off every inch or so by the force of bad habits. The flesh sagged against the cords of his throat. The mouth parted a little. The guy looked like he wanted to scream, but the needle they had given him was too strong. He looked sixty-five, but at the most he was forty. They had brought him over in a squad car, handcuffed so he wouldn't try to grab the wheel and crash the car. The U-Haul Squad, which is in charge of picking up drunk cops and taking them to Straight and Narrow, is always wary of its clients. A young boy, fourteen or so, terrified, his head hanging in shame at the same time, helped the handcuffed father up the steps of Straight and Narrow. The boy had short hair with plenty of machine on the sides. His dark-blue All Hallows School blazer was a little short at the wrists, which showed how quickly he had been growing. The father had just short-circuited the main switchboard at Brooklyn Headquarters on Bergen Street. The father kept seeing cunts coming out of the holes you put the jacks in. He began tearing at the extension cords; after that he got at the wiring behind the switchboard. By the time they had him under control, emergency power had to be used to handle the calls for almost all of Brooklyn.

This was Johno's second trip to Straight and Narrow. Both he and Dermot made it to the building under their own power. The first time for Johno the U-Haul Squad came into his house in the middle of Thanksgiving dinner. Johno was sitting there with his wife and nine kids, the oldest thirteen, and he was making all the young kids laugh because he was eating with a knife. The peas and mashed potatoes kept dropping from the knife onto Johno's belly. Johno had no shirt on and he would rub the food all over his belly. He told the kids, "I can make the food go through my skin and fill up my stomach."

Johno put down the knife, picked up the gun, dipped the barrel into the mashed potatoes, and stuck the gun into his mouth and stared at his wife until she screamed.

17

The U-Haul boys didn't say a word when they walked in. One of them grabbed the pistol. The other two hand-cuffed Johno. They lugged him out of the house. All the kids were screaming and the mother began to cry.

Dermot was on his bed looking at the ceiling. The depression was so deep he could not talk. Just the idea of being in the place, of coming down this far, meant to him that he had lost. He tried to brush it off with a sports score. Life twenty-nine, me zero, he thought. Even that was putting it too lightly, he told himself. He became more depressed when he understood that for a long time now he seemed to have no other way to go.

One night, a year and a half before this, he figured, he had been working a four-p.m.-to-midnight shift in the 125, which is in Glendale, in Queens. He was called off the regular run and told he had to drive the sergeant. When Dermot got to the 125th, here was Johno, roaring, out on the sidewalk.

"Hello, hump," he said. "Let's give these humps something to talk about." He made Dermot put on his sergeant's tunic and he wore Dermot's tunic with the buttons open. Johno switched the radio off and turned on the roof light. They started rushing through the streets, the roof light twirling in the evening darkness, it still was only six o'clock, and they stopped first at the Glen on Myrtle Avenue and Sixty-fourth Place. A guy named Leo, a five-hundred-pound guy, runs the place. When he saw Dermot in the sergeant's tunic, he let out a yell. "I studied hard," Dermot said. Leo clapped his hands. "Christ, but that's great," he said. He went into the refrigerator and came out with a bottle of champagne. He had the bottle uncorked and on the bar when Johno shambled in, wearing Dermot's tunic.

"El Humpo!" Johno yelled.

"Fuck you guys," Leo said. He tried to pull the champagne back. Johno got both hands on it. He lifted it up and chug-a-lugged a third of the bottle.

At eleven o'clock at night, they were coming from Duro's, down at Eightieth Street and Myrtle Avenue.

They were all the way up to the A&P on Sixty-eighth Street, right on the corner with St. Pancras, when Johno saw this kid running along and pushing one of these wire carts from the supermarket. Johno made Dermot pull the car over, and he grunted and lifted himself out. He rolled around the fender and caught the kid. The kid was about twelve. Johno clouted him on the shoulder hard. The cart rolled into the middle of Myrtle Avenue.

"Get that fuck-ing cart," Johno told the kid.

The kid stood there looking at Johno. Dermot could see the kid was afraid of Johno. The kid started to the curb to get the cart. Then the kid dropped his head and took off. Running for the corner, with his young feet beating the pavement. Johno reeled backward, trying to keep his balance. Something made Dermot come scrambling out of the car and onto the sidewalk. Johno had his pistol out. His feet were set and he was down in a military crouch. He had the pistol aimed at the kid's back. Dermot pulled Johno's arm down.

"Get away from me, hump," Johno said.

"Jesus Christ, come out of it," Dermot said.

The kid was around the corner and gone into the night. Johno was still in his military crouch, the pistol out. "Fuckin' hump kid," he said.

Later, when they came in for the night, Dermot said to Johno, "Jesus, what happened to you?"

"You shoulda let me scare the hump," Johno said.

"What 'scare'? You were aiming right at the kid's back."

"Why, you hump, I had the fuckin' thing up in the air. You hump. What do you mean I was aiming it at the hump kid?" Johno was drooling.

And then last year, in 1969, Dermot was working another four-to-midnight shift in the 125. It was a Sunday. The saying in the 125 is that the most commotion in the precinct on a Sunday comes from a German rolling over in bed.

They had the Giants football game on the television

19

in Frenchy's Car Service on Sixty-second Avenue, and Dermot stopped in to watch. Frenchy's cars are radio dispatched and the big fat guy, Patty Rolls, sits at the desk in the storefront with two phones, a radio set, and a television in front of him.

"They got to have all these niggers playing halfback," Patty Rolls was saying. "Look at this yam. What a piece of shit he is, I don't have to tell you. Giants got too many niggers on defense."

On the television there was this one small tangle of hands clawing from one side and elbows hooking from the other and a step or so away from it, Gabriel, the Los Angeles quarterback, beginning to rock on his feet so he could throw.

"There you go, look at this!" Patty Rolls said.

The television showed a big white guy running, his face turning up and the hands coming up past the face and into the air. A black arm was in the picture but the white hands grabbed a ball out of the air and now there was a full picture of the big white guy running with the ball and a little black guy throwing himself at the white guy and missing and the white guy striding into the end zone.

Patty Rolls was yelling. "That fuck-ing spade prick, what do we need them for? That's it! That's the mother-fuck-ing ball game."

He got up and another guy in the room took his seat in front of the radio and phones and television. "We get a drink for a minute," Patty said.

"I don't know, I'm just starting," Dermot said.

"Then start drinkin' too," Patty said.

They went into a doorway that was the back entrance of the Prosit, which has its front entrance out on Fresh Pond Road. Dermot, in uniform, stood at the end of the bar, back far enough so you couldn't see him from Fresh Pond Road. He had a beer. It was cold and the glass was clean and the beer had a taste to it. There are three big breweries in the area and so many workers live in Ridgewood and Glendale, Germans making beer, that the bars wind up with the best beer

20

out of the breweries. Dermot finished the beer and put down his glass for another. The shift he was on, the four-to-twelve, is the worst physical enemy of the Police Department.

He left the Prosit after three beers and walked Fresh Pond Road. He walked up past Pelligrini's without looking in the window. A block away, Dermot turned around and came back to Pelligrini's.

At twelve-thirty a.m., through with his shift, Dermot was back on Fresh Pond Road, out of uniform, with no reason to go right home—his wife Phyllis and the three children would be asleep. Standing on Fresh Pond Road eight hours after he had gone into the Prosit for the first time. His breathing was heavy and when he started to walk he rolled just a little bit. He had short dark-brown hair that was almost black. Blue eyes were narrowed and set well back under dark eyebrows. His nose had been broken once and had a bump in it but was not spread. The skin over the cheekbones was taut. The chin had a little square to it, it could be a tough chin, and the neck flesh under it was firm. The wrestler's bridge. You had to look under his eyebrows into his eyes and see tiny lines of blood to know anything.

He was dressed in the clothes he had worn to church. A dark-blue jacket, blue slacks, white shirt, and a solid blue tie. He had a .32 in a clip holster behind the arch of his back. He liked having it there. That way, when he walked along with a good jacket on, like the one he had on now, there was nothing sticking out on his hip to bulge the jacket and rip the lining if he moved too much. He was five-foot-eleven and he weighed a hundred ninety pounds, fifteen more than he should have. The dark-blue jacket hid the weight very well.

It was twelve-thirty a.m. and he had hours left in the night. He went into the Prosit, through the front door, for a drink.

"Morrison played good," a man of about fifty, with a crew cut, was saying. The man had on a zipper jacket with lettering on the back saying MIRACULOUS MEDAL.

"He should play good," the bartender said. "What the fuck else does he have to do with his Sundays?"

Dermot had a couple of drinks, Scotch and water now. He was alone at the end of the bar by the window. He left and walked up to Pelligrini's. They were talking football in there too. Dermot was tired of it. He walked around the corner and down two blocks to the Swallow's Nest. Young kids were in there, heads rocking, loud guitars coming out of the juke box. Dermot sat in the noise and stared at his drink. He walked out without paying. He went over to the Lounge, under the El station on Myrtle Avenue. Jackie Scannon, from the Steamfitters, was at the bar.

"What's happenin'?" Scannon said.

"Fuck," Dermot said.

"Oh my God, give him a gazzazza," Scannon said to the barmaid.

"What kind of gazzazza?" the barmaid said.

"Scotch," Dermot said.

He went back a step because he had his weight on the feet wrong. He bumped into a short guy with horn-rimmed glasses who was walking to the men's room.

"Look out," Dermot said.

The short guy looked back. He was in a black suit. His hair looked like it had been sculptured.

"Look out what?" he said.

"Guinea," Dermot said.

Jackie Scannon's hand came out to Dermot's shoulder. "Come on, come on, have a gazzazza."

Dermot picked up his drink. He could feel the guy standing there, halfway to the men's room, staring at him.

"Are you a cop?"

"Bet your ass I'm a cop," Dermot said, not looking at the guy.

"So come on in with me and cop my joint."

Dermot pushed himself away from the bar and was in the middle of the floor ready to go after him. And the guy was standing there waiting. Jackie Scannon grabbed Dermot and put him up against the bar and then he went up to the Italian and spoke to him and followed him into the men's room and they came out smiling. The Italian guy walked up to Dermot, his hand out. "Come on, what are we talkin' crazy for?" he said. "We're supposed to have charity."

"Well don't fuckin' bounce me around," Dermot said.

"Ah, come on," he said.

"Gazzazza!" Jackie Scannon said.

When they finished a drink, the Italian guy pushed three dollars at the barmaid. Dermot stared at him. "All right, boys," the Italian said.

"I'm coming with you," Dermot said.

"Hey, come on," Jackie Scannon said.

"No, I want to take care of this right. I was wrong," Dermot said.

The guy was at the door. "Don't worry about it, pal, I'll see you around, pal."

"No, I'm going with you," Dermot said.

He pulled away from Scannon and went outside and came alongside the Italian with the black hair.

"I'm sorry I was a ballbreaker," Dermot said.

The Italian guy threw his right arm around Dermot's shoulder as they walked along. "Don't worry about it."

Dermot put his left arm around the Italian guy's waist.

"I just want you to know I had the fresh fuckin' mouth," he said.

"Don't worry about it, pal," the Italian said. His leather heels sounded on the pavement.

"I'm going to shoot you," Dermot said.

The Italian guy dropped his right arm from Dermot's shoulder.

"I'm going to walk you around this corner and I'm going to put a hole in you so fuckin' big that I could reach in and pull out your heart," Dermot said.

"You talk crazy," the Italian said.

Dermot tightened his grip on the guy's waist. Dermot's right hand started to come around his back, for the .32 in the clip holster behind the arch of his back. The Italian guy got the flat of his right hand against Dermot's side. The Italian guy pushed. Pushed as hard

23

as he could. Dermot went off balance. He still was holding on to the Italian guy's jacket with his left hand and the Italian guy hit him in the face with his right hand. Dermot felt a pain, like a needle going into him, when the Italian's pinky ring cut into his left eyebrow.

Dermot went to the Interlude, where the Italians hang out, looking for the guy. When he described him to the bartender, the bartender said the guy had just left to go up to Tippy's, way up on Myrtle Avenue, into Brooklyn. The bartender gave Dermot some cracked ice wrapped in a bar rag. Dermot held it to his left eye. He told the bartender he was going to get a cab and go to Tippy's.

Dermot woke up at home in the middle of the afternoon. He woke up because he had to throw up. He had been sleeping on his face with his clothes on from the night before. He was leaning over the toilet, waiting for the second heave, when for some reason his right hand went back to the pistol. He was looking down at it and tried to puke past it. The cylinders were empty. Right away, he heaved.

He sat on the top of the toilet seat and tried to put the night before together in his mind. He remembered the music in the Swallow's Nest. He shook his head. What came after that? He remembered the Lounge. Somebody yelling "cop my joint." He saw the Interlude now. Dark, smoky, a rock band in the back. But was that last night, he said to himself, or was it the other time? He ran a hand over his eyes. He felt the crust in his eyebrow. He looked at himself in the mirror. The eyebrow was tufted, dry blood on the dark hair. A small hole, the blood dried to dark red, was in the skin under the eyebrow hair. Blue seeped out of the top of his eyelid and spread down the right side of the eye. Jesus Christ, Dermot said to himself. He was frightened.

He went to work hardly able to walk to the bus because of the nerves. Water was streaming from his eyes. In the locker room in the basement nobody said anything to him out of the ordinary. They hardly looked at the wide Band-Aid Dermot had over his eyebrow. At

24

roll call the sergeant did not mention anything unusual.

On Dermot's first tour of the area, he drove down Sixty-second Avenue and had to stop in the traffic behind a bus which was blocking the way, right in front of Frenchy's Car Service. When Patty Rolls, inside the storefront, looked up from the television and saw Dermot in the squad car, his fat arm waved. He scrambled up from the desk and came lumbering out onto the street. Dermot was terrified. He gagged. He did not have anything in him to throw up. Rolls had him park the car and come inside the storefront.

"Now, I don't want to get you upset. We're all drinkers. I just want to show you."

He took Dermot into the back and tapped the red Coca-Cola machine in the room where the drivers sit while they wait for calls. The red tin machine had bullet punctures in the front. The plaster-board wall alongside the machine had a hole in it.

"You just come in here last night and started fuckin' wingin' away," Patty Rolls said. "I don't know what the fuck you had on your mind. One of the drivers, Billy there, was gettin' a Coke for himself. You never seen him. You fuckin' near belted him out. It's a good thing. It's a good fuckin' thing. Whack a guy out like that. I mean, Jesus Christ, Davey."

Nobody ever heard about the night with the guns. Nothing stronger than missed days showed on Dermot Davey's record. He was put in the Bow and Arrow Squad, with his guns locked up, and then he was let out of the Bow and Arrow Squad, given guns, and returned to regular duty. The record showed he had turned himself in for Bow and Arrow duty. Some policemen are in and out of the Bow and Arrow Squad several times during a career. With Dermot, he was first reassigned from the 125th Precinct to a job handling auto-identification files in Manhattan. After six months of good attendance records on both the job and the weekly alcoholics' meetings, Dermot was given his guns back and returned to duty in the 125th. Six weeks after returning from Bow and Arrow Squad duty, on a Thursday, in January of 1970, Dermot Davey was scheduled to work an eight-to-four tour at the 125th.

Nobody in his house woke Dermot up until seven-thirty. In fact, nobody woke him up at all. He heard his mother-in-law in the kitchen downstairs yelling something to his wife, who must have been in the cellar. Thursday was their day to work together in the house, both apartments, the Daveys' upstairs, and the mother-in-law's downstairs, and for all they cared about anything else, you could drop dead on the kitchen floor and either one of them would pour wax on you.

"Phyl," Dermot called over the banister.

"Oh, my God," his wife's voice yelled up the cellar stairs.

"Well, I mean, what the hell," he said.

She came running up the stairs and looked up at him with one hand over her mouth.

"Don't you know what eight-to-four means yet?" he said.

"I'll drive you. Get ready quick and I'll have a cup of coffee ready and I'll drive you."

"No, it's all right. I have to go to court."

"Oh. Then what's the matter with you? You've got time."

"Yeah, and it costs me five dollars."

"Oh, give it to him. What's the difference? It's worth it this time."

Dermot called the precinct and got Gene McGuire, the clerical man. He told McGuire he was going straight to court. You're supposed to report and turn out with the eight-to-four shift and then leave for court. He asked McGuire to sign him in. McGuire said, "Pleasure." Which it was. You had to give him a five-dollar tip for doing it. A few years ago clerical men got only two dollars for a favor. Now it's a pound.

"Am I going to see you today?" McGuire said.

"Maybe in the afternoon. Maybe. I don't know."

"If you get in here before two o'clock I'd like to see you," he said.

"Do the best I can," Dermot said. Gene McGuire

goes sick two, three times a year on a Thursday afternoon. He gets chest pains. The police surgeons all take Friday, Saturday, and Sunday off. So the soonest Gene gets to see a doctor is Monday. They send him for X-rays. He gives the girl working in the X-ray place a few dollars. She loses the plates. By the time he's finished screwing around, McGuire can get eleven or twelve days out of chest pains in the afternoon.

Dermot took·his time getting dressed and came downstairs at eight o'clock. The wife called up from the basement. "I'm just puttin' some wash in."

"Here, I'll get you a nice cup of coffee," his mother-in-law said.

The front of the stove was lined with Clorox bottles and sprays to clean the stove. When she put a cup of coffee on the table her hands were wet with soap suds and the coffee was lukewarm.

"You got the paper?" Dermot asked her.

"It's a good thing you mentioned it. I was just putting it out."

She went into the garbage can under the sink and came out with the *Daily News*. Coffee grounds were stuck to the front page. The headline said, MILLIONS LOST ON UNWED MA'S. Underneath the big headlines was a picture of Marzullo, a City Councilman, shaking his finger at the Mayor during a confrontation at City Hall.

His wife sat down at the table. "Is that the thing about the day-care centers?" she said.

"I don't know, I didn't read it yet."

"All that money for them," Phyllis said. "What about a day-care center for my children?"

"You said it," her mother said. "We had a day-care center, all right. A day-care center cleaning shit diapers right in this house."

"They had the babies, let them take care of them," the wife said. "Why should we pay?"

"They had the fun too!" her mother said. "Want to have fun in Harlem, that's fine. Just don't ask me to pay for your fun, sister."

"What time did the kids leave?" Dermot asked.

"They ran up to Aunt Grace's house at seven o'clock. You know how they love doing that. Then she walks them to school."

"Is there anything in there about the school?" the wife said.

He had the paper open to the sports section. "I don't know, I didn't notice it," he said. "You can look for it after I'm gone."

"Oh, I don't know if I have time. All I care is that they keep the school just the way it is."

"I heard one whole floor is empty," Dermot said. "I don't think they can keep a whole floor of a school empty."

"Well, it's better empty than filled with a lot of troublemakers."

"Our kids don't even go to the school, what do we care?" he said.

"Because we live on the same block with a school that's paid for with our taxes. And I don't want troublemakers walking around our block."

"Thank God our children don't go there," the mother-in-law said. "Could you imagine poor Tara trying to learn something with these nigger kids shouting in her ear?"

"All I care is my kids learn something and go to college," Phyllis said.

"That's all I care about," Dermot said.

"Well, nothing else counts," the wife said. "And they're going to Catholic schools right through. I don't care, it's the only place to learn. You should have seen when I came out of Dominican Commerical and went for jobs. All these other girls from public schools, they came walking in chewing gum and combing their hair. Imagine that! Thank God for the nuns. And least I knew how to act."

"They make you sit on your ass and pay attention and have a little respect," her mother said.

"I'm going to have one cup of coffee with you and then get going on the house," the wife said.

28

She was wearing an old chenille robe that had a design of blue flowers all over it. She had a big safety pin holding it together in the front. When she stood at the stove you could see on the bottom of the robe this inverted V bloodstain that had dried black.

"Hey, Phyl!" Dermot said.

"What?"

She saw him looking down. She took the hem of the robe and twisted it around the front and looked down at it.

"Oh. Look at me. I have everything in the wash. I don't know where this was. I guess I dug it out of the bottom of the hamper someplace. I got so busy."

She poured herself a cup of coffee. The mother-in-law got busy.

"I wouldn't know when you have a period or when you don't. You couldn't prove it by me."

"Dermot!" She pointed with her eyes at her mother.

"Fuck it, I'm going to work," he said. The two of them jumped like a gun had gone off.

"What can I tell you?" he said. He walked down the hallway, picked his coat off the banister, and went out.

He walked down to Jamaica Avenue and over to 111th Street for the bus. It took ten minutes to get up to Queens Boulevard. You get off by the subway entrances at Kew Gardens, where people take the subway to the city. At the top of one of the subway staircases at Kew Gardens there is a big white statue of a naked warrior standing with a sword in his hand and his foot on a naked woman's neck. The statue used to be over in the city. Right by City Hall. When LaGuardia was the Mayor, he had to look out his window every day and see the statue. One day LaGuardia said, "I have enough big pricks right in this office without having to look out the window." The statue was sent out to Queens. Quite often, lesbians take turns climbing up the statue and sitting on the woman's face.

Dermot walked down Queens Boulevard and went into the coffeeshop across the street from the courthouse. It has a sign in the window saying eggs are forty-four cents. Johno was sitting at the far end of the counter, on the last stool. He was directly under a fluorescent light. He had a bald spot. So he sat there with his hat on. He was the only cop in the place who kept his hat on.

Johno was eating an egg sandwich on a seed roll. He always eats the first half of a sandwich in one bite. He keeps it in the side of his mouth and swallows it as he goes along. He had the *Daily News* open to the sports section. Under his elbow was the brown manila envelope with the evidence for court.

"You watch the Knicks last night?" he said.

"No."

"I watched the Knicks game," he said.

"Good game?" Dermot said.

"Bradley done pretty good." When Johno watches a basketball game, he only sees the white players. The Knicks usually play two of them. If one white guy doesn't have the ball, or if one of them isn't guarding somebody with the ball, Johno doesn't know what's going on in the game. Because he only watches the white guys. Then in the morning Johno only looks up the white guys in the box score. He reads how many shots they took, how many assists they had, the points they got. Sometimes he doesn't even know who won the game.

There was a seat at the other end of the counter, nearest the door. Dermot went down to it. He sat with his elbow hemmed in by the cash register. He ordered coffee and an English muffin. A few feet away, at a long table set against the coffeeshop window, five lawyers sat over coffee and talked with the owner, a bald man with a body consisting of a white apron wrapped around a barrel. The lawyers tripped a small anger cord inside Dermot. One of them had mutton chops turning to white at the bottoms, and the mutton chops ran into the collar of a salmon-pink shirt. Another had very little hair, but it had been so arranged and blown and trimmed by razor that it looked as full and almost as unnatural as a toupee. Another one was wearing glasses that were so thick Dermot tried to make up

30

his mind whether the lawyer looked like a frog or a trout. The one with the thick glasses was short and pudgy and his hair seemed to have been trimmed one strand at a time. Dermot knew the pudgy lawyer's last name. Klein. Klein began talking so loud that Dermot had to listen to him whether he wanted to or not.

"The one kid of mine this morning, he's sixteen, he comes into the bathroom while I'm shaving. He says, 'I got to talk to *you*.' I go really, what about? I keep looking at the mirror shaving. He says, 'I think you're fucking around.' I just keep shaving. Humming while I'm shaving. I go dum dee dee dum do, and he says, 'Yep, I think you're fucking somebody. You can't bull-shit me you're out till three four in the morning on *business*.' I keep the razor moving. Do do dum dee dum. Then what do you think he says? He says, 'Well, I guess it's all right. It relieves the tension at home.' How do you like him. Talking like that at sixteen? Then he says to me, 'Well, of course, if it's only one girl, then I don't know about that. That would be bad. That would mean you're in love with another woman. It would kill Mom.' "

"What did you say to him?" one of the others asked him.

"Nothing," Klein said. "I just kept humming and shaving."

"What did the kid do?"

"He finished talking and went to school."

"You still better watch," one of them said. "Do you remember in *Death of a Salesman* when the son catches the father in the hotel room with a hooker? Remember what that did to the kid? It may be all right for your kid to talk like he does. But it could be a lot different if he found it to be true."

"Not with kids today," the first lawyer said.

"I know, they're so different," the other guy said. "That's why Arthur Miller is as good today as he was twenty years ago. Come off it."

"All I know is I love to fuck my girl friend," Klein said.

A black kid came up to the register. The old woman who takes the money was dumping water into the coffee urn at the middle of the counter. The black kid took a toothpick from the glass alongside the cash register. He stood there with the toothpick hanging from his lower lip.

"Say, my lady," the black kid said.

"One minute please," the old lady said.

"Whose minute you play with?" The toothpick worked up and down. He was wearing a black leather jacket, a real good jacket. Dermot's leg began pumping under the counter. An old black woman came up behind him. She was wearing a thin cloth coat. Bet me it had half the warmth of the kid's leather jacket. She went through her cracked purse and came out with a dollar.

"Say, my lady, le's go," He was tapping his fingernails on the top of the cash register.

"Henry," the black woman said.

"Henry, my ass. Hey, old lady, le's go."

The woman came down to the cash register. She was drying her hands on the front of the apron. The hands were scalded. When the mother got her change, the kid walked ahead of her to the door. There was no way not to notice his cowboy boots, boots with the thickest soles you ever saw. Had to cost fifty dollars for low. The kid swung the door open and went out. The mother shuffled behind him. She had her head down while she put the change into her purse. The door swinging back hit her.

"You see that?" the counterlady said.

Dermot paid for the coffee and muffin and went through the door. Outside, the sidewalks were wet from the rock salt which had melted the snow during the night. At the curb there was a wall of dirty snow—newspapers, and cigar butts stuck in it. The old black woman balanced herself on one foot on top of the pile of snow. The son in his thick boots was already halfway across Queens Boulevard. The old woman steadied herself and stepped down off the pile of snow onto the street. Then she didn't move. Dermot stepped over the top of the snow and here was the old woman standing in a long puddle of black ice water that was up to the top of her shoes. Her stockings were dark with the water. She was almost crying. He jumped over the puddle and turned around and held out his arm. "Let's go, here you are," he said to the woman. She took his arm and came out of the water. "Look at me, now I gots to go all mornin' maybe sittin' like this. I gots to be sick, doin' this."

The mother rolled like a boat when she walked. The wet stockings bunched up on her thick ankles. He got her to one of the traffic islands in the middle of the boulevard, slipped his arm away, and walked by himself.

The son was on the other side of the boulevard already, swaggering along. You could see that he was singing out loud. Nigger is the only person in the world sings going to court, Dermot thought. There was a break in the traffic and Dermot trotted through the last lane and came onto the sidewalk. The kid stopped to light a cigarette. Dermot was walking up almost behind him now. The sidewalk in front of the courthouse was empty. It gets like that on a cold morning. One minute a bus comes and there are a hundred people running into the courthouse. After that, there might be nobody. The kid had his cigarette lighted. He was starting to walk again. He still hadn't turned around to see where the mother was. Dermot took one big step and was walking right behind him. He hit the kid in the space between the bottom of his Brillo hair and the collar of his leather jacket. The Brillo head went flying forward and he fell down. Dermot didn't look. He just walked fast, as if nothing had happened, and turned into the courthouse. The room where the police check in is just inside the entrance. He went into the corner of the room and sat at a desk and picked up a *Daily News* and put his face into it. The room was filled with cops signing in. The rules are you have to be all signed in and sitting in the courtroom at nine-thirty. It was nine now.

"Who can I report?"

Dermot put the paper closer to his face.

"Report what, ma' am?" one of the cops said.

"My son just got hit by a cop."

"What do you mean, he just got hit?"

"Jes' outside the courthouse. No reason at all, this cop hits my son right in the back of the head. I was walkin' right behind and I could see it. Henry! Come in here, Henry. You tell the man, Henry."

"Man hit me from behind and knocks me down."

"Now wait a minute," another of the policemen said. "You say it happened right outside here?"

"Right outside."

"And you saw it?"

"Yes, I did. I was walking right behind my son."

"And it was a policeman in uniform?"

"No."

"Well then how do you know this man was an officer?"

"He come in here."

"Here? In this room?"

"Yes, he did. I see him just as he turn in."

"Well, lady, many people come in here. Do you see him right now?"

Everybody in the room was moving around. Somebody called out excuse me and left. Another guy said excuse me very loud and walked out.

"Tell me, did anybody else see this man who struck your son?"

"No."

"Nobody else?"

"Uh uh."

"But you know this man who struck your son when you see him?"

"Sure do."

"How do you know?"

"He cursed at me 'cross the street by the luncheonette."

"He cursed at you?"

"Sure did. He try to get past me on the street and when I don't move fast enough he call me a bad name."

"What bad name did the officer call you?"

34

"Double motherfucker."

"What?"

"Yes, he did. He call me that and then he hit my son."

"Now wait a minute. All right? That's no language for a lady."

"I don't say that. The cop the one call me that."

"Say, what time is it getting to be? What brings you to court today anyway?"

"Judge Levine courtroom," the mother said.

"What for?"

"Somethin'."

"What something?"

"Somebody say that he take a television out of an apartment."

"Oh, he's here for housebreaking?"

"He not. The superintendent tries to say so. Henry nowhere near that day."

"But you still have to be in court for this today?"

"Uh huh."

"Any bail on your case?"

"Five hundred."

"Five hundred? Well Jesus, lady, what are you doing here? You better get right into court so they don't mark you missing. If they do that, they'll revoke the boy's bail. You can lose five hundred just standing here. You go to the courtroom right now and when you're through you come back here and we'll have the complaint forms ready for you."

"Right back here?"

"Right back here."

"All right."

After they left the room, the cop said, "Whoever did it better get the hell out of here."

Dermot dropped the paper and ran to the door. The guys all laughed. "Dinge'll be rubbin' his neck all day," the lieutenant who runs the room said.

The hallway was so crowded you couldn't see to the other end. The building's smell was a thick municipal small. Disinfectant, cigarette smoke, overcoats against radiators, green cleaning dust, folded newspapers, hair tonic. The only ones laughing in the hallway were policemen. The rest of the noise, all up and down the hall, was made by a lot of people making a lot of little noise. A lawyer near Dermot, a sharp guy in a three-piece suit, started backing away from a family group. "I have to be upstairs in Part Six for a few minutes and then I'll be back. Just go in and sit down and if they call you, go up and say your lawyer is in another part and he'll be right down." An old woman in a black kerchief said, "But why can't you. . . ?" The lawyer was gone already. That's all you hear from the families, "But why can't you. . . ?" The old women stand in the hallway and their faces are pouchy gray. The younger ones, the girl friends and wives, talk in whispers and bite their lips when they don't talk. The guys they come for, the defendants, smoke cigarettes and bitch that they even have to be in court. "For bullshit," they keep saying. Always bullshit. A holdup. Bullshit. Grand larceny. Bullshit. Assault. Bullshit. Dimes binged in the pay phones.

The floor was covered with newspapers already and shoe heels made a scraping sound when they caught the newspapers. Dermot stood outside the doorway to the police room and looked down at his cigarette. At nine-thirty he went into the courtroom, Part Three. He sat in the front row. The room was crowded. Johno was standing at the table with the Assistant District Attorney, Carty. The Assistant was starting to read the complaint. While Dermot stood alongside them, he looked around and saw these two kids in the third row. Twins. Cuomo was their name. They had on dungaree jackets. One of them had his hair down over his ears. He didn't look as bad as the brother. The brother had hair all over his shoulders. The mother was sitting with them. She had a knitting-mill face.

The hearing was to determine if there was enough evidence to have a trial against the twins. They wouldn't plead to a possession of. It's like spitting, but they wouldn't plead. They wanted to go to bat on the case. The judge came in. Curtin, a big fat guy with a sunburn you get at night. He used to be an assistant district attorney. The bridge man had a long calendar to call out. When they came to the twins' case, the judge put it off until the afternoon. Which didn't bother Dermot. He had the day to stand in the hallway and talk with guys he knew, go for a cup of coffee, get the afternoon paper, hang out. In the hallway he saw the Cuomo mother looking nervous on the phone. She was probably calling her job to tell them how she wouldn't be able to come in for the afternoon either.

It was almost a quarter after three in the afternoon before they got to the twins. Carty, the Assistant District Attorney, called Johno up before the case came on. Then he called Dermot. He was going over the complaint sheet. "No," he said to Johno, "it doesn't say so here."

"All right then," Johno said. "Dermot, don't say anything about the money because you don't have nothin' about money written up in the complaint."

"I never said anything about money," Dermot said.

"Your partner here told me that you saw one of the defendants get five dollars passed to him and then he passes the marijuana to the buyer."

"Yeah, well, you see," Johno said.

"All I see is what you have on paper. All I care about is that you don't go one inch past what you state in the complaint."

"It's all right," Johno said.

"Just make sure."

On this arrest, Johno had gotten out of the car and done everything himself. Dermot never even saw what was going on. Johno came back to the car and threw the twins in the back of the car. The minute they got back to the precinct Johno started whining. He had forgotten that he had to pick up his wife at his sister's. That was way out on Long Island, in Commack. It takes seven or eight hours sometimes, when a policeman arrests somebody. Defendants have to be taken for fingerprinting and photos and then to court for the arraignment. To avoid this, Johno talked Dermot into putting Paltrolman Davey down as the arresting officer. Johno went home. Dermot had to stay making out papers and getting the twins to court for arraignment on a case he never knew anything about.

Now Carty had the envelope with the evidence open. He was reading the report from the Police Laboratory. Johno looked over his shoulder. He came flopping over to Dermot.

"They'll shit," he whispered.

"So?"

"They found something else in there besides marijuana."

"What?"

"I don't know, some long thing. I just see it on the report."

Dermot went over to have a look. "Did you know about this?" Carty said to him.

"What?"

"They found a drug called phencyclidine mixed in with the marijuana."

"What is it?"

"I think it's what they call angel dust. I don't know. I know that it makes this different. It's listed as a dangerous drug. I have to go upstairs and ask them what they want to do about it. I don't think I'm allowed to handle it just like another marijuana case."

"They must of got it off some guy home from Vietnam," Johno said.

"I'm talking only to the arresting officer," Carty said.

"I don't know anything about it," Dermot said.

"That's exactly right. You don't know anything except what you have sworn to on this complaint."

When the case was called, the attorney for the kids and Carty and the judge were talking up at the bench. The lawyer turned around and whispered to the mother and the two kids. The kids came out of their chairs together.

"He's lyin'!" one of them yelled.

"He wasn't even there!" the other one said.

38

The attorney got a hand on each of their shoulders and pushed them down.

Dermot sat in the front row and looked straight ahead. He didn't move. When your body moves in a courtroom it always gives something away. It wasn't easy, because Johno had started the whole thing. He got out of the car and ran over to the kids and started the hassle. Dermot never asked him, but it figured he'd put the sticks of shit on them. But where did Johno get the sticks with this drug, whatever the hell it was, in the marijuana. Could they move the thing up to a felony on these kids? Well, it was too late for that now.

Johno leaned over. "They deserve it. Look at the two of them. Did you ever see such walking shit in your life?"

The judge said something and Carty called Dermot and told him to take the stand.

Carty asked him to tell about the arrest.

"While I was on patrol in my sector at eight-thirty in the morning I observed the two defendants in front of seventy-twenty-two Sixty-seventh Place. They were in an automobile. The doors were open. One defendant sat in the front seat, the other in the back seat. I was driving slowly along Seventieth Avenue when I observed a group of young boys and girls around the open doors of the automobile. I slowed my car down. I observed one of the young boys stepping up to the open car door, the front door, and then after a very short time walking away. I became suspicious. I stopped the patrol car and got out. The young people at the curb quickly dispersed. The Cuomo twins were in the car when I came up. One in the front, one in the back. Immediately I detected the odor of marijuana. Immediately I advised them of their rights. I then asked the defendants to empty their pockets. When they did so, on the ground, at their feet, I observed four marijuana cigarettes, two of which apparently had recently been snuffed out. They made no statement to me. I placed them under arrest."

The two kids were sliding all over the bench. The pros

never move. They sit there and they don't even blink when you do it to them. Amateurs like these two kids start twisting around. The mouth always open. One of them slapped himself in the face and grabbed his hair.

The defense attorney got up. A thin guy, his hair half gone, he was dressed in one of these tight suits. The kind that have only half a jacket and big patch pockets. A foreign suit.

He said, "Officer, did you have a warrant for this arrest?"

"The defendants were holding the marijuana in their hands and I could see them bringing it to their mouths."

"You could see," he said.

"Yes."

"And how far away were you that you could see this so well?"

"I was approximately fifteen feet from one defendant and seventeen feet from the other."

"You're certain of this?"

"Yes."

"Are you always so conscious of distance? Do you look at people and say to yourself, Well, he is twelve feet away from me and the woman is fourteen feet away from me? Are you always conscious of this?"

"When I am on duty I am trained to observe things in many ways," Dermot said.

"And at that distance you could recognize the defendants were smoking pot and not ordinary cigarettes?"

"Yes."

"And what told you this? By the length of the cigarette? Or the thickness? Or was it by the color?"

"I recognized it by the smell when I got out of the car."

"Oh, but you couldn't tell this at first?"

"I presumed it was marijuana."

"I see."

He turned and walked away. He went up the aisle. He stopped and held up a pack of cigarettes.

"Tell me, officer, what brand is this?"

40

"I don't know, but light one of them and if it is pot I will know it."

"And you could tell it was pot they were smoking?" the lawyer said.

"Certainly. I have been trained. I consider myself thoroughly familiar with this sort of thing."

"And you also could tell the presence of phencyclidine in the cigarette?"

"No, I only could detect the marijuana smell."

"And when did you learn of the presence of phencyclidine."

"The report from the laboratory."

Dermot got off the stand and sat down. Johno whispered, "That's it." Like he had something to do with the testimony.

"You done it to them good," he said.

Dermot put his mouth to Johno's ear. "Where did you get the butts from?"

He shook his head. "In Ridgewood. Who the fuck knew what was in them."

"Well, what if it's trouble?"

"Oh, fuck them. Look at them. Did you ever see such walkin' shit in your life?"

They set a new date for February 11. Johno and Dermot went through the door in the courtroom wall to the pens behind the courtroom. The place is a long hallway with tan tile walls, block glass windows, and great big detention pens with green bars. Sometimes as many as fifty guys can be fitted into one of the pens. Now it was so late in the afternoon that only a few guys were in them. Three women prisoners sat on a bench just outside the detention pens. A matron stood over them. Johno and Dermot had a cigarette.

One of the women on the bench, a white woman, an older woman, her head gray, said, "Hey," to Johno.

"That's it," the matron said.

"I'm talking to the bulls, nothin' the matter with that. Hey, you."

"Yeah?" Johno said.

"What'd you move us for? I spent all day gettin' used to the bench at the other place."

"Lady, I got nothin' to do with you."

"Ain't you two fellas from the one twelve?"

"No."

"Oh, I thought you was two of the bulls we seen at the one twelve."

"I can tell you one thing about the bench you're sitting on," Johno said.

"What?"

"After this they all get soft. Tonight'll be the softest one of them all. A matress in the Women's House." Johno laughed. "The Women's House," he said. He laughed some more.

"Shit on that," the woman said.

"The Women's House." He kept laughing.

"Shit on that."

A black woman, a tall black woman with lips that stuck out, leaned out so she could see past the matron. "Say officer . . ."

"A courteesian from the Third World," Johno said.

"Come on, off'cer."

"Come on, what?" Dermot said.

"Come on, give me a cigarette."

"Sure," Dermot said and took the cigarette out of his mouth and handed it to her. Johno started to laugh.

"Thank you," she said.

"Don't mention it," Dermot said.

She ripped the filter off the cigarette and dropped it onto the floor.

"What'd you do that for?" Dermot said.

"Well, you had it in *your* mouth."

She closed her eyes and took a big drag on the cigarette.

When they got on the street, it was five after four. They walked up Queens Boulevard to Moran's. The glass door to the bar was locked. Moran's is a night joint, an Irish kid joint, and it still was early for him to be open. They stood on the little brick stoop under the canopy and Dermot tapped a quarter against the glass

42

door. The old porter came to the door. He put his hand over his eyes to see out. When he saw the shield, he let them in.

Moran, the owner, looked out of an office at the end of the bar.

"Be right with you fellas. Lou, give these gentlemen a drink, will you please, Lou?"

The bartender was slicing oranges and lemons down at the far end. He put down the paring knife and came over. They ordered Scotch and water. Johno put a five-dollar bill on the bar. When Moran came out of the office and sat down with them, that meant the bartender wouldn't be taking Johno's money. Moran used to be on the job himself. He worked narcotics in Manhattan.

"Luck, fellas," Moran said.

"Luck," Johno said.

"I don't know what makes me mention luck," Moran said. "What I really want to do, I really want to fuckin' kill myself."

"Bad?" Dermot said.

"I got murdered by Dallas."

"That was a tough game to lose, too."

"Yeah, well you see, you think you know and you really don't know."

"What a shame," Johno said. "I thought that Brewster got all the money for you when he made that run."

"So did I," Moran said.

"What a shame," Johno said. On Sunday he had rooted like a bitch against Dallas. He hates Dallas because once he saw the coach, Landry, on the television at a Billy Graham revival meeting. Johno can't root for anybody who isn't a Catholic. But for a free whisky, Johno will say anything.

"You know what hurt you Sunday?" Johno said.

"Losing," Moran said.

"Uh huh. Yeah, that's right. That hurts. But do you know what helped you lose? The nigger cornerbacks. Why do they use niggers as cornerbacks?"

43

"What are you going to do?" Moran asked. "The sport is full of niggers."

"Yeah, but you see what they do. They jump in then they jump back, then they come all the way up again. Quarterback like Unitas, he called an automatic right at the line and caught the nigger Dallas was using. Caught him comin' in and threw the bomb right over his fuckin' head. That's what really killed you."

"Yeah, well you see, sometimes you just do the best you can."

"I have to agree with you," Johno said.

They had another drink. Moran started talking about the races.

"You seen how that Woodhouse's kid rides fillies?" he said. "Geez, the old man was the best jock for a young filly in the world. Now the kid comes along and he's just as good."

"I have to agree with you," Johno said.

"What the hell do they have?" Moran said. "They must have some way with young fillies. It's in the touch, I guess."

"I tell you," Dermot said. "I think he wins with a lot of young fillies because he rides a lot of good young fillies that win. I think it's as simple as that."

"Never," Moran said. "He got to have a touch. Some little touch that fillies respond to."

"I have to agree with you," Johno said.

Dermot never argued with a guy buying drinks. He took another one and walked over to the doorway with the drink in his hand. The mother and the twins were standing in front of the place talking with the lawyer before he went down into the subway. The mother was doing the talking. The lawyer kept his hands in his overcoat pockets. The mother was too excited to notice the cold. She was talking with both hands. The breath came out of her like smoke. One of her kids started talking. He took his index fingers and used them to push the hair out of his eyes. He did it just like a girl. Pushing the hair and keeping on talking.

Dermot swallowed the rest of his drink and went

back to the bar and put his glass out for another.

"I think you're right," he said to Johno.

"Yeah?"

"They're outside talking with the lawyer. I got to tell you you're right this time."

"Oh, listen, don't worry," Johno said. "Do you think I'd put anybody decent into a jackpot? Don't worry. These two deserve anything they get."

"Junkies?" Moran said.

"I'd say so," Johno said. "Yeah, two junkies. Or about to be junkies. Who the hell cares anyway? Anything you do to a kid who uses narcotics is all right. Anything."

"They infect a whole neighborhood," Moran said.

"Fuck them kids," Johno said. He put his glass down. The bartender gave him another.

"What time is it?" Dermot asked.

"Five o'clock," the bartender said.

"Who cares," Johno said. "Drink."

Moran said he had to go back into the office and do some work. The bartender gave them a drink and didn't take out for it. The bartender began to talk about himself. Johno listened like it was the President.

"I'm working construction one time. We had these brass chits. You got one in the morning and you handed it in at quitting time. They kept track of the time you worked that way. All right. So I used to go home and give it to a guy. I'd go to sleep and at three o'clock the guy would go to the job for me. He'd hand in the brass chit for me and they'd mark it down. Give me credit for the time. So one day the whole cellar caves in. They're goin' crazy diggin' guys out. Everybody had to hand in the brass chits. So they could see if anybody was missing. Well they don't have mine. They start diggin'. Call the police emergency. Call the fire department. I'm home sleepin'. Out like a light. Wound up getting fired."

"That's a pisser," Johno said.

"Wound up gettin' fired," Lou the bartender said. He took a drink. He held the glass, laughing to himself.

"Wound up gettin' fired," the bartender said.

Then he began to talk about how professional football players shouldn't be asked to pay taxes. "What's the difference to the rest of the country?" he said. "What's as important as a good pro football game? Nothing, right? So why not encourage people to play it. Pay them big enormous salaries and don't take no taxes out."

"I have to agree with you," Johno said.

"A thing important like that, we should make sure the caliber of play stays good," Lou said.

The waiters and the other bartenders started coming in for the night. The band, kid musicians with long hair and mustaches, began warming up on the bandstand. One of the loudspeakers made a foggy sound, then the foggy sound became a whine and the whine got louder and began wavering. There was a crash of noise and the band started playing. Moran was saying hello to customers.

Dermot broke a five-dollar bill for drinks. Now that it was business time, Lou was taking the money out. When he leaned over to say something he had just thought about, Johno didn't even come close to listening. Dermot put a second five down and that was gone too. He went to the men's room. When he came back, Johno was standing between two girls who couldn't have been much over eighteen. The girls hunched forward talking to each other, trying to make their backs a wall against Johno. Dermot put his hand out to tap one of them on the arm and by accident hit her drink and spilled it. He started to mop it up with his hand. One of the girls called the bartender. Lou walked over, making a face. Dermot touched the arm of the girl whose drink he'd spilled. She jumped. Lou grabbed Dermot's hand. Moran came down, shouting at Johno. The music was very loud.

Johno must have gotten his car because Dermot was standing out in the cold air under the bright-yellow light coming from the canopy and then he was in the back seat of the car. He had the window a little open and his head against the window. They were at the curb in front of a candy store down in Jamaica. The place stayed open all night selling the papers, the *Morning Telegraph,* mainly, and the *News.* When neither of them came out of the car for a newspaper, a black girl, a tall one, the hips swinging, came out of the candy store and over to them. She bent down with her head cocked on the side and this little smile, the kind when they have something on you.

"Hel-lo," she said. "Oh, I see two of you gentlemen."

"We got a basketball team, you want to play for us?" Johno said. The way he talked gave him away. He was used to coming here. In the summers the sidewalks are so full of black prosses they tackle you right on the street.

"What position you put me at?" the black pross said.

"You look like you could play the pivot," Johno said.

"That isn't what I like to do," the pross said.

"Yeah, and what do you like to do?"

"Suck cock."

"What do you want for making that kind of a shot?"

"For you, daddy. Twenty dollar."

Johno held up the shield to her. "Do I get a discount?"

"Po-leece is my *personal* friends," the pross said. She looked at Johno's shield and smiled and said ten dollars.

A block down from the store Johno was driving with one arm around the black pross. "Say hello to my friend Dermot," he said. The black pross turned around and said, "Hel-lo. My name is Dora." The pross had on so much perfume that Dermot gagged. He put his head out the car window like he was a dog. Then he fell asleep. When he woke up they were in the municipal parking lot a couple of blocks from the candy store. Johno was sitting sideways in the front seat, looking down. Johno was mumbling to the pross and making little sounds. The smell of the perfume was too much. Dermot got out of the car and leaned against it. He was trying to focus on the streetlight at the entrance to the parking lot, but he couldn't. He kept seeing two lights. The glare ran together, watery, and even when he squinted it did not clear up. When he shut one eye he could just see the one light.

The pross was out of the car, crouched down in front of him and he looked at the streetlight and felt the warm mouth all over him. He looked down at the pile of black curly hair. He reached down for the front of her dress. The pross grabbed his hand and held it away. He tried to pull his hand free. The pross wouldn't let go. He gave a yank and got his hand away. He stuck his hand inside the coat and down the front of the dress. The first thing he felt was the shaved hair on the pross's chest.

Dermot started to push the guy away. The head came in on him more, the tongue lapping now. Somewhere, down at the bottom of the whisky, was this huge fear. He pushed the guy on the shoulder again. He was going to get both hands and shove. But now he was warm with pleasure. It made him tremble a little. He had his hand on the guy's shoulder and the hand relaxed and he felt everything release. Right away, the fear exploded inside Dermot. He tried to shove the guy away. But the head was immovable and the tongue was lapping and Dermot pulled his arm back and swung at the guy. He punched down a second time. The black went down onto his side. Dermot kicked. He could feel his toe going full into the stomach. It was the fullest kick he ever had given anybody. Dermot kicked again, this time at the head. The black hair rolled out of the way. Dermot was shouting something and Johno was out of the car now. He came at the black from the side and kicked hard. There was a popping sound as Johno's foot went into the side of the black head.

Dermot was leaning back against the car, trying to focus on the streetlight. Johno had the black guy against the chain-link fence. The fence rang as metal hit it.

"I'll kill this cocksucker!" Johno yelled.

"Put the gun away," Dermot said.

"I said I'd kill the cocksucker," Johno said.

"Just put the fuckin' gun away," Dermot said.

Dermot said it without looking. When he brought his head up, he saw Johno with both hands around the black's neck. "Cigarette!" Johno said. "Give me a fuckin' cigarette!" he shouted. Johno was coughing and heaving with effort. Dermot did not move.

"Light me a fuckin' cigarette!" Johno shouted.

Dermot got out his cigarettes. He missed the cigarette the first time. He had the match too far from it. Then he measured it and got the end of the cigarette into the flame.

Johno took one hand off the black's throat and took the cigarette from Dermot. He held the cigarette between his thumb and forefinger, the other three fingers spread out, and the tip of the cigarette became a little shower of sparks as Johno put the cigarette out on the transvestite's eye. The black shrieked. A loud male voice. Dermot was leaning back against the car, trying to focus on the street-light.

When he drove out of the lot, Johno's face was all twisted up. He was screaming that he should have shot the black. Johno had a handkerchief with blood on it wrapped around his hand. Dermot had his head against the window. He woke up looking at the hardware-store window two blocks from his house.

On the fifth of February Dermot walked into the 125 at three-thirty in the afternoon. He was listed for a four-to-twelve. He didn't even get to the desk. A pink-cheeked fat guy from the Internal Affairs Division stepped right out from the desk and told Dermot he was detailed to him. They drove to a white stone building attached to the Poplar Street house. The pink-cheeked fat guy held the door for him. They went into a room upstairs with six or seven guys in it. Johno was over in the corner. The pink-cheeked fat guy closed the door. There was a mirror on the door. Dermot knew it had to be that the nigger was on the other side of the one-way glass, looking in on them.

The lawyer's name was Nussbaum. He handled most of the tough trials for PBA members.

"If we shot the fuck, we'd be up for a medal," Johno told Nussbaum.

"Well, I don't know if that would be so good either," Nussbaum said.

"Be better than this," Dermot said.

"Suppose you shot him and somebody saw you shoot him?" Nussbaum said. "Let's start talking about where we are now, not where we could be. First, can either of you get any help?"

"A good rabbi," Johno said.

"The only thing better would be two of them," the lawyer said.

Dermot began to think. He knew the people who would know his name would be useless. Johno was talking about captains and inspectors he had known over the years. Dermot knew they would do nothing. Dermot began thinking of the first time he was in Room 615. The Monsignor's gentle handling. The word "confession" ran into his mind. That was one thing Dermot had learned forever in grammar school. Always go to a priest and tell him you did wrong. The priest would be almost elated. And he would immediately look to help. Whenever Dermot was in trouble with the nun in class, he would go to one of the priests and tell him something. Tell him anything. Once, he told the priest he had been stealing things. The priest patted him and went to the nun in Dermot's class. For weeks, the nun let Dermot get away with almost anything. Dermot remembered this. He began to think about the Monsignor. He mentioned to Nussbaum that both he and Johno had been in the Counseling Unit.

"Gold," Nussbaum said.

"That good?" Johno said.

"The only thing he could do for you is save your life," Nussbaum said. "Let me tell you, I had a Puerto Rican woman claiming she was pregnant by one of the men. The Puerto Rican had a landlady backing up her statement that the policeman came to the house every day and went to this Puerto Rican woman's flat. The man's captain appeared as a defense witness at the departmental trial. Here's what he testified. He said it was impossible for the man to make the woman pregnant because the man was a good Roman Catholic with five children at home. If he ever fucked this lousy Puerto Rican he would have worn a condom. The patrolman was too good of a Catholic to get inside a Puerto Rican and then go home and sleep with his wife. The trial board asked the captain what the patrolman was doing in the Puerto Rican's apartment so much. You know what the captain said? 'The man has a problem with the drink.' That's all the board had to hear. They had the out. They whipped the man over to Straight and Narrow and in six months he was back on regular tours.

"What this story means to you is that the best chance against any offense, particularly a sex offense and most particularly a sex offense when there are Irish Catholics on the trial board, is to cop out to alcoholism. It's way easier to be guilty of misuse of whisky than misuse of the prick."

The lawyer only had to say it once. Dermot and Johno knew that if they could not work themselves out of the trouble they were in this time, they both might as well be dead. Without a pension, Johno would wind up sleeping in the streets. Even for Dermot, it was too late to think of anything else except his pension. Half pay for life after twenty years. Every two weeks, Dermot Davey received a check of $387.90. The check represented two things to him. Food for his family. And fourteen less days to wait until he could go out on pension. He knew it was bad to be this way at twenty-nine, to be looking forward, awaiting the day when you are forty-one.

He thought about what he would do then. Security was a business that always would be, Dermot thought. He would be at an airport probably. Sometimes he thought about a bar with a screen door open and sunlight coming onto the floor. A bar in Florida. He liked that. Other times, when he was depressed, he kept thinking of faces of bank guards. Retired New York City policemen who

51

are bank guards stand by the glass counters, putting pens back into the holders, and the pens are black and shiny and the guards are enveloped by a thick layer of dust that stays on them until a mortician rubs it off.

2:

Dermot Davey comes out of St. Monica's Parish in Jamaica, in Queens, in New York City. He was living now in Holy Child Parish, in Richmond Hill, in Queens, in New York City. Richmond Hill is only twenty-five minutes away from Manhattan. But everybody in Queens always thinks of Manhattan as another place. The people say, "I'm going to the city," or, "I'm going to New York." Queens begins at the East River, directly across the water from midtown Manhattan. In Manhattan, you have the United Nations building on the water, sun exploding on the windows, sprinklers throwing water on the lawns and gardens. Directly across the river from the United Nations is the Pepsi-Cola plant in Long Island City, in Queens, its red neon sign bare and ugly in the daylight, eerie at night in the smoke rising around it.

Eddie Kieran, who lives next door to Dermot on 109th Place, was standing outside one Saturday night having a cigarette while he waited for his wife to fall asleep upstairs.

"Where'd you go?" he asked Dermot.

"Picked them up at the Maspeth Bingo," Dermot said.

"Oh, somebody says you went to the city," Eddie Kieran said.

"City? I haven't been to New York with Phyllis in, what, six months?"

"Oh, so you just went to the bingo."

"Picked them up at the Maspeth Bingo. What did you do?"

"Done nothin'. Went to her mother's."

Kieran had on a brown windbreaker with GROVER CLEVELAND HIGH lettering on the back. It is the jacket he wore on his high-school baseball team. Eddie is thirty-nine and he takes very good care of the jacket.

"Another couple of weeks," he said. He was swinging his arm in a circle.

"For what?"

"Jones Beach softball league. The start, anyway. The first meetin's and that."

"You play again this year?"

"What're you, kidding? Play every year."

Eddie took a drag on the cigarette as if he were a general. When he talks about playing ball he always is like this. Otherwise, Eddie is afraid of speaking to people. He had a job as a laborer at St. John's Cemetery. People looking for gravesites asked him too many questions. He quit and now works nights in a bakery. He puts jelly buns into paper bags and loads them onto a delivery wagon.

"I think I'm gonna play short this year," Eddie Kieran said.

"What'd you play last year? I saw you play shortstop."

"That was only the one game, against the Grumman. I played centerfield all year. I could throw, for Christ's sake, I was the only one could throw. The one game there, Mahon from the West Babylon, I threw a strike on him at the plate. What a fuckin' throw."

He took the cigarette and threw it out into the street. It made a little red arc in the darkness under the big old maple trees along the sidewalk.

"The fuckin' school is breakin' my back, too," Eddie said.

"What do they want now?"

"The same fuckin' thing. They want her to go college. Fuck them."

"How much would it cost you?"

"She got a fuckin' scholarship to the place."

"Which place is it again?"

"The Middlebury. They give her a scholarship for speakin' fuckin' French. That ain't it. For Christ's sake. Let her go out and work and help out at home. What is this here, a fuckin' paradise I got?"

"What's the wife think now?"

"She ain't allowed to think. I'll do the thinkin'. I just wish the fuckin' schools would butt out. This here woman at the high school. Fills my daughter up with a lot of bullshit. I tell them all. I tell them, I didn't go to no college. It was good enough for me, it's good enough for my daughter. We got no money. Let her start bringin' home a coupla dollars. Bucks. That's what we need. Bucks. That's what we need. Bucks. Not some fuckin' French."

They were standing on a street of dusty wooden houses with gingerbread all over them. Small patches of lawn are in front of each house. Most of the lawns are more rutted dirt than grass. The houses are separated from each other by common driveways, so narrow a car can barely fit between the houses as it inches back to the garages in the back yard. Most men when they bring their wives home on a Saturday night open the door at the front of the house and the wives get out. The man takes fifteen minutes inching his car into the driveway. Then he comes out and stands on the sidewalk, smoking a cigarette, waiting his wife out, waiting for her to be undressed and asleep by the time he comes into the house so they will not have to as much as talk. On the blocks in Richmond Hill on a Saturday night you always can see pinpoints of cigarettes in the darkness in front of the houses.

The house Dermot Davey and his wife and three daughters live in is owned by his mother-in-law. Dermot lives on the top floor, his in-laws downstairs. The house is tan, with green trim. The house is in the middle of the block. At one end of the street is the main avenue, Jamaica Avenue. El tracks run on top of Jamaica Avenue. A throw-up-green El with rust coming out from under the ties and black pillars lining the sidewalk. At the foot of each pillar, the crevices and ledges are stuffed with cigarette and candy wrappers. The light comes through the slats in the tracks and falls on the street in wavy rectangles. The El is old and noisy. Often, as trains clatter along it, bolts loosen in the tracks and drop through to the street, two stories below.

Under the El, yellowing attached two-story buildings of Jamaica Avenue push the street into even more dreariness. As you come up Jamaica Avenue from Lefferts Boulevard, a main cross street, you pass a wallpaper shop, a Cheap John's Bargain Store, a wedding photographer's shop, two real-estate offices with nervous young men sitting at scarred desks, a candy store with plastic toys in the window, an old A&P supermarket, several bars, Irish dungeons, with withered old men sitting in them and staring out at another day wasted. Once it becomes dark the doors to the bars are locked. The bartender lets in customers he knows by pressing a buzzer under the bar which automatically unlocks the door.

While Dermot and his next-door neighbor stood on the sidewalk, it was still early, before midnight, on a weekend night. Nearly all the houses were dark anyway. Dermot knew that day or night made little difference in the activity in the houses. In the daytime, the people were afraid to come to the door if the doorbell rang. They stayed back in the kitchens, peering down the hall. Nearly everybody in Richmond Hill has a dog. On Dermot's block, the people were buying big German shepherds. Black gums wet and flapping, yellow teeth bared, nose thrashing against the inside of the storm door, the dogs answered the doorbells for the people.

On this night, there were lights in the Laurino house in the middle of the block. On Saturday nights, the Laurinos always go to New York for plays and things like that. Laurino is an accountant. His wife, Laura, used to be a schoolteacher and now she substitute-teaches once in a while.

One time, Dermot and his wife went to a party in their house and late, while everybody was going home, Dermot was pouring himself another drink and Laura put a hand on his wrist. "You're too young to be drunk like this," she said. Ever since then, whenever she sees Dermot

56

on the street she looks at him carefully. He turns his face from her as much as he can.

Next to Laurino, where Jackie Collins lives, is a different story. He drives a truck for Piel's Beer. His brother delivers for New Arrival Diaper Service. The two of them are always together at one of the bars on Jamaica Avenue. Jackie Collins in a zipper jacket with PIEL'S stitched across the back and his name, JACKIE BOY, stitched on the front breast pocket. And his brother in a zipper jacket with NEW ARRIVAL DIAPER SERVICE stitched across the back and his name, EDDIE BOY. In the summers, Jackie works overtime. He goes to the race track as much as possible. In the winters, work is slow. He hangs out in bars. Dermot always notices his wife walking on Jamaica Avenue with her head down. She doesn't want storekeepers to notice her and come running out with one of her bad checks in their hands. The only time Dermot notices her picking up her head is when she passes the Blue Marlin or McLaughlin's or JB's, and she does this because she is looking for her husband. It is easy to spot him, in his PIEL'S zipper jacket. Usually he is right alongside his brother, in his NEW ARRIVAL DIAPER SERVICE zipper jacket.

The other people on the block are older. Toner, across the street, has a good job in the Fire Department, driving a Battalion Chief. Toner has fourteen months to go on his pension, thirty years. His wife never leaves the house. She keeps sending neighborhood kids down to the corner for ice cream and stays inside with the curtains drawn, watching television. The house is a mess and the furniture torn. The wife, when you see her in a house coat once a week or so, seems to be nearing three hundred pounds. The Taylors live next to the Toners. Taylor is a retired bank teller. The women on the block all say they see him naked and hiding behind trees at night. The rest of the people on the block Dermot knows only by name. They all are in their sixties. One of them, Mrs. Metcalf, a shriveled woman, stopped him one day when she heard that Dermot's wife had gone to the hospital during the night to have her first baby. Mrs. Metcalf said, "Did her water break?"

"I guess so," Dermot said.

"That's bad, dry babies is very hard to have," Mrs. Metcalf said.

Dermot's mother and sister lived in Ozone Park, less than ten minutes away from his house in Richmond Hill. He had not seen or spoken to his mother in the last three years. Since the christening party for Dermot's third daughter, Tara. His mother had arrived for the party with her eyes bloodshot, her lip curled. She started an argument with Dermot's mother-in-law. The argument started for the same reason his mother's fights always start, whisky. Dermot's mother-in-law looked to him for help. He walked out of the house and went down to the avenue, to McLaughlin's. While he was there, his mother left the christening and went home. Dermot's mother-in-law came down to McLaughlin's to get him back. He said something fresh to his mother-in-law. She walked out of the bar. Dermot never went back to the christening party.

In the days following this, he first tried to call his mother and hammer at her, but he found he was always stopping short of calling her the one word, drunk, which kept running through his mind. He decided not to call her or take calls from her. Dermot still had a marriage at that time. He knew his mother was capable of keeping two families at once living in the misery of whisky rages. He stopped going to visit her although she lived only ten minutes away. Once in a while over the months, Dermot's mother called his house. The voice snapping, "Let me speak to my *son*." If he was home, Dermot would grab the phone and hang it up. That would start her calling every ten minutes until either she fell asleep or Dermot took the phone off the hook. For the three years this went on, Dermot knew that his sister, living with his mother in a four-room apartment, was giving up her years and her nervous system so the mother would not have to live alone. The mother continually tried to pick fights with neighbors, who by this time did not speak to her. When his mother would be sober, she would not understand why people ignored her. Depressed, she would start the cycle of drinking and fighting again.

Because of age differences and because of the occupation—policemen rarely speak to anybody but policemen, and policemen's wives rarely speak to any other women but policemen's wives—Dermot and his wife had little to do with the people on the block. Most of the policemen with whom Dermot works live out on Long Island. They live in places called Deer Park and Massapequa Park, in split-level and ranch and Cape Cod houses costing twenty thousand dollars. The houses have lawns that the policemen mow in the summer. The houses have walks that the policemen shovel in the winter. There are barbecue stands covered with plastic in the back yard and a picnic table with a garden hose on it and the television set always is on and the cop leaves the house for only three reasons. The ride to the supermarket with his wife. The ride to the hardware store by himself. And the hated trip, the ride on the Long Island Railroad to the job in Queens. For eight hours a day the policeman patrols streets he hates, watches people he despises and, if the people are black, people who make him apprehensive or even afraid. Many of the policemen who still live in Queens live cheaply with parents or in-laws. The one Dermot Davey knows best in Queens is Johno O'Donnell.

When he was straight, before he began swallowing too much whisky, everybody always said Johno was one of the best cops they had seen. Johno had two citations. The one Dermot knew by heart—Johno had told it to him so many times over so many drinks—came from a payroll holdup of a bakery plant in Long Island City. The plant was on a dead-end street. A girl inside the plant had been able to sneak a call. Johno was in the first car to respond. The holdup men were coming out the metal door from the factory office. They jumped back inside. They were either going to take hostages or shoot it out from inside. Johno was out of the car and had the factory door open and was firing so quickly up the metal staircase that none of them got past the first landing. One was shot in the back, another in the leg, and the third quit.

If you saw Johno stumbling around Glendale and Ridge-wood, you would have trouble believing it. But once Dermot had seen the Johno the old-timers talked about. There was a call from Schmidt's Restaurant on Myrtle Avenue. Dermot was driving Johno in the sector. When they arrived, a German waiter was standing with a group of women around a booth. The waiter was wringing his hands. In the booth, slumped against the wall, her legs on the seat, was a heavy woman with frightened eyes. They had a coat thrown over her.

Johno started the moment he came through the restaurant doorway.

"All right," he called out, almost happy, "here we are."

He put a hand on the waiter. "Excuse me, sir. That's fine. All right. Here we are."

"She's havin' a heart attack!" the waiter shouted.

The woman slumped in the booth looked even more frightened.

Johno leaned over and ran a hand over the woman's forehead.

"Well, dear, you're not having a heart attack," Johno said. "How can you have a heart attack when you don't sweat? You ought to know better than that. What did you eat? That's what's bothering you."

The frightened eyes closed. When they opened, the woman in the booth looked five years younger.

"Pain is in the chest, right?" Johno said.

She nodded yes.

He had her hand and was feeling for the pulse. "I'll tell you," Johno said, "I play horses, lady. I'm betting gall bladder. That's a four-to-five shot, dear. Relax, nobody died from gall bladder."

By the time the ambulance came, he had the woman in the booth quiet and smiling a little. The other women were calmed down. The waiters were relaxed. When the place cleared, Johno sat in a booth as if it were a broken car seat. "Hey, you," he said to the waiter, "bring me a straight VO."

Johno said to Dermot, "You see that cocksucker standin' in everybody's way when we come in? Doin' fuckin' nothin'. Scarin' the poor woman half to death. I would of done some scream job on him, but I was afraid I'd make the woman scared. What the fuck do I know what was the matter with her? She could've gone out right there on us."

"It was gall bladder," Dermot said.

"That's what you say," Johno said. "I don't know what the fuck she had. I told her she wasn't sweatin'. Chrissake, I touched her head, it was like a faucet."

Johno lives in Ozone Park, down by the race track. When Dermot and Johno and their wives go out, every fifty or sixth week, Dermot and his wife drive down to the Cross Bay Theater, on Rockaway Boulevard in Ozone Park. The wives go into the movie and Dermot and Johno walk up the block, past Shep's Army & Navy Store, Aid Auto Supplies, Chen's Chow Mein to Tommy Madden's bar. Always, in Tommy Madden's, it is the same. Dermot and Johno sit at the end of the bar, near the window, and Tommy Madden, bald, his ears lumps of skin, sits on a stool and talks about his days as a fighter.

"Al Weill managed me," Tommy Madden said one night.

"He was a hump," Johno said.

"He was a cutey," Tommy Madden said.

"A hump," Johno said. "I may be a prick, but I'm not a hump."

Nobody talked for a while. Then Johno said to Dermot, "You know, that play never worked once."

"What play?"

"What play? For Chrissake, what's the matter with you? Hump. The Long twenty-two. How many times do you think it worked?"

Dermot was trying to think. "Fuck, I don't know," he said.

"My ass you don't know. Hump. We had the Long twenty-two when I was playing and when I come to see you play, you had the same play. Don't shit me. You humps couldn't make it work either."

"Christ, I don't know," Dermot said.

"Well, I'm tellin' you again, it never worked when I played. We couldn't even make it work against Flushing

61

the year we beat them thirty-seven points. We used to make it out of a double wing. Second and short yardage. Or right after you recover a fumble and you're lookin' to—boom!—hump 'em. The ends go away down and cross over. You throw the fuckin' thing as far as you can. What are you tellin' me you can't remember. Chrissake. You had the same thing. I seen you try it against Styvesant. Out of the T, but the same thing. Long twenty-two. You humps couldn't make it work, either."

When the movies got out, the wives came to the sidewalk in front of the bar. Johno and Dermot came outside and took them to the pizzeria two doors down. They ordered pies. Johno swallowed wine. His wife, Emily, kept her cloth coat on. She was so fat that she wore the same smocks, faded and worn, that she used when she was pregnant.

"We don't have long to go," Emily said.

"Twenty-three months," Johno said. "Then right to Fort Lauderdale. No geese there. People down there know what to do with the niggers. They're not humps, the people in Fort Lauderdale."

"Maybe someday we all could be livin' in Fort Lauderdale," his wife said.

Dermot's parents were born in Queens. His father in Woodside, his mother in Jamaica. His father played the piano in taverns in Sunnyside and Woodside, and in the summer at Long Beach, out on Long Island. All the saloons in the west end of Long Beach, the Irish end, had piano players on Sunday afternoons.

Dermot can remember only two scenes involving his father, both of them during the winter.

He came home one day and said to Dermot's mother, "I saw Carmen Cavallaro today."

"Did you?"

"He was having a cup of coffee in the Automat."

"Really? What did he look like?"

"Looked like a million dollars."

And Dermot remembers the afternoon in the winter. He was in second grade then, and he and his sister, who wasn't in school yet, were running toy cars over the linoleum on the floor of the apartment in Sunnyside. Dermot and his sister kept asking the father if they could go downstairs and play out on the street. All the father did was stand at the window with his hands in his pockets. The day was cold and became dark early. Dermot and his sister sat on the couch and the sister began picking on him and he pushed her and she began crying. The father kept looking down at the street and not seeming to hear them. Finally, his mother came in from work. She had a city job with the Department of Purchase. His mother did not talk. She put on a light, stood there with her coat still on, and glared at Dermot's father. Dermot remembers his mother going into the kitchen and his father walking into the bedroom. In the kitchen, dishes still were on the table and sink. Dermot heard his mother taking ice out of the refrigerator. When the father went in to see her, she had her back to him.

"Just stay out of here now," she said.

He and his sister were on the couch, pushing each other, when Dermot's mother came out of the kitchen and walked into the bedroom. She slammed the door behind her. First, there was whispering. Then his mother shouted, "You!"

There was a big noise now, and his father was shouting and his mother shrieking. One shriek after the other. Dermot opened the bedroom door. His father, standing nearest to Dermot, was trying to ram the bed against Dermot's mother and pin her to the wall. Dermot grabbed at his father's arm. His sister came into the room crying. His mother threw herself onto the bed. She was half sitting, half kneeling, grabbing for her husband's face. The father shoved Dermot away and walked out of the apartment. The mother sat on the bed crying with her mouth open. His sister had her arms wrapped around her mother. Dermot went into the kitchen and got a can of Campbell's tomato soup. The same red-and-white label they have today. He put the can of soup against the apartment door. This made him feel like he was protecting his mother and sister and he stood by the door, watching his can of soup that kept the door shut. He heard his father come back to the door. The lock turned. He still can see the apartment door swinging in, the can of soup rolling into the dimness in one of the corners of the living room.

Dermot does not remember ever seeing his father after that day. His mother took his sister and him to his grandmother's house, her mother's house, in Jamaica. The grandmother was a widow. Dermot's two uncles lived in the house. The grandmother's other child, an aunt, was married and lived in White Plains, up in Westchester. Nobody ever mentioned his father's name in the house. Whenever somebody in school asked Dermot about him, Dermot said his father was dead. Dermot was terrified that one of the kids would find out that his father really was alive and was not living in Dermot's house.

One day when he came home from school, Dermot found his grandmother in the kitchen talking to an older woman and the older woman made a fuss over Dermot.

"Looks just like his mother," Dermot remembers his grandmother saying.

"And he's got a lot of somebody else in that face too," the other woman said.

The grandmother held a finger to her lips and Dermot remembers her saying, "Shhhhhsh now," and the words went through him and he ran out of the kitchen.

One day, Dermot was in the bedroom he shared with one of his uncles, and his sister was trying to get in and Dermot tried to keep her out. He slammed the door on his sister's hand, cracking one fingernail badly, and she ran downstairs screaming. His mother stood in the hallway looking at the finger, and Dermot remembers hanging over the banister and his mother looking up at him and saying to him, "You're no good. You're just like him. He's no good and you're no good."

At home, all Dermot ever heard from his uncles was police talk. Early one morning when he was about nine, he came downstairs, it was about six-thirty, and he found his Uncle Tom had his pistol and blackjack on the table and he was drinking beer out of a Kraft-cheese glass that had blue flowers on it. Uncle Tom took a quart bottle of Piel's beer and poured it like ketchup. The beer splashed and foam ran up over the sides of the glass. Uncle Tom's head dropped like an elevator and he began sucking up foam. "The people dyin' in the desert!" he said. Dermot went over to the refrigerator to get milk for his Rice Krispies. On the wall alongside the refrigerator was the Proclamation of Irish Independence of 1916. Everybody in the family, the uncles first of all, had Dermot memorize it. "Irishmen and Irishwomen: In the name of God and of the dead generations from which she receives her old tradition of nationhood, Ireland, through us, summons her children to the flag and strikes for her freedom. . . ."

Dermot remembers sitting over his cereal on the opposite side of the table from Uncle Tom. Tom patted the blackjack. "Ah, your Uncle Tom got plenty use out of this last night," he said.

"Where?" Dermot asked.

"Bedford-Stuyvesant."

"Bedford-Stuyvesant?"

"Niggers," Uncle Tom said.

He produced some whisky to slop into the beer and he threw one big drink down, this one so quickly that it splashed against his bottom lip and brown drops fell on his undershirt. He took the pistol out of the holster. He released the cylinder, dropped bullets onto the table, pushed the cylinder back, and held out the gun. "Listen to your Uncle Tom now. Good boy! Go upstairs and poke your Uncle Jack with this. Just poke him and say, 'Post time!' Do that now. Good boy!"

Dermot took the gun and ran upstairs. The grip and the ridges of metal felt nice in his hand. The finger on the trigger gave him the same feeling he has had every time he ever holds a gun. It starts between the legs.

Uncle Jack was alseep on his face. Dermot shouted, "Post time!" and poked the gun into his ear. He moved his head and his face rolled out on the pillow and Dermot held the gun steady so that when his Uncle Jack opened his eyes for the first time he was looking into the barrel of the pistol. His mouth popped open. In one motion he grabbed the pistol and gave Dermot a clout on top of the head.

He remembers his Uncle Jack walked into the kitchen, opened the cylinder, poked it with a finger, and a bullet fell onto the kitchen table. Gray and brass rolling around in the spilled beer, the sun from the kitchen windows shining on the wet metal. Dermot reached to grab the bullet. Uncle Jack hit him on top of the head again, this time so hard that everything went black.

When Dermot came home from school that day, Uncle Jack was still in his pajamas at the kitchen table. He was sitting across from Dermot's grandmother and they both were drinking from a quart bottle of Piel's beer.

"You really saw it?" the grandmother said.

"I saw my whole life," Uncle Jack said.

Uncle Tom was back on the living-room couch. He was snoring loudly. He smelled so badly from his breath, armpits, and socks with caked soles that Dermot could not stay in the room with him.

Dermot Davey came out of St. Monica's grammar school with the same grounding in life as so many other policemen in New York. The girls in his class were told by the nuns never to wear patent-leather shoes. The nuns said, "They give you headaches." In the higher grades, in the boys' room, Dermot learned that the nuns were against patent leather because a man could look down at a girl's shoes and see up her dress.

The rest of the education which stuck, the religious education, came out of the Baltimore Catechism. The name "Baltimore" comes from the Council of American Bishops, which first approved the book. The Baltimore book used by Dermot had a blue cover, which he still remembers, and it taught him the basics of the Roman Catholic belief, which he, like everybody else, still can recite with no preparation.

Q Who made the world?
A God made the world.
Q Who is God?

66

A God is the Creator of heaven and earth, and of all things.

Q What is man?

A Man is a creature composed of body and soul, and made to the image and likeness of God.

Q Why did God make you?

A God made me to know Him, to love Him, and to serve Him in this world, and to be happy with Him forever in heaven.

Q Are the three Divine Persons one and the same God?

A The three Divine Persons are one and the same God, having one and the same Divine nature.

Q How do we know this to be true?

A It is a mystery.

Q What is the Sixth Commandment?

A The Sixth Commandment is: Thou shalt not commit adultery.

Q What are we commanded by the Sixth Commandment?

A We are commanded by the Sixth Commandment to be pure in thought and modest in all our looks, words and actions.

Q What is forbidden by the Sixth Commandment?

A The Sixth Commandment forbids all unchaste freedom with another's wife or husband; also all immodesty with ourselves or others in looks, dress, words or actions.

The last one always sticks. Dermot and his wife had their first two children in the first two and one-half years of marriage. They spoke of not having any more children for some time. Dermot came home one night after working a four-to-midnight and having a couple of drinks on the way home. Phyllis was sleeping with her back to him. He reached over her shoulder and ran a hand over her. She shook her shoulder. He began kissing her neck. She moved away. "Come on now, it's a very bad time," she said. Dermot said he would be careful. He put a hand onto her breast. She shrugged her shoulder to get his hand away and pulled the cover up over her. "Come on now," she said. "I'm telling you it's a bad time."

Dermot went to sleep irritated with her. In bed, Phyllis

always took the last look to be sure the bedroom door was closed. She never wanted sex in the daytime, and Dermot worked many nights, and when they were having sex she seemed to be trying to control her breathing. She was now going even beyond this.

When they got up the next morning, Dermot was even more irritated with her. Phyllis acted as if nothing had happened. Phyllis's mother had agreed to take care of the kids for the day, and they were going to take a drive out to Long Island. Dermot gave Phyllis the car keys. He sat in the front seat with his eyes closed. When Phyllis got in next to him, his left side, the side touching her, squirmed. Phyllis drove on the Northern State Parkway.

It was the last week of October and the trees were changing colors. As they got farther out on Long Island, the trees had brighter reds and yellows. Dermot said nothing during the drive. For an hour and a half he sat in the car and looked out the window and he did not speak to his wife and she did not speak to him. Finally, when they were out at the end of the parkway and were going onto Montauk Highway, Dermot turned on the car radio. It made a loud static and nothing else. They were going down an incline at Eastport, with a pond in the incline covered with red and yellow leaves on one side, and on the other side the sun glinting off the bay that leads to the ocean. And Dermot said the only words he was to say all day. "Just take me home."

She pulled into an old gas station with thick trees and a portico hanging over the gas pumps, turned around, and started back for Queens.

They were almost home when she said, "That's why you're mad."

Dermot didn't answer.

"You're mad because of that," she said.

He still didn't answer.

"You don't understand," she said.

Sometimes, Dermot felt that if he and Phyllis had been born a little later, just a couple of years later, they might be like so many of the young Catholic couples of today. Dermot always noticed that younger people do not seem to become embarrassed or to lapse into Queens words at the subject of sex. He and Phyllis received the old Diocese of Brooklyn schooling. She was taught that sex is solely for having children who will become good Catholics. And never to wear patent-leather shoes. Dermot was taught that it is perfectly natural for a young man to have severe temptations, but there is no temptation which cannot be overcome by an Our Father and ten Hail Marys. The one line that stayed with Dermot the most during his life was said to him late one Saturday afternoon by a priest in confession. Dermot was in his first year in high school. Eyes closed, highly nervous, he told a priest that he had committed a sin of touch.

"How?" the priest said.

"I touched a girl with my hand," Dermot said.

"Externally or internally?" the priest said.

"Internally."

"Would you like somebody doing that to your sister?" the priest said.

Dermot and his wife, like so many others from the same background, were unable to discuss sex. Many times they went two weeks without sex. And immediately after that, two or three more weeks. It seemed to Dermot that his wife was always heaving herself onto her side, her back to him. It would make him angry and he would move out onto the edge of the bed on his side. And then he would not come near her for weeks. Once, they went seven weeks without sex. There was no way for them to handle the subject in conversation. It always came out to be a fight over wallpaper or weak coffee.

Phyllis had light-brown hair that she had brushed the same way for so long that it was almost unnoticeable to Dermot. Her face was still thin and together enough to be acceptable for a twenty-eight-year-old. The extra years were in the eyes. A greeting would produce some reaction. A conversation with her about anything would produce almost no movement, no brightening or dimming, no coupling of her eyes with anybody else's to show interest. Always, no matter what was going on, she was a woman staring at the stove waiting for coffee water to boil.

Her body fell apart at the hips. Three children had weakened the muscles, and the weight spread her hips and went down through the tops of her thighs. From behind she began to look like a bell buoy. What saved her was her legs from the knees down. They had the form and spring of youth. When she walked through the house quickly, she made Dermot remember Sunday afternoons, walking in Forest Park, before they were married.

The afternoon Dermot was taken in by the Internal Affairs Division, two detectives from the IAD came to the house to talk to Phyllis. One of them had a briefcase. He put his hand inside it, but never took any papers out. They asked Phyllis if she had noticed anything abnormal about Dermot's sexual instincts. They asked her if Dermot had undergone any psychiatric treatment.

When Dermot finally was allowed to leave the IAD office on Poplar Street that night, he came home and found Phyllis in the kitchen in silence. The next afternoon they started an argument about newspapers on the floor. During the argument, Phyllis did not look at Dermot. Through the weeks that followed she rarely looked at him the few times they talked while they were alone.

The catechisms in the higher grades began to intermingle conservative religion, patriotism, and obedience and produced the special doctrine of Diocese of Brooklyn Roman Catholic American.

Essay question:

Giles is murdered by a Communist just as he leaves the church after his confession. Giles has been away from the church for 28 years. He just about satisfied the requirements for a good confession, having only imperfect contrition, aroused during this week's mission. The Communist demanded to know if Giles was a Catholic, threatening to kill him if he was. Fearlessly, Giles said, "Yes, thank God!" The Communist murdered Giles. Did Giles go immediately to Heaven, or

70

did he go to Purgatory for a while? Given a reason for your answer.

Nobody in Dermot's class ever considered Giles as anything but a martyr who ascended to heaven immediately. All people killed while resisting Communists essentially were Catholic saints and needed only the publicity drive to force Rome to recognize them as such, according to the priests and nuns in charge of schools when Dermot attended.

Giles is murdered by a Communist.

Other questions had their own answers underneath.

243

Q Does the Fourth Commandment oblige us to respect and obey others besides our parents?

A Besides our parents, the Fourth Commandment obliges us to respect and to obey all our lawful superiors. All are obliged to respect and to obey legitimate civil and ecclesiastical authorities when they discharge lawfully their official duties.

Q Name three moral virtues under the Fourth Commandment.

A Obedience, which disposes us to do the will of our superiors.

Liberality, which disposes us rightly to use worldly goods.

Chastity, or purity, which disposes us to be pure in mind and body.

252

Q What are we commanded by the Fifth Commandment?

A By the Fifth Commandment we are commanded to take proper care of our spiritual and bodily well-being and that of our neighbor.

(*a*) Man does not have supreme dominion over his own life; he was not the cause of its beginning nor may he be the deliberate cause of its end. Man must use the ordinary means to preserve life. He is not, however, obliged to use extraordinary means which would involve relatively great expense or intolerable pain or shame.

(*b*) The life of another person may lawfully be taken: *first*, in order to protect one's own life or that of a neighbor, or a serious amount of possessions from an unjust aggressor, provided no other means of protection is effective;

second, by a soldier fighting a just war;

third, by a duly appointed executioner of the state when he metes out a just punishment for a crime.

The rest of Dermot's education, the nonreligious topics, prepared him for nothing but a badge.

Dermot Davey's grandmother, who owned the house he grew up in, was a widow. She died when he was ten. One of his uncles' wives came running into the hospital room, Mary Immaculate in Jamaica, hysterical. She had an enormous black crucifix in her hands as a gift. She thrust the crucifix at the grandmother. The grandmother thought the crucifix meant she was dying, and she fainted and died later that night. At the funeral, they began to talk of the grandfather. Dermot didn't remember him. He had worked as a messenger for a big Wall Street lawyer named Dufficey. The lawyer used to help support Irish actors and poets. When Yeats came to New York, the lawyer subsidized him. Dermot's grandfather had the job of delivering the envelopes to Yeats. In an album they were showing around during the wake, there was one newspaper clipping which mentioned Dermot's grandfather. That got Dermot's mother excited about Yeats. Then when some old relative from Brooklyn said that somebody else on the grandfather's side had been the editor of a weekly newspaper in Brooklyn, Dermot's mother began talking of her family as if she were a Pulitzer.

She took Dermot into the living room on a few Saturday mornings and had him read from a book of Yeats poems. She wanted him to read out loud so he would memorize it. She was always tense in the morning. Tense and snappish. Dermot would have his thoughts on playing ball in a lot down by the railroad tracks and his mother would be snapping at him and making herself nervous and her son nervous and trying to learn "Cathleen Ni Hoolihan." It was, Dermot remembers, a fuck of a way to learn and of course he never did.

In St. Monica's school one day in June, in the last week of school when Dermot was in the seventh grade, the nun was trying to spend the day collecting books and putting them away for the summer and she had to keep the class busy so she had them write a composition on anything they wanted. Dermot put down his "JMJ" heading, which means Jesus, Mary, and Joseph bless this work. He started doing something he never had done before in school. In St. Monica's all the composition topics were mandatory. They were all of the "My Trip to the Planetarium" type. Dermot started to write about an old man who worked at the stables at Jamaica Race Track. The track is gone now. When he was growing up all the kids used to play baseball in an empty lot in the stable area. There was an old man who used to stomp around on a wooden leg. He used to have a big tub of boiling water. The lower part of a race horse's legs are so thin that almost no blood circulates. A race horse can have something bad the matter with his ankle and never feel it and keep walking on it until he starts dying of gangrene. So the old man used this boiling water on leg injuries, and it was fine except his stable was right by the fence. Just outside the fence was a bus stop. All the people looking out the windows of the bus would see was an old man torturing a horse with boiling water. People bombarded the ASPCA with phone calls. Finally, the ASPCA sent inspectors to the stable. The old man started fighting with them. All the kids came over from the baseball lot and watched. In the middle of the argument, the old man said, Here, I'll show you the water doesn't hurt anybody. He walked over to the tub and put his leg into it. The people from the ASPCA, particularly this one woman, got hysterical. They didn't know it was a wooden leg the old man was sticking into the water. All the kids were jumping up and down.

So on this day in St. Monica's school Dermot began

to write a composition about the old man. He couldn't write fast enough to keep up with the things he wanted to put down. After a while his hand started to hurt because he was gripping the pen so hard. When he finished, he took the composition up and put it on the Sister's desk. He slid it right in front of her and stood waiting.

"Well," she said. She began reading. When she finished the second side, she told Dermot to take it to Sister Rita, the eighth-grade teacher. He ran it down the hall to Sister Rita's room. Usually he was nervous about opening the door and walking into another class, the whole room always looked at you, but this time he couldn't wait to get the composition onto Sister Rita's desk.

She took it and read the one side so quickly he couldn't understand how anybody could be that fast, and when she turned it over and only glanced at the second side, and when he saw she wasn't reading, the bottom fell out of him.

"Well," she said.

"Yes, Sister."

"Do you know why Sister had you bring this up to me?"

"No, Sister."

"Well. Come over here. Look at this handwriting. Just look at this handwriting. Do you call this penmanship?"

"No, Sister."

"Well. Neither do I. And neither does Sister. Do you know why she sent this up to show me? Because she was so ashamed of such a sloppy piece of work. She wanted to know just what kind of sloppy boy I am getting in my class next fall. Now let me warn you about something. The summer goes very fast. And then you are going to be sitting right here in this class with *me*. So you better not embarrass Sister and arrive here next fall from her class and not have better penmanship than what you have just shown us here with this."

Most policemen, particularly policemen out of parochial schools in Queens, have language problems along with their penmanship problems. Their word usage, restricted so much in grammar school by stilted religious phrases, rarely improves once out of grammar school. In preparing for the police examinations, they attend schools that specialize in Civil Service tests. The schools teach such phrasing as "apprehend the perpetrator" and the policemen cling to the official language. Dermot was in court one day when Harry Feeney of the 112th Squad, testifying in a homicide, referred to the dead man as "the alleged victim." They rarely read anything at all. In a room where there are both police and defendants, the common rule is that if the *Daily News* is opened to the centerfold, the picture spreads, it has just been thumbed through by a policeman. If the *News* is open to a page with stories on it, a defendant has been reading it.

One day while he was working in the 125, there was a call from the subway station at Myrtle and Wyckoff. When Dermot came downstairs to the change booth a doorman from one of the trains was holding a little bald man against the wall. A Puerto Rican girl was standing to the side. She was looking down at her coat, a black cloth coat. The doorman said the little bald man had been sitting next to the girl on the train. "The man playin' with himself behind the newspaper, you know, and then he let go of the newspaper and come all over this poor little girl's coat. She called me then."

Dermot noticed a miraculous medal around the Puerto Rican girl's neck. She had her handkerchief out, trying to clean her coat. Dermot told her to stop. The coat was evidence.

Ray McBride, the second cop to get to the change booth, gave the little bald man a shove.

"Cut it out," the bald man said.

Ray grabbed him again and threw him against the wall. "He just resisted arrest."

"Shit, yeah," the doorman said.

Dermot handcuffed the bald man. They walked him upstairs, the Puerto Rican girl behind them. The temperature was close to ten degrees. Dermot stopped to button the collar of his overcoat. The girl was holding her handbag over the spot on the coat, down at the bottom. But

75

when she came up into the lights of the pizza stand alongside the subway steps, Dermot could see the purse wasn't enough. The stuff was all the way to the hem of the coat. Dermot said to himself, This filthy old bum must have had to get off something fierce. He also knew he could not have her walking around like that. The coat was black cloth gook, Dermot said to himself, little kids in the street could see the gook and know what it is. He told the Puerto Rican girl to take off her coat. "I'll carry it for you," he said. The girl had on a thin yellow dress underneath. She crossed her arms and closed her eyes against the cold. Dermot held the coat way out in front of him and the girl and he stood on the corner in the ten-degree cold waiting for a patrol car to come for them. Dermot thought it was better for her to freeze than to have people see her in the coat with the come on it.

At the precinct, Dermot looked up the charges. Harry Myers was the name of the little bald man. Dermot charged him with assault in the third, PL 120.10 in his book; sexual abuse, PL 130.55; disconduct, PL 240.20; and resisting arrest, PL 205.30. McBride wanted to charge Myers with assault on an officer but the desk lieutenant said he needed some marks as proof. McBride put his hand into his mouth and bit down on it. The lieutenant shook his head no.

"It's all right," Dermot said to McBride. "We got this degenerate good."

Dermot walked down to the end of the long desk to where Jerry Ahearn, who was the 124 man on this day, sat at an old typewriter. A 124 man is the clerical man. He types out the arrest charges. When Jerry Ahearn types out a normal arrest, a stabbing or a robbery, he doesn't put anything in capital letters. Even proper names are always in small letters. As Dermot started to give him the case, Jerry Ahearn typed out the complainant as "juanita rivera" and the person arrested, "harry myers" and the arresting officer, "dermot davey." He kept going as Dermot told him about the case. Dermot looked over his shoulder at the arrest sheet in the typewriter.

complainant juanita rivera states that on the 16th day of february, 1968, the defendant harry myers did commit a violation of section 130.55 of the penal law in that he did place himself on a seat alongside and next to said complainant miss rivera on the bmt subway train, said complainant charges that as said subway train was approaching the subway station at myrtle and wyckoff avenues in ridgewood, queens, said defendant myers

As Dermot went on with what had happened, the red flushed through Ahearn's face. Ahearn types with two fingers. He usualy holds the fingers a half inch or so off the keys and flicks them out after he hears you say something. This time his shoulders drew back and his fingers began coming higher off the keys and pretty soon he was pulling his fingers back all the way to his shoulders and punching so hard at the keys Dermot thought he was going to bang right through the typewriter.

did have his trousers open and his PENIS IN HIS HAND and said defendant myers did then work HIS PENIS BACK AND FORTH! said defendant myers' said PENIS was in proximity to said complainant's coat. said defendant myers then did CONTINUE WORKING HIS PENIS BACK AND FORTH UNTIL SAID PENIS of said defendant myers DID EJACULATE! SAID EJACULATION CAME ALL OVER THE COAT OF SAID COMPLAINANT WHO WAS ASSAULTED BY SAID EJACULATION! SAID EJACULATION WAS IN THE GENERAL PORTION OF SAID COMPLAINANT'S COAT COVERING SAID COMPLAINANT'S VIRGINIA!

When the case went to court, the judge was shaking his head as he read the arrest sheet. He set a date and let the defendant out on his own recognizance.

Dermot became angry. "How can you let a pervert bastard like this out on the street?" he said to the assistant district attorney. "Now they'll let him take a plea for being fucking alive."

The judge couldn't hear Dermot, but he saw his face. After Myers walked free, the judge called Dermot up to the bench.

"Officer, the way you fellows treat this thing, you'd think it was a homicide. I haven't seen this many exclamation points since I did a paper on comic books when I was in college. One thing perhaps you should think of, officer. Did it ever occur to you that sometimes a case like this might be love?"

3:

When he had started, when he was twenty-one and clean
and still trim and strong, Dermot Davey walked the beat
with the same feeling that he had when he came home
from receiving Communion. He felt as if he was somebody in the uniform, and that he was doing something
worthwhile. He had tried a construction job when he
finished high school. He had a temporary book in the
Operating Engineers Union. He ran a hoist on the construction of a new building. All day he sat in a plywood
booth watching a huge drum of cable which ran an elevator up and down the side of the building site. The
elevator was for materials only. Bells on the wall of
Dermot's shack told him which floor to run the elevator
up to. He never saw the elevator or any of the men working. He simply sat in a shack, with the drum of cable, a
clutch and brake, and watched the cable come in or go
out, white chalk lines on the cable showing him the distance between floors. He found the job boring.

The idea of being the one who pushed through the
crowd to see what was going on instead of just another
person in the crowd was important. He was elated the day
he left the shack for the last time. Now, eight years later,
Dermot wondered how it had happened to him. How the
cleanliness had been covered over with a layer of slime.
All he held important now was his pension. Half pay at
twenty years.

It was different when he started. He was on the job

seven months in the 83rd in Brooklyn, walking Knickerbocker Avenue on a midnight-to-eight-a.m. shift on a
Saturday night. It was in February. The sidewalk had a
thin covering of crusted snow. Near the end of one block,
a lot of Puerto Ricans were out on the sidewalk in front
of an apartment house. The street was lined with six-
story apartment houses that had a piss smell in the hallways. The Puertos were babbling. The hallway on the
ground floor was crowded with them too. Dermot pushed
into the building and through the people in the hallway
and came to the open doorway of the superintendent's
apartment. The door opened into the kitchen. The super,
a black Puerto Rican, was at the window in the kitchen.
The window opened onto a courtyard. The courtyard
really was just a wide air shaft. Pieces of wood and an
old door, faded yellow and dirty, were ugly on top of
the snow. In the middle of the wood was the body of a
woman all huddled together, on her side, and next to her,
a thin line of snow separating them, was a baby in pajamas
with feet. The baby's head was split to the white. The
superintendent leaned out the window and pointed up in
the blackness to an open window with light showing in
it on the top floor of the building. Dermot stood with
the super and kept staring at the pajamas with feet.
    He cleared the doorway and the hallway and waited
with the super for the emergency squad and the detectives to come. The super told him the woman had to be
very young, twenty-five at the most, and that she spoke
no English. Her name was Gonzales and she was from
Colombia. Every morning the woman went out with her
son, the boy actually wasn't a baby, he was closer to
five, and took him to an apartment house halfway down
the block and across the street. She left the boy with
somebody in the building. She came back at night, picked
up the boy, and went up to the sixth floor with him and
never came down. Nobody in the apartment building
knew the woman. The Puerto Ricans spoke too quickly
for her to understand them well, and she couldn't say a
word in English.
    When the emergency squad and the detectives got there,

Dermot didn't know why but he went upstairs to the woman's apartment. In the kitchen, where you came in, there was a table with loose aluminum legs and two chairs. The refrigerator had a half-finished bowl of chicken noodle soup. Otherwise there wasn't even a cracker in the place. The next room, the bedroom, had two mattresses on the floor with old covers on them. The living room was a playroom for the baby. The floor was covered with puzzles and rubber balls. One of the window sills had fur bears sitting on it. The other window sill was the one with the open window. The detectives had the woman's purse out and they were going through the closets. The purse had no money in it. Dermot took a look at the bankbook one of the detectives found. It showed the woman had a balance of $1.23. The super was telling them that she had two months' security paid on the apartment and that she had stopped paying the rent and was letting the security get used up. He said she had told him with hand motions and the like that she had lost her job. Dermot was looking out the open window and thinking that at least it was easy on the little boy. In the middle of the night you take a kid out of bed and even if he has his eyes open he really doesn't know what's going on. The window frame was dusty and the detectives showed him there were no marks on it at all. The kid never even put his hand out to touch anything when the mother threw him out the window. Then she went out after him.

Dermot went downstairs onto the avenue and finished the tour and went home. When he came to work the next night, Sunday night, he went up to the detective squad room and asked about the woman and the boy. The guy working, Rand, told him the bodies were in the morgue. They hadn't been able to find out anything about her or whether she had any relatives. They had come up with a form she had from Goldwater Memorial, the hospital for welfare people. Dermot asked Rand about the apartment house where she used to leave the boy. It turned out nobody knew exactly which apartment house she took the boy into, and that it takes three hours to canvass an apartment house. Even then, you can't do it unless you have at least two families home on every floor. With Puerto Ricans, you never know when they're home. It could take a week.

When Dermot finished his tour at eight o'clock in the morning, he left the precinct and called his wife and said he'd be home late and he went back to the avenue and started in on the first building across the street from where the woman lived. The detective was wrong. It didn't take three hours to canvass a building. It took over four hours of Dermot's talking with his hands to Puerto Ricans and trying to convince people he wasn't there to arrest somebody. He came out with nothing.

When he came to work for the Monday-night midnight shift, Dermot told Rand that he'd be in the neighborhood after work if it would do him any good. Rand said he'd help canvass a couple of buildings.

He wasn't around when Dermot finished in the morning, so Dermot went to see the superintendent himself and he got the name of the real-estate office where the Gonzales woman had rented the apartment. It was up on Broadway, in Brooklyn, and Dermot had to hang around an hour waiting for it to open. The two guys gave him a whole pile of old applications. It took two hours to go through them. The full name was Aura Gonzales and she listed two adults and one child. That meant the husband must have run out on her. Where it said employment, she had put down "Stein form. 6 W. 36." The place was not listed in the Manhattan book.

Dermot got on the subway and went over to Manhattan and got onto Thirty-sixth Street, which is in the middle of the garment center, and he went from place to place about "Stein form." until late in the afternoon. Finally he found a freight elevator guy in one of the buildings who said that was an old name, Stein, and now the place was called Berger. He took Dermot up to the floor the place was. It was after five and it was locked for the night. Dermot went down with the elevator guy to where they kept a book on the building's tenants. This Berger's home address was Great Neck, out in Nassau.

Dermot went to a cafeteria and had a cup of coffee, then looked him up in the book and called him. A woman answered and said he wouldn't be home for another half hour. Dermot sat in the cafeteria reading a paper and falling half-asleep. He called again at six-forty-five. The guy said he couldn't remember the woman working for him, he runs a girdle factory and a lot of women work sewing machines for him. Dermot asked if he could come back to his place so he could go through some records with him. The guy moaned like a bastard. Dermot told him if he didn't come in he was coming out after him.

Dermot walked around to stay awake and then stood in front of the place on Thirty-sixth Street. The street was deserted and cold. The guy pulled up in a Cadillac at eight o'clock. He was hissing his breath out while the night watchman took them upstairs. Berger went through his records, and he found her name and a husband's name, Jorge, and an address up in the Bronx, 1401 Teller Avenue. Berger said the Gonzales woman hadn't worked in his place for four months, so the address might be old.

Dermot took the subway up to the Bronx. There was no Gonzales on the doorbells. So he got the super, who had only been working a month, and he didn't know anything about a Gonzales. But he gave Dermot the name of a woman on the third floor who was from South America and who might have known the woman or the husband. The woman was home and she was pretending she didn't know what it was all about, but she did know, and Dermot kept pushing. Finally, she said he had moved across the street to 1404A Teller Avenue.

He wasn't home and Dermot couldn't go any more. He had the next day off. He went home to get some sleep. It was midnight by the time he got to bed, and he lay there telling Phyllis about it, every step of the thing. They were both excited. Dermot fell asleep. Phyllis went out and slept on the couch with the alarm set for four-thirty a.m. so she could make breakfast and not have to wake him up until exactly five.

He was at the apartment in the Bronx at six a.m. He pounded on the door for five minutes before Gonzales answered it. He understood what Dermot was telling him. He giggled when he heard the bodies were in the morgue. Sometimes South Americans giggle when they're shocked and they don't mean anything by it. The guy was like a little boy. He didn't know what to do. He had been separated from the woman for six months. Dermot asked him why he hadn't sent her any money. He shrugged. He said he didn't even know where she was living. Dermot took him to the morgue on First Avenue in Manhattan and had him claim the bodies. Now he needed some money. They went all the way up to the Bronx again, got the bankbook, came back to the garment center, and almost emptied the bank account. Gonzales had $310 in the bank. That is a hell of a lot of money for a guy like this, although not so much when you realize that he walked out on a wife and baby and never paid anything.

From the bank, Dermot took him over to the Holy Redeemer Church on Central Avenue in Brooklyn, a few blocks away from where she had jumped, and told the story to the priest on duty. After he heard how much Gonzales had, he finally said he would handle it, that there could be a funeral on Friday morning. Dermot told Gonzales to call his job and say he wouldn't be in for the next two days, Thursday and Friday. Gonzales said, "Should I tell it to my boss that you said I should not come to work?"

Dermot told him, "Just tell him your wife and baby died."

He said, "Oh, that's good, that I will tell him."

The uniform kept Dermot from stopping to celebrate on the way home. He told himself he would go home and change and go out and party. When he got into the house, at one in the afternoon, he didn't feel like going out again. The house was empty, the bed made, and pajamas fresh out of the dryer were folded on top of the pillows. He put them on, got into bed, and stretched out. He was not going to report finding the husband. He didn't want to spoil the thing with a detective or a desk lou saying anything, good or jealous, about it. He wanted this one for himself. He wanted the feeling, pure, clean, to run through him without anyone touching it. He lay in bed listening to the daytime sounds of the neighborhood. A hammer knocking on wood, a United Parcel truck squealing while stopping for a delivery, a carriage squeaking while the mother walks the street jiggling the baby to sleep.

Usually, just before Dermot fell asleep, there was this little knife-blade pricking his insides: What happens if I die while I'm asleep? This time there was no knife. Everything inside him, right to the back of his brain, was under a warm blanket.

He never came close to feeling like this again.

4:

In 1964, Dermot Davey was in plainclothes in Brooklyn, which is like saying he was President of the United States. The first day he went out with his partner, Buddy Lennon, they drove to a restaurant in Brooklyn where there was a numbers business. They got there at eleven o'clock on a cold, bright morning. The inside of the place was a barroom with a white tile floor that was clean enough to eat off, with a couple of tables along the wall, and then in the back was the main restaurant. There were five or six guys sitting at a round table in one corner of the barroom, and Lennon started to walk over to them and one of them held up his hand. "Be right with you fellas," he said.

Lennon changed direction and went to the bar. He and Dermot sat on stools. There was an old man bent down polishing bottles along the bottom of the back bar. He did not look up. One of the men from the table came walking across the floor. His heels sounded like hammers on the tile floor. He was a little under thirty. Black hair slicked straight back, even with the sunlight flooding through the windows you couldn't see a dot of dandruff or lint or dust on the hair. His skin was smooth, the way you look from barber-shop shaves. He had olive oil in his skin and big white teeth.

"Hi, guys," he said.

"Nicky," Lennon said.

"What's your name?" he asked Dermot.

"Davey."

"Davey what?"

"Davey's my last name."

"Oh. What's your first name?"

Anger ran through Dermot, but Lennon looked at him hard and said, "His first name is Dermot."

"Oh, that's your name. Dermot Davey. Now I know."

His hand slapped the bar. "Give us a drink here," he said. The old man behind the bar stood up. Lennon and Dermot ordered Scotch. "Good luck to you, fellas, I got a lot of things to do," he said. He picked his hand up from the bar, turned his back, and walked away. His heels tapped hard on the tile floor. He liked to hear himself walk.

There was a hundred-dollar bill on the bar where his hand had been. The old man took it and made change. He put tens, singles, and silver in front of them. Lennon sipped his Scotch. Dermot gulped his. Lennon picked up his half of the change and Dermot quickly did the same. They walked through the door without a word, without looking back.

From there, it only was a matter of time until retirement. The standards were gone. Dermot and Lennon arrested a bookmaker named Russo, who was working out of an apartment in Williamsburg. Russo was charged with taking bets on a phone. The true charge was that he took bets on the phone without getting an O.K. from the plainclothes division. A few weeks later, Lennon told Dermot there would be a thousand dollars if court testimony made it clear Russo was not on the phone and was in another room when the arrest took place. Which would make the affidavit useless and force the judge to release Russo. On the morning of the case, Russo was in the hallway outside the courtroom. Lennon and Davey came up to him. Russo turned his palm up. His thumb covered several hundred-dollar bills, folded in half. "First say something good," Russo said.

Russo's lawyer was hit by a virus on the way to court. He called the judge and the case was put over for five days. When Dermot and Lennon walked out of the building, they saw Russo standing at the curb, snapping his fingers and whistling. He was looking up at the sky.

Five days later, when Russo came to court, his face was scratched and his suit badly wrinkled. Lennon got on the stand and said Russo was in the living room and not on the phone. The assistant district attorney muttered about stupid affidavits. Russo swaggered out. Dermot and Lennon hustled after him. In the hallway, Russo's bloodshot eyes squinted as his hand went into his pocket. "Thanks, guys, buy yourselves a hat," he said. He handed Dermot a bill. At this time, when you bought a cop a hat it meant you gave him twenty dollars. Which is what Russo handed Dermot. When Lennon saw his twenty-dollar bill, his face turned beet-red. He started shouting. The courtroom door swung open. The attendant said the judge wanted to know what the trouble was. Russo waved good-by. "Thank you, gentlemen," he said.

"That fuck," Dermot said later. "That dirty fuck robbed us."

Dermot lasted in plainsclothes for seventeen months. When he was flopped out of the division and put back into uniform he had sixteen thousand dollars in a bank under his mother-in-law's name. In uniform in the 125th in Ridgewood, he depended on small things for extra money. He went around with the men from the gas company, shutting off the gas in houses where the bill had not been paid. A city marshal accompanied the men from the gas company. The city marshal had legal papers which he said allowed him to enter any house, even if the people were not at home. The gas-company men still wanted a cop with them when they went around. One of them told Dermont he would get three dollars a house.

"Hey, there should be a pound," Dermot said.

"We're doin' seven houses, it's not like you're only gettin' the one," the gas-company man said.

"Still it should be a pound, you're from a big company," Dermot said.

"It's not a company, it's a utility. What's the matter with you, all utilities are cheap."

Nobody was home at the first stop, in a six-family apartment. The landlord, a German, saw the big seal and the signatures on papers that looked legal. The German nearly saluted. He opened the tenant's apartment. The gas-company guys pulled out the gas meter and capped the pipes. When the people who lived in the apartment came home they would have to set the couch on fire if they wanted coffee.

The second house they went to was on Wyckoff Avenue. The apartment was on the ground floor. A black guy with half-shut eyes opened the door. He was in a sweatshirt. The city marshal showed him the papers. The black guy stood in the doorway looking at them.

"Well, you see . . ." he said.

"No, you have to let us in or he'll arrest you and put you in jail," the city marshal said.

"You an officer?" he said.

One of the gas-company guys took Dermot by the arm and brought him into the light. "See, police," the gas-company guy said. "You got to let us in or he'll arrest you."

The black guy shrugged and let him in. A fat woman sat on a broken couch in the living room, holding a little girl. The girl looked at Dermot wide-eyed.

"You take out the gas?" the woman asked.

Dermot didn't answer.

"He police," the little girl said.

The next house they went to was a two-story shingled place on Irving Avenue. Nobody answered. The city marshal brought out a tool bag and went to a first-floor window. He took the window out of the frame and climbed in. The gas-company man, McDonough his name was, said he was glad Dermot was with him. "These people here aren't like niggers," he said. "Niggers are so dumb, you see that, all you have to do is tell them they're going to jail. But white people, they know you're full of shit."

The city marshal opened the front door and let them

in. The two guys from the gas company were halfway down the front hallway, going to the cellar door, when a door opened. Black curly hair came out. Under the black curly hair was enormous shoulders. The curly hair was shaking. The man was trying to wake up.

"Gas company," the city marshal said.

The guy pushed the door open. He hissed at them. "Sssssss!" And a German shepherd flew into the air in the hallway. The dog was stopped in mid-air because the guy in the door was hanging on to the collar. The marshal stumbled back. The gas-company men began pushing to get out of the hallway. One of them swung a wrench while he was trying to run. It hit Dermot on the back of the head. Dermot's scalp froze, and he stopped to hold his head.

"Ssssss!" The man was crouched down, walking the dog right at Dermot. The dog fought the air to get free. Dermot's hand moved automatically to his right side. He had backed out onto the stoop before he had made his mind up. The man stopped with his dog at the doorway.

"I'll arrest that wop fuck," Dermot said.

"Forget it," the city marshal said.

"Forget my ass. You got a court order."

"What we got is a lot of bullshit to fool the niggers with," the city marshal said. "This paper is good for only toilet paper. Don't get into it or you'll get yourself in trouble too."

The gas-company men decided they had enough for the day. One of them handed Dermot six dollars. "Two houses," he said.

"What about the threesky for this one?" Dermot said.

"We didn't shut no gas off in this house," the gas-company man said.

"Yeah, but we went in there," Dermot said.

"The gas got to be off."

"Come on."

"Hey," the gas-company man said. *"You* come on."

Dermot was involved in one outside activity in his life. On a Sunday in March of 1968, he and Phyllis went to mass at Holy Child Jesus Roman Catholic Church on 111th Street. The church is a tan-yellow fort. Catholic architecture is defensive. Only the gun slits are missing from most Diocese of Brooklyn complexes. Massive church, rectory, grammar school, the building sides forming walls. Young boys, altar boys and sons of Holy Name Society members, were in front of the church with leaflets. One, on green paper, announced a meeting of the Senator Joseph McCarthy Memorial Mass Association. Once the Joseph McCarthy Memorial Mass was a big thing in Queens. When Dermot was a grammar-school kid, he attended one of the masses outdoors in Forest Park when five thousand attended. This time, Dermot was not interested in the pamphlet.

"It's funny," he said to Phyllis. "Look at a great man like this and I don't even care any more. I guess it's so long since he died now."

"Mother was saying the exact same thing about Roosevelt," she said.

He was putting the leaflet into his pocket when a young boy handed him another leaflet announcing a meeting of the South Queens Committee to Elect George Wallace President. The meeting was for Tuesday night. The address was only a few blocks from Dermot's house. "Maybe we'll go," Dermot said.

The meeting on Tuesday night was in a storefront that once was a real-estate agency. It was next door to the Triangle Hofbrau Restaurant. Chairs from O'Brien's Funeral Home in Richmond Hill were set up. A young guy named Kelly, with a blond crew cut, a member of the Ushers' Society of Our Lady of Grace in Howard Beach, introduced a man named George Creel, who wore two-tone shoes. He was from Montgomery, Alabama. Creel explained the mechanics of petition-carrying. He told the people sitting on the funeral chairs, pinched Richmond Hill people, that the objective this time was to put Wallace's name on the ballot for the June Presidential primary in New York.

"Now, we up here in overcoat country for that purpose alone," he said. "You folks got opposition, that's for sure.

91

You got McCarthy people—the wrong McCarthy people, as we all know—you got Bobby Kennedy people . . ."

An old man sitting behind Dermot began to hiss.

"Now, we gonna take a second here to talk about somethin'," Creel said. "Y'all see, Governor Wallace isn't in politics for sport. Y'all can boo and hiss in a sportin' game. Governor Wallace is a pro-fessional politician. Now, you been so disillusioned by politicians that you probably get nervous when you hear me say the Governor is a pro-fessional politician. But he is. Every inch of that little fightin' rooster's body is pro-fessional politician. That's why we respect other politicians. We may not agree with them. The Governor get out there and attack them. But we never waste time in a closed meetin' like this gettin' worked up over opponents. Hell, they in the same business as we in. They out there tryin' and workin'. A Bobby Kennedy campaign worker, they out there workin'. You got to admire anybody out there workin'. They wrong, but they think they truly tryin' to do some good. Don't be hissin' at that worker. Respect that political worker. And say a little-bitty prayer that we could win that worker over. Now, don't tell me we don't want Kennedy workers. Evey one of them come through the door here, they in trouble. Automatically. 'Cause they goin' get loved to death by me. Anybody doin' anything out there in politics, you can rap 'em in public in a campaign. That's part of the business. But don't ever take it personal.

"Now lemme give you a little-bitty lesson about politics. In every endeavor in life, you try to succeed. Business-man tries to succeed. Student tries to succeed. Man will do certain things to succeed. But in politics, the word is survahval. You must survahve no matter what the cost. And a man does anything to survahve."

He pointed to the man who had hissed the Kennedy name.

"And, mister, I take second to no man, to no man in my worry about the Kennedys with all their money and all their pointy-headed pro-fessors. But we here this year is interested in survahval. We want to get by. And then we goin' make George Wallace the President of the

United States come nahnteen-seventy-two, or, if we got to, we can wait. We can wait until nahnteen-seventy-six. But we goin' make him President. Right now, our job is to survahve. And to survahve, the first thing we goin' do is go out there and shake hands with ever' Kennedy supporter we can find. We goin' cultivate them. We goin' survahve."

He asked for questions. The man who had hissed Kennedy asked, "What about the Jews? All they ever do is mollycoddle criminals."

"Welfare!" a woman said. "The Jews put everybody on the welfare."

"That's because the Jews got all the jobs in the Welfare Department," a huge blond woman said.

"Hear this now," Creel said. "The Jew like everybody else. They keep sayin' to you folks, 'Open up your hearts.' That's fine. But you also happen to be gettin' your haids opened up. And the Jew got a haid like anybody else. When the Jew gets his haid laid open by some bully comin' out of a dark alley, then the Jew goin' be out lookin' for George Corley Wallace jes' like you. So this is our year of survahval. And we goin' out shakin' hands with the Jew. Gentlemen, you goin' to see a day in this city, in this state, in this whole country, when everybody, from Jew to the pointy-headed pro-fessor, is goin' to be standin' up and cheerin' for the po-leece. Cheerin' for them! Supportin' 'em. The po-leece and the President of the U-nited States, George Corley Wallace."

When he had finished, Dermot clapped. It was the first time he had ever experienced any excitement outside of the job or watching a football game. He went up to the blond kid at the desk and signed his name and took a sheaf of green petitions.

"I'm a policeman, am I allowed to go out with these?" Dermot asked Creel.

"Don't sign your name no place," Creel said. He smiled. "But when you goin' door-to-door, let them see your weapon. Just a little-bitty glimpse of it. People like to know that security people goin' 'round for Governor Wallace."

"There's a lot of cops around the area," Dermot told him. "Do you pass something out in the precincts?"

"Why don't you write me up somethin' to give to them?" Creel said.

Dermot barely noticed the walk home. He was walking quickly, so quickly Phyllis had to almost trot to keep up with him. He wanted to get to the kitchen table and sit down and write something out.

Once, in the middle of the block, he stopped. "Where's the petitions?"

"I have them right here. You gave them to me."

"Oh, Christ. I thought I left them back there. Goddam, they're important. Don't lose them on me. This thing could be important."

When they got home, he sat down and began writing, using his daughter's looseleaf paper. The words looked strange and amateurish when he wrote them out longhand on the lined paper. They looked better when he printed them. His eyes were tired and he went to bed. He fell asleep right away. He had one idea out of the night. In the next two days, he worked on a leaflet. He finished one that said:

Don't tell your partner. He knows.
Don't tell your wife. She knows.
TELL IT TO THE VOTER! HE DOESN'T KNOW!

Under the block headlines, he printed, in body type,

A policeman of the City of New York works eight hours protecting the lives of the citizenry. Yet we are on duty twenty-four hours a day under law. Well, let's live up to the letter of the law. Let's protect the public from commies and rapists. Let's finish our tours and go out and inform the public of what they can do to help us. We need their prayers. We live under God and everybody must ask His help for us. After prayers, we need their temporal support. The citizenry can best support their peace officers and fight commies and rapists by making Governor Wallace the President.

He took it down to the Wallace storefront. Kelly, the one with the crew cut, gave it to a black-haired woman. She typed out a stencil. When she finished, she put it on the mimeograph machine. She pressed the button and it began flipping out neat copies of Dermot's statement. He watched the drum spin and the paper shoot out with a squeak, and he could not take his eyes off it.

"Gives you a feeling, doesn't it?" the black-haired woman said.

Dermot didn't answer.

"At least we're doin' something," the woman said. "At least we're just not sitting around. We're trying to make ourselves better than what we are. That's all we can do. Try to make ourselves better."

Again, when he walked home, Dermot never noticed the blocks. He could smell the air. He never remembered doing that before this. When he got home, he asked Phyllis about the petitions.

"They're in the kitchen cabinet," she said. "I couldn't do anything with them today. I had to go shoppin'."

In April of 1970, Dermot Davey's life, on paper, was in the hands of Nussbaum, the lawyer, and Monsignor Carrigan of the Counseling Unit. How they handled the Police Department's Internal Affairs Division would determine Dermot's future as a policeman. In this, he also had the tremendous help of being an Irish Roman Catholic from Queens. In any dispute between an Irish Roman Catholic policeman from Queens and a black transvestite, the policeman is a fine man, a bit mixed up but still a fine man, and the black transvestite becames a dirty sick nigger son of a bitch who should have his balls cut off so he not only thinks he's a cunt but he can have a cunt in the bargain.

There was no criminal action taken against Johno and Dermot. The transvestite never appeared before a grand jury. Any grand jury would have to meet in Queens. The District Attorney in Queens, Devlin, had his family roots in Cookstown, in Northern Ireland, the center of the Devlins in that country. Dermot Davey's father was from

Maghera, in Northern Ireland. Dermot knew that his father had a brother who had moved from Maghera to Derry. He had heard this over the years. Dermot's mother had an uncle and aunt, the Meehans, living in the Ardoyne section of Belfast. The complaint had to go through Assistant Chief Inspector McKinney, who lived in Rego Park, in Resurrection Ascension Parish, in Queens. McKinney's grandfather came from Strabane, in Northern Ireland.

Monsignor Carrigan's recommendations were all Assistant Chief Inspector McKinney cared about. The Monsignor had made whisky, not assault, the problem. He noted that both men in question, Davey and O'Donnell, had entered the sanitarium in Paterson of their own accord and now were reporting to the Counseling Unit. McKinney felt this was fine. Both men were assigned to light duty in the auto-identification bureau. It was the second time Dermot had been pulled out of a precinct and put on the Bow and Arrow Squad. He hated pulling out file drawers for eight hours a day. And he regarded the Counseling Unit meetings as trips to the dentist. But he knew it all was better than what could happen to him. He had had several nightmares about being jobless and in jail since the night in the parking lot.

Even with these natural things going for him, Dermot knew nothing was to be taken as permanent. The Irish-Americans Dermot was dealing with allowed strong bonds to dissolve rapidly. George Brennan, a business agent for the ironworkers, was probably the most popular union man in Queens. Brennan got into trouble in the Bronx. A Jewish assistant district attorney, out of the Reform Democratic movement, secured a highly questionable indictment for extortion. The ironworkers in Queens sat in bars and saw Brennan's indictment announced on the evening news. Several of them immediately ran to the phone to begin campaigning for Brennan's job. They now considered Brennan to be a convict. Dermot Davey understood that the protection he was being given could not be taken as final. I'm no Jew, he reminded himself. Jews know how to take care of each other. Irish are nothing, he kept saying.

Throughout parts of Queens—Woodside, Sunnyside, Rockaway—and into Bay Ridge and Greenpoint in Brooklyn and up through the Inwood section of Manhattan and the Fordham section of the Bronx there are great outward signs of Irishness. A network of neighborhood travel agencies keeps the Irish Airlines waiting room at Kennedy Airport filled with people taking advantage of low-cost tours. Saloon after saloon has a shamrock on its neon sign. And once a year everybody stops and goes to the St. Patrick's Day Parade on Fifth Avenue. After these things, it ends. Dermot Davey's father was born in Ireland. His mother had an uncle and aunt in Belfast. This is unusual in New York. Most people in New York with Irish names go back at least three generations before they reach Irish-born in the family. The heritage of being Irish is more a toy than a reality. A drink, a couple of wooden sayings, and a great personal pride, bordering on the hysterical, in being Irish. The bloodlines were present. But they were being thinned out by time. You could count on some help if you were Irish. But there was no way to count on the help lasting forever. Dermot Davey understood the implications.

"Thank God we're out of that," Johno said one day.

"Remember Gene Monaghan?" Dermot said to him.

"Do I," Johno said.

"How long did he go around saying his case was killed?"

"Year."

"Then what happened to him?"

"He got humped."

"Six months in the slam, that's all he got," Dermot said. "But they said they were sorry."

"So we got to be careful," Johno said.

"I think so," Dermot said.

One day when he came home from work Phyllis told him that his aunt had died. The aunt was his mother's oldest sister and she lived in White Plains. Dermot showed no emotion about it. He tried to forget about it as quickly as his wife told him. If he had to begin thinking about his aunt, then he also had to begin thinking about growing up in the house in Jamaica. He knew he was better without any of it in his mind.

He heard about his aunt dying on a Tuesday. He called the funeral home on Wednesday and found that the final night of the wake was to be Thursday. Dermot knew he could use work as an excuse for not attending the funeral mass on Friday morning. He had no way to get out of Thursday night. He took the car with him when he went to work at the auto-identification bureau in Manhattan on Thursday morning. He got to the funeral home in White Plains at seven o'clock. It was a floodlit white wooden house with a blacktop driveway and parking lot. Dermot sat in the car in the parking lot and had two cigarettes while he tried to get himself ready to go inside. When he finally went into the funeral home, he walked down a long carpeted hallway. Two dark-suited morticians were standing at the entrance to one of the chapels.

"I don't know," one of them said.

As Dermot walked past them, he looked into the chapel. It was small and not in use. On a couch against the wall, in dim funeral-parlor light, Dermot's mother was asleep on her back.

"No, she just snored," the other mortician said.

Dermot walked into the chapel. His mother was motionless but her breathing was whisky-heavy. A liquor smell hung over her. Her face had more paste in it, lumps of paste, than it had the last time he had seen her. The auburn hair had a change in it. The start of gray. He looked down at her and something came into him naturally. He felt sorry for her. He started to bend down to kiss her. It would be good to kiss her when she was asleep. There would be no embarrassment that way. But as his face came down, the liquor smell from his mother's breathing was so heavy that he straightened up. He put out a finger and touched her hand.

He went into the next chapel. There were only fifteen people sitting on folding chairs in front of a closed coffin. A few sprays of flowers were alongside the casket. Dermot knelt at the casket and said three Hail Marys. His mind wandered as he said them. He thought about walking directly out. It would be perfect, he thought, to leave while his mother was still asleep.

He got up and started to walk to a seat. The faces he saw were mainly from the husband's side of his aunt's family. He sat on a seat for a moment, nodded at a couple of them, then got up and walked outside for a cigarette. The smoking room was down a flight of stairs.

"Here he is." His Uncle Tom sat on a couch with a cigar in his mouth. He was completely bald. He had several layers of pouch under each eye.

The other uncle, Jack, said nothing. He nodded. Jack had thick gray eyebrows that kept much of his face from showing age or bad habits, both considerable.

"How're the kids?" Uncle Jack said.

"The wife's home with them," Dermot said. He started to take off his raincoat but remembered he had no pistol. He kept it on so the uncles wouldn't know.

"When is she going to come up with a boy?" Uncle Jack said.

"It's half his decision," Uncle Tom said.

"Maybe he's lettin' his half of the decision run down his leg," Uncle Jack said.

The talk embarrassed Dermot.

"We were just talking about Louis Goldstein, do you remember him?" Uncle Tom said.

"I heard the name," Dermot said.

"Christ, that's the only name you ever heard growin' up around me," Uncle Tom said.

"Best Jew ever lived," Uncle Jack said.

"Louis Goldstein was a deputy chief. He had Brooklyn South," Uncle Tom said. "He taught me how to steal. God Bless Louis Goldstein, I say."

"Oh, he was some fuckin' Jew, Louis Goldstein was," Uncle Jack said.

"What did he have, the division?" Dermot asked them.

"Christ no, he had the whole fuckin' half a borough," Uncle Tom said. "Stole half the fuckin' borough too."

"I guess you were too young," Uncle Jack said. "I don't even know if you were living with us then or if you were still over in Sunnyside with your father. With Jimmy. Christ, isn't that funny? I haven't heard the man mentioned for years. Now I mention it here. And just a couple of weeks ago, a fella told me he was back in Ireland for a while. And here the name comes up again tonight."

Dermot spoke to his uncles without looking at them. "Who's in Ireland?" he said.

"I told you, your father. I met this fella from the docks. Met him down at Mutchie's one afternoon. Fella tells me he knows my brother-in-law. I says to him, which fuckin' brother-in-law. He told me. Sure enough, it's Jimmy. He got a job with the ILA in Lauderdale. Port Everglades is the name of the docks there, you know. Well, he got sick or somethin' in December and he went to Ireland. Stays with whatever's left of the family, I guess."

Dermot shrugged. "What the hell does that do for me?"

"Nothin' at all, what could it mean to you?" his Uncle Tom said.

"Sometimes you wonder if kids need anybody," Uncle Jack said. "You grew up like a weed, Dermot. A weed. Couldn't cut you down or pull you out."

"Who was the fellow that knew he was in Ireland?" Dermot said.

"Fellow name of Murphy. He's in charge of the Belgian Line piers. Eastside piers. I saw him down at Mutchie's."

Slow footsteps, a squeak at a time, sounded on the staircase. His Uncle Tom's wife lumbered down. Some women Dermot remembered only vaguely, the other side of his aunt's family, followed her. Everybody began talking and greeting each other. Dermot waited until they all were talking and he slipped upstairs. He was walking past the doorway to the funeral chapel when he saw his mother sitting in the front row. He stopped. He was about to start walking out again when his sister came up to him.

"Are you going?" she said.

"No, just outside for some air," Dermot said.

"Oh, I thought you were going."

"No, I wouldn't walk out."

"Well, I thought if you were, that we could meet you. There's no sense staying late tonight if we all have to get up early in the morning."

"Where?" Dermot said.

"Well, we all were going to this little place right on the road. Just before you go onto the parkway. The whole family was going."

"What's the name of the place?"

"Acerno's. The reason I'm saying it is that I've got to get her something to eat. She hasn't eaten all day."

"Acerno's," Dermot said. "If anything happens and I decide to stay outside in the air, I'll meet you in Acerno's."

"In about an hour, we're not going to be so much longer," his sister said.

Dermot went outside and sat in the car. He turned on the radio and smoked cigarettes. He was surprised at how much the small mention of his father bothered him. The name was just mentioned in passing. It moved something around inside him. He could not figure what it was that had moved, or how it had moved. He smoked the cigarette and thought about it. He did not know how long he sat there. But when he saw people starting to move out onto the porch of the funeral parlor, he drove out of the lot. He did not want to talk to anybody. Instead of driving home to Queens, he simply went around the streets of White Plains. When it was nearly nine o'clock, he came down the hill from the funeral parlor and onto the avenue leading to the parkway, and the restaurant, a small roadhouse, was on the right-hand side. He wanted to keep going, but he pulled in.

When he came through the door, Dermot heard his mother and his sister laughing. They were sitting in a booth. One of Dermot's uncles was walking away with a big smile. The mother was laughing over a glass of wine which she held, on the ready, at her chin. She was laughing deeply, like a man, and too loud. "Aha . . . aha . . . aha." She threw the laugh out like a challenge. Big, irritated eyes looked around the room. Dermot's sister was laughing like a high school girl, a high-pitched laugh, a tone higher and it would have been hysterical. The laugh

101

had no fun in it. The sister had hair that was lighter and had more hue than the mother's. The sister had the mother's face—large eyes, the sharp nose, and the pointed chin. But it was too full for a girl of twenty-six. The sister was always on a diet and always gained weight.

Dermot's uncles, and three or four others, were at a table against the wall. Dermot started to take his raincoat off. He remembered he had no gun. He kept the coat on and slid into the booth. Right away, he felt his mother's eyes. The mother and sister were on the opposite side of the booth, the mother directly across from Dermot, glaring at him. Her fat eyes did not blink or move. They glared at her son. Dermot did not say hello. He looked at his uncles against the wall.

The waiter was a young boy in a white coat who handed out small typewritten menus. Dermot reached for one, and his eyes met his mother's. She had a menu in her hand, but she was still glaring at him.

"How old are you?" Dermot's sister asked the waiter.

"Seventeen," the waiter said.

The mother's eyes finally moved. "Do you attend school?" she said.

"No ma'am."

"My, you certainly start life in a hurry."

"Long as I don't finish it so fast."

The mother gave this laugh that sounded like a snarl. "Aha . . . aha . . . aha." The sister's body convulsed. Her laugh was near a shriek.

"On that I'll have a whisky sour," the mother said.

"Ma'am?" the waiter said.

"A whisky sour."

"I'm sorry, ma'am, but we only serve wine and beer here," the boy said.

"I said a whisky sour."

"Bring her an orange soda," Dermot said.

"Hey, you!" the mother said. She said it with her teeth and her bottom lip. Her fat eyes glared more intensely.

Dermot picked up the menu with his right hand. He leaned across the table so his face almost was touching her and the menu became a screen. "Go ahead, say some-

102

thing," he said to his mother. "Let me see you say something."

His eyes were narrow and the words came through his teeth. His sister was whispering something, her eyes wet, and Dermot began to shake. He pushed himself out of the booth and walked over to the table with the uncles. He put his head against the wall with his eyes shut. He was breathing as if he had just run half a mile.

One of them at the table asked him if he wanted anything. He kept his eyes closed. "Get me a cup of espresso," he said.

A few minutes later he felt the cup being put down in front of him. He opened his eyes and picked up the coffee. It was too hot. Dermot glanced across the aisle. The mother had the tablecloth in front of her pulled up. She was knocking her glass of orange soda against the bare wooden table. It was a thick glass and, without the tablecloth to muffle the sound, thick glass hitting right against the wooden table, the glass was making a steady sound that ran through the room. Dermot's mother was glaring at him with her fat eyes and her bottom lip out. Dermot kept looking into her eyes and the knocking, knocking, knocking was all he could hear and it was getting louder and louder and his temples were throbbing.

The sister had the menu open and she was looking at it. The sleeves of her blouse showed motion from the trembling arms inside.

Nobody at the table with Dermot paid any attention to the mother knocking the glass against the table. Dermot closed his eyes to the throbbing of his temples. When the knocking finally stopped, he opened them. His mother was asleep in the booth with her head against the side of it. His sister was slumped down in the booth with her head thrown back. She had one hand clamped to the back of her neck. She looked up at the ceiling. Dermot went over.

"Can I do anything for you?" he said.

"I can supervise," his sister said.

"Well, I'm going to go, then."

One of his sister's shoulders moved in response. He went back and said good-by to his uncles and left. He got home by ten-fifteen and went to bed at eleven o'clock. He woke up at two o'clock. He was wide awake. He got out of bed and went into the living room and had a cigarette and put on television. The movie on Channel 2 was *Captain's Paradise* with Alec Guinness. Dermot was lucky. It was a movie which held him. The movies were not so good in the nights that followed, nights of waking up at the same time and smoking cigarettes in the living room until light came through the windows.

He tried walking. If he worked days, he walked at night. Walked for miles through Richmond Hill and into Wood-haven and back. He still did not sleep. When he worked at night, he walked in the daytime on the beach.

For the first time, he stopped and asked himself who he was. He looked at the white sand blowing and he remembered the nun in school teaching that the life of a human being was so much less than one grain of sand on a beach. When Dermot looked up at the sky, he saw it solid with people. A mass of people, millions of people, moving slowly across the entire sky. Moving, moving, and yet never moving because there were so many millions of them and so many millions more to come, the millions on the other side of the horizon, that there was no room for anybody to move. They shifted and swayed and exchanged positions but never went anyplace. Dermot Davey stood in the cold by the sea with the sand blowing and he felt his mother next to him, tearing at him, and his sister on the other side of his mind like a weight. The guilt came through him. He did nothing to help either of them. He wondered why he thought about them and not about his own children. He felt guilty about having children. His mother and sister kept coming up first in his mind. He had three daughters and the only thing he could remember automatically about them growing up was the Sunday afternoon he took the two oldest ones to a puppet show at the library in Jamaica. The youngest, Tara, wasn't three yet and he was leaving her home. She stood on the stoop screaming. When her mother tried to soothe her, Tara stuck her thumb in her ears so she wouldn't hear. At the same time the rest of her fingers were tearing at her hair to punish them. Dermot's wife laughed and he laughed with her. He remembered he felt sad under the laugh. He stood on the beach and wondered why it was the only thing he could remember about his three children. He knew it meant he was wrong, the way he had been living. He began to think back, looking for something that would make him feel sorry for himself, that would give him an excuse. As it always did, everything became a red can of Cambell's soup rolling across the floor of the apartment in Sunnyside. Jesus Christ, Dermot Davey said to himself, I wish I knew how to think.

It came quickly, and out of nowhere. *Suicide is a mortal sin.* He shook his head quickly. He was frightened of himself and he walked off the beach quickly.

On the way back from Rockaway, he stopped at a roadside place. Nobody was inside and he had a bowl of clam bisque at a table while the counterman stared. The day was gone now, and Dermot looked out the window at the start of the night traffic. He thought about his father. He couldn't remember the face completely. Only the presence. He wondered what the father looked like now. He didn't know why he was wondering about his father. One guy fucked this whole thing up, he thought. He thought of his mother and his sister in sunlight. How it should be. He got up to go home. Thinking of the house in Richmond Hill gave him a closed-in feeling. He had to be at work at midnight. That made him uneasy too.

The next time he came on the beach he began to lope so he would begin to run out of wind. The job of gulping for air kept his mind busy.

Through February and March and April of 1970, Dermot Davey, troubled, walked the beach whenever he could. One day he came off the beach and walked up 116th Street, past Sullivan's Hotel and Duffy's Bar to the Emerald Cottage, a store ran by Terry O'Keefe and a woman named Mae. They sell sweaters from Donegal, records from Dublin, tea sets from Belleek, crystal from Waterford, maps of Ireland suitable for framing, and Easter Rebellion Proclamations. To priests, Terry and Mae sell the idea that they are married, which is unsupported by such temporal authorities as the city clerk.

When Dermot came in, Terry was preparing for his major business, the Sunday-night radio show he does out of the back of the store. For one hour, at eight o'clock every Sunday night, Terry O'Keefe sits in the back room and sends out over Station WKIL a constant stream of music, "Mother Malone" by the Liffey Boys, "Irish Soldier Boy" by the Corkmen. Between records he delivers a fierce, thumping hard-sell of tours to the old country. Station WKIL carries Terry O'Keefe's show as far away as White Plains. Each Sunday night at about seven-thirty, the Irish, those who immigrated or are first- and perhaps second-generation, after that they care not, begin fiddling with radio sets to put on WKIL. All week, WKIL is a black station. To pay respects to integration, WKIL allows Terry O'Keefe his Sunday-night hour.

Terry uses it for his tours. From late May on, the Aer Lingus terminal at Kennedy Airport in New York is packed with people flying to Ireland on special charters. Two and three charters a night leave New York for Shannon. And all during the year, at Christmas and Easter and St. Patrick's Day, for the All-Ireland Hurling Championships, for the trip to the shrine at Knock, for a special anniversary mass in honor of the Cork City Brigade, Terry O'Keefe puts together charters with travel agents in Woodside in Queens, and Inwood in Manhattan, and the Fordham section of the Bronx.

When Dermot walked into his store this day, Terry O'Keefe was leaning against the wall reading his script for Sunday night's show.

"Attention the boys in blue! John Mackell, PBA delegate from the Hundred and First Precinct, Far Rockaway, announces a fourteen-day tour for PBA members and families only. One man in each party must have a shield. Fourteen glorious days under bright blue skies for boys in blue and their loved ones. A special free cocktail party in the wonderful Aer Lingus lounge at Kennedy Airport. A first-today drink at Shannon free-duty bar. Fourteen days. One hundred and forty-five dollars.

Contact Francis Troy Travel Service, Twining nine-eight-five-three-one. Or go to Francis Troy Travel at seventy-two dash ninety Roosevelt Avenue, Jackson Heights, Queens. Patrolman John Mackell announced that for special inspiration, the Very Reverend Monsignor Michael Carrigan will serve as official chaplain for the tour!" He finished with a shout.

"That was very good," Mae said. "You've got a grand speaking voice."

"When is it?" Dermot said.

"When do you want to go?" Terry O'Keefe said.

"You don't have a date yet?" Dermot said.

"What difference is it?" Terry said.

"Well, just for the hell of it."

"The tour leaves when we got a tour together."

The next day, when he finished work at the license bureau, Dermot walked through Chinatown and across East Broadway and down to Mutchie's. The owner was behind the bar, in sunglasses, snapping a bill between his fingers to see if it was good.

"Murphy?" the owner said. He shook his head vaguely.

Dermot ordered a beer. He mentioned his uncle's name. The owner said, "What are you, a cop too?"

"It's personal," Dermot said. "My uncle told me to stop by. It has nothin' to do with the job."

The owner walked away to serve people at the end of the bar. He stayed down there and had a drink with the people. Then he came back to Dermot. "He's usually here, Murphy, he's usually here at about four o'clock. You won't catch him no more today. What time is it now?"

"Five-thirty," Dermot said.

"Oh, you won't catch him no more today," the owner said.

Dermot came back the next day. He waited and then the owner told him, "You see, he starts at seven in the morning. So he's out of there by, who knows, two, three in the afternoon."

The next morning, Dermot left the house at five-forty-five. He took the car. He drove down the East River Drive and got off at South Street. He pulled in front of the

Belgian Line piers at six-twenty-five. He asked a watchman what time Murphy came on. "The Murphy that's the boss? He be here any time now."

Fifteen minutes later, the watchman pointed to a man who was getting out of a Buick Electra. He had a hat perched on top of a big head and a blue topcoat pulled up around red jowls.

"Well, there's nothin' to it," Murphy said. "I don't know the fella, you know. But Mickey Lynch said this fella was layin' dead in Lauderdale. Tommy Meehan's brother-in-law, Mickey told me. Some sort of a musician, right? Mickey Lynch *ast* me to put him to work, so I called Hughie O'Donnell down Lauderdale and I says, put this fella to work. Which he did. I happen to be down there last month and I say to Hughie, how is Tommy Meehan's brother-in-law doin'? He tells me the guy got hurt. Fell under a hoist, I think. He got compensation and said, fuck it, I can live on this money in Ireland pretty good. So he went over there until he was feelin' better. That's all I know. He went to Ireland. He's probably better off than all of us."

At lunchtime at work, Dermot maneuvered the switchboard operator into a call to the ILA office at Fort Lauderdale. The man there had his father's name and Florida address. Dermot asked him to get the mailing address for the compensation check. When he called back, the man said the checks were being sent to the post office in Bundoran, County Donegal.

"For how long are they supposed to go there?" Dermot asked.

"Doesn't say. That's the address."

On the way home, Dermot stopped at Johno's house. He told him about the PBA tour with the Monsignor.

"What the fuck good is that going to do us?" Johno said.

"I just think we better stay close to this Monsignor. I told you that when we started and you agreed with me."

Dermot did not want to go alone. He knew Johno could not be moved more than ten yards east of Rockaway Beach. Dermot knew he had to make it important

108

or Johno wouldn't listen. If he brought up his father, he was sure Johno would laugh. He had to make it Johno's life or nothing.

"We could feel a lot safer," he said. "A good insurance."

"Fine," Johno said. "How am I going to get there? Swim?"

"It's only a hundred forty-five dollars," Dermot said.

"Oh, then I'll borrow it off Rockefeller," Johno said.

"Well, we'll see what comes up," Dermot said. "Where is Bundoran over there, do you know?"

"It's in Donegal someplace, isn't it? It's up north. It's like a Rockaway Beach, I think. What's Bundoran got to do with it? Is that where the rat-fuck Monsignor is going?"

"No, I don't know where he's going. I was just wondering. I heard somebody mention the place and I was wondering."

"Well, I got no money," Johno said. "If you want to go, then go. You sit next to him and hold his hand for the two of us. Make sure it's his hand too."

"I don't feel like going alone," Dermot said.

In the kitchen that night, Dermot mentioned the tour. His wife frowned. His mother-in-law said, "By airaplane? Oh, Jesus, I'm afraid of them. I'll go by boat before I die. I want to go on a cruise without being stuck in a wheelchair with the plaid blanket tucked around me. But oh, Jesus, not by airaplane."

Why bother even talking, Dermot said to himself.

One night two weeks later, a sergeant from the 106th Precinct in Ozone Park, Nativity Parish, called Dermot at home. He said he had gotten Dermot's number through the precinct. He said, "We have been receiving a number of calls from a woman who identifies herself as your mother. The woman in question lives on Ninety-seventh Street. That is your mother? In that case perhaps you should know that we have been receiving these calls. She calls in regards to an animal, a cat or a dog, scratching the floor in the apartment upstairs from her. We send an officer up of course. He hears no noises. Then she will call again later for the same thing. Apparently, she is just looking for somebody to talk to, and I thought I'd let you know about this. The calls are coming quite frequently and the men keep reporting back on them to me." The sergeant spoke in these flat mechanical words, and Dermot thanked the sergeant and said he would do something about it.

He called his mother. When she came on the phone, after five rings, the voice was high, whisky-defiant. "Yea-yes," the voice snapped. Dermot hung up without speaking.

A couple of days later, a patrolman at the precinct called him. The patrolman worked the switchboard. He said the sergeant had instructed him to remind Dermot about calling Mrs. Davey. He said the sergeant sounded as if he wanted the job done. "Gettin' a lot of calls here," the patrolman said. "She ought to call the Sanitation."

"What do you mean?" Dermot asked.

"Give the wops somethin' to do."

Dermot called his mother. She was out someplace. His sister spoke to him in that high, nervous voice of hers. She said she would have the mother call Dermot back.

Two days later, when Dermot was in the middle of dinner, the call came.

"Yeah?" he said.

There was no sound on the phone, only breathing. He knew who it was.

"Yeah," he said, softer this time.

"You never see me," she said. He could hear her crying through the whisky.

"Well, what can you do?"

"I'm all alone."

He muttered something and she kept sobbing and he said he would see her within a couple of days. He hung up. He was disturbed and he showed it. "I never even tell you," Dermot's wife said. "She calls here all the time."

He sat alone in the kitchen with cigarettes and coffee. Dermot Davey has not had as much as a swallow of beer inside his house in his life. He drinks only in saloons. His mother drinks only in the house. You drink at home, you're an alcoholic, Dermot always told himself.

Three days later, his mother called the house again. Dermot came on the phone with a bright voice.

"Punk," she said.

"Oh come on," Dermot said.

"You punk."

He didn't talk.

"Bum."

He held the phone and looked at the ceiling.

"You're a punk and you come from a punk."

Dermot hung up and took the phone off the hook. His mother was fifty-four. He wondered what she would be like at sixty-four.

In the basement that night, before dinner, one of the girls began howling. Dermot walked to the basement staircase and looked down. Kim, the six-year-old was standing on the bottom step.

"Kelly and Jane Leary locked me out," she said, sobbing without tears.

The door to a storeroom in the basement opened. The oldest daughter, Kelly, eight, looked out. She was grinning.

"We did not, she could come in."

Kim turned and ran to the door. Kelly slammed it in her face. Kim began screaming. Dermot didn't say a word. He went down the front hall and stood outside with a cigarette. It was hot and tasteless. His wife opened the front door and told him dinner was ready. Dermot did not answer her and he did not come into the house for an hour. Later, in the middle of the night in the living room, he decided he had to do something. Sitting alone, with his religious training, he believed it all be to the work of the Devil. Torment him, have others misunderstand, frustrate him, lure him, trap him. Catch another strong body and soul and shove it through the Gates of Hell. He began to think of an old saying. The Devil you know is better than the Devil you don't know. The trouble is, Dermot thought, he did not even know the Devils in his

111

own life. Somehow, he had to put his hand on the evil in his own life.

He got dressed and went out. McLaughlin's, on the avenue, was still open. It was two-fifty-five a.m. Dermot began drinking straight shots with beer chasers while the bartender sat and watched television. A German shepherd was asleep in the middle of the room. The bartender had a drink with Dermot at four a.m. Then he shut the lights off. He and Dermot had another drink in the darkness. Dermot only grunted to the bartender. By the time he got home to bed, it was after four-thirty.

He dreamed of a hockey game at Madison Square Garden between the Detroit Red Wings and the Rangers. Before the game, when the teams warmed up, there was trouble. Each team skated in a circle and, at the part of the ice where the circles passed each other, in the middle of the arena, the players were sticking out elbows and jabbing each other with their sticks. When the game began, Gordie Howe of the Red Wings hit a slap shot and it missed and he became angry and hit Rod Seiling of the Rangers in the face with his stick. Seiling went down. Howe tried to jump on Seiling's face with his skates. When the referee came up to stop the fight, somebody punched him and knocked him down. Now both teams were fighting and fist fights were starting all over the arena. Men were punching each other and tumbling into the aisles. In the upper tier, a man stood up with a small boy held over his head. He threw the boy off the upper tier. Policemen ran up, firing guns at the man. Outside on Thirty-fourth Street, there was a traffic jam. A cabbie jumped out with a tool in his hand. He reached into the car in front of him and hit a man on the head. The traffic patrolman ran up to the cabbie. The cabbie hit the patrolman. The patrolman went down. He pulled his gun and fired from the ground and the cabbie went down. Screaming. A loud scream. Now all of Thirty-fourth Street was filled with people kicking at each other. The fighting spread off Thirty-fourth Street. Black men were running down Seventh Avenue, in front of the Americana, in orange light from torches. Inside Madison

Square Garden, Dermot gripped his seat. He was in the upper tier. The upper tier began to go out like a swing. Now it pulled back, far back, and everybody in it began to spill out of the seats and Dermot looked down, far down at the ice, it was so far down it was a tiny oval, and he saw little policemen on the ice skidding and falling as they shot at people who were lying on the ice. Now there was a tangle of people fighting. In Washington, two men with attaché cases walked past each other in a building hallway. They dropped their attaché cases, black cases on white marble floors, and they lunged for each other and one of them got his leg out and tripped the other, and the minute the guy was down, the man on top of him, a gray-haired man with thick eyebrows, began slamming the head against the white marble floor until the head split open and blood ran on the white marble. First just a finger of blood. Then a circle of blood becoming a pool. The gray-haired man pulled the head high up, his knuckles tense as he gripped the hair, and then he brought the head down, brought it down with his shoulder blades, jerking to give leverage, and the head hit the marble in a spray of blood. Little gray tufts, pieces of brain spit out from the head and into the blood. A uniformed guard came running down the hall, his feet echoing on the marble. The gray-haired man turned to face the guard and the guard shot him between the thick eyebrows. Down the hallways, in brown wooden chambers, men were fighting in dim light while desks fell over. Now, in the dream, the men fighting had on uniforms and they were thin Americans with long noses, hands out and fingers spread as they went for each other's faces. Then the men fighting had shaved heads and the backs of their necks were creased with fat. They were grunting in Russian. A Russian got free and began punching buttons and an American got free and began turning keys in boards covered with blinking lights, and missiles, white with frost, roared through the black night in the sky. Dermot was on a catwalk hanging from the ceiling at Madison Square Garden and there were all little bodies, like dead rats, far below him and the black metal catwalk creaked and

113

one end of it started to break. Dermot was on his belly on the catwalk. He was taking out his pistol to shoot himself before he fell. This woke him up.

He sat on the edge of the bed with the nerves in the inside of his elbows throbbing. His head was fuzzy from the whisky. The inside of his mouth was sour from too many cigarettes.

Before he went to Rockaway the next time, Dermot went to the bank, the Ridgewood Savings Bank, on Myrtle Avenue. He kept some of his money, forty-five hundred dollars, in the Ridgewood. Most of his money, sixteen thousand dollars, was in the mother-in-law's account in the Richmond Hill Savings Bank.

The Ridgewood Savings Bank has as its centerpiece an enormous mural rising two stories to a cathedral ceiling. The mural is of an angel with a halo of sunrays standing against a misty sky and with one hand clutching part of an American flag. The angel's other hand rests on a white headstone with the inscription:

Saving Is
The Secret
Of Wealth

The lines are always long at the bank. On the days when interest is recorded, the lines go out into the street. The Germans in Ridgewood do not trust the bank. They want the interest posted in their bankbooks. A few times a year, the interest-posting day coincides with the day rents are collected. A passerby would suspect the bank to be under siege.

It took Dermot a full half hour on the line before he could withdraw three hundred dollars. He drove to the travel service in Jackson Heights and bought two tickets. While he was there, he looked up Bundoran on the map. The travel agent told him the train from Dublin to Belfast, and then a car rental, was the fastest way. He drove over to Johno's house.

He handed Johno the ticket. "Forget about the money,"

114

he said. "We'll even it up with a score someplace. Even if we get off and sit in the waiting room in Shannon for fourteen days, it's worth it. We hold hands with the Monsignor all the way to Ireland. He's our insurance policy. We've got the perfect excuse to hang around him."

"Well, I don't know," Johno said. He fingered the ticket. "Yeah, but I need more than this."

Dermot did not answer. He was not going for any more money.

"Christ, I need a few bucks. Can't be a hump walkin' around fuckin' empty."

Dermot said nothing.

"Fuck it," Johno said. He got his coat and went out with Dermot. They rode over to the Falls Pub on Greenpoint Avenue in Sunnyside. Once, when Johno had been in the Sunnyside precinct, he had done the owner, Jimmy McManus, a favor. Over the years, McManus was always good for a twenty, sometimes as a gift. Now Johno wanted to borrow one hundred and fifty dollars. That figure made Jimmy McManus's blue eyes glaze over. He was not listening. Then his eyes came back into focus.

"Could ye not do somethin' in return?"

"Holy Christ, Jimmy, are you kiddin'. What is it?"

"Bring a piece of machinery to my brother-in-law," Jimmy said.

"Hey, we'll bring him a whole fuckin' arsenal."

McManus went into a drawer behind the bar and took out a sheet of writing paper with a big Rheingold letterhead. He carefully printed the name and address of his brother-in-law. The lettering said: JOE O'NEIL, O'HAGAN'S PUB, LESSON STREET, BELFAST.

"It's just a wee little way down the street from the Falls Road, you know," Jimmy McManus said. "Everybody in Belfast knows of the Falls Road."

On the day Dermot Davey left for Ireland, he went to Criminal Court in Manhattan to pick up a pistol from Jack Sherdian, who worked out of the 32nd Squad and was in the Police Department Gaelic society.

He found Jack in the R.O.R. room behind the arraign-

115

ment part. He had his prisoner being interviewed by one of the hippie law students who work in the R.O.R. program. R.O.R. stands for "release on recognizance." If the people working for R.O.R. can write down enough good things, to show roots in the community, on the sheet going to the judge, the prisoner can be released without having to put up cash bail. The police hate the program automatically.

Jack Sheridan had arrested this black prostitute, and he was standing behind her while the whore sat at the table and talked to the R.O.R. girl. The R.O.R. girl was in a yellow T-shirt. On the front of it was this big drawing of the alligator from the Pogo comic strip. She was going out of her way to be nice to the black prostitute. The whore said to the girl in the Pogo shirt, "Put down that this man says he wouldn't 'rest me if he could stay with me. And I let him stay with me and he still 'rest me."

Jack Sheridan said, "Hey, I'll kiss your ass."

"Then you put down that beside takin' my body, the man take my money. And he still 'rest me."

"Hey, I'll kiss your ass, I'll kiss your ass," Jack Sheridan said.

The black whore turned around and looked right at Jack. She said it loud so everybody in the room would pay attention. "You had your chance to do that last night when you had your head between my legs."

Jack Sheridan stood there with everybody looking at him. Sheridan started to say something back to the whore but he didn't. Then he and Dermot went into the toilet. Sheridan still had the whore's words sticking into him. He was more concerned with that than he was with handing the gun to Dermot. It was a police .32 in a holster. Dermot put it onto his belt.

"I don't know," he said.

"What?" Sheridan said.

"I don't know what the hell I'm doing this for."

"Then don't do it, give me the thing back. I mean, Christ."

"You know, I think I will," Dermot said. His hands

116

went to his belt. "No. Thanks, Jack, I promised. So I'll do it."

"Well, Christ, don't go hangin' around now," Sheridan said.

"I'm leaving tonight," Dermot said.

"All right. Just don't be hangin' around."

When Sheridan was finished with court, he and Dermot went over to Carmine's. Carmine's is always the same. At two-thirty in the afternoon, when there were only police brothers at the bar, somebody went over to the juke box and punched the numbers N-5 and P-5. The same record sides have been on N-5 and P-5 on the juke box in Carmine's since anybody can remember. Carmine's is the bar on Bayard Street, behind the Criminal Court building in Manhattan, where the cops and court attendants go. With the courts back in session for the afternoon, the only ones at the bar were cops who had finished up in court before lunch. Carmine's smells as if it has river water in the basement. A couple of drinks and you don't notice the smell any more. The place is kept very dark in the daytime. A lot of the guys have been up all night and the last thing they want is bright light stinging their eyes while they drink. The first of the two records to come on the juke box was N-5. The rule in Carmine's is that this record must always be played first. The N-5 record was Kate Smith singing "God Bless America."

Sometimes it takes a little while for the music to get through to all the guys drinking and bullshitting. This time Kate Smith did only the first two words of the song, "God . . . bless . . ." and Jack Sheridan picked it up as loud as he could, and Jack Sheridan can be very loud. "A-mer-i-cuh . . ."

Everybody started singing. There wasn't a place open at the bar, so there was a solid line of brothers, holding their drinks and singing this hymn. "Brothers," sometimes it sounds a little strange to use that word because the Black Panthers and the Communists say it so much. But when you work in a job where you can get hurt, killed sometimes, it is natural that guys should be very

117

close and call each other brothers. A few drinks had taken the empty feeling out of Dermot's shoulder blades and instead of being depressed like he'd been for the last few weeks, he felt good and proud. As the song went along, all the brothers at the bar pulled themselves together while they sang. Stomachs were sucked in. The chins came up as high and as far out as they could go. This made the flesh underneath the chins pull a little tighter and not look so bad. Most cops are fat and look at least five years older than they are. When Dermot sucked in his stomach, his shoulders came up and one of them brushed against the shoulder of Jack Sheridan. He never moved and Dermot never moved and they stood there with their shoulders touching and they sang "God Bless America." At the end, when you get the idea that Kate Smith is putting her whole life into the notes, Jack Sheridan's fingertips held Dermot by the elbow and they sang the last lines together from the bottom of their stomachs.

There was a cheer when the music stopped. The brothers were putting their glasses down all along the bar and the ones sitting on barstools were getting up. Carmine, the owner, came through the swinging doors from the kitchen and stood in his apron. It takes a couple of seconds for the inside of the juke box to work its way around between records, but everybody was getting ready for P-5 to come on. Jack Sheridan looked around the place and saw three lawyers sitting over coffee in one of the booths along the wall opposite the bar.

"Everybody up!" Jack Sheridan yelled at them.

All the brothers at the bar stood at attention. Carmine, the owner, put his hands to his sides and squared his shoulders and stood like a sentry. A sound of static came out of the juke box. The record came on the same way it has been coming on at Carmine's during every afternoon for years. Kate Smith, in that great American voice of hers, began "The Star-Spangled Banner."

The lawyers in the booth did not get up. "I said everybody up!" Jack Sheridan yelled back at them. The lawyers sat in the booth and looked at each other and pretended not to hear Sheridan or the music. They were lawyers.

The bartender bent down and turned the key that controls the juke box volume and he made the record so loud, and everybody sang louder because of it, that it was hard to hear Sheridan when he yelled out, "Get up, you fuckin' mockies," but it was one of those things you could feel being said rather than actually hear it being said. Dermot touched Jack's hand to calm him down.

Everybody was up to " . . . And the rockets' red glare . . ." The voices trailed off badly but that was because the national anthem is harder to sing than "God Bless America." All along the bar the brothers were standing motionless, a few of them with their eyes shut, and Kate Smith's voice filled the room and her voice was louder than all their singing together. Sheridan's shoulder and Dermot's shoulder pressed into each other while they sang. Somebody's arm touched Dermot on the other side. He could feel the gun in his holster. He had never felt warmer or safer in his life.

The national anthem ended and everybody yelled out "Yea!" and reached for a glass. Jack Sheridan stepped back from the bar. He called out in that big voice of his, "Fuck all commies, niggers, and liberals."

Dermot put his glass on the bar and hunched over it and began staring into it. The letdown was on, and some of the others were leaving. The small glass of Scotch and ice in front of him looked greasy instead of cold. His mouth was hot from cigarettes.

He waited through half of the next drink with Sheridan. He went to the men's room and he grabbed his change and coat and went out of the place.

He stopped in a pay booth at the corner. He dialed the number.

She answered on the second ring.

"Yeah?" he said.

"Well. And where are you?"

He had a little dry patch in the back of his throat. The whisky had hit him. "Oh, I'm around," he said.

"Around?"

"What are you doing?" he said.

"Nothing." She spoke very softly.

"What would happen if I came up?"

"Why don't you come up here and see what would happen?"

"A half hour," he said.

"A half hour," she said.

He hung up. He felt like a baby and he took one deep breath. The apartment house where she lived was straight down Queens Boulevard. It was across from the courthouse in Kew Gardens. It still was only a little before four. That gave him four and a half hours until he had to be at the airport. With the liquor from the afternoon wearing off, he felt tired. It was the kind of tired where you fall asleep with your head against the window of a subway or a bus and wake up feeling sweaty and dirty.

She had on a dark-brown dress with a gold watch hanging around her neck on a gold chain. Thick, long light-brown hair that was almost blond against the shoulders of the dress. The hair was always brushed until it glistened. It smelled of perfume, not a lot of perfume, just enough to let you know it was there. She had the door shut when he put his finger into that thick hair and they pressed into each other. He put his hand on her back and walked her to the bedroom.

At the doorway, her mouth came up at him. She kept her lips an inch or so away from his.

"You're right on schedule," she whispered.

"I said a half hour and that's what it was."

"No, your schedule is every five weeks," she said.

"What do you mean, every five weeks?"

"After four years, you don't think I know you? I hear from you every five weeks. I knew I'd hear from you today."

He leaned against the closet door and took off his shoes. She pulled the bedspread down. She stood by her bureau and lifted the dress over her head.

"You're lucky, we got through early today," she said.

"Uh huh."

"At first I thought we were going to have to type the whole day's testimony. We would've been across the street until midnight."

"Uh huh."

"But at lunchtime they must have changed their minds. Somebody came upstairs and said we wouldn't have to do it. So I knew enough to leave early so I could be here for your call."

"Uh huh."

"What time is your plane?" she said.

"What plane?" he said.

"The plane you're going to Ireland on."

"Who told you that?"

She put her hands on her hips. "Dermot, please. Half the police in New York are in the building where I work. How wouldn't I hear what somebody I know is doing?"

"How do they know to bring up my name when you're around?"

"Oh, Dermot, grow up. People know."

"You must tell them something," he said.

"I don't say a word. But after four years, what do you expect?"

"Well, I don't want anybody to know anything."

She had her hands behind her back unhooking her bra. She took it off slowly, the shoulder dropping and one breast appearing and then the other shoulder dropping and he took her into bed on top of him, with the breasts pressing into his chest. Her body on top of his was soft and warm and with a form to it. You forget how good it is to run your hands over the hips of a woman who doesn't have maternity-ward fat billowing from her ribs to the tops of her thighs. He ran his hands through that thick hair. One of her hands, just the fingernails, glided along his legs. Her green eyes were looking right into his. She had a little smile.

"I love you, Dermot," she said. The words smothered him.

"Say something," she said.

He was silent.

He touched her on the top of her thick hair. A light

121

touch. All she ever needed from the first time he did it was this light touch on the top of the thick beautiful hair. She was kissing his chest. She brushed against the rest of him and she nestled between his legs with her hair draped onto the insides of his thighs and he couldn't tell the difference between lips and her tongue and then she brought this soft warm mouth completely over it. There was an instant before he came when he wanted her down farther and then there was this rush through him. Right away he pushed at her hair to get her away. Her head pressed against his hands and he felt her body rustle while she tried to stay there. He pulled himself away and pushed her head up in the same motion and she fell against his chest and he could feel himself spreading over her belly.

Now he could hear the sound of traffic from Queens Boulevard. He buried his face into the pillow.

"Why didn't you let me?" she said.

He kept his face in the pillow.

"I wanted to," she said. "You never let me. I love you and I wanted to."

He said nothing. "Oh well," she said. She lay down alongside him. He got up on an elbow and looked at her clock. It was four-twenty.

"I got to run. I'm so late I'll be dead."

"I knew it," she said.

"I got to go," he said.

He swung out of bed and took his clothes into the bathroom. He turned on the shower and leaned against the wall while the warm water came over him. He dressed quickly and came out looking for his shoes and pretending he was in trouble for time. She was putting on a robe and he had the coat in his hands and she started for the door.

"Can you at least let me open the door for you?" she said.

"I'm late as hell," he said.

At the door he had to look at her. He couldn't kiss her good-by. So he reached out and tweaked her nose. She smiled.

"Take care," he said.

"You too," she said.

"Don't you tell anybody I was here," he said.

"No, don't worry, I won't tell people your business," she said. She said it a little bitterly, but he was telling himself this would be the last time he would ever be there.

It was only seven o'clock and the kids were in bed. His wife's aunt came down the block to babysit. He did not have to be at the airport until eight-thirty. Dermot decided to drive his wife and her mother to the Maspeth Bingo Game. He showed his badge to the two men in American Legion hats who were at the door.

"You got to pay for your cards, though," one of them said. He had his arm on a stack of thick cardboard bingo cards folded in half. Dermot's wife and her mother had already bought their cards from the guy in the Legion hat.

"I'm not playing, I'm just going to sit here for a few minutes with them," Dermot said.

"You could sit all night, you just got to pay for the cards."

The Maspeth Bingo Game is in an old moviehouse on Grand Avenue. Usually Phyllis and her mother play in the bingo game at the old RKO Keith's, on 117th Street, only nine blocks from the house. But for the last two weeks they had been going to the Maspeth Bingo Game. The Maspeth Bingo Game runs every night at seven-forty-five. The inside of the place is green cinder-block walls and, high up, a black ceiling. Long rows of fluorescent lights run across the hall. It looks like an old fight club. Bright lights on dinginess. When you get inside the place there are three more men in Legion caps sitting at a table with Phillies cigar boxes in front of them. They sell the super jackpot, the sheets for the special prize games they have during the night. You buy your regular cards at the admission door and then you pay extra for the supers inside.

"The big super here pays a hundred seventy-five dollars," Phyllis's mother said.

Every night, a thousand people come to the Maspeth Bingo Game. Women mostly, a few old men wedged among them. Dermot's wife and her mother went to a table along the wall. The moment they sat down they started unloading a big purse. Five little plastic bottles of Speed Dot Bingo Ink Marker. "Girls in Brooklyn get three for a dollar," his mother-in-law said. "Big, big bottles too. They sell here for sixty-five cents each. Isn't that something?"

Plastic margarine containers filled with metal chips to use as markers. Three small silver-foil ashtrays that looked like miniature pie plates. Cigarettes, matches, super sheets, regular bingo cards. Dermot's wife and mother arranged everything in front of them. Across the table from them a tall woman, chest sagging in a tight short-sleeve wool sweater, unwrapped a sandwich. The woman had thick lipstick on and a ciagrette sticking straight out of her mouth. She closed her eyes against the smoke. An old lady got into the seat next to her. The woman in the sweater said hello out of one side of her mouth.

Dermot's mother-in-law got up. "Have a cup of coffee?" she said.

"Uh huh."

"You, Phyllis? You want a cup of coffee?"

"I'll get it, Ma."

"You sit and talk to your husband. After all, he's going away. Jesus, he's got to go in an airaplane."

"Why don't you come along?" Dermot said.

"Oh, Jesus, not me. Not me in an airaplane."

The mother-in-law walked to a sandwich stand set up along the wall.

Dermot looked at his wife. She took a drag on her cigarette.

"Well?" he said.

She exhaled slowly. "One way it's good you're going," she said. "The bathroom is going to be a mess. There has to be a leak inside the wall. Remember I told you I was

124

sure the leak had to come from inside? Well, Bob came over and he said he's going to have to take all the tiles down and go right inside the wall at the pipes."

"When is he coming?"

"He works eight-to-four. I called Estelle. She said he'd be here Saturday morning."

"What else?"

She took another drag on the cigarette. She gave her head a little cock and said nothing.

He reached in front of her for a match.

"Here's coffee," the mother-in-law said. She had a small tray with three white plastic containers of coffee and two apple turnovers in plastic wrapping.

"I was just talking to Mrs. Shaffer," the mother-in-law said, "and she was telling me her sister had open-heart surgery."

"How is she?" Phyllis said.

"I'm telling you. Oh, brother. They really cut her open this time. Cut her from the neck down and spread her all out like a chicken. Here, have an apple turnover. Dermot, do you want an apple turnover? Do you know what they did? Took out two arteries this time. Do you know how long it takes the doctor to replace a heart artery? Seventeen minutes for an artery. Can you believe that?"

"I thought it would take hours and hours," Phyllis said.

"Only seventeen minutes for each artery."

"That's hard to believe."

"That's only the heart surgeon, dear. Somebody else had to prepare her first. I don't know how long that took. They had her spread open like a chicken."

"Uh huh."

"That's how it is. When something is old and rotten, you just have to cut it out and throw it away."

The old woman across the table stood up. "There's that one," she said.

"Who's that?" the woman with the cigarette in her mouth said.

"She plays twenty boards at once, she doesn't put a marker on a board. Keeps it in her mind."

"No chips at all?" Phyllis said.

"Not a one," the old woman said.

"This I admire," the mother-in-law said. She took a bite of the apple turnover. "Yick," she said. "Soggy. Ain't it soggy, Phyllis?"

"It is, Ma," Phyllis said.

"Here, give it to me. I'm going right back with them."

She gathered everything into one plastic wrap and went back to the counter.

Phyllis sat with a thumb against her teeth.

Dermot got up. "I've got to get to the airport," he said.

"You put the car in parking lot two," Phyllis said.

"That's right. Right across from the Aer Lingus terminal."

"That's the International Building," she said.

"That's right."

"I'll have Ma drive me over tomorrow when we go out shopping."

"You've got the keys?"

"Yes."

"All right." He almost leaned over and kissed her. "It's only two weeks," he said.

She nodded.

"I'll see you." He brushed his hand against her arm.

"Sweaters. I can put them away for the kids for the fall."

"Fine."

He reached out and brushed his hand across her arm again. He walked away from the table and she sat with her thumb against her teeth and stared out into the smoke that was starting to form in the hall.

His mother-in-law was arguing with the man at the counter.

"Look, baby," he was saying, "it just came in this wax paper. That's moisture inside. That's good. Why are you telling me it's bad?"

126

"Eat it, it tastes awful," his mother-in-law said.

"Don't tell me it tastes awful."

"You eat it, then."

"Baby, I only sell fresh. Despite what you say."

"Goddam cake is no good," she said.

Dermot touched her arm. "I'm going," he said.

She turned around. "Oh, Jesus, have a safe trip." She shivered. "No airaplane for me. You'll take care of yourself now?"

"Only two weeks," Dermot said.

"It'll be good for you to get away. She's got so much to do with the bathroom."

"I know."

He turned to go. The counterman was telling other people, "Telling me it tastes awful."

The mother-in-law turned to the counterman again. "Goddam cake."

As Dermot went out the door, past the men in the Legion caps, he looked back into the Maspeth Bingo Game. It was seven-forty now and getting crowded. He had to look past a sea of gray hair and curlers to see Phyllis, sitting with her thumb against her teeth, looking out into the smoke.

A little girl, rubber pants showing, stood on top of the waiting-room stairs in the Aer Lingus terminal at the airport. She held a plastic bottle of milk up like it was a trumpet. She started to come down the stairs. Dermot was afraid she'd topple and he started to run up the stairs to get her. The girl's father reached out for her. He was flat-faced and had short hair. He might as well have had a sign saying COP hanging around his neck. Dermot was wondering why the guy brought a kid along for a trip like this. When he got to the top of the stairs, Dermot found a nursery. Babies, screaming, sucking, drooling, were being jiggled on laps all over the waiting room. Older babies stumbled around the room. A little boy was running and yelling. He tripped over a foot and fell. He lay on the floor screaming. Two nuns smiled as the boy's mother picked

127

him up. The nuns were with a crowd of women. More nuns were on the other side of the room. Priests were everywhere in the room, which was so crowded there was no place to sit. The charter had a hundred seventy-five booked. There were about five hundred people in the waiting room. As Dermot edged off the staircase, he had to walk around a group of about twenty people, sitting and standing in a circle around a big cooler. The cooler had ice inside it. Everybody held out a plastic glass. One man had a fifth of rye and acted as bartender. Somebody turned around with a glass in his hand and bumped into Dermot, spilling some of the drink onto his sleeve.

"Oh, Jesus!" the man said. Pouches over and under the eyes, red dashes through the cheeks, and a suit jacket and pants that did not match were as good as a neon sign saying OLDER COP.

The Monsignor sat with a nun and an old inspector named Horace Mulligan. "Mayo," the Monsignor was saying. "It's such lovely country. Ah, it's good to go home. It's good for you lad to come, too," he said to Dermot.

There was loud laughing at the staircase. Johno was standing with the ones who were drinking whisky. Dermot gave Johno the eye. When one of the drinkers held out a plastic glass, Johno shook his head no. The Monsignor saw Johno turn down the drink. The Monsignor waved to Johno. Dermot felt good. The fat bastard, now he probably thinks I'm Jesus Christ.

Once they got settled on the plane, over the sound of the engines, there was the crackle of brown paper bags as the tour members pulled out the whisky bottles. After a while, the stewardesses moved down the aisle with a cart that had racks of canned beer. The tourists went for the canned beer with both hands. The plane was an hour out of Boston when the first kidneys leaked. Cops swung out of the seats and headed for the toilets. The aisle soon was crowded. The plane was out over the Atlantic with a solid line crowding the aisle from one end of the plane to the other. At first, the line was in good humor. That changed to irritation. Once a man gets going with beer he takes bigger leaks than a race horse. Now and then even a couple of women came on line. And always, all through the night, babies cried and the older babies squeezed past the men waiting in the aisle and wandered through the plane.

5:

The white clouds were dissolving into thin mist, and there were rocks covered with ocean foam and large squares of dull winter green and brown. The plane came in low over the cold flat waters of Shannon. At the airport there was nothing to look at except construction workers putting up buildings at the edge of the airport. Everybody went to the bar. An hour and a half later, the plane came through blowing fog to land at Dublin. The group was staying at the Gresham, which has the bar in the basement. With everybody in the bar from New York and with nothing to look at that was Ireland, the talk was the same as you would hear in the Green Derby in New York.

The Monsignor drank Dubonnet. Johno and Dermot had ginger ale. Horace Mulligan, the old inspector, took over the conversation.

"It was on the second, no, let me see, the third, that's right, the third night of the riots in Harlem," the inspector said. "That was in nineteen-sixty-four, July. Jiminy crickets, Monsignor, will I ever remember that. I was up on Saint Nicholas Avenue looking down a Hundred Twenty-third Street. The street was solid with these people. They were spilling onto the first avenue down from me, that would be Eighth Avenue. If they got across Eighth Avenue and started going down a Hundred Twenty-third Street some more, why they'd be right at the precinct, the Two-eight, and who knows what would have happened then? I walk back up to Saint Nicholas to a Hundred-Twenty-fifth Street where all the commanders were kind of grouped about. I was going to see if I could get some men for a Hundred-Twenty-third Street. Don't I get to a Hundred-Twenty-fifth Street just as these two busses pull up with men from the Academy. You could see just by looking through the bus windows at them that some of them couldn't of had their Police Academy uniforms on more than two or three times, the shirts looked that new. Brother, did I know what to do with them. I didn't ask nobody. I swung onto the first bus and grabbed a lieutenant in charge there and told him to line up the men, both busses of them.

"Out they come. Big, fine-loookin' lads. Monsignor, they would bring tears to your eyes, they were so good-lookin'. I stand out in the street and I explain to them who I am. I'm in plainclothes and half of them I guess didn't even know my name. I tell them, Assistant Chief Inspector Horace Mulligan, chief of detectives. You should of a seen the faces perk up at that. I say to them, all right now, we've got a real job to do. I tell them just spread out and follow me. And get them sticks right out in front of you. I start walking down Saint Nicholas Avenue to a Hundred Twenty-third Street. I'm right out in front of them, naturally, and I turn around and spread them out some more. I want them from the building line on one side of the street to the building line on the other side of the street. Wall-to-wall cops.

"Now we're gettin' closer to a Hundred Twenty-third Street and we could hear all the noise coming out of the street. Oh brother, you should of seen these men pick up the pace. I'm walkin' right out ahead of them and all behind me I could hear them takin' bigger steps, the feet were really coming down, and of course I start steppin' out myself. Boy, what a feelin' that was. I had a good solid line of these lads, I'm telling you, Monsignor, they were beautiful. Just between you and I, they were all white too. That was all right with me, I don't have to tell you that. Now we're walkin' along and just before we get to the corner I take out my blackjack and I turn around, and I keep walking backwards fast on account of I didn't want to lose any of the rhythm we had going, and I held up my blackjack and they brought the sticks up and out, and I said to them, 'Are you ready, gentlemen?' Boy, you should of heard them holler back, 'Yes!' So I said, '*After me!*' I charge around the corner and the whole line of them come right after me and here we come onto a Hundred Twenty-third Street and this whole block is full of people and they're all lookin' down the street, down towards the Two-eight, you see, and they never seen us comin'. Ah, I'm tellin' you, what a feeling. We were on those derelicts so fast, and we chased them so hard, they had no place to go. They went down cellar stairs. One of my lads was right after them givin' them a good beatin' for their troubles, the derelicts. Oh, Monsignor, if you could of only seen them. You'd have tears in your eyes. The way those wonderful men went to work on that crowd of street bums."

The inspector was half crying himself. He stared down at his drink. "You know, I never was in the war. The one thing in my life I always regretted, that I wasn't a Marine landing at Saipan or one of those places. But when I turned around and looked at those men and I said to them, 'Are you ready, gentlemen? *After me!*' When I did that and I came running around the corner, leading these wonderful men, and we went running straight at the backs of these derelicts, well I knew just how it felt to come ashore with the Marines at Saipan."

He took off his glasses and began to wipe the wetness away from his eyes. "That was the greatest day I ever had in the Police Department of the City of New York."

At dinnertime, the Monsignor had made reservations at the Russell, which is supposed to be the best food in Dublin. They walked up O'Connell Street and were on the bridge across the Liffey, the inspector and the Monsignor walking in front. A woman was sitting in a heap on the sidewalk on the bridge. Her head hung like she had a broken neck. A dirty brown shawl covered her to the ankles. Shoes that had no laces in them stuck out from under the shawl. When the woman saw the group coming, she unfolded the shawl and held up a baby wrapped in rags.

"The wee baby," she said. She held the baby out in the drizzle.

Two little girls came out of the drizzle and stood in front of them. One was about eleven. She had on an old frayed man's suit jacket and a dirty red housedress underneath the jacket. Ankle socks were hanging over shoes that were so big they flopped when she walked. Even in the dim light and the drizzle you could see the grease in her hair. When she opened her mouth she showed teeth that were yellow with deep brown lines along the bottoms. Green was spreading from the gums at the top. The second girl was about nine. She had bright-red hair that was a tangle of knots. A blue rain-jacket covered whatever she had on underneath. Her legs were wet from the drizzle and smeared with dirt. Her feet were in sneakers that had rips along the toes.

"Please, for the baby," the eleven-year-old said.

"The wee baby," the red-haired one said.

The inspector and the Monsignor kept walking, in silence now, and the two little girls walked alongside of them and looked up at them and then looked at the others trailing and one of them kept saying, "Oh please, mister, please, mister, for the wee baby."

The other kept saying, "Please, a few shillings. Oh please, mister, a few shillings. The baby, mister. Oh please, a few shillings."

The woman sitting on the bridge kept holding the baby in rags out in the drizzle.

"Fucking thing," Johno said.

Dermot had his hand out first. He glanced down and saw that he had pulled out a five-dollar bill. He started to put that away and fish for a single when the green gums and yellow-and-brown teeth began moving.

"Oh please, mister, the wee baby."

His hand stopped and she grabbed the five-dollar bill.

"Oh, God bless you," she said.

They walked over the rest of the bridge in silence in the drizzle. They were on Grafton Street when the

Monsignor pointed out a saloon called McDaid's, on a side street, where the writers drink. On the other side of Grafton Street he pointed out Davey Byrnes' and the Old Bailey, two places where Behan had hung out. The Old Bailey had a big crowd around its two entrances. Most of them had long hair.

Up at the top of Grafton Street there was a movie-house showing a Charlie Chaplin movie, *City Lights,* and the Monsignor shook his head when he noticed it. "How do they let a traitor like this show his wares?" he said. He turned his head away from the theater. There was a long line waiting to get in. At the end of the line, a boy and girl in military ponchos and dungaree pants were huddled in the doorway of a shop. The girl wore one of these Indian headbands and the boy had black hair that fell into the hood of his poncho. The girl was taking a deep drag on a home-rolled cigarette. She held it between the thumb and forefinger and handed it to the boy. He took a deep drag and held it.

They were at the corner of Stephens Green when footsteps came running. The little red-headed girl in sneakers spoke to Dermot. "Mister, you gave the girl the money, mister, and she was supposed to give me half of it and she ran away and now I have nothin'."

"Hey, that was your sister," he said.

"No, mister, 'twasn't me sister. It was just a *goil.* I never seen her before and you give her the money and she runned away."

"Well, go find her and make her give you your share," Dermot said.

"Oh, I can't find her. Please, mister, just a few shillin's. Me mother's sick."

Her eyes filled as she looked at him. He put his hand in his pocket and tried to come up with some change. He couldn't find any in one pocket and he stopped walking so he could go through his pockets. As he stopped he glanced back. The other girl was staring from a doorway on the other side of the street. She stepped back in the doorway when she saw Dermot looking at her.

"Oh please, mister," the other one said.

"Come on now," he said. He motioned to the one across the street. "Now the two of you are playing me for a sucker."

He walked away from her.

"Mister."

He kept walking.

"Mister!"

"What?"

"Fook you, mister."

They all laughed. The monsignor said that, aside from the language, you had to love them for their brazenness. Good tough street kids.

The next day, the Monsignor led most of them out of the hotel early for the golf course. Dermot and Johno checked out after lunch and took the afternoon Enterprise to Belfast. A pale-green light was coming through the glass roof of Connolly Street Station. The train left exactly at two-thirty. It is supposed to be one of the world's most punctual trains. Many Irish are afraid of the train because of this. A few minutes after the ride began, passing through a town called Malahide, the first raindrops hit the windows of the dining car. Dermot sat by the window. Johno had his legs sticking out into the aisle like construction horses. The waiter was a young boy in a white coat who handed out small leather menus.

"You serve drinks?" Johno said.

The waiter nodded.

"Paddy's and water," Johno said. "Fuck the Monsignor."

Dermot said he didn't want anything.

"How long are we going to stay in the North?" Johno said. "We got to hang around our man a little bit, you know. That's what we come for."

"He's just going to be playing golf every day. We can catch him any time we get back to Dublin. Don't you want to see anything?"

"Yeah, but going to that Portmaronock clubhouse with a Monsignor from New York, they'll treat us like kings."

"What the hell do you want with golf?" Dermot asked him.

135

"I don't. But while he's playing, I'll sit in the fuckin' clubhouse and live," Johno said.

"I want to go to Belfast and then over to Bundoran and then we can drive back," Dermot said.

"What do we got in Bundoran?" Johno asked.

"My father's there, and I want to look him up," Dermot said.

"Why the fuck would you want to see him for?" Johno said.

Dermot didn't answer. It angered him when great things which he built up in his own mind were dismissed by somebody who didn't know. He put his head against the train window. "We'll be at the golf course with that son of a bitch in a couple of days," he said.

He fell asleep with the motion of the train. He woke up with the train going past black and white cows huddled together in rain at the foot of empty green hills that climbed sharply into the mist. Johno was talking to the waiter.

"In Northern Ireland, the Catholic Church doesn't run the country, right?" Johno said.

"Aye."

"Does that mean the policy on pornographic literature is different in Belfast than it is in Dublin?"

"Aye?"

"Pornography. Books with big dirty pictures in them."

"Oh, the dirty pitchers. You can't buy them in Belfast station. Just because it's the North that doesn't mean the people is dirty."

"Do they have a customs when we get off the train?"

"Aye."

"Will they search me very closely?"

"They're old men and they just stand there."

"That's good. Because I have a lot of dirty magazines with me and I don't want to be searched and have them confiscated."

"The tings you bring in is your own business."

"Gee, that's good. Do you know why I have so many magazines with dirty pictures in them?"

136

The waiter was starting to go away. Johno held his arm so he couldn't.

"The reason I have so many dirty magazines is that I'm here without my wife. I go to bed all alone."

Dermot moved in his chair and he could feel the gun in his belt. Johno was looking at him. Dermot opened his jacket. The gun was stuck into his belt.

"If they search us, we're going to be in the shithouse," Johno said.

"You'll be wishing you were in a shithouse," Dermot said. "They don't have them in a British prison. You use a bucket and it stays next to your bed all night."

"I don't care about the gun. I care about the magazines. I have to have them."

Dermot said nothing.

"Do you know what I have in my bag? An Italian *Playboy*. You should see it. It's way better than the American *Playboy*. The Italian *Playboy* shows you pubic hairs. I have to get somebody to teach me Italian. I'll bet the whole of Italy jerks off the day the new issue of Italian *Playboy* comes out. The Pope does it before the people do. He gets an advance copy."

Dermot said he was worried more about getting caught with a loose gun. The top half of the train window had a handle on it. He pulled the handle up and pushed the window out, like a slat of louvered glass, seven or eight inches. Wet, chilly air blew into his face. The sound of the train wheels was limited to a loud click as they went over the spaces in the rails. He stuck his hand out of the window. If there was any trouble with customs before leaving the train, he could drop the gun out the window. In case of any problems out on the platform, one of them could duck back into the dining car and drop the gun onto the tracks.

The train made one stop, at Portadown. The station was empty and there were no people or cars on the streets of the town running out from the station. A printed sign on the station wall which said H.M. CUSTOMS told you what side of the border you were on. About the only real thing Dermot knew about the North and the

137

South was the names of the counties. An aunt had made him memorize them. She would say, in a soft voice, the counties of the South: Sligo, Mayo, Galway, Kerry, Cork, Wexford, Waterford, and the rest. There are twenty-six counties in the Republic. Her voice had razor blades in it as she chanted the six counties of the North: Antrim, Fermanagh, Down, Derry, Tyrone, Armagh.

6:

The train came out of the farmlands and was running alongside a six-lane highway leading to Belfast City. There was a golf course and after the golf course a white cement fairgrounds auditorium and a big green wooden soccer stadium, and then the train was running in an alley between the first streets of red-brick row houses. British flags, new flags with bright reds and blues, big flags too, flags large enough to fly on government buildings, hung from flagpoles over each doorway on each side of each street. Strings of pennants, alternating red and blue, were fluttering over the little streets. The lines of pennants were fastened to the chimneys and they hung over each street like a cloth roof. When you looked down at a street from the train window it was like passing a baseball park on opening day. Somewhere under all the bunting there would be one empty patch. Kids in short pants standing in wet garbage in the middle of the street and kicking a stone or a can while a scrawny dog with matted hair sniffed at the garbage.

The bare walls at the end houses of the rows were covered with large signs painted in white. They were for train passengers to read. One said NO POPE HERE. Another house said NO SURRENDER. The wall of the last house of the blocks with flags said REMEMBER 1690. The train was coming into the platform. A porter put the bags on a cart and walked ahead into a little shed. A couple of old men in unpressed uniforms, the white caps dirty, stared at luggage and marked it with pale-green chalk. They opened nothing, and did not look at the people. Dermot and Johno came out of the shed into a bare cement place which seemed more like a men's room than a waiting room. It was nearly five o'clock. Outside, the street was crowded with double-decker busses and trucks. Old buildings of rough brown, dull stones, the corners of the buildings rounded, green shades showing in the big square windows, stood six and seven stories high.

A line of high Austin taxicabs was in an alley beside a saloon directly across the street from the railroad station. The porter walked the bags through the traffic. As they were walking across the street the door of the saloon swung open. It was crowded and painted in circus colors, lights and glass gleaming everywhere. The saloon had a long bar with six bartenders working. The wall along the back of the bar was covered with huge mirrors made of engraved glass. The engravings along the top of the mirror glass had scrollwork and inscriptions saying BLENDED WHISKIES.

"How old is that glass?" Dermot asked the bartender.

"Hundred fifty years old," he said.

The rest of the saloon was a long row of semicircular booths with tables that were behind partitions. Each booth had a door to it. If you got in the booth, closed the door, and hunched down over your drink, nobody could see you from the bar or through the window from the street. On the door of each booth was a polished silver plate with the word MATCHES on it.

A man a few feet down the bar said something to Johno and Dermot, but it was unintelligible to them.

"How's that?" Johno said to the man.

The man spoke again. Johno leaned toward the man so he could listen to him more carefully. Johno still could not understand the words. In the booth directly behind Johno and Dermot, a man raised his voice. Dermot concentrated on what the voice was saying. Still, only a couple of words had any familiarity to them. Dermot found that at first his ear was a quarter-beat off in picking up the flat, sparse, Scottish-base Belfast inflection. There was not a trace of the familiar stage-lilt Irish heard in the counties to the south. The brogue Americans know from the movies. Northern Irish is a winter language. Words to be spoken in a cold rain.

The bartender nearest them called out to somebody at the far end of the bar and Dermot missed most of it until one phrase spoken by the bartender came through to him.

". . . . they *doan* want to know *ye*."

The last word, the *"ye,"* rose a full tone higher than the words before it.

The man at the far end of the bar called something down to the bartender. The bartender listened. Then he called back, "Well, *ye*'ve got. to get to the *rut* of the matter."

The voice went up on the word *"rut"* and immediately came back down and finished the sentence in a monotone.

As Johno and Dermot continued to listen, some of the strangeness came off the tongues around them in the barroom.

"It's a goddam nice bar," Johno said to the bartender.

"Oh, it's a civilized place to drink, all right," the bartender said. "The only trouble is that sometimes the fuckin' customers go out and get fuckin' killed."

They finished the drink and went out to the cab. The center of Belfast, Royal Avenue, was thick with traffic and people coming from work. A jeep swung in front of them. Four soldiers in flak jackets and Scottish plaid caps, the tail ribbons whipping in the wind, sat with their weapons held up. An Army truck came out of a side street and onto the Royal Avenue. It was filled with soldiers sitting across from each other. The two at the end faced out, their rifles pointing at the traffic behind them.

"Get alongside that truck," Johno said.

"Aye?" the cabdriver said.

"I said get alongside the truck. I want to tell those kids about how to handle a weapon. You don't point it at traffic."

"You sure the fuck do," the cabdriver said. "In Belfast you point a gun all day. Or someday they'll be pointin' fingers at you and sayin', 'Jesus, but he was a lovely fella before he got killed.' "

The cab turned onto the Crumlin Road. It is a busy cobblestone street which rises slowly up a long hill. Both sides of the street are lined with two-story wooden buildings with small shops on the first floor. Nearly every corner had a saloon which was boarded up, but people walking in and out through the plywood door showed it was open for business. On three consecutive corners the sign for the saloon was on the building, and underneath the sign was a charred cavity. Across the side streets there were wooden barricades with coils of barbed wire around them. Three and four soldiers stood at each barricade. Women in kerchiefs held on to little children and walked under the barrels of the rifles. The little children kept looking back at the soldiers as their mothers pulled them up the street. The small shops ended and the road became factories, a hospital, and on the left side, standing alone, a courts building, and on the right, directly across from the courts, a dark-gray stone archway with huge newly painted green doors and black metal ring handles, the entrance to the Crumlin Road jail.

"Bookin' office on one side, your reserved rooms on the other," the cabdriver said.

They went a few more short blocks and the cab started to turn into a side street but stopped in the middle of the turn. Men in old suit jackets and work pants, their faces red from the air, stood on both corners of the side street. A man in a shapeless topcoat, the top of a black turtleneck sweater showing, walked toward them. He had the thickness of a light-heavyweight put on a body that was far too short. He was no more than five-foot-nine, for the bulk. He was not fat. The shoulders of the topcoat were strained. You could trace the contour of the tops of his arms through the topcoat. His hands were in the coat pockets and he walked with a swagger that had the hint of a waddle. His thighs were so thick that they probably rubbed into each other when his legs moved. He stuck his face into the cab. High cheekbones pushed his eyes into slits. Black hair was brushed straight back.

"Lansdowne Road, they told me," the cabdriver said.

The slit eyes had a street cruelty in them as he looked at Johno and Dermot.

"Who is it you're lookin' for on Lansdowne Road?" he said.

"Meehan," Dermot said. He pulled out a piece of paper with the address on it. "Sixty-seven and a half Lansdowne Road. Ardoyne. Meehans are relatives. We're from New York."

"Aye." He pulled his head out of the window. The cabdriver started away. He went only a few yards down the side street and he was at a cross street. Three and four men were standing on each corner. One looked back at the corner of Crumlin Road. As his face showed he'd received a sign, he stepped back, waving them on. The cabbie made two turns, came onto this street of identical houses running down and up a hill, slowed down while he hung out the window, looking for the address.

Dermot's mother's uncle was at the front door, his finger in the pockmark in the bricks. Behind him, down a hallway that was four or five steps long, Aunt Cathy was at the stove. As they walked in, she said, "Oh there are two of you. Which one of you is which now? Oh, I can see who you look like." She pointed a spatula at Dermot. "So now, who might you be?" she said to Johno.

"I came with him all the way from New York and I have to have a room all by myself tonight," he said.

"What's that?" she said

"I need a room all by myself because I have a copy of Italian *Playboy* and I have to be alone."

Nobody knew what he was saying. Aunt Cathy looked at the stove, the mother's uncle slogged into the kitchen, limping slightly, and opened a cabinet. "Have a drink?" he called out.

"I don't think we need anything to drink," Dermot said to him.

"Oh, you have to have a wee drop."

The uncle was reaching up into the cabinet for small glasses, ducking under the cabinet for a bottle of Paddy's, pouring the whisky, putting the bottle away, handing out

143

the glasses. Aunt Cathy sipped her glass without looking up from the stove.

In the living room there was a couch on which you could sit two people. The couch took up one wall. The mother's uncle sat in an easy chair which filled a corner of the room. A fireplace with an electric heater glowing under false coals, a television set with the screen the size of the ones in New York in the early fifties, a straight-backed chair, a small table, two lamps, and two windows with clean curtains on them made up the rest of the room. A picture of the Sacred Heart was on the mantel of the fireplace. A candle in a wine-red holder, a church candle, flickered beside the picture. On the other side of the mantel was a framed color reproduction of John F. Kennedy and his wife standing together with their foreheads touching.

The uncle sat in the easy chair and held up his glass. "Give 'em the warks with a Wabley!" He swallowed the drink in a gulp, slumped down in the chair quickly, dropped his left hand to the floor, poked the hand under the chair, came out with a bottle, dug his heels into the floor, and sent his body zipping back up the chair until he sat like a medical student.

"We had a Gaelic football field right across the way," he said. "The B Specials got in there with Lewis guns in a sandbagged post. They'd fire all the time at night. No reason atall atall. Just fire at night. A wee girl, three years old she was, she run out of the house the other night onto the field. She goes runnin' across the Gaelic field with the mother chasin' after her. The B Specials opened up with Lewis guns. Cut the wee girl in pieces. Cut her right up like butcher meat. The mother was bendin' over to pick up the wee girl, they shot her through the top of the head. When they found her, the hair and all that on the top of the head laid open, well, they thought she'd been shot from an airplane. She was bendin' over to pick up the wee girl, you see." He rolled over the arm of the chair for the bottle. "Here." Johno took a drink, but Dermot didn't want one.

144

Aunt Cathy stood in the doorway with a drink. She did not mention food.

"Why didn't your mother come?" she said to Dermot.

"She couldn't this time," he said.

"Does she not like us?" she said.

"Oh, never," Dermot said.

"We be sendin' her *lattars* in the *mayel* and she never sends a *lattar* back."

It took him a couple of seconds to realize she was talking about letters in the mail. It was not just whisky on the edge of her voice. Dermot stood up. "I want to go out and see what the place is like," he said.

The aunt waved a hand at him. "Sit you down and tell me why your mother or you never send us a *lattar* back in the *mayel*."

Dermot stepped past her and went out into the street. He could feel her eyes glaring at him. Johno lumbered after him. Dermot heard the woman's voice rising inside. His mother's uncle, muttering, came out the door. When he came up to them on the sidewalk his face eased. "How it was," he said, "with the head laid open like that, everybody thought she got shot from the sky. Took a while to realize when she was bendin' down the top of her head was sittin' there like a target for the bullet. Laid her head open somethin' terrible."

The mother's uncle led Dermot and Johno down the hill to a cross street. To the left, four corners up, a burned-out double-decker bus blocked the street.

"Protestants live on the other side of the barricade," the mother's uncle said.

The houses on one side of the burned-out bus were the same as the houses on the other side. Dermot mentioned this to the mother's uncle.

"There's a big difference," he said.

"What difference?"

"In the morning everybody down there gets up and goes to work on a job. Up here, most of the boys don't bother gettin' up. Nothin' to get up for. No jobs. The one's got jobs on account of bein' Protestant, the other's

145

got no jobs account of bein' Catholic. That's the difference."

"There's no work at all?" Johno said.

"Where would you work?" the mother's uncle said. "The shipyard hires ten thousand. Five hundred of 'em are Catholics. And the five hundred do porter's work. Dunno a Catholic with a good job in the shipyard. Huh. The Mackie Works is on the Springfield Road. It sits facin' a whole Catholic section. They must have four thousand workers in there. Only a couple Catholic. A couple of sweep-up men, that's the only Catholics in the place. All the Catholics sit across the road, watchin' Prods go to work at Mackie."

"They turn you down just because you're Catholic?" Dermot said.

"Notatall, notatall," he said. "They don't hire because we're lazy and we're too dirty to have around. Catholics are lazy and dirty, you know. Oh, you'll hear that around here, you will."

He was punching the palm of his hand. "Where would we work? On a job like you fellas have, on the police? No Catholic policemen in Ulster. Just as well, because when the Army goes away we're gonna kill all the fuckers on the police. If Catholics was police, we'd wind up killin' some of our own by mistake maybe. No, let the Prods be police. Greatest moment of a policeman's life is when he gets a chance to shine at his own funeral."

He started walking in the opposite direction from the bus barricade. They crossed two blocks of these row houses with gates in front of them and came to the side of a school building. They went through an alley alongside the school and came out in front of the school. The school was on a street which consisted of a long row of one-story cement houses painted gray with windows and doors every few feet—there were about a hundred doors. The roofs were so low that the coal smoke from the chimneys rolled across the sidewalk. The windows were dark with soot and the doors were scarred. The street was the first of a network of streets with these low houses on them. There were no hedges or gates in front of the doors,

146

just cracked sidewalks. A chimney sweep, his face and clothes as black as the brooms tied to his back, came by on a bike.

The sign over the doorway to the school said it was the Holy Cross Boys' Primary School. Four men were smoking cigarettes just inside the entrance.

"Larry there?" the mother's uncle called to them.

"Who?"

"I said Larry."

"He said he'd come back."

The mother's uncle nodded. "We'll have a look around and come back," he said to them. They walked down the street the school was on and came to an empty dirt lot. A crowd of about fifty, young guys of about fifteen and sixteen all the way up to old men who looked like they were seventy, were crowded around something.

"You call this a pitch-and-toss school," the mother's uncle said. Everybody in the crowd was throwing money into a pot, the way you do in a crap game. One guy stepped into the middle of the circle. He began swinging a thick chain, the end of it dragging in the dirt. Everybody began stepping back as the chain swung in a wider arc, then lifted off the ground. The guy swinging the chain started to spin around, whipping the chain around at knee height. The chain cut into one pair of baggy dungarees and the baggy dungarees jumped back. Whoever was in the dungarees made a little moan. The chain slapped against the top of a pair of rubber boots and the boots jumped. The guy in the boots swore loudly, but nobody paid any attention to him. The chain whirred in the air now, clearing a wide circle around the men. As the chain stopped, an old man in a greasy suit jacket came into the circle. He crouched down. He held a small wooden block between his hands. On top of the block were two big copper coins. "Yup!" he said. He flipped the board. The coins came down to bounce in the dirt. The crowd tried to push closer, but the chain man came back into the circle swishing the chain to keep the legs back. The flipper went to the coins, shook his head and picked them up.

"Nothin' that time," the mother's uncle said. "The

coins have to come up both the same side. Two harps or two faces. That's what you bet on. Flip this time come up a harp and a face. So you just toss again."

They all began throwing coins into the pot for the next toss. Nearly everybody in the crowd had a bottle of beer or stout to drink from. At the edge of the crowd, a couple of dogs screwed on the sidewalk in the coal smoke.

There was another yell while the two coins hung in the air, flipping, then falling.

"Game goes on all day, most of the night," the mother's uncle said. "Nobody got anything else to do. Just stand around drinkin' and gamblin'."

"Where do they get the money to gamble?" Dermot said.

"The bru."

"The what?"

"The bru, the dole. Where else would you get it from?"

"The dole. You mean unemployment?"

"Unemployment, welfare, whatever you want to call it."

"They take the money and gamble with it?"

"What the fuck else do you do with your day?" he said. "Take a few bob, get somethin' to drink, and come to the pitch-and-toss school. We call it a school because that's where you start in the game, you see. Start playin' when you're in school. And where else would you get money except the bru? Can't get any work. So you go down and collect the bru every week."

"Everybody here is on welfare?" Johno said.

"Aye."

"And it's the best they can do?"

"Aye. Oh, exceptin' one thing."

"What's that?" Johno said.

"Stealin'."

They walked back to the entrance of the primary school. One of the four men smoking cigarettes inside the front entrance nodded to the mother's uncle. He shuffled through the door. The fellow pointed down a dim hallway. They went down it. "You see, Larry's in charge of everything in here," the mother's uncle said. "This is his station if something happens. Everybody has a post. Do ye know

148

Cathy's job? She has to keep the front door open, no matter what's going on, account of our kitchen is first-aid headquarters." He began looking in doorways. "Where are we going here for fuck's sake, oh, Jesus, I'm sorry to be cursin' inside the Lord's school." He blessed himself. "Oh, here ye are."

In a classroom there was a girl in a brown sweater, her arms folded, leaning against a desk. A baby sat on the floor playing with a low stack of diapers. A young man sat on the edge of a coat, a cigarette hanging from his mouth. A comforter and pillow were on the floor.

Larry was standing by the windows, but he didn't bother to say hello. Dermot had seen only pictures of him. They were cousins.

"This is where a family lives," Larry said. "How do you like this?"

"How's everything tonight?" the mother's uncle asked the girl.

"Ah dunno," she said.

Larry said he had to take a walk around the area, and the mother's uncle and Johno said they would rather sit down someplace. Dermot said he'd go with Larry, who said he knew where to pick them up later.

They came out onto the Crumlin Road at a point two blocks below the church. The entrances to the streets were all barricaded and on the opposite side of the road the streets were covered with British flags and red and blue pennants. At each corner of the streets with the flags, there were five or six guys standing around, one of them always with his hands in topcoat pockets, the same as there were groups at every corner of Catholic blocks.

"See," Larry was saying, "this was Pope's Row. Look at it all burned out." Stores, two and three in a row, were blackened and windowless. "The stores that you see open are owned by Prods," he said. At Number 378 there was J. Moorcroft Carpets, the store untouched. "Prod," Larry said. Then there was The Eagle, Fishmonger and Hot Pies, also untouched. "Prod," Larry said. David Savage, Hairdresser, was gone and only his sign and a chopped-up floor were left. "Catholic," Larry said. Next door to it,

149

Jacqueline Fashions also was gone. "Catholic," Larry said. At 386, John McGinty, Hairdresser, was untouched. "Protestant," Larry said. The Logue saloon was on the corner. When you looked down the Crumlin Road, for as far as you could see, there were curtains blowing in the second-story windows over Protestant shops, and over the Catholic shops there was black broken glass.

They were past the church and coming up to the corner when a voice came calling up from one of the Protestant street corners behind them.

"How's old red stockin's today?"

On the Catholic corner, a heavy-set guy jumped out into the gutter.

The voice called out again. "Oh, it's about that time in Rome now. Old red stockin's, he's really givin' it to her now!"

"Dirty bastards, talkin' about our Pope like that," Larry said.

"How's the Immaculate Conception doin' today?" another voice yelled.

The heavy-set guy stood in the street, cupped his hands, and yelled down toward the Protestant corners. "How's about your man Williamson? He still got that nice little boy helper?"

Larry laughed. "Williamson is the head of the Protestant defense organ-i-zation. He has this wee boy helper livin' with him."

"How's your man's little boy?" the heavy-set guy yelled again. He drew the outline of hips with his hands.

The Protestant corners had become crowded. As the heavy-set guy yelled, they shifted in agitation. When he drew the rear end in the air, the crowd on each corner jerked as if they were on a rope somebody had yanked.

From down the block a voice shouted, "Old red stockin's, he's really givin' it to her now. He's all the way up her now!"

The heavy-set guy's face became beet-red. He ran into the middle of the street and threw a rock down the hill at the Protestants. Everybody began picking up rocks. Larry was crouched, groping for a rock and cursing.

150

"Did you hear what he just said about the Pope? Did you hear what he said about the Pope? That's our fuckin' Pope he's talkin' about."

The first Protestant rock hit the pavement a couple of feet from Dermot, who ducked and headed for the corner. Everybody around him was throwing rocks at the Protestants and they were throwing them back. The shouting became loud and unintelligible. The faces were becoming a deeper red. Spit flew out of their mouths while they screamed and threw rocks at the crowd down the hill. Both groups were edging into the road, walking toward each other. The Protestant crowd was much larger, too large for the Catholics to handle. The heavy-set guy was glancing around. A look of fear came on his face and he ran onto the side street leading to Lansdowne Road. He had his arms held out. Halfway down the short street he threw himself against three guys and began pushing them back. One of the three was carrying a rifle. The other two were putting pistols back inside their jackets.

"Oh, it's a good thing we got leadership here," Larry said.

"They would have showed those things?" Dermot said.

"Showed them? Christ, we'd of been in a shootin' match in two minutes."

The heavy-set guy shoved and argued until the three with the guns went back down the block. On the Crumlin, the Protestants were coming up, the crowd moving up a step or so at a time, and then they started to spill out into the street. The Catholics began darting forward to throw rocks. Traffic was stopped. The groups moved at each other gradually for fifteen minutes. They were a block and a half from each other. When this whining sound came from the top of the Crumlin. And down the hill the top of an armored car showed in the Protestant crowd. It came through the crowd slowly, forcing them to get off the road. Another armored car skirted the stalled traffic and ran down the road as the Catholics jumped out of the way. The armored cars met in the space between the two crowds. Jeeps were pulling up around them. Soldiers

151

stepped out and formed a line across the street between the two gangs. The fight was over before it really started.

Larry and Dermot walked past the house on Lansdowne Road and down the hill to an empty lot. In one corner there was a large green corrugated metal shed. It was the same kind of shack construction companies around New York put up for the offices on the site of a big job. The entranceway was lined, sandbag style, with wooden beer cases. Larry turned sideways and slipped down a narrow passageway between the beer cases. Dermot could barely squeeze through. They came into a large room that was crowded with men sitting on chairs at small tables, drinking from bottles. There were no windows. There was so much smoke you couldn't see anybody sitting on the other side of the room. Johno and the mother's uncle were bunched in a corner with a man who had steel-colored hair and deep-set eyes and a false hand inside a brown leather glove. More than a dozen empty bottles were on the small table in front of them. Johno had a full bottle in each hand. The mother's uncle dropped down in his chair, his hand went under the table, and he pulled himself up with a bottle of whisky in the hand. Dermot sat down. Larry went over to a small wooden bar against the wall to get some beer. He brought back an armful of bottles. The guy with the false hand knocked all the empty bottles onto the floor. "Give ye some room," he said.

"This is a real good cellar club," Johno said.

The noise of the talking in the room was very loud, but suddenly the room became quiet and Johno was standing on a chair which was shaking and seemed ready to fall apart. Everybody in the room was looking at him.

"I came over here from New York with a terrific present for you people," Johno said. He was swaying on the chair.

"Look at this!" He whipped out his magazine and held it up. "Italian *Playboy!*"

They could not understand what they were looking at. Then, slowly, they began to realize what they had on their hands with Johno. A total lunatic.

"Naked women and dirty jokes on every page," Johno

152

said. "Pubic hairs! We can all read it together and jerk off."

The noise started up in the room again as everybody shifted around in their seats, talking while they returned to their bottles.

"A circle jerk!" Johno screamed.

People were talking loudly. Johno shouted at them. "Wait one minute. I brought something else with me. Look!"

When he opened Dermot's coat and pulled the gun out of Dermot's belt, they all shouted.

"What would you rather have?" Johno said. "A rotten old gun or the Italian *Playboy* with the naked women?"

"Even if the girls were real!" somebody yelled.

They were all clapping. Dermot reached over and pulled the gun out of Johno's hand. They all whistled at Dermot. He put the pistol into his pocket.

"Give me it," Johno said.

"I'll take care of it myself," Dermot said.

He left Johno swallowing beer and he walked up the street to the house and went upstairs into the tiny bedroom and went to sleep. The pistol was under the mattress.

He slept well into the next afternoon. Downstairs, his mother's uncle and his cousin were looking in at the living room. Johno was on his back on the floor snoring off a drunk.

Dermot shrugged. He mentioned the errand to Leeson Street. His mother's uncle looked at the Rheingold stationery. "O'Neill?" he said. "Wee fella called O'Neill? Do go right to the Falls and look for him. Leeson Street. That's another district, you know. We've our own command here. But we'll go to Leeson Street right off."

7:

Dermot should not have had the gun with him at all. Walking on the Falls Road, in Belfast, with a gun in his belt under his jacket, all he could do was be nervous inside and keep going straight. Indecisive walking is evidence in Belfast. The night before, Paddy, a wine victim, had come onto Raglan Street holding a bouquet of flowers —nobody knew where Paddy got flowers in Belfast— and he stood in these clouds in the middle of the street, the flowers held out, his knees melting in the gas. A Saracen came down the street very fast. Paddy wanted to hand the bouquet of flowers to the tank. The Saracen veered a little to make sure Paddy was centered. Paddy was still holding the flowers out when his head hit the Saracen and came off.

All along the Falls Road the sidewalks were crowded with people out doing their Saturday shopping. Everybody was talking about Paddy. A jeep swung out of the thick traffic and came to the curb. Three soldiers in Scottish plaid caps, black tail ribbons whipping in the wind, sat with their weapons pointing up. An Army truck came in behind the jeep. The truck was filled with soldiers sitting across from each other. The two men at the end sat facing out, their rifles pointing over the tailgate at the traffic.

Dermot was walking on the outside. His mother's uncle was in the middle. The old man's right leg did not bend and he dragged it as they went along. Larry was on the other side. He said the next corner, Leeson Street, was the one they wanted. The cold spring wind blew paper into the coils of barbed wire at the corner. Three soldiers turned their faces from dust swirling in the wind, turned their faces so they were looking directly at the two younger men walking with the old cripple. The three soldiers had on Scottish caps too. The rifles were pointed up, the butts jammed into the space on the right hip between the bottom of the flak jacket and the cartridge belt.

If the soldiers stopped the three of them, the first pat would have found the police .32 in Dermot's belt. He had an American passport and a shield to show he was a member of the New York City Police Department. He also knew how the soldiers would respond to both credentials. Push the passport into his mouth and shove the badge up his ass.

The mother's uncle kept talking, which was good because it kept the three of them acting natural. The soldiers, short, had cold ridges for faces. "From Glasgow, they are," the mother's uncle said. "Glasgow's only place in the British Isles got organized blackguards. Bloody fuckers probably couldn't last with an organized gang in Glasgow, they joined up and come over here bullyin' us."

As they came up to the three soldiers standing at the entrance to Leeson Street, his mother's uncle was muttering in this Northern Irish accent, "Give 'em the warks with a Wabley."

At the barricade, he was saying, "We had barbed wire all around the Admiral Bar, place I was born, and it gets to be like the gaslight on the street. You don't notice it. And it's only been up since the last time there, the riot in twenty-one. Same trouble, always the same trouble."

He kept talking and walking and they went past the soldiers, walked under their rifles and stepped through a space in the barbed wire and started down Leeson Street.

"I have to be crazy," Dermot said.

"As an actual fact, I should have been thinking better," the mother's uncle was saying. "I let my mind wander. I keep forgettin' that I let you go stridin' around here with the machinery on your person and you don't even come from here."

"I shouldn't even have the goddamned gun with me in New York," Dermot said.

They were down in the middle of Leeson Street before he stopped concentrating on the soldiers behind them and saw what the street was like. Leeson Street is an alley, not a large alley either. The alley runs between red-brick row houses, the smallest houses you've ever seen. The houses are two stories, but they are not even as high as a garage behind a house in Queens. He began to measure the row houses while he walked. Each house was exactly four of his steps wide. When his mother's uncle started to cross the street and head for a boarded-up saloon on the corner, Dermot dropped behind. He put his back against the wall of one house and began pacing. Two steps took him to the curb. The street was six steps wide. The sidewalk on the other side of the street was two steps. The distance from a doorway on one side to a doorway on the other side was ten yards. There was not a tree, bush, or patch of dirt on the block. Not a single flowerpot. Just gray cement running between tiny red-brick houses. The houses had sharply slanted gray slate roofs. From sidewalk to rooftop couldn't be more than thirteen or fourteen feet. Every four yards on the roofs there was a stumpy chimney with a television antenna lashed onto it. The street was a toy street with toy houses, only it went on and on, with little alleys running across it to form corners. The street, a doorway every four yards, went on until it faded into a haze of coal smoke.

The mother's uncle and Larry went into the pub on the corner. When Dermot pushed through the door, which had three layers of plywood, the smell of the saloon came at him like an opponent. It came from damp coal fires along the block, from wet suit jackets at the bar and shoes soaked by rain puddles. Four men in old suit jackets and baggy pants stood in olive-drab light and drank stout from pint glasses at a bar that only came up to the waist. Dermot and his two relatives ordered pints. When the barman brought them over, the smell of his black sweater was stronger than anything the rest of the room had to offer. One old man was to their right, on the side nearest

156

the back of the saloon. To the left was a man with a plaid cap pulled down until the peak touched the top of black horn-rimmed glasses. Wide green eyes stared through the thick glasses. Down at the end of the bar an old man, flesh sagging under the chin, sat with a younger man in a gray cap, who was looking out at the street through a gap in the plywood covering the space where the saloon windows had been. When the young man turned from the plywood to pick up his drink, Dermot could see he was much younger than old clothes and a cap made him look. A kid really. The kid looked up and saw that Dermot was looking at him. The kid's eyes intensified. He was going to stare Dermot down. The old man, flesh hanging from the neck, sat next to the kid and looked at nothing but the glass. The kid stared hard at Dermot and Dermot looked down at the bar and smiled to himself.

"Saturday night in Rockaway Beach," he said.

"What's that?" his mother's uncle said.

"Nothing," Dermot said. He looked at the man in the plaid cap. The man was out of a movie about the IRA.

Nobody spoke. Dermot tried to start the conversation off.

"How come the bar is so low?" he said to the barman.

"Because it is," he said.

"Oh," Dermot said.

"Just as well," one of them at the bar said. "Anybody here tries bendin' over the bar, the arse's come through his britches pockets."

Behind the bar was a large blackened metal urn, with metal spigots and knobs everywhere on it. Alongside it were three silver measuring cups and a copper funnel.

"What's that for?" Dermot asked.

The barman tapped the urn. "Geezer for hot water."

"What's the hot water for?"

"For hot water."

"Oh."

He was pulling a pint from a small aluminum tap. There were big wooden tap handles still on the bar, but they weren't being used. In New York, any saloonkeeper

157

with half a brain would fight you in the streets for the wooden handles.

Dermot asked the barman what the cups and funnels were for.

He motioned with his head while he was pulling the pint. "They're for pouring the dregs from one bottle to t'other. Christ, ye ask so much, what are ye, a policeman?"

"Oh, Christ no," the mother's uncle said quickly. "He's no policeman."

"He's from New York," Larry said.

"New York?" the man in the cap said.

"New York," Dermot said.

"Uh huh," the man said.

"A good friend of mine has a saloon in New York, Jimmy McManus. He told me to come in here and say hello. He has a place called the Falls Pub on Greenpoint Avenue in Sunnyside."

The guy in the cap turned and looked out at the street again.

"You don't know Jimmy McManus in here?"

"Notatall, notatall," the barman said.

Dermot leaned over to his mother's uncle, who had his small face stuck into the glass of stout. "Let's get out of here then," Dermot said.

The barman quickly asked, "Where do you come from?"

"Ardoyne," Larry said.

The guy in the plaid cap said nothing.

"Know MacCormack?" the old man up at the end, the one who had flesh sagging from his chin, said. The kid with him did not stare at Dermot now.

"John?" Larry answered.

"Aye," the old man said.

"Ridder!" Larry said.

"Aye," the old man said.

"Lives next door to us," Larry said.

"Oh," the old man said.

"I saw Jem this morning. She took the baby to the hospital."

"What's the matter with the baby?"

158

"Same as everybody else. Two and a half vomits from the fuckin' CS gas."

The old man nodded. The barman said nothing. The old man in the plaid cap turned and looked out at the street again.

"I got something here that Jimmy McManus in the Falls Pub in Sunnyside, New York City, told me to bring in here and give to a man named Joe O'Neill," Dermot said. "I'm going to finish this drink and leave with the thing if I don't see Joe O'Neill."

The place was silent. Dermot swallowed the pint of stout. When he put the glass down, the old man with the flesh hanging from his neck said, "Tell me."

"Yes?"

"Is Jimmy McManus's ass still so fat?"

The barman said, "The last time the fat fucker was in here, his wife come in after him and he told her to fuck off, he wasn't leavin'. So she punched him right in the ballocks. He fuckin' well moved then."

They spoke with straight faces. The barman reached out and started shaking hands. Dermot went under his coat and came out with the pistol. The old man reached for it.

"You O'Neill?" Dermot said.

"Aye."

O'Neill had a face like a cell wall. Gray hair was combed straight back. Dark-brown eyes looked right at Dermot but were seeing things that were a thousand miles away. The chin was square. When O'Neill stuck the chin out, the flesh under the chin grew taut. O'Neill seemed to know this. He kept pushing the chin out.

He took the pistol and handed it to the kid. The movement of O'Neill's hand, deliberate, nearly exaggerated in its slowness, was familiar to Dermot. The kid with O'Neill shook like he had been in an accident. From drink and no sleep and excitement, Dermot guessed. The kid fumbled the pistol under his suit jacket. He went past Dermot without looking and walked out the door.

O'Neill lifted his glass. A little of the pint dripped onto the cuff of his jacket.

159

"Goddammit," O'Neill said. He put the glass down and took out a handkerchief and carefully wiped the cuff. The jacket was gray tweed which once was good.

He put the handkerchief away and picked up the glass. He stared at Dermot over the glass. Dermot knew the style by heart. He held out his glass for another pint.

"How long'd they have you for?" Dermot asked.

"Seven years. The Crumlin Road jail. Four the first time, three more in 1960."

"Rough."

"It's a cold place, that."

He stepped back from the bar. "I'm best gone from here now."

"Take care," Dermot said.

O'Neill stared, the eyes not blinking, and he nodded and walked out. Dermot had seen a kid named Ryan in court one day who could have been the guy's younger brother. The kid Ryan had held up a doctor in his house on 110th Street in Forest Hills. In the middle of the holdup the dry-cleaning man came to the door. This kid Ryan answered the door, paid the dry-cleaning man four dollars, and shut the door as if nothing were going on. If the dry-cleaning man had said one word out of line he would have had his head blown off. When Irish eyes are smiling. Somebody should do a song about Irish with cuckoo eyes. Dagger eyes.

When the old man left, Dermot asked who he was. "That man is the Assistant Chief of Brigade Staff, Second Battalion, Provisional Brigade, IRA," the barman said.

"What does he do with a job like that?" Dermot asked.

"He does what the job requires," the barman said.

"He arranges funerals for fuckin' policemen," the man in the plaid cap said.

Dermot got up and walked to the door and looked out the window. In the doorway directly across the street from the saloon entrance, a guy of about twenty leaned in a doorway with his hands in the back pockets of his dungarees. A cigarette came straight out of his mouth. He looked up the street at the Falls Road. On the sidewalk in front of the doorway next to the saloon, two women stood and talked. The heaviness made their cloth coats, very old coats, stretched and shiny across their rears.

A little boy was in the middle of the street. He had long hair that was in knots as much as it was curly. He wore an imitation-leather zipper jacket. Short pants ended at the tops of his thighs. Black rubber boots flopped against his legs. His legs were thin and dirt-streaked. He ran up to a rock and kicked it, the right leg coming across the left in a soccer kick. A dog with a rib cage showing through a black coat trotted after the rock, picked it up, and stood in the street trying to chew the wet rock.

The day had turned into a haze that was almost a drizzle. Nobody else was out on Leeson Street. But feet hung from every doorway. Feet in ripped sneakers, shoes that once were the mother's; feet in rain boots, feet in low shoes with dirty ankle socks. As you looked up the street in the haze, the doorways and the feet sticking out of them—three and four and five pairs of feet sticking out of each of the tiny doorways—started to come together. There was the feeling that if the sun came out, the houses would empty and you'd suffocate on the street from the smell of all the people and their clothes.

Dermot turned back into the saloon. Nobody was talking. The barman rubbed his hand over the side of his face, the heavy beard scratched loudly. The man in the plaid cap put his pint glass down; it made the noise of a thrown rock. The mother's uncle swallowed. The sound of the swallow started in the back of his gums came next from the top of his throat, ended with a clunk in the bottom of his throat. Everybody made noise breathing. At first, it sounded like four or five people hurt in an emergency room, but as you listened it grew to a steam pump. Dermot tried to talk to the old man nearest him. He had an enamel insignia held to the lapel of his suit jacket with a safety pin. The safety pin kept the lapel bunched up. The insignia was a green disk with a silver harp on it. Dermot asked the old man what the insignia was for. Long, watery eyes came up from the stout and focused on the lapel. "Ah dunno," he said. "I just found it on the

161

road and I got a friend to run a wee pin through it and I wear it."

Which ended that conversation. The sound of breathing rose again. Dermot was finishing the pint when there were voices outside and the door opened and people came in.

"Hel-lo," the first one said. He had long sideburns and curly hair and he was slouched over, but he walked quickly.

"Ah, there's Jerry," the one who came in next said. The barman nodded to her. She swung as she walked, her hands stuck into the pockets of a navy-blue wool parka. Black hair fell behind her into the hood. Rain and mist had trickled color through her face. She was in her early twenties and she was tall. She came into the space next to Dermot and she was so busy saying hello to each of the old men, her eyes filled with energy, head moving, mouth in a smile that was almost a laugh, that she did not notice how everybody was looking at her. She went from one to the other and now the eyes looked right at him. Her chin made a little half-smile. It is the same facial motion you use in New York when you are asked to do something hard and you say, "Gee, I don't know." In Ireland, it is the way they greet somebody they don't know.

Another girl, thirty probably, with straggly light hair and a few freckles on her forehead had come in too. She was with a guy who was much younger. He stood back against the wall, his wet hair hanging into the thick glasses he wore.

"Gentlemen," the one with the sideburns said. He rubbed his hands and looked around at everybody.

"Liam?" the bartender said to him. Liam looked at the ones with him. "Vodka," the dark-haired girl said. The other girl and Liam ordered the same. The dark-haired girl turned around. "Damien?"

The one against the wall shook his head no.

"Oh, come on now, Damien."

"I don't prefer anything."

She turned her back to him and picked up her glass of vodka. "Damien, are you not comfortable here?"

Damien muttered something as he was turning his head to look at the door. Dermot didn't hear what he said, but the girl did and she broke into a laugh. Her laugh was like a hand reaching around the room and poking people. Everyone laughed with her.

"What did he say?" Dermot asked her.

She turned to Damien. His face was solemn and his eyes very wide. Between syllables of her laugh she said, "Damien, tell the gentleman what you just said."

"They'll have our balls," Damien said.

"Damien is scared to death of being castrated by the Prods," she said.

"They will, too," Damien said.

The barman was almost smiling. "They think they can do it."

"Isn't he safe on this street?" Dermot asked.

The mother's uncle made a noise. "There's no safety around here," he said.

"Fookin' millions of Prods all around us," Damien said.

"And they could come swarmin' down the block just to castrate you," the dark-haired girl said.

"I got nothin' else," Damien said. He was holding himself. "If they take it off me, I just as soon go kill my fookin' self."

The dark-haired girl exploded into more laughter. "He means it actually," she said to Dermot.

Damien tapped her on the arm.

"Do ye not have a few bob, Deirdre?"

"Yer fookin' not on," she said.

"I've a few quid," Liam said.

"Ah, that's very good," Damien said.

"Ye are a fookin' greedy bastard, so ye are," Liam said.

Dermot said to the girl, "Where do you come from?"

"Derry. We're not from Belfast."

"I notice you don't talk like the other people here." They spoke with more lilt than the Belfast people in the bar.

"Derry people speak differently because Derry should be the capital of Donegal, and that is part of the Republic of Ireland," she said. She had very little accent as she

163

spoke. From going to schools, Dermot thought. She pronounced "fuck," the one most used word in Northern Ireland, as "fook," which is how Dermot had heard it in Dublin. "You see Belfast is good Unionist," she said. "Good Scottish Presbyterian. You can go to a wee little town out in the country and people talk with more Belfast than anything else. Then you can go to another wee little town that are only eleven mile away and the accent changes considerably and you would think you were in one of the counties in the South."

Dermot could feel he was looking at her too much, so he held his hand out to Liam and said, "Say, my name is Dermot Davey."

"Ah hah," he said.

"I'm just here from New York having a drink. This is my mother's uncle, Mister James Meehan. He lives near here."

"Ah hah," Liam said. He nodded pleasantly, his eyes were friendly. He went no further.

The dark-haired girl took out a box of cigarettes, pulled a few up, and reached past Dermot to offer them to the mother's uncle and the old man with the pin. The man with the pin took one. He said thank you, and she gave him the little nod and smile. She offered one to the barman, who said no, and then held out the pack to Dermot.

He grabbed one and said thanks and she gave the little nod and half-smile and turned to the people with her. They all were smoking. He held out his lighter for her, but she didn't notice it. She was striking a box match.

"How's your drink?" Dermot asked.

She held out the glass. "I believe it's brilliant."

"Have another one then," he said.

Her eyebrows raised and her eyes looked right over the glass at him while she drained the glass and held it out to the barman.

Dermot asked Liam if he'd care to have a drink.

"No, I have too much to do," he said. He waved his hand at the others. "They'll keep you busy, however."

The four of them were wearing small red-and-gold insignias. Dermot leaned over to look at the one pinned to the girl's coat. The insignia was made of a gold profile of a man's head. The lettering under it said 1870—NEVER! The man, bald and with fierce eyebrows, looked exactly like Lenin.

"Who's that?" Dermot said.

Her eyes widened. "You don't know?"

"I tell you the truth, to me it looks like Lenin."

"Well, it is."

Dermot pulled his head back. "What do you have that for?"

"Labour Party," she said.

"Oh, for a second there I was going to say—"

"Say what?"

"Well, what am I supposed to think, I just come here from New York and I see somebody wearing a pin with Lenin on it."

"If I were civilized," she said, pronouncing each word slowly, "I would think that the person with the pin was interested in working-men and -women."

"Yeah, but the Labour Party isn't the Communist Party."

"Ah dunno, I guess you could call us Communists. Although we're a bit more radical than Communists, you know."

Larry put his hand on Dermot's arm and said, "I want to take a walk around and look up a few people."

"Well, go ahead."

"Don't you want to come?"

"I'm fine here," Dermot said. He poked Larry's father.

"Oh, I can see you're interested in the old man here," Larry said. He was smiling. His father chuckled.

"No, I just want to talk to her."

"Don't even try," Larry said. "We're always arguin' with them. All they do, the whole fuckin' lot of them, is talk, talk, talk. Every time we advocate doin' something all they want to do is talk about it."

Larry walked out, and Dermot turned back to the girl. He tapped her on the back. "Let me ask you something."

She was watching his face closely. "Look at you, you look like you're afraid the pin is going to bite you. If

165

there's any way to scare an American to death it's mention the word 'Communist.' "

"I'm just wondering," he said. The drink was pushing the words along, but he kept going. "I was just wondering if you understand Communism."

"Understand what about it?" Her eyes were wide and her mouth was parted just a little. Even with the heavy parka coat she had on, you could almost see her body coiled.

The drink pushed the words out again. He pointed to the old man with the harp insignia pinned to his lapel. "Well," he said, "he's wearing an insignia and he doesn't know what it stands for."

She let out a shriek.

"She reminds me of the woman just got killed by the Gaelic football field," the mother's uncle said, pointing at her. "Shot her right through the top of the head, everybody said they used an airplane to do it."

"When was this?" she said to him.

"Oh, this past riot. They had a pillbox on the field and they shot Lewis guns all night."

"Oh," she said.

"Yep, used to shoot all night. One night here the wee child run out of the house onto the field. The women went chasin' after the wee child. The woman was bendin' over to pick up the wee child when they opened up with the Lewis gun. Shot her right through the top of the head while she was bendin' over."

"That's fine, that's fine," she said, taking her drink.

"You see, when she bent over the shot went through and laid her head all open. But we thought when we first seen it, the head laid open right to the brain, you know, we thought they'd shot her from a bloody plane."

"That's fine, that's fine," she said.

"Bloody Black and Tans," he said.

"They're the worst, I hate them myself," she said. She smiled. That seemed to take them off the other subject, so Dermot said to her that Leeson Street seemed like a crowded place to him.

"In this immediate area there are one thousand houses,"

166

she said. "Best put it at two thousand couples in the houses. Because the people are Catholic, it doesn't take a wizard to estimate thirty thousand people live right around here."

"How can anybody live in places this small?" he said.

"And who informed you they were living?" she said.

"I guess they're not," he said.

"Neither are your Negroes in America," she said. Dermot felt a little burn run through him.

"The people here keep having children?" he said.

"Aye, children, children, children," she said.

"Nobody practices birth control?"

She laughed. "Birth control? With Father McPriest breathing down your bloody neck?"

"Why don't they tell the priests to get lost?"

"Some of the women would love to," she said.

"Then why don't they?"

"They wouldn't know what to do after that."

"Wouldn't know what?"

"They don't have a clue, not a clue," she said.

"Get somebody to tell them."

"Who's going to tell a girl? Her mother who had nine?"

"Go out and buy a woman's magazine, it's all in there, isn't it?"

"The people here live on eleven pound a week," she said. "A magazine costs two bob. Most of the people here see meat once a week. Every week they come down to the last day and a half, probably the last two days, with no food in the house. No food for anybody. Perhaps a few scraps for the children. So now, who is going to spend two bob to learn how to commit a mortal sin?"

"Are you a Catholic?" Dermot asked.

She looked at him very coolly. "Can you not be a Catholic and a Communist too?" she said.

"Oh, I don't know, leave me alone, I'm here from New York and I'm just having a drink, and if I say six more words, you're going to claw my eyes out. Let me finish my drink and get out of here alive."

"Ah, we're not that mean," she said, smiling. She was relaxed.

"What brings you here from Derry?" he asked.

"Questions, questions, you Yanks ask personal questions every half second. Next you'll be asking me what I do for a job."

"What kind of work do you do?"

She clapped her hands and laughed.

"And how much money do I get and what address do I live at and what kind of car do I drive?"

She was saying it with some lightness, but he was still that half step behind her. He motioned to her to drink up.

They didn't talk for a while. Then she said, "Well, I can tell you what type of employment I'm not allowed to have."

"What's that?"

"Can't teach."

"Because you're a Communist?"

"Because I wrote a poem in my last semester at Queens and the Bishop shit himself when he read it."

"Then teach in other schools," he said.

"Not if you're Catholic. You can only teach in Catholic schools."

"How bad a poem was it?"

"Oh, horrible, horrible. Blasphemy it was."

"What did it say?"

She took a drag of the cigarette and looked up at the ceiling, squinting while she spat out the smoke.

"I read *News of the World*
Because I am bound
By stringent Catholic laws
That say I must
Not have intercourse
Or enjoy by
Any other source
Premarital simple pleasures
And so to the *News of the World* I go
And sex myself through another girl's endeavors."

The mother's uncle began clapping. "Oh, very good, very good."

"The *News of the World* is some kind of a scandal sheet?" Dermot asked her.

"It's the world's largest newspaper," she said. "Comes out every Sunday. Who's doing it to who. Christ, it's great."

"The poem doesn't seem so bad to me," he said.

"Well, it was enough to get me banned from teaching."

"It's too bad you're not down in the South," he said. "At least they respect a poet there."

"Says who?" she said. "Christ, they'd shit themselves down there too if anybody put this out. The South? Huh. Do you know they've just had a major breakthrough in the South? Bishop McBishop there, he finally relented. Now they are allowed to publish *Borstal Boy* in Dublin."

"What are you talking about," he said. "That's an Irish book."

"What does that mean? So is *The Ginger Man*. Christ, they'll never let that book see the light of day. All over the world it's a fookin' classic. If you want a copy of *The Ginger Man* in Dublin, you have to ask somebody to bring it to you from London. What they need in Dublin is about six months of Mailer walking around abusing them. He'd fix the bloody asses."

"Mailer?" he said.

"Do you not agree?"

"He's a fuckin' nut."

"A *what*?"

Dermot had seen Mailer once in his life. Dermot was going through the police gate at Shea Stadium to see a fight and in the tunnel there was a big crowd of police shoving each other. In the middle of them here was this stocky guy with wiry hair, talking in a southern drawl. One look at him told you he could get into trouble in a telephone booth. All the brothers were pushing so they could get closer to Mailer and break his fucking head if he did anything.

"What do you do, come here to teach classes?" Dermot said.

"Political educating," she said. "We've an election."

"Are you down here getting votes?"

"No, the election we're in isn't in Belfast. It's in Mid-Ulster. Do you know where that is?"

"No, I don't even know about the election, either."

"Do they not tell you of the general elections in your New York newspaper? The Parliamentary elections? The House of Commons? Westminster?"

He kept shaking his head no.

"And then they want to govern the world," she said.

He shrugged. "All I want is another drink."

"Ah," she said and smiled. "We have this wee girl candidate and all we ask of the people here is that they control the violence until the election is over. The situation is so fragile. Things could break out any second. But we think we are doing something far more important than violence and we can get so much more done. We no longer can indulge ourselves in violence. We've done that for a half century. Now we have to go out and truly bring a government down. You cannot do that with the gun any longer."

"What we need here is more guns," the mother's uncle said. "Give 'em the warks with a Wabley!"

"To shoot the soldiers," she said.

"Aye, shoot the soldiers."

"And shoot the Prods too."

"Aye, shoot the Prods too."

"Ah, there's a good churchgoing Catholic." She said it softly but her eyes flashed and snapped.

The mother's uncle put a hand on Dermot's shoulder. "Well, he brung us a—"

Dermot cut in. "Drink it down, we'll have another." He pushed his hand toward the drink.

The door opened and a man put his head in and made a motion with his chin. "Up, let's be on our way," Liam the one with the sideburns, said. He was picking up his change. "Good luck," he said.

"Cheerio," she said with a wave.

"What the hell is your name?" Dermot said.

"More questions!" she said.

"I at least want to say good-by by name."

"Name of O'Doherty," she said.

"What O'Doherty?"

"Deirdre O'Doherty. Cheerio." She started walking to the door. She stopped for a moment. Then she spun around, the Lenin pin in her hand. She shoved it into his face.

"Boooooo!"

She went away laughing, her hair swinging while she walked. Even with the coat and the slacks she had on you could see she had a strong, young body, one of those with no waist and big curved hipbones. When the door closed behind her, the barroom fell into silence, the energy from her still hanging in the air.

"That's the first Communist I ever had a drink with in my life," Dermot said.

"It didn't appear that it was particularly painful," the barman said.

"They told us everything about them, but they never told us they were fucking beautiful too," Dermot said.

The barman clapped. He bent over to get something from under the bar. "Oh, they're well meant, I suppose," he said. "They're here the same reason you are too. For Joe O'Neill. But they think different. They have their wee girl and they'll try to get her reelected to Commons. Speaks like a marvel, the wee girl does. For that matter, so does this one here. Christ, they can persuade."

He folded his arms and looked down. "I think the machinery you brought here speaks our language a bit more," he said.

Dermot held out the glass for another pint and drank it in silence. After you're on stout for a while, you get over the fact that it's warm, that it puts fizz in your nose and at first gives you the feeling of swallowing phlegm. By now he had to take a piss. The barman pointed to a doorway in the back room. There was no door, just an opening. He stepped through it and found himself outside, standing in a good rain. He was in an enclosure made up of a cement wall that was almost black and stood seven feet high. The wall separated the open door of the saloon from an alley running between the saloon and the backs of the houses on the street behind the saloon. The wall had a gutter running along the bottom. He stood in the rain and pissed against the wall. The rain came harder and he could barely follow his piss in the rain. He came back into the saloon with the rainwater dripping from his hair. The front of his pants was streaked with rain.

The barman was in the back room, climbing up the stack of Guinness cases to turn on a dusty television set which sat on top of the pile of cases. The back room was stacked from floor almost to ceiling with cases of Guinness bottles. The picture was wavery when it came. The picture came on, horses, their rear ends swinging, walking to the post. The white lettering under the horses said FOURTH AT NEWCASTLE. The picture showed one horse and the white lettering underneath the horse said the horse was Tillinghast and the jockey was Lester Piggot.

"Aye, there's your man," one of them at the bar said.

"Aye, that's him," the barman said.

Dermot looked up at the set. Piggot was standing in the stirrups on the way to the post. He always rides that way, standing almost straight up. Once he came over to Aqueduct and rode for a whole month. One day Dermot bet a horse called Assigned with Bobby Ussery riding him and Ussery got in the middle of the track all down the back stretch and Piggot's horse was along the rail. Piggot standing up in the stirrups like a soldier. When they started to come into the turn, Ussery got down flat on his belly and he headed for the rail. The horse came down the hill from the mound in the middle of the track and dropped right into the gutter along the rail. Piggot never knew what happened. Ussery had the horse rolling down the hill and he picked up lengths like nothing. In the stretch, Ussery put his face into the horse's mane and here was this Piggot still standing straight up. Dermot's horse paid sixteen-fifty. You never forget what you had a ten-dollar ticket on, and he went home whistling that day. His friend, Herbie, let him off at the corner. His kids were down the block in front of the house. When they saw him getting out of the car, the three of them gave a little skip and came running up the block. Running with their hands out and calling his name once and carrying it for the whole

172

time they were running up the block with their hands out. You know how kids do that, "Daaa . . . aaaa . . . deeeeeee." That was the last time he'd seen Piggot.

He told the barman he wanted another pint, and this time some whisky with it.

He was drinking by himself now. Everybody else was watching the race. He looked up once. All the jockeys were standing up while they rode. He swallowed the whisky. The barman leaned on the back bar and watched the race. Dermot asked him for another whisky and while he was getting it for him, he downed the pint of stout and told him he wanted another one of those too. The mother's uncle nodded his head when he asked him if he wanted another.

Dermot was taking the pints in big gulps. He had to piss again and went out into the rain and began to lean forward, to put his forehead against the wall, but the smell of the piss coming out of the cement stopped him short.

He walked back to the front of the saloon and looked out at the street. The guy who had been standing with his hands in the back pockets of his dungarees still was leaning in the doorway looking up the toy street to the Falls Road. His shoulder came off the doorway and he stuck his head out. His hands came out of his pockets. He yelled something back into the darkness of the house. He came running into the rain in the middle of the street. His top lip dropped down over the bottom lip and he made a high, clear whistle.

"Wup!" the barman said. He came over the bar and pushed against Dermot in the doorway. The others in the bar left the television and jammed in the doorway around him.

Across the street a woman came churning out of the dark to see. Her tits were flopping inside a brown sweater that buttoned down the front. She fell to her hands and knees and began banging a garbage can cover on the sidewalk. Out of every doorway women were stumbling and kicking at the legs of the children as they stepped over the legs and came out onto the sidewalk to fall down on

173

their hands and knees and bang garbage can covers. Both sides of the street were lined with women. They were banging the garbage can covers in rhythm. There was a clang, clang, clang, each cover hitting the sidewalk at the same time and the noise echoed off the little brick house and filled the street. The women were looking off to one side, the way a dog does when somebody comes to grab a bone from him. They were looking up to the end of the street. At the corner of the Falls Road there was an armored car with two jeeps behind it. The soldiers in Scottish caps were pulling the barbed wire away so the armored car and the jeeps could turn into Leeson Street.

"Let's get out of here," Dermot said.

"Notatall, notatall," his mother's uncle said.

"Oh, shit, I forgot about Larry."

"It's me. Larry must be on the run somewhere. I can't make it around so fast. I'm stuck."

"Well, what's to worry about now anyway?" Dermot said. "They must come down the streets all the time. As long as I don't have a gun on me, I'm just a tourist. I'm all right."

"Not on this fuckin' street," the barman said. "Any man they see they lift. You could be in all day."

The street was crowded with women and kids. The garbage can covers kept banging. A girl came out of the doorway next to the saloon, a girl with kinky red hair pulled back and a cigarette in her mouth. She was buttoning a green sweater. Shapeless tan corduroy pants had a zipper fly that was broken. She had the fly bunched together with a safety pin. She pulled the sweater down so that it covered the broken fly. Dark-blue socks were sticking out of the toes of her shiny black imitation-leather boots. She had a garbage can lid in one hand and a stick in the other. She began beating the garbage can cover. Kids started running to her and the women began picking themselves up from the sidewalk and walking to her. They stopped to pick up rocks and sticks to beat on the garbage can lids. The redhead leaned over and spat her cigarette out. She kept looking around. When she saw Dermot standing on the sidewalk, she snarled.

174

"Come on, you," she said.

Dermot said nothing.

"Come on," she said again.

"He's no business here," the mother's uncle said.

"Fuck," she said to him. "Come on, you," she said to Dermot.

She was a roughed-up twenty-five.

"Come on, come on, you're a man, aren't you?"

The mother's uncle started back into the saloon. "Get inside," he said.

"Ginny Ann!" the redhead yelled at Dermot. She began grabbing women around her.

"Ginny Ann!" one of the women yelled at him.

"Ginny Ann, Ginny Ann, Ginny Ann," the redhead yelled at him in a singsong.

The crowd of women and kids, there must have been two hundred people out there now, all were looking at him and all were chanting, "Ginny Ann, Ginny Ann, Ginny Ann!"

A whine from the top of the street, the armored car starting to move, made them all turn around. The redhead began beating her garbage can cover again with the stick. They all picked up the beat. A kid in short pants ran up the block and threw a rock at a head sticking out of the top of the armored car. The jeeps were coming behind it. The redhead began walking straight up the middle of the street. The crowd followed her. The redhead kept going at the armored car. The soldiers in the car tried to bluff her and keep coming. She never took a weak step. The car had to stop. The soldiers jumped out of the jeeps behind the car, and right away the women were around them. They held the garbage can covers up to the soldiers' faces and began to bang faster and faster. The soldiers were wincing from the noise.

The mother's uncle kept shouting at Dermot from the saloon doorway. He went back inside. The mother's uncle was alone with the barman. The barman closed the door and the place went dark. One shaft of light came from a narrow space between two pieces of plywood covering the front window. The light fell on the middle of the bar. The

175

mother's uncle put his glass down exactly in the light. Some more light was coming through the open door to the piss wall. Otherwise the whole place was in the night.

The barman put his face against the gap in the plywood and kept looking out. The noise of the garbage can covers was so loud now that it hurt to listen.

"Bloody fuckers," the barman said.

He pulled the plywood piece out so Dermot could watch with him. The women, they all had wide behinds and fat legs, ankles bulging out of their shoes, were being pushed back by the soldiers, there must have been fifteen of them now. A couple of soldiers began shoving with their hands until they got to the doorway across the street from the bar, the doorway where the guy with his hands in his pockets had been standing.

"Now we're in for it," the barman said.

"Who lives there?"

"It's not who lives there, it's what's behind the house. That's a warehouse around the corner, you can't see it from here. It's sealed off so you can't get at the front entrance. But you go through the house over there. You can crawl from the back of the house, into the back of the warehouse. We got all the stuff in the warehouse."

"The people in the house can say they don't know anything about it," Dermot said. "The stuff isn't on their premises, is it?"

"Christ, what does it matter about the people in the house? We've the machinery for the whole Falls in there. We can't let them have that. We're gonna have to have a go at them right here. Oh, look at the bloody fuckers comin' from all over."

Soldiers were coming from the other end of Leeson Street, pushing toward the house. A tubby soldier was swinging his shoulders and coming through the women. One of the women reached out and slammed the garbage can cover on his face. The tubby soldier got a hand in the woman's face and pushed hard and she fell back and the crowd of women went berserk and tried to get at him. The tubby soldier kept swinging his shoulders and the women wound up squeezing against each other and popping him out of the crowd and into the doorway of the house.

"That's it," the barman said. "There'll be a go now."

"Somebody gave them good information," Dermot said.

"You could buy the whole fuckin' block for twenty pound," the barman said.

"They're goin' in only one doorway?" the mother's uncle said.

"Aye. One doorway."

"Can't have holes house-to-house any more." The mother's uncle was talking as he was moving, bad leg and all, around the end of the bar in the darkness and advancing on the Guinness tap. "Can't have holes house-to-house. Used to have them like tunnels, you know. Never knew who'd come into your house. Guy fixin' his fly racin' from a husband came into our kitchen."

There was a thump on the ceiling. Somebody was up on the roof of the saloon. The barman left the plywood right away and went to the back of the saloon. Empty bottles began clinking. He came into the light of the doorway to the piss wall carrying two cases of Guinness bottles. He went out the door, came back, and carried out more cases. Out against the piss wall he had two cases on top of each other, in another spot three cases on top of each other.

"Take you man and put him up on this one," he said, tapping the top of the three cases. "Over the wall he goes. Don't use this one here." He tapped the two cases. "I'll be runnin' for this one myself. Myself, at least."

He went back to the front of the place. The armored car still was stuck up the block with a circle of women and children around it. There was another crowd of women, the redhead leading them, pushing against a couple of soldiers, four or five of them, who were trying to keep the doorway across the street clear. The redhead had her garbage can cover a couple of inches away from a soldier's face. His face didn't even twitch. He could have been one of those guys who stand in front of Buckingham Palace.

It stayed this way, milling and banging garbage can

177

covers, for a full five minutes. "Why the fuck didn't we run?" Dermot said. "Come on, why don't we try gettin' the hell out of here now?"

"You can't move now," the barman said.

"We'll just duck out the door and get out of your life." He didn't answer. He put his arm out like a bar in front of the closed door.

"Why?"

"Because you can't," he said.

"The man's in charge," the mother's uncle said. His face was right over the pint, hanging in the shaft of light as if he were praying for the pint.

"Come on, there's yours here too," the barman said. He had another pint and whisky alongside it.

The banging out on the street stopped. There was a loud moan. Across the street there were two men with their hands on top of their heads. Soldiers pulled them by the arms toward the armored car. A soldier came out of the doorway holding a rifle up in each hand. The soldier after him had three rifles cradled in his arms. When another soldier came out carrying two grease guns, the women went crazy and tried to attack the soldier. The other soldiers trying to keep the doorway clear held night sticks across their chests and kept pushing them out, trying to keep the women away.

The redhead was standing alone with her back to the saloon, hands on her hips. A fat woman in a black rainjacket and a dirty housedress came out of the crowd on the other side of the street. The fat woman's feet were flopping in sandals. She came through a puddle, the bare feet in the sandals splashing black water onto her legs. Her face was concentrating on running. When she came close to the redhead, the fat lady's top lip curled up and she threw a left hook the way a man does. She caught the redhead on the side of the head. The redhead put a hand into the fat woman's face and began clawing. The fat woman went back a step. The redhead started swinging both hands, her hands in fists. The fat woman threw punches back. She had her eyes wide and her mouth open, sucking in air. The redhead had her legs very wide

178

and the imitation-leather boots kept slipping while she punched. Trying to keep her balance, she looked like her hips were disjointed in the baggy corduroy pants.

A little girl in a parka ran up alongside the fat woman. The little girl's bare, dirty legs began jumping up and down. Her fist was in the air, cheering the fat lady on. Women began flocking around now, but instead of stopping the fight they formed a circle of mean, shouting faces. The redhead had both hands in the other woman's hair. The fat woman ducked, trying to pull away. Her face looked out through the crook of one of the redhead's arms. She was a cow somebody was torturing.

The barman was opening the door. The soldier was across the street, the one who had kept his face straight. He was craning his neck to see over the heads of the cheering women. Then he shook his head and came out onto the street toward the crowd of women. The barman opened the door wider.

Dermot started to walk out the door and the barman grabbed him and snarled, "Get away!" as the women in the part of the circle between the soldier and the fight pulled away like a curtain. The redhead let go of the fat lady and ran to her left and the fat lady went the other way into the crowd of women and children. In the middle of the semicircle was the old man, Joe O'Neill, in a crouch, his arm straight out, holding a pistol. The soldier dropped his club. He sat down in the street as the sound of the shot registered. The women shrieked and held up their arms while Joe O'Neill still in a crouch, slipped through the wall of women between himself and the saloon and, down even lower, came through the doorway with the gun in his hand, his eyes popping. The barman reached past Dermot and slammed the door. As it swung shut, he could see that an incredible amount of blood was coming out from under the soldier's chin. And a lot of skirts and rain-jackets and bare legs of kids in front of the saloon. A gun went off on the roof of the saloon. With the door shut, it was dark inside the saloon again. Dermot got on the floor and closed his eyes. On the street, women shrieked and you could hear men, the soldiers, cursing. Footsteps were

179

sounding in every direction. The gun on the roof went off again. Guinness boxes were falling over out by the piss wall. The barman's voice was shouting curses. Dermot started crawling on his stomach toward the back of the place.

His mother's uncle couldn't get on the floor. So he worked his way along like a hunchback. When he got into the light coming through the doorway to the piss wall, he still had the pint in his hand. He was rocking a little bit. "Always the same trouble, same trouble," he said. The sound of gunfire came through the doorway from the piss wall. Between the gunshots there would be this quick whine. The Guinness boxes at the piss wall were overturned, the empty bottles all over the place. A bottle jumped in the piss.

"Well, Jesus, I'm not going out there," the mother's uncle said. He groped in the darkness, pushing the stacks of Guinness cases around.

Dermot made a narrow space between the wall and a line of Guinness cases that were stacked almost five feet high. He crawled into the space and began to think about the old man, Joe O'Neill, crouched down with the women around him and with his arm straight out and holding a pistol—a police .32.

8:

The shooting lasted for fifteen minutes. Which seemed to be hours. Jeeps out in the street were swerving and running up the block, away from the saloon. A heavier sound had to be an armored car backing up. There was a loud curse from the guy up on the saloon roof. He must have been perched directly above the piss wall. His voice came clearly through the open door. Something hit the piss wall and bounced around. Right away Dermot's eyes were stinging. He shut his eyes. There was a strong smell of sour metal. He put his hand over his face against the smell. His mother's uncle was coughing. Dermot pulled himself up and crawled over to the stacked cases of stout the mother's uncle was behind. Dermot's fingers clamped on a bony shoulder. He yanked it up. The sour metal was at Dermot's face now, suffocating him, the pain going through to the back of his eyes. He gripped the bony shoulder and pulled up. Then he yanked him from behind the cases. Eyes shut, one hand out in front of him, the other holding the uncle, Dermot went toward the front of the saloon. He was afraid to open the door and step onto the street. But he could not stay inside. The sour metal was pulling a sheet of black around the inside of his head. He opened the door.

"Don't rub the eyes," a man's voice called out.

Dermot wobbled down the saloon steps and crouched on the sidewalk. Next to him, he could feel the uncle standing straight up.

181

"Here," a woman's voice said. The vinegar smell pushed one of Dermot's eyes open. The woman was holding a plastic bowl under his chin. Her rough hands were shaking so much that the vinegar spilled over the sides. Pieces of ripped cloth, diapers, were in the vinegar. Dermot put one over his nose and mouth, the other over his eyes. He bent down and splashed more vinegar onto the rags. He blinked to let the vinegar get into his eyes. The woman in front of him holding the bowl could not have been thirty, but her face was so pasty and drained she might as well have been fifty. She was shaking from her shoulders to her hands, and she kept looking around to see if anything was coming from the corner of the Falls Road. But she did not move. She stood holding the bowl out for Dermot and the mother's uncle. Up and down the block, women with bowls were standing in the doorways. One woman came onto the sidewalk with a dripping towel. She bunched it up and threw it on the roof, toward the chimney. An arm came from behind the chimney and pulled the towel in. Halfway up the street there was a fine white mist. All the way up, at the corner of the Falls Road, the gas was in clouds.

A priest came around the corner with a white cloth in the air like a flag. Dermot asked the priest how to get out of the area.

His mother's uncle interrupted him. "They block off the whole section," he said. "Last riot here they blocked us off ten days with no food or water. Black and Tan pigs comes along the streets hittin' the women."

The priest paid no attention to what the uncle was saying. "A soldier are shot," he said. "Be difficult to move about."

The woman was still standing by Dermot with the bowl held up to him. He dipped the diaper into the vinegar and put it over his eyes again. The woman said, "What can yer man do with his leg?"

Dermot looked at the priest. "Why don't you go with him?" he said to the uncle.

"Notatall."

"I can see why," the woman said. She was smiling. Her

finger touched the lapel of the priest's rumpled suit. He wore a bright-red pin, a Sacred Heart, of the Pioneers, people who take a pledge of total abstinence.

"He'd prefer death to thirst," the priest said.

The mother's uncle was clutching a bottle of stout.

The priest started around the corner. Both of them followed him. They went past the last house on the other side of the street, turned the corner, and came into Balaclava Street. It was the same as Leeson Street, the same toy houses and toy sidewalks. On the left-hand side of Balaclava, seven or eight yards from the corner of Leeson Street, was a gray cement warehouse. The right side of the warehouse was attached to the rear of the last house on Leeson Street. About ten people, a couple of old men and some young ones in their very early teens, were in front of the warehouse doors. The windows and entranceway were boarded up with wood that was wet and thick, like railroad ties. There was a cracking sound. A crowbar was being used inside the warehouse.

The priest walked up to O'Neill and the barman and two other men, old nervous men with uncombed hair and heavy beards showing against red cheeks.

Liam came around the corner first. His head nodding, the jacket collar turned up so you couldn't see he had sideburns. Footsteps were sounding, and out of the side street, running with her body held together, the legs not going out sideways the way most girls do it, head up, cigarette in her right hand, came Deirdre. She stopped at O'Neill. She took out a box of cigarettes and offered them to the priest, who took one, and then to O'Neill and the two older men. She held out the box to Dermot. He took one. She did not look at him. She was looking straight at Joe O'Neill.

"We need the television to come here," she said.

"That would be fine," O'Neill said.

"If there were no shooting, then the BBC could come all through the area," Liam said.

"Been shooting already," O'Neill said.

"If it could end at that," Deirdre said, turning to them. The timber cracked, the crowbar working from inside

183

the warehouse had the top half of the timber ripped off the doorway. The crowd of kids. began reaching up. The hands were out like people reaching for food. A hand came over the top of the timber covering the lower half of the doorway. A rifle came up from inside the warehouse. An old bolt-action rifle. A hand grabbed it and a red-haired kid came pushing out of the crowd, holding it like it was a prize. He had a long, bony face with sunken eyes and lips that barely made a line in his face. His suit jacket was much too big for him. His pants were wet and wrinkled and fell over the tops of a pair of pointy shoes that had no heels left at all. If he was sixteen, he was old.

Dermot's mother's uncle waved at him. "Good boy! Give 'em the warks with it."

"Can you not get the arms out of the area without using them?" Deirdre said to O'Neill.

O'Neill grunted something.

"Then we could get the telly in. It would be extremely beneficial for us to have something on the telly showin' wee children with no food."

"We all know there's no food," O'Neill said.

"The people in London tonight and tomorrow would see hungry children," she said.

"London? And what would we get from London. More bloody troops?"

"And who'd defend us today?" one of the men with O'Neill said.

"The telly would defend us," Deirdre said. "Soldiers are afraid of it."

They laughed.

Her voice rose. "If we are all shootin', the telly won't come close. We want to make a political issue of children havin' no food. All the people will see it on the news programs. If you are shootin', there'll be nothin' for the telly camera to do except hide for his life."

"We'll defend the area," Joe O'Neill said.

"With what?" Deirdre said.

"We've enough," O'Neill said.

"There's troops by the hundreds and you are here with a dozen people at best."

"We'll have a go at them," O'Neill said.

"And when you be gone the troops will be everywhere. The people here will be stuck. Jesus, try the television today. Anybody can pull a wee trigger."

"We fight for a nation," the priest said.

"Aye. For justice," O'Neill said.

"What justice can you get today with women and children in the line of fire?" Deirdre said.

"A man must have justice no matter how many people must be hurt," O'Neill said.

He had his handkerchief out. He was rubbing a hand against it. The hand was smeared with dirt from climbing the wall after he shot the soldier. He looked down at the hand. He began rubbing it again.

In front of the warehouse, a boy, about ten years old, started out of the crowd. He popped free and stumbled toward them. Out of the crowd after him came an older boy of perhaps sixteen. The older boy came up and threw a headlock to the kid. "Give it, you fucker," he said.

"Here now!" the priest said. He held out his hand. The younger one dropped his eyes. "Dennis!" the priest said to the younger one.

The boy, still looking down, brought out a pistol from inside his jacket. The priest took it from him. The older one jumped in front of the priest. Thick yellow coated his stumps of teeth. "Father?" he said. "Father?"

"Now, Paddy," the priest said, shaking his head.

"Yes, Father? Yes, Father?"

"What've ye to say of your language?"

"Oh." Paddy was relieved. "Sorry, Father, I'm excited. Sorry, Father."

The priest grunted and nodded. He handed the pistol to the boy. "Just remember," he said.

"Yes, Father, yes, Father."

At the half-open entranceway to the warehouse, kids straddled the timber and passed pistols and old rifles into the cluster of hands reaching up. Somebody inside held up a cardboard shoe box. A man pushed through the kids and took the box. The crowd got out of his way as he began moving. Another cardboard box was held up and another man pushed through the crowd to get it. Nearly everybody else was in the teens. Hair uncombed, old suit jackets wet and shapeless. Or they were even younger, eleven and twelve, wearing imitation-leather jackets with decals of soccer players on the sleeves. All the feet shuffling on the sidewalk were in ripped sneakers or imitation cowboy boots with ground-down heels or in black street shoes with wrinkled backs and no heels left. When the feet in the shoes pressed and strained while hands reached for a gun, brown mucilage squeezed out from the insides of the shoes through broken stitching.

"The telly will only show the shooting from a distance," Deirdre said.

The priest sniffed. O'Neill's face did not change.

"All the blackness, a few big spotlights, here and there a soldier scuttling across the street, that's all they'll see on the telly."

"We're not the Abbey," the priest said.

"I think we should be," she said. "The gun wins nothing. The one who can be brilliant on the telly, there's your winner."

Joe O'Neill spat. "Would the telly show the Crumlin Road jail? They give you the big jail key. They turn it right up your rear end. Excuse me, Father, but you know what I say. That's nothin' to what's happenin'. They put electric wires to your other fellow here." He tapped the front of his pants.

"Would the telly show half the men from this section in prison or on the run?" the priest said. "Would it show soldiers comin' through here all night, night after night, blowin' dog whistles to keep wee babies awake?"

"We've only two cheeks and now both of them are smashed in," Joe O'Neill said.

"It's all they do in America you know," Liam said. "They throw rocks and gather big crowds just to get the telly camera. Then they state their case."

Joe O'Neill waved at Dermot. "Here's your man from America. He brought us somethin' to help us state our case good and proper, he did."

Deirdre's eyes were weapons as she glared at Dermot.

186

He turned his face and started walking over to the mother's uncle. A rifle went off. Kids in broken shoes were running every place, climbing the front of the warehouse to the roof, then jumping to other roofs. Or they simply scattered on the run through the toy streets. Another shot went off. This time you could tell it was from a rooftop around the corner of the first side street. Deirdre's body shook inside the coat. She was alone. Liam was running up toward the dead-end street, the priest was going around a corner, and Joe O'Neill and the two men with him were hurrying down the street, shouting to faces looking out from behind chimneys.

"Do you know where you're going?" Dermot called to her.

"Ah dunno just yet."

"Well, where's he going?" Dermot pointed at Liam.

"Far and good and quick, I hope," she said. "He can't be caught here. They'll lift him."

Dermot took her by the arm, grabbed the uncle, and went to the corner of Leeson Street. He could see the first few doorways on the other side of Leeson Street without sticking his head around the corner. In the doorway next to the saloon, the edge of a plastic bowl was showing. Single shots were sounding from almost every direction now. Any cop would have to be edgy about ricocheting. Outside of the windows and doors, every inch of each street was hard surface. Any kind of firing would turn the street into a pinball machine. The woman holding the bowl in the doorway must have known. She stayed there. The three of them headed for the woman's doorway. Dermot and Deirdre had to drag their feet to keep with the uncle. His head was bobbing around. There was blood in front of the saloon. They were walking on a diagonal. The uncle began pressing into Dermot, trying to change their direction; he was trying to get to the saloon, but there was shooting up at the Falls Road. Gas, much more gas than before, billowed. Dermot hustled them along as best he could, and they came onto the sidewalk and into the doorway of the woman's house. She stood aside, moving her chin from one side to the other, her mouth forming a

187

half-smile. When they were inside, she started to inch up to peer out the open doorway again. Dermot put a hand on her stomach and pushed her back. She stiffened when he touched her, and he pulled the hand back. "I'm just afraid of the street," he said. He shut the door. She acted like she wanted to open it.

Inside the doorway, it was only a full step to a tiny staircase. Halfway through the step there was a space to the right. The space was so small you couldn't call it a doorway. They went through it into a room where babies were on the floor and older kids sat with their legs drawn up on a couch with ripped fabric. The woman, Deirdre, the mother's uncle, and Dermot could not move. The air in the room was smothered with mold. It was the kind of smell you get in some rattrap when you open a closet where a wet floor mop has stood for weeks. Another smell, not quite as thick, came streaming out of the diaper of a baby who sat on the floor playing with a cardboard box. One of the children on the couch said something, running the words together incomprehensibly. The mother pushed through the room. A small white television set with a tiny screen was on the table against the wall. An indoor antenna was suctioned to the wall over the set. A rerun of an American space-adventure series was on. The kid on the couch said something else. The mother turned up the sound. When she moved to do it, a wave of heat came from a little mound of red coals in a fireplace. When the mother stepped back from the television set, her body blocked out the entire fireplace. There was a noise outside. The Venetian blinds were drawn on the one window in the room, but they gave no feeling of safety. Anybody tripping on the sidewalk would come right through the window. With people shooting on the street, being in the room was the same as walking around a pistol range. Dermot started to say something but the woman reacted to the noise by herself. She picked the one baby off the floor, putting him under her arm like a loaf of bread, his dirty diaper fuming, then scooped up a baby girl whose diaper was sopping wet and hung down to the insides of her knees. She went upstairs.

At the sound of another shot somewhere up the street, the oldest one on the couch, a boy, darted to the front door, pulled it open, and flopped on his stomach, his hands out as if he were firing a rifle. He was going "Chew! Chew! Chew!" and inching out so that his head was going to be showing in the doorway. Dermot moved quickly and hooked his foot in front of the kid's shoulder and shoved him back while he slammed the door shut. The boy scrambled up and was trying to slip past to open the door again. Dermot called for the woman. She came to the top of the tiny staircase.

"Aye?" she said.

"Can you tell him, please?"

"Martin, back to the telly."

"Oh." Martin went back to the couch, stamping his rubber boots.

The front door was made of frosted-glass squares. You could see the darkness now on the other side of the glass. Dermot told the woman he didn't think they should be showing any light in the house and that he'd turn off the television.

"Oh, everybody watches the telly during a riot," she said.

In the room, four heads were in the blue light from the television set, the heads higher than the window sill. Dermot shook his mother's uncle, who was asleep in a straight-backed chair. His eyes opened but he didn't see anything. Dermot got him off the chair and onto the floor. He sat with his legs stretched out and his head propped against the seat of the chair. His eyes closed. Dermot told the three kids to get off the couch and onto the floor. They looked at him as if he was crazy. "Come on," he said. They slid off the couch and onto the floor. They watched television with their legs out and their heads resting against the seat of the couch. That was still no good. All the heads were still above the window line.

Deirdre was in the narrow frameway separating the front room from the kitchen. Dermot stepped past her into the kitchen, a kitchenette, really, a square of dirty linoleum. If you turned quickly you hit either a sink with

189

rust streaks in it or a stove with thick crusts on the burners.

"Where do they keep the refrigerator?" Dermot asked Deirdre.

"The fridge? Oh, the fridge. In the back of course."

There was a door opening onto an enclosure about the size of two telephone booths. The back wall of the enclosure was part of the cement wall running behind all the houses on the block. An outhouse took up one side of the enclosure, a coalbin and garbage cans the other. A half-filled pint milk bottle and a roll of butter were on a window ledge.

"That's some refrigerator," he said.

"As a matter of actual fact, I thought you were codding me about a fridge," she said.

He shut the door. It was cold. The topcoat was no help to Dermot because it was damp from being out in the rain. The woman was back downstairs now. She picked her way over the legs and edged past him to the kitchen door. She brought in the milk bottle. "Jesus sake," she said, "I've not enough." She went to a shelf and reached up into the darkness and brought down two plastic baby bottles. Both of them were discolored. She held the baby bottles in the sink and ran water over them. She split the half pint of milk between the two baby bottles. "Jesus, I've not enough, I've not enough," she said. She put the nipples on and stood rubbing the baby bottles across her blue raincoat to dry them. "I hope the wee ones can sleep on this little amount," she said. She shook her head. In the dim light her face, deep lines running through pouches, held more years than it had seen. Dermot told her his name and asked hers.

"Marie," she said.

"Marie what?"

through the room. A small white television set with a tiny

"What's it matter, Marie what?" Deirdre said. "Her name is Marie."

"At least let me ask her if somebody else is expected here tonight. I would like to know what to do if somebody starts coming in here."

"That's different," Deirdre said.

190

"He's workin'," Marie said.

"What time does he get off work?" Dermot asked her.

"About this time."

"He's got a problem getting home tonight," he said.

"He could be doin' somethin' else too, but I suppose he's workin'."

"Is he Provisional?" Deirdre said.

"Aye, Provisional."

"Think he's doin' something else too," Deirdre said.

"Oh, he went to work, he always goes to work. He must be the only man on this end of the street what's with a job. Oh, he goes, all right. But just now. I don't know what he'd be doin' just now."

"What's Provisional?" Dermot asked Deirdre.

"The provisional wing of the IRA," she said. "They've two groups in the IRA. One is the Official IRA. The Official IRA are Socialists and would prefer other ways than violence. The Provisionals, the Provisionals are here. They believe in, well . . ." She looked at the woman. "No mind what they believe in, we're all here and that's all there is to it."

"They believe in people havin' two legs to stand on, not two knees to bow down on," Marie said.

"Of course," Deirdre said. She went into her coat pocket and came out with cigarettes. She offered the box to Marie, who took one. Dermot took out his lighter for her.

"I'll go up and blow smoke in their eyes to keep them shut," she said. "Maybe that'll do it. There's not enough milk for them, that's as sure as Christ."

She stepped back over the legs with the cigarette sticking straight out of her mouth. On the television there was a Popeye cartoon, the big guy who looks like an ape was holding Olive Oyl in one hand and with the other he was trying to put a huge thumbtack through the top of Popeye's head. Dermot sneezed, and sneezed again; his eyes started to sting again. The woman, Marie, had left her bowl of vinegar and water on a little drainboard next to the sink. He cupped his hands and splashed his face. "I forgot we're next door to the goddamned saloon," he said.

"Takes a bit more for us," Deirdre said. "Coming from

191

Derry, you get used to the gas. It's like breathing out and breathing in."

"I'm just realizing," Dermot said.

"Realizing what?"

"Realizing how, excuse me, but just how fucked we are. If a lot of gas gets around here, what the hell are we going to do? Where can we go?"

"I don't see why you should be concerned. You thought enough to bring them a wonderful gun; then you certainly must have thought about all else that would go on."

"I'm just worried about all these kids here," he said.

"Why worry about them? Every house on the street is filled with wee children. You must have taken them into consideration when you arrived here with your gun."

"I don't know what I thought or what I did. All I know is that I wish to Christ I'm out of here and in some place where I belong."

"Ah ha." She crouched down, picked a spot on the floor, and sat down, her knees drawn up. She took a quick drag on her cigarette and blew it out. "Best make yourself easy. We might be here a long time."

Dermot sat down on what was left of the floor and squirmed around until he had his head up against the kitchen door. "Who is out there, just the Army?" he said.

"Just the wee British Army."

"And where are the Protestants, right behind them?"

"Oh, the Protestants are over on the Shankhill having a celebration. The Catholics are committing suicide."

"Oh, no, they weren't celebrating when I saw them last night. They were out on the street looking to fight. Christ, the Army had to come to break it up."

"The Army are supposed to stand between both sides. But all they do is stand between us and liberty. Now and then, when it moves them, they stop Protestants and Catholics from murderin' each other. Just now and then."

"Why the hell do people have to fight over religion?"

"Who was it that told you that everybody fights over religion?" she said.

"Well, that's what it's about."

"Oh, is it, is it?"

"Well, fuck, isn't it?"

She took another drag of the cigarette and waved it at him. "I don't think you know so much about the history of the situation."

"Well, I know something."

"Whatever it is you know, I can tell you it isn't as much as it should be. Religion, sectarianism, is a great weapon of the aristocrats. They're livin' in their manor houses and they're runnin' their factories. All the Scottish Presbyterians are livin' in wee kitchen houses just like this one. Whenever the situation gets so that the Prods and the Catholics seem to be talkin' to each other, the wee rich men in their factory offices yell out that Rome is threatenin' all of us."

"Were the Protestants and Catholics getting together?"

"We had this civil-rights march last year. We had some wee Protestant girls and boys and we had some wee Catholic girls and boys. Comes a bridge we're marchin' across goin' to Derry and all these men are attackin' us. The government are up on the hill watchin'. Next the B Specials run into a Catholic housing off the Springfield Road and set fire to everythin'. The factory bosses let the men off the jobs early so's they could set the fires. Jesus, they couldn't allow Catholic and Protestant working-class people to get together. We'd all look up the hill at the aristocrats and find out who the real enemy is."

She started stamping her foot on the floor and singing in a voice that was between a wail and a moan.

"... bayonets flickerin' in the sun
and the Tans they flew
Like lightnin' to
The rattle of the Thompson gun ..."

She stopped singing the words and hummed it for a while. When she stopped she said, "Do you not have that on your music boxes in America?"

"Only on about three thousand of them on the East Side, and in Sunnyside."

"Ah, Christ, I'll bet they do. They run out and send guns to the Bogside and go home to their warm beds."

"Oh, I don't know what they do."

"On your music boxes, do they sing any songs about the wee children of the Falls Road being smothered by gas while they lay in their beds?"

"I don't know all the songs."

"Or do they have any songs about a wee girl in Derry trying to run to her mother and being shot through the head by a British soldier who was shooting at a shadow?"

Dermot said nothing.

The foot was stamping again and she let out another moan and wail.

> "The only thing they did that night
> That filled my heart with fear,
> They took the ice right off the corpse
> And put it in the beer."

"How's that one?" she said.

"I don't know if I ever heard that."

"Why would you not? Certainly it's on your music boxes."

"I don't know, how would you know?"

"In university we looked up many of the songs and books you have in America. Tracin' the legend, you see. We chose this song as our favorite, being there isn't a piece of ice in all of Ireland big enough to cool your finger."

A shot went off in the street right in front of the house. She sucked in air and her body shook. He crept into the front room to turn off the television and get the kids upstairs. He moved just in time to find the one kid, Martin, off the couch and at the front door again. He was opening the door and Dermot came off the floor and made one leap to catch him. He had his hand out as if he had a pistol and he let one "Chew!" go and then Dermot had the door shut, him by the shoulder and onto the stairs. He gave him a push and told him to keep going, then got down and crept over to the television set and turned it off. The two kids on the floor in front of the couch gave

194

this "Oh gee. Thanks a lot!" Dermot said come on and gave them little taps on the head. The two started to stand up to go upstairs and Deirdre put her hand out to push them down. "If you stand, you'll frighten us to death," she said. The kids giggled and went up the stairs crouching.

Deirdre and Dermot sat on the floor directly under the window. She put her head back against the wall and let her breath out. "Ah, that feels so good on the back of my neck," she said.

"Nerves," he said.

"Always nerves. Nerves always get me in the back of the neck, the nerves do."

"You shake like a leaf," he said.

"I'm so afraid of guns," she said.

"Well, what did you come around here today for? It's bad enough I didn't know what I was doing and I'm here. But at least you knew."

"Oh, ah . . . dunno." She held the cigarette between her thumb and forefinger, but the red ash was still so far down that another drag or so would have it touching her fingers. She did not look at the cigarette and took another drag. "As an actual fact, it doesn't matter where you go. Guns are everywhere. We used to have no shooting in Derry. Now we've all you can hear."

"Are you always this scared when you're in Derry?"

"Why wouldn't I be?"

The shot that went off this time made the window shake. Right away there was another shot. She flinched badly and had her eyes closed tightly. There was shouting on the sidewalk directly outside the window.

"Has this place got a cellar?" he said.

"No," she said, and smiled.

The mother's uncle was awake now. He began working his big mouth around. He gulped, swallowed, licked his lips, choked, worked the saliva back and forth over his gums and then began gulping again. The little noises went through Dermot and made him squirm.

"No cellar, only floorboards here," he said.

Dermot twisted himself around and came up to the window. He poked a finger in front of the tin blinds and drew them back a couple of inches, then brought his head up and looked out into the street. It was night by now. There were fires on the other streets, and probably somewhere up at the head of Leeson Street, because there were wavering patches of half-light, reflections of fire, on the dark cement outside the window.

A man came running out from Balaclava Street, running out from the corner the saloon was on. He put one foot into the gutter and had the other one on the sidewalk. He crouched down and the arm came straight out and he fired a pistol up toward the Falls Road. He started back toward the corner but when he tried to push off his right foot, the one in the gutter, the shoe slipped and he nearly went down and he had to stumble back around the corner. Dermot pulled his fingers from the blinds and put his head down on the floor. He could hear the whine and slap of bullets going against the brick walls. He looked out to see if the guy had been hit. The street was empty and dark.

"The guy is completely infuckingsane."

"What?" Deirdre said.

"I don't know, they run into the street, I don't know, they'll get themselves and everybody else killed," Dermot said.

"Where do they run?" she said.

"Right into the middle of the fuckin' street."

"Oh. That's proper form."

"That's what?"

"Aye, that's proper form. If a man stands out where the soldier can see him and then he shoots and kills the soldier 'tisn't as bad as it would be if he were to sneak up and kill the soldier. This way he kills the soldier in a fair battle. He killed the man, but he also gave the man a fair chance to kill him first. When you die and are judged by the Lord, He will take this into consideration. You will not be a murderer. You will be judged as a soldier. Therefore, the Lord will only send you to Purgatory for killing the soldier. Christ won't doom a person to Hell for that. The way He would if you murdered a soldier."

"Yeah," Dermot said. "Well, what about this old man O'Neill today? For Chrissakes, he hid behind women."

"Oh, Joe O'Neill is not a soldier. He's a bona fide gunman," the mother's uncle said.

"Murderer is more to fit," she said.

"Notatall," the mother's uncle said. "He gave 'em the warks like a good Irishman should."

"What about the ones up on the rooftops here? They stay behind chimneys. I don't see them standing up to get shot."

"Once again, they are your gunmen, your murderers," she said. "But the others, these wee boys and many of the men, they believe it's a mortal sin to kill a soldier if he cannot see you."

"What the fuck do you call this?"

"Irish Catholic," she said.

9:

He woke up with Deirdre's hands digging into his coat sleeves. Her face was down inside the top of her parka coat. Somebody in the street was screaming without stopping. He was either on the sidewalk outside the window or in the gutter. No farther away. The more he screamed in the street, the more Deirdre's fingers dug into Dermot's coat. There was plenty of shooting at the end of the block. Single shots and then little bursts of triple-tonguing of automatic fire. He did not want to move a fraction of an inch, but the screaming was loud and ceaseless.

"Let's go, I have to see," he told her. Her hands came off his arm. She shivered and hunched herself more into her coat. He moved his head up the wall, the plaster like ice cubes pressed to his forehead, until the edge of the window sill hooked into his cheek. He fingered the blinds and looked out. The guy was in the gutter, on his back, the top half of his body rocking from side to side while he screamed. The legs were still. A couple of others were on their bellies, trying to drag him. Something buzzed and whined into the bricks right under the window. Dermot's head jumped back a foot. When he came back to the window the ones on their bellies in the street were motionless. Dermot saw there was no fucking around now, they were shooting pretty good from up at the Falls Road. Then one of the three got into a crouch and got his hands under the screaming guy's shoulders and he began pulling him backward, like he was walking a wheelbarrow. The other one came off his belly and grabbed the body under the rear end, and they got to the corner quickly. There must have been shots close to them, because they all seemed to jump while they were going past the edge of the saloon.

Dermot crept the few feet to the staircase and went up the little flight of steps. At the top there was a one- or two-step turn and two doorways, one to the front bedroom, the other to the rear. Not bedrooms really, a pair of freezing closets under a low ceiling. The beds in the rooms were almost flush against the doorways. Martin and the little girl were crouched on the end of a bed which came almost to the window over the street. They acted like they were watching a football game.

"Go away from there!" Dermot snarled.

"Go where?" Martin said.

"Just get your head down."

In the back bedroom, one of the babies was standing in a crib which barely fit between the end of the bed and the wall. The baby's hands chased the reflection of the fire on the next street as it snaked across the wall over the crib. The reflection kept moving in the water which streamed down the wall in the coldness. The mother was in bed with a dark coat buttoned to the neck. She had a hand pressing against the back of the other baby, who was in bed next to her struggling to get up.

In the front room, Martin still had not left the window. Dermot stepped in to grab him. Two of the kids were on a bed that was almost flush against the doorway. The kids weren't asleep. They were in a tangle of sheets and bedspreads that smelled of cold piss. Dermot got around their bed, pushed Martin back onto his own, and looked out the window himself.

It was like watching a war movie. An armored car was inching along, it was halfway down to the street. Machinegun bursts came out of the turret of the armored car. From what Dermot could see, the firing was at a house on the other side of the street. But everything seemed a hundred miles away. He was in a half-trance watching an armored car with a machine gun hitting the same kind of toy house he was in. The toy house bulged as the machine-gun slugs hit it. The bulges grew larger and larger and the walls folded in on each other and the slate roof collapsed. When Dermot's focus came back to the real street, the armored car was about thirty yards away. It stopped and backed up. It stopped again and the machine gun went to work in short bursts. There were plenty of single shots from every place on the street.

Dermot got back from the window and pulled the blinds down. The kid had pulled them up again. Dermot took him by the arm out of bed and through the doorways and into the mother's room.

"Keep him in here, I don't want any problems."

"They fancy bein' at the window and lookin' out and pretending," she said.

"Let him pretend here."

"They all like to pretend."

"Bad as the street, being here."

" 'tis, 'tis."

"For Christ's sake now, keep Martin right where you have him now. Right next to you. Martin, don't you move. Christ we all can get killed."

"Aye. It's a wonderful thing that you get for bein' a Catholic, isn't it?" she said.

"What about your husband?" he said. "Is he coming here or what?"

"I haven't a clue."

"Tell me one other thing."

"Aye?"

"Have we got anything in here we don't want the soldiers to find?"

"Ah, he takes care of those himself."

"You're sure now?"

"Aye, I'm sure. We've not a thing. Not a thing. It's a wonderful thing that you get for bein' a Catholic, isn't it?"

Downstairs Dermot put a hand on Deirdre's shoulder. The shaking came through her coat.

"If I could get you out of here."

"I'd only be someplace else."

"Anyplace is better than this."

200

"I see no safety in hiding."

He worked his hand through the folds of her parka until he came to the back of her head. He ran his thumb and forefinger onto the softness of her neck. He began massaging the neck cords. Her neck arched against his hand. "There's shootin' and riotin' wherever you go," she said. "That's my trouble, I guess. Too much shootin' for my Christ-forgotten nerves."

The shooting up the block was coming closer. Over the shots now you could hear the whine of the armored car. It moved a few feet. It would stop and make this different noise as it backed up. After machine-gun bursts, the car would whine forward again. The car was close, three or four doors away, when Dermot sneezed. The right nostril held the lightness in it and he could feel the lightness run up into the sinus over his eye and then curve through his cheek inside his face and he sneezed again. Tears came out of his eyes. The eyes started to hurt. Right away, one of the babies upstairs was crying. Deirdre's neck came out of his hand. "Get whoever it is," she said. She was crouching and moving quickly to the kitchen. Upstairs, everybody was coughing. The woman had the baby from the crib in her arms. The baby was screaming, the bare mouth wide open and the eyes shut. Tears came out of the slits. There was plenty of gas in the room, more than there was downstairs, and Dermot closed his eyes and held his breath and felt for the baby, took the baby from the woman and came downstairs. The baby's arms were thrashing. Deirdre had the back door open and he went into the little enclosure. He put the baby's face right up against the cement wall. Dermot put his own nose into the wall and took deep breaths. The baby kept crying and Dermot's eyes felt like they had razor cuts in them. The air at the wall was moist, almost a drizzle. Wind blew in the enclosure. Gas wouldn't last long in this. The gas coming into the house had to be coming from the front from one of the rooftops. Once it got inside a house it was critical. But wet air could dissolve it.

"Tell her open the window," Dermot said.

Deirdre shouted inside the house. The window over him

opened. There was a noise above the window up on the roof. A leg hung in the air from the roof. The leg lifted and began crabbing up the slate roof. On the other side of the enclosure a rifle was pushed up. Whoever was up on the roof reached down. The hand grabbed the barrel, a young voice cursed when the hand nearly dropped the rifle. The rifle was lifted. Whoever was up on the roof— because of the sharp slant and the darkness you couldn't see—gathered the weapon in and crawled up in the blackness at the peak of the roof.

A woman's voice on the other side of the wall said, "Now how's that?"

"Good girl yourself, Mary," the voice on the roof said.

"Get the fuck inside," the voice said to Dermot.

"He's minding where he is," Deirdre said. She came out of the doorway and looked up to try and see him.

"And he'll get himself and the wee baby fuckin' killed."

"And they were chokin' to death inside, your man had no choice," she said.

"We're sayin' to get in," another voice on the roof, an older man's voice, said.

"And we're sayin' fuck off," she said.

A chink spat out of the bricks around them. There was a whine. A window broke. Now you could hear something automatic firing from up the block, firing down the space between the backs of the houses trying to belt out anybody climbing around. Dermot got down and came through the doorway, the baby in his arms like a package. Deirdre was erect in the doorway. She dropped wet cloths onto the baby's head. Deirdre's face showed she was concentrating only on the baby. There was a ping! close, only a couple of feet away. Deirdre still showed nothing. Dermot ran upstairs with the baby. The cold moist air coming through the open window had cleared the gas from a space over the bed. The woman was on her back on the bed. She held out her arms and Dermot gave her the baby.

Downstairs, Deirdre was sitting up, the top of her head just below the window line. She was smoking a cigarette.

"There's Dermot," she said.

He said nothing. The armored car was two, maybe three doors away at most.

Deirdre called upstairs. "I'm your sister from Derry. Which wee baby is mine?"

"The wee girl," the woman called down. "Kathy her name is."

"Aye, Kathy."

Deirdre dragged on the cigarette. "You're the uncle," she said. She tapped Dermot's hand. "And you're the cousin visiting from America. We all came here to see the wee baby Kathy. Only the bloody villains livin' here started a war."

The vibration of the armored car filled the room. The car moved past the house and was in front of the saloon when shots went off from the top of their roof. There were shots from the street and a lot of shouting. The front door banged open. Some glass squares of the inside door were slapped in. A rifle butt came through the rest of the glass, splattering it over the room. A hand came through the broken glass to turn the doorknob. Dermot stood up as a soldier in a steel helmet and gas mask stepped in with his rifle. Another soldier crouched in the vestibule. The one in the room said something through the gas mask. He poked Dermot with the rifle. He came out with a small flashlight and played it around the room. The mother's uncle sat on the floor next to Deirdre with his hands over his head. Deirdre smoked the cigarette as if the soldier wasn't there. A couple of shots sounded from up on the roof and the soldier in the vestibule jumped into the room. His shiny boots creaked as he inched back out to the doorway. He stuck his rifle out the doorway and began squeezing off shots. In the house it sounded like cannon going off. With the sharp slant of the roofs, he hit nothing but the sky. Through the broken front door Dermot could see the tail of the armored car right outside the house. A soldier was on his stomach on the sidewalk alongside the tail of the car. There were shots from one of the roofs. The soldier on the sidewalk threw himself into the doorway and the armored car backed up. Its side was covered with luminous paint somebody had thrown. In the light from the fires in the neighborhood you could see the machine gun in the turret pointed up at the roof of the house now.

"Boy, I hope those kids—" Dermot said.

He went for the stairs. The soldier in the room kicked sideways without looking at him. His boot missed Dermot's groin and caught him on the inside of the thigh. He sat down on the couch. Deirdre was off the floor, brushing past the soldier, and up the stairs yelling for the kids to get under the beds. There were shots from the street and the soldier in the doorway began pumping more shots in the direction of the roofs up the block, but he still couldn't have been coming close. The machine gun on the armored car turret swung and then stopped. The pivot went only halfway around and the machine guns could not shoot behind the car. The car began backing up. On the rooftops they must have been waiting for the armored car to pass, and then they were firing down at the soldiers following the armored car. The men and kids up on the roofs were taking on armored cars and a full army. There was a racket out in the back. The soldier turned around and hunched over to see out onto Leeson Street again.

The armored car came back in front of the door and kept going past it. The soldiers left the doorway and followed the car. The one who had kicked Dermot was pushing against them to get out.

The mother's uncle giggled. "He didn't feel like stayin' here case a stranger comes through the back door."

"The fuck," Dermot said.

"A fuck with a gun," he said. "Best ye can do is keep the wee soldier nervous."

"I'd like to fucking kill him."

The shooting in the street stopped. The sound of the armored car faded a little when it whined around the saloon corner and went down Balaclava Street. Martin was down the stairs and in the doorway.

"Get out of there," Dermot said.

The kid flopped on his stomach and made believe he was shooting. Dermot kicked his foot. "Get out of there," he said. The street outside sprang into light. The Army had

204

turned on searchlights. Martin was yelling out the doorway and kids across the street were calling back to him. Dermot reached for his jacket collar but he was gone, running out into the middle of the street, and two other kids came running out from doorways across the street. They began playing that they were shooting each other. Then they began making believe they were shooting at the rooftops. They got prone and started crawling and stopping to shoot and then they'd crawl again. For kids, they knew how to do it right. Then the last kid got up. He pretended he was shot as he got up. He doubled over and began staggering toward the doorways across the street. Staggering the real way with the feet shuffling. No kid ever played this real. A soldier was standing a few feet away from them. He was taking off his gas mask like one of the Giants football players taking his helmet off at the end of the game.

The little soldier who had kicked Dermot was strutting in front of the saloon. There was an explosion around the corner from the saloon, on Balaclava Street. The soldier brought his rifle up and ran around the corner and some others went with him. Dermot turned to yell at Martin but he was gone already, running with the other kids onto Balaclava Street so they could see what was happening. The soldiers were shouting and ducking and there were shots on Balaclava Street and the armored car started for them. In the light from the searchlights Martin gave a little skip into the air and fell on his shoulder. At almost the same instant the kid with him jerked and went down on his side. For a moment it was crazy, soldiers playing for real while kids stand alongside them and pretend. Then a soldier on his belly was pointing to the two kids and Martin's leg was moving back and forth in slow motion and Dermot was out on the street running for the kid, when the lights went out. A soldier came off his belly, holding his rifle at high port. He pushed it at Dermot, who tried to go around him. The soldier swung the rifle butt. Dermot stuck out his left hand to stop it. The butt hit the tips of his fingers like a foul tip in baseball. The soldier slapped the rifle against his chest and pushed him back

205

into the house. He got into the vestibule and stood there, pointing his rifle out onto the street.

Deirdre and the mother were down the stairs and bumping against the soldier as they tried to get outside. The soldier leaned backward into them and spread his elbows. The mother made a hissing sound and clawed at him. All she could get was the back of the flak jacket and, with the shoulders hunched up, the back of the steel helmet coming to the top of the flak jacket. The mother was snarling to him that one of the boys in the street belonged to her. The soldier didn't move. None of them had bothered to chase the kid out of the street. He gets shot and they won't let the mother out of the house to go to him, Dermot thought. It was insanity. Give a moron soldier like this some authority and look what happens. Dermot reached out with his right hand and shoved hard. The soldier went forward. But he spun around with the rifle butt swinging. The mother and Deirdre were thrown against Dermot. The mother began screaming. Deirdre's hands flew at the soldier. A jeep ran past the house and you could hear it stop at about where the boys were on the street. Now the mother shook all over trying to get out of the house.

"Here's your door," the mother's uncle said. He was still flat on the floor and Dermot didn't pay any attention to him. "Here's your door," he said again. He was tapping the blinds. Dermot yanked them open. The cord broke and the blinds hung crazy. He pushed the window open with his right hand and stepped through the space. A rifle butt hit him in the back of the head.

The blackness went away very fast, but he couldn't move. He was down on the sidewalk grabbing his hair with both hands. He was running his hands through the hair on his head and opening and closing his eyes. When the searchlights went on, the jeep started up. The soldiers sat on the sides of the jeep, holding the kids in the back. One of the heads in the back was flopping. The mother came out of the doorway, her flat shoes flapping on the cement, and she tried to grab the jeep as it went past her. She began screaming. Deirdre walked past her. She was

206

pointing at the soldiers in the street as if she were in charge of them. A tall guy, an officer's cap on, was standing with his hands behind his back. One of the soldiers with him jumped up to block Deirdre.

Deirdre was shouting past the soldier to the officer. "Her son's shot, we've got to get her to the hospital."

"Yes?" the officer said.

Deirdre pointed to the mother, who was in front of the house wailing.

"Her son's shot."

"Yes," the officer said. He talked through his nose.

"We've to go to the hospital," Deirdre said.

"Oh," the officer said. "Well, actually you are not permitted out of the house."

"It's her *son*."

"Oh. Well. I see. Her son." His head was craned forward to listen. "If you'll just stand there a moment," he said. He walked away, the hands clasped behind his back, leather heels sounding.

He must have said something to one of the soldiers in the street, because the soldier came running with his arms out. "Back in the house," he said. "Come now, come now." Deirdre was saying something and the woman was shrieking now, but two or three of the soldiers pushed them into the doorway. One of them reached for the door. "Two of 'em got it with the same bullet, they did," he said. "One in the stomach, t'other in the leg, I think." He pulled the door shut.

"Now who's this?" somebody said. Dermot was on his feet now, and soldiers were looking at him through slit eyes.

"Comin' out the window, he was," the soldier standing in front of Dermot said.

"Fenian bastard."

"Go on you fuckin' Fenian bastard, we'll do you," one of them said.

Dermot brought one hand down to get the passport out of his jacket. "I'm an American," he said.

The soldier stopped his arm with the rifle. "Put yer hands back on yer head or ye won't have a head."

207

"I got an American passport in my jacket," Dermot said.

"Who cares what you got, ye're scum to me. Scum, that's all ye're, scum."

Another soldier poked his boot against Dermot's ankle. Just enough to sting. Dermot put his hands on the back of his head. In the searchlight, he could see what looked like over a hundred soldiers on this one street alone. They were in groups of four and five. They were standing in this strange light, the kind of light they always have at bad auto accidents and big fires. Light like this always means somebody dead. The soldiers were starting to go inside houses. The officer standing in the middle of the street was sending sergeants running up and down the street. One of the sergeants came up to the soldiers around Dermot.

"Man from this house here?"

"Aye, from this house here. Man tried to scuttle out the window."

The sergeant walked the soldier into the middle of the street and began talking to him. Dermot did not like it. The minute a policeman gets called away by another one and the two of them stand there talking, with the arrested guy left alone, it means somebody gets in worse trouble.

A few feet farther down, against the door of a house, standing in a little circle of dark shadows, three soldiers had a man and a young boy up against the wall. The man was small. He had his hands in the pockets of a suit jacket that fitted him like a car coat. The boy with him was about eleven.

"What're the hands doin' there?" one soldier said to the man. "Up on yer head with them."

While the man was taking his hands out of his suit jacket pockets, the soldier hit him in the face with a right hand.

"Fuckin' Fenian."

One of the soldiers said, "Give 'em yer IRA number."

"I'm not IRA," the man said.

The soldier had his right hand shoulder-high. He made a fist, his hand bathed in the bare light of the searchlights. He dropped the fist out of the bare light into the shadows, into the man's face.

208

"I'll shoot yer face off," the soldier said.

The familiarity of it all began to bother Dermot. A dirty street at night, emergency lights, people screaming, broken glass, uniforms in charge, this was where he had lived his life. He was used to having the responsibility. He was the one who walked down the middle of the street and told people to stand back. Dermot's head throbbed from the gun butt. But that wasn't bothering him as much as the soldier threatening him. He'll do fuckin' nothing with his gun, Dermot said to himself.

"Ye saw a soldier murdered today," one of them said to the man.

"Notatall, notatall," the man said.

"Or were ye too busy helpin' murder him to see it?"

"Where's your head, lad?"

"On the Sacred Heart, I'm no IRA."

"What's yer father's IRA number?" one of them asked the boy.

The boy's eyes widened but he said nothing. The soldier brought a hand out wide, a little bony hand. The boy started to wince. The soldier held the hand up in the light, showing it to the boy. He brought it down and slapped the boy in the mouth.

The man had his hands off his head. He held them out like a beggar. "The wee boy. Please, the wee boy," he said. The soldier slapped the man.

One of them said, "Fenian fuck," and went into the pocket of his fatigue pants. His front teeth were missing. He took out a revolver and held it up. It looked like a police .32.

The soldier cocked the pistol.

"What's it now?" he said.

The man had his mouth open but he couldn't talk.

The soldier grabbed the boy's hair. The pistol muzzle went hard into the boy's forehead. The soldier held the boy by the hair. Dermot had seen it all his life. A gun in a nigger's ear. The soldier this time had the gun on single action. The trigger did not have to be pulled back against the spring. A flick could make the thing jump forward.

The boy was frozen. His forehead was tilted upward. Saliva bubbled on his lips. The father's face collapsed.

Dermot moved as if he were practicing in the Police Academy. The left hand went out to hold off the soldier standing directly in front of him. The right hand went at the soldier with the pistol. He couldn't reach the soldier with the pistol, but he waved his hand as he reached, to distract the soldier. Eight years of pushing to the front of crowds at accidents, eight years of knowing that if anything happened he was the one supposed to handle it. It became stronger than fear.

"Shoot me!" Dermot said. Said it like a command. He was going to say, "Shoot me, cocksucker!" but the last word never came out. The official mind cut the last word before it reached the mouth.

The soldier looked out the corners of his eyes.

"Shoot me, I'm a man!" Dermot said.

The soldier who had been in front of Dermot, the one Dermot had pushed off with his left hand, banged the rifle stock against Dermot's side. The soldier with the pistol pulled it away from the kid's forehead. He threw the boy's head against the wall and let go of the hair. His mouth was open, the gaps in his teeth wide. He lunged at Dermot. The pistol came hard into Dermot's chest. The boy and the father were screaming. The soldier with no teeth snarled something and his small eyes danced under his soup-bowl helmet. He pulled the trigger. The empty pistol made a metallic sound and nothing else.

Whichever soldier swung the rifle butt around on Dermot did it sloppily. Half the slapping noise came from Dermot's shoulder coming up as a reflex. The rest of the blow caught Dermot behind the ear someplace and it drove him a step or two to the side and then down on the wet pavement.

Screams started coming from the windows along the block. Heads came out of second-floor windows and shouted into the bare light. Soldiers began yelling back and the heads sticking from the windows screamed louder.

A soldier stood over Dermot. "Name?" he growled.

Dermot's hand moved slowly. It missed, going inside

210

his jacket for the passport. The soldier slapped the hand away and went in and grabbed the passport. While the other thumbed through the passport, Dermot slid his hand into his back pocket. He brought out the shield and held it up for the soldier. Dermot's hand was trembling.

The soldier took the shield from him. He went out into the middle of the street to talk to somebody. A few feet down, the man stood with his arms around the boy, who was sobbing against his chest.

"God bless ye," the man said.

Fuck you too, Dermot said to himself.

He could see in the light up and down Leeson Street that the soldiers had men in front of nearly every house. Most of them were spread, hands against the wall. A couple of men were kneeling with their hands on their heads. In front of one house, a man in a cap with his hands against the wall had a cigarette hanging from his mouth. The smoke was bothering his eyes. The man took a hand off the wall and reached for the cigarette. A stumpy soldier hit the man across the back of the legs with a club.

One of the soldiers came back to Dermot with the passport and shield.

"Which house ye in?" he growled.

Dermot turned the wrong way at first. Everything spun in the bare light. He turned around again. He was two doorways down from the house. The soldier put the passport and shield into his hand. "Be off with ye," he growled.

As Dermot stepped up to the doorway, the soldier took him by the elbow and swung him into it, swung him hard.

As the door pushed in and Dermot went into the vestibule, Deirdre was coming out, pushing past him, a baby in her arms.

"The wee baby's sick," she was shouting. "He's to go to the hospital."

Dermot stepped into the house. He stumbled over a chair that was upside down and had wet diapers hanging from the rungs. The stairs were covered with thrown clothing. One end of the couch had a broken leg. The woman sat on the end that wasn't broken. She was holding the other baby and she looked old as hell. The mother's uncle was on the floor in the corner. The television above him was smashed in. Glass bits were all over the floor and the clothes piled on the floor. There was loud noise upstairs. Dermot looked up. Soldiers were banging with rifle butts to break a hole in the front bedroom ceiling. In the back bedroom a soldier was punching a mattress with a rifle butt until the springs came through. He stuck his hand through one of the holes and felt around. There was more noise at the back door. Two of the kids watched soldiers dump coal out of the bin and kick through it. Deirdre was still out in the front doorway. She was yelling very loud.

The soldiers came downstairs, squeaking and stomping. The last one walking out said, "Scumoftheearth."

The mother's uncle said, "Sacred Heart of the Lord, Holy God, if we're the scum of the earth, Lord God what are they?"

"They told me if the wee baby cried they'd stick him with a bayonet," the woman said. "That's as true as that Sacred Heart picture." The picture was knocked off the wall next to her. "The Queen's Second," she said. "I'm sure she's very proud of them."

"Silly little bitch, he's too stupid to know what's right and what's wrong," the mother's uncle said.

"So we live in kitchen houses," the woman said. "So at least they're clean."

After a while she said, "Oh my God Jesus, Martin, where are ye? What did they do to ye?"

"Listen to your girl there, Deirdre, she's out there tryin' for you," the mother's uncle said.

Sticking out of a pile of dungarees and jackets was a wedding album. The white leather cover was yellow. Dermot sat on the floor and opened it. "Let's see what you looked like when you weren't crying," he said to her. He read the title page out loud.

"The marriage of Marie Flynn to Patrick Kelly. At Saint Peter's Pro Cathedral, July twenty-third, nineteen-sixty. Well I'll tell you one thing, Marie Flynn. You're letting the years show too much."

"Aye, what've I got?"

"What have these girls got?" He read her the brides-maids' names. "Sylvia Flynn, Olive Flynn, Marie Lewsley." She didn't answer. He began to turn the pages of the album. White tissue paper covered each page so the pictures were in good shape. In one picture she and her husband sat at a table with a wedding cake, a bottle of ketchup, and a bottle of HP sauce in front of them. The husband looked about sixteen. His neck was so thin the white dress shirt looked like it went around him twice.

"He looked real young then," Dermot said.

"Ah, sure, he was beautiful then."

"You got a nice look too. What were you thinking about here?"

"Ah, just about comin' to this house."

"You moved right in here?"

"Aye, moved in the next day, we did. We bought it for two hundred pound. We put four hundred pound into it. Ah, I thought we'd come here and have a life together in this house. And look what they've done to my house. And look what they've done to me."

"You were going to stay here your whole life?"

"Ah, sure, where else would we live? Only so many places for a Catholic."

"What's the husband do for a living?"

"Asphalter. Well, you know, that's when he works." She buried the baby into her. "I wonder where he is. Jesus, if he's lifted."

Deirdre stuck her head in the door. "Come on, come on with you," she said. "The father too, the father too." Her eyes were telling them to hurry more than her voice was. The two of them scrambled up.

A soldier's voice outside said, "The Royal Horsepital."

The mother said, "Oh, the wee ones in back," and Deirdre pushed her out the door. "I'll keep them organized," she said. The woman and the mother's uncle each held a baby and went away with a soldier.

Deirdre closed the door against the cold. The two kids stood in the room. Dermot sat on the floor. The room was cold and smelly and the walls were wet.

"You were fantastic," she said.

"I don't know what the fuck I'm doing here," he said.

"You were fantastic."

She gave him a cigarette and they sat in the darkness and smoked and said nothing. The pain in his head was making him twitch. He could feel her looking at him. She couldn't have understood that this was his business, streets like this, and he had done it without thinking. The pain bothered him too much to get into it with her.

To Dermot, it seemed like a long time later when he felt well enough to speak. "What time is it?" he said.

"Half four, the last I heard," she said.

"And how long are we going to have to stay here?"

"Could be till Monday morning."

"Fuck that."

"There was a great big fat man from America who was here with his wife, visiting relatives. The soldiers raided the relatives' house. The big fat man woke up with a soldier aiming a rifle at his head on the pillow. The fat man had a heart attack right there. He's still in the hospital. Well, you know, you're doing better than at least one of your Yank tourists."

"I don't know what the fuck I'm doing here."

"It's good you were here, you were fantastic," she said.

"That's not helping my head."

"You just called their bloody bluff," she said. "Fantastic."

"I'm used to all of it except getting hit on the fucking head," he said.

"The boy will grow up remembering you and he'll tell his sons stories about you," she said.

"That does me a lot of good," he said.

She gave him another cigarette. "Do you not go around doing this to people in America?" she said.

"The hell I do."

"Ah, Jesus now, come on. The whole fookin' police force in America gets medals for shootin' blacks."

"What are you talking about?"

"Are not the blacks on the bottom in America?"

"I don't know what you mean by the bottom."

"The fookin' blacks are on the fookin' bottom and the

214

fookin' police beat them bloody, the same as we're on the bottom here and the fookin' police and the fookin' soldiers beat us and shoot us like animals."

"Well, I don't know what it's like here, but I don't do anything like this," Dermot said.

Something came into his mind, an afternoon on Knickerbocker Avenue when this old Jew from the jewelry store was hollering about two spade kids coming around and stealing a new watch. Dermot wrote down the complaint and the description, and later, at a quarter to five, he went past Grover Cleveland High. The schoolyard was crowded with kids playing basketball. Nigger kids playing a nigger game, Dermot remembered. They stand under the basket and jump. You can't expect them to think out a play. They just do what comes to them natural. Stand around and jump. Nobody jumps like a nigger. Dermot was remembering the crowd around one basket, black hands, a little pink showing, going up for the ball. And a little higher than all the other hands was this one, the fingers spread, the gold watch standing out against the black wrist. Dermot remembered getting out of the car and walking into the schoolyard. He could still see the faces, some of them stopping their game to watch him, others, the fresh spades, not even bothering to look at him. The one with the watch on never looked. All the others playing at his basket stopped to watch Dermot walk up. The kid with the watch kept playing. He threw the ball up against the backboard and then jumped up and tried to tip it in. "Reboun', reboun'," he was saying to himself. Dermot remembered how he said to the kid, "Stop rebounding, I want to talk to you." And the kid said, "Talk to me on the reboun'." Dermot put a hand on the kid's shoulder and stopped him from going up. The big eyes, with nigger-blood flecks in them, stared at Dermot. "Get your hands off me, mother," the kid said. Dermot had the index and middle fingers of the right hand spread out, on the ready. He remembered now how the kid never saw it coming. He remembered the tips of both fingers catching moistness as he stabbed at the nigger spade's eyes.

215

He sat on the floor and thought about it for a moment. No, Dermot told himself, that was different from this. That was a nigger kid who stole something.

Fuck it, Dermot said to himself. He didn't know why he was on the block, he didn't know why he'd stepped out at the soldier and he didn't know why he had to stay in this small, smelly house. His head throbbed in the two places where he had been slammed. The pain ran into the corners of his eyes. He closed them. The blackness inside him made him dizzy. He opened his eyes again and kept his head still. He did not move or say anything and finally the sleep rose up through the pain and his eyes drooped and closed.

10:

The small boy pulled Dermot's arm to wake him up. The searchlights were off. In the cold, natural light the street looked like somebody had dumped a bucket of dirty water over it.

"Terlet are broke," the kid said.

A bottle came out of the saloon doorway and broke on the street. There was a loud laugh in the doorway of the saloon. A lot of them must have been inside the saloon. Another bottle flipped in the air and broke on the street. The breaking glass sound was no good at all.

"Terlet," the kid said again.

Dermot went out in the back with him. The door to the outhouse hung on a hinge. The toilet inside was smashed. One big triangular chunk of china was jammed point down in the mouth of the pipe. The tank hanging over the toilet was smashed. Water spilled down the tank pipe. The water was spreading in a puddle because the drain was covered with the coal the soldiers had spilled out of the coalbin. Dermot kicked the coal away until the puddle rushed down the drain.

Dermot had to go himself. He started to take a piss in the corner of the enclosure. Even the slight effort of pissing caused his head to throb. "Come on," he said to the kid.

"Shit," the kid said.

"We'll have to take care of that, then," Dermot told him. He went to the front door, the kid in front of him so

217

the soldiers would see him when the door opened. The soldier in front of the house had his rifle under his left arm. A bottle of stout was in his right hand.

"Toilet's broke. Can I take the boy here next door?"

"Get yourbloodyfuckin' face back in there."

"You guys broke the toilet and the little boy here has to go."

"Shit himself." The soldier swung his hips to make the rifle under his arm wave forward.

He threw the bottle of stout into the street, pulled the door out of Dermot's hand and slammed it.

Deirdre was on the stairs behind him. "You'll just have to take him out back," she said. "I'm tryin' to make the place livable for the kids upstairs." When Dermot didn't move, she said, "Oh, use your flamin' mind. Don't be standing there like an eejit. Find something to use. We've no time for your Yank niceties."

There was no paper bag in the kitchen. Dermot looked at the cereal boxes on the shelf. They were American cereals, corn flakes and puffed rice and Quaker Oats. The round cardboard container with red-and-blue paper and the guy with the Ben Franklin hat on. He took the top off. There was only a little bit of white oats left at the bottom of the container. He shook them into an empty dish. He took the kid out in the back and told him to pull his pants down. The inside of his undershorts was crusted. The mud streaks came up his legs right to the cheeks. Dermot reached into the outhouse for toilet paper. It was sopping wet and came apart in his hand. He pulled off chunks of it and gave it to the kid. He put the Quaker Oats box up against his rear end and pushed him on the head and told him to get himself down and go to the bathroom.

Dermot turned his head away. The kid grunted like a cow. Finally, he stood up straight. "All gone," he said.

"Here, wipe yourself."

"Wipe my shitter," the kid said to himself. He took some sort of a pass at his rear end, dropped the toilet paper on the ground, and pulled up his pants and went into the house, leaving Dermot with the steam coming

218

out of the Quaker Oats box. He put the toilet paper into it and left the box in the outhouse. He went right for the kitchen sink. There was a sliver of brown translucent soap which did nothing in the cold water.

"Afraid of dirt?" She was downstairs with the little girl now. "Only thing around here that won't kill them is dirt, you know."

She sat the kids at the small table alongside the sink. She looked through the kitchen. "I guess we've no milk." She took out a box of corn flakes and made games out of eating dry cereal. In the front room she pulled one thing at a time off the pile on the floor because of the bits of broken glass from the television screen. Her hand came out with a coloring book that was wet, then a few broken crayons. She patted the book pages with a rag. Dermot used his feet to clear out the fireplace. When he got the fire started, Deirdre sat the kids down with coloring books in front of the fire.

Outside, two soldiers stretched out on the sidewalk, using their helmets as pillows. Another soldier sat on the saloon steps. He held a bottle of whisky up and took a suck. He held the bottle up again. It was empty. He threw the bottle out onto the street. He got up, tripped coming off the steps, and nearly fell on the two soldiers sleeping. One of them woke up. He rolled onto his side, pulled himself up, and took a dizzy step. He picked up two stout bottles from the saloon steps and went into the middle of the street. He threw them down hard. The breaking glass sounded dangerous now. The soldier began kicking all the glass in the middle of the street into a pile. Brown glass, some of it in big chunks, the necks of stout bottles, the curved bottom halves of whisky quarts. The soldier's foot began to swing through the pile of glass. The boot kept swinging, spreading the glass wider. He spread the glass so wide that he had to take two full steps in one direction to spread around one end of the pile of glass and a few steps back to run his boot through the other end of it.

The soldier came lurching back to the front of the saloon. He waved. Across the street, in front of the doorway of the corner house, the one with the warehouse behind it, they had a man who was in his stockinged feet. The soldier in front of the saloon waved again for the man to cross the street. A soldier ran up and slapped the man on the head. He grabbed the man by the arm and ran him into the street. The man wore black socks and bare skin showed through a hole in the ankle. The bare skin kept moving and then it stopped and hung over the glass while the man tried to keep his balance. Then the foot came forward, the toes picking a spot between pieces of glass. But he couldn't balance himself on the one set of toes and the other foot came down on top of a curved chunk of whisky bottle. He tried to keep his weight on the toes but his head was too far forward and his body began to follow his head and all his weight came down on the foot on top of the piece of whisky bottle. The foot crushed the piece of whisky bottle. The man's body came straight up. He tried to leap clear of the glass, but the good foot couldn't reach an open place and the foot came down full onto a choppy-topped sea of brown glass. He threw himself straight out on his stomach, the feet coming up in the air behind him. He made it clear of the glass. He landed almost at the soldier's feet, his body moving in pain. The soldier's thick boot came across in a soccer kick. The boot went deep into the man's side.

Dermot started for the door, but Deirdre had a hand out and she was out the door and into the middle of the street before anybody could stop her. She was looking up the block and yelling. "We've no milk for the wee children!" she shouted. Women began to hang out from upstairs windows. They started shouting with her. A soldier had Deirdre by the arm and another tried to take her other arm but she kept waving it and screaming about milk. The noise on the street was very loud now and the soldiers were looking up at the windows and waving their rifles but the women were leaning far out now and their arms moved while they started a chant for milk.

They pushed Deirdre back into the doorway when the officer came into the street. His hands were behind his back. His head was bent while one of the soldiers with

Deirdre ran up to him. The officer said something, the lips barely moving. He walked over to Deirdre. He watched the tips of his shoes and brought his foot down with the leather heel first.

He had no eyebrows. The eyes under the forehead were colorless.

"Yes?" he said through his nose.

"We've no milk for the wee babies," she said.

"Yes," he said through his nose. Behind him, soldiers were walking around in the street with bottles of stout. Deirdre pointed at them. "Your fine men have their sustenance. Now the wee children need theirs."

"Milk, yes, milk," the officer said to himself.

"Is it official military policy for children to be hungry while soldiers are drunk?" she said.

"Here!" one of the soldiers with the officer said.

"We've two wee children who've been up vomitin' all night and now there's no milk in the house for them."

"Well," the officer said.

"I'm sure there are wee babies ready to die all up and down this flamin' street."

"Well."

"I'm sure that's how you gain advancement in the Army, by allowin' wee babies to die."

The soldiers started to push her back into the house.

"While your soldiers get drunk."

The officer said something to the soldiers and they stopped pushing.

"Milk. Well, actually, we've got to do something about milk."

He spun around on his heels. The soldier pulled the door shut in Deirdre's face.

She stood in the vestibule with her eyes closed. "That should keep them."

The man was sitting on the sidewalk, his socks off. He was picking at the glass, covered with blood, in his foot.

"He needs more than his hands for that," Dermot said.

"They wouldn't have stopped if I even looked at him," she said. "Christ but they would've run him through thirty more times. Wee children, the smaller and sicker the better, that's what you must use against them."

Deirdre sat on the floor smoking cigarettes and playing with the kids. She told them that while the soldiers were watching the house, their father was helping the IRA steal all the soldiers' trucks. It was almost noon when the fat woman across the street came out onto the sidewalk. Nobody stopped her. She was waving to others. Soldiers walked in the street, but there was no trouble. Deirdre was up and at the door. The man with the cut feet was gone. Now, in the street, wearing a bright-red stole, the old priest clutched a missal against his chest and kept nodding his head at people. Down Leeson Street a crowd was out walking to church. In the other direction, up at the corner of the Falls Road, soldiers were in a line in front of armored cars. The area was sealed off.

Deirdre was in the next doorway, talking to the woman. "She's gone to the hospital, the big boy was hurt."

"Aye, Martin," the woman in the doorway said.

"She's got the two wee ones."

"Aye."

"Royal Hospital, you know."

"Aye."

"All right then," Deirdre said.

A girl of about fourteen stepped onto the sidewalk.

"Go on, now," the mother said.

"No!"

"Be off with you!"

"Why?"

"I said."

The girl stamped her feet and went past Dermot into the house. The kids inside shouted when she came in. "You little fuckers," the girl said.

"Cheerio," Deirdre said. She and Dermot were in the street walking with the stream of people going to church. Soldiers stood in groups at each corner, rifles pointed up, red eyes searching the crowd. Kids ran past them sticking out their tongues. Women far outnumbered the men. The women had lined faces which sagged against handkerchief knots. They paddled by in loose shoes, not looking at

222

the soldiers. Nearly all the men had no hats on and their hair was matted and uncombed. They were hunched over, heads down, staying as close to the largest clump of women they could. A couple of streets down and over, the charcoal-gray church climbed out of the red row houses. The doors of the church were open and people were backed into the vestibule already. Most of them still coming would have to hear mass in the street. Deirdre edged up the side of the crowd and got to the side of the vestibule. A young priest stood in the archway of the room where they had the baptismal font. The priest stared through thick glasses with his mouth open. Deirdre pushed to get to him. The priest drew in one shoulder to allow her into the baptismal room. His shoulder came back out to block Dermot. Deirdre said something to him and the shoulder pulled in again. All the time he stared ahead with his mouth open. They sat on the floor alongside the legs of the copper tank holding the baptismal water. The bells sounded dimly for the start of the mass. The exaggerated rising and lowering of the priest's voice, the altar boy ringing the bell during the consecration, and the people coughing through the silence. The praying out loud and the feet shuffling as people started down the aisles at the end of the mass brought him awake.

They stayed there while the church emptied. The priest came and shook car keys at them. Deirdre and Dermot got up and followed him through the empty church and out a door on the Epistle side of the altar. The back of the church came onto a school building. The door opened as they came to it. They walked through a dim hallway. Some guys jumped out of one room to see who was coming.

"A school's a school," the priest said. "Got to hide guns someplace. School's as good a place as any."

"We tried to keep them out of use," Deirdre said.

"Couldn't be done," the priest said. "Why would they listen to us? With my own pastor frothin' to bless their grand efforts."

"Aye."

"And why didn't you come here right off?" he said.

"Stayed too long and then there was no way out," she said.

"For Jesus' sake 'twill teach you to be early."

They went out a door and onto an empty street. A blue car was at the curb. Deirdre and Dermot got in the back. "Jesus, you could look a wee bit sick for me," the priest said. Deirdre's head came onto Dermot's shoulder. "For Jesus' sake, I said sick, not sufferin' headache." She turned onto her side, burying her face into Dermot's coat. The car rolled slowly, the priest waving his arm out the window. Soldiers saw him and turned back to themselves as the car went past. They drove for a couple of minutes until they came onto a factory street. At the end, soldiers leaned on a jeep parked alongside a barbed-wire barricade. The arm waved while the car rolled toward a space at one end of the barbed wire. Two soldiers jumped off the jeep, pointing their rifles. The car jerked to a stop and the priest jumped out.

"Are you blind? Are you blind? Can't you see I'm a priest? Are you blind?"

The authority ran out of them. They didn't move while the priest got back into the car and rolled past them, around the barricade, and out onto an avenue.

"The bloody bastards would've shot us," the priest said.

He went up the avenue for several blocks and stopped. Deirdre was off Dermot's chest and out of the car.

"There's a good Father Miles," she said.

"Aye," he said. He drove off.

"We're out of it now?" Dermot asked her.

"Aye, we're out of it now."

"Well, what do we do about the kids back there?"

"Do you want to go back and sit with them?"

"No."

"Come on, then."

They walked up the avenue. Small leafless trees shook in a wet wind. They hailed a taxicab. The taxicab came over a low bridge by the railroad station and into center Belfast. The International Hotel was behind City Hall. Past the registration desk a narrow staircase led to a barroom in the basement. The mother's uncle was at the bar talking with two men. He picked up his pint to wave hello. He had a small basin of Irish behind the pint.

"Too many visitors, the man on the horsepital door says to us, said he wasn't lettin' us in to take the wee ones to the horsepital tea room. She tucks the wee one under the arm and she has a go at him. She says to him, I've an eleven-year-old son there and if yez don't let me in I'll ransack the lot of you. She's pushin' while she's yellin'. In we went. There was lots of people to look after her in the tea room. So out I went. The doctors seemed to be lookin' after her boy. Shot in the belly, they told her he was. This is Joe Donahue. He came today up from Tipperary. He was here last year for the trouble over the Springfield Road. And this is O'Brien. Dublin lad. So. These houses on Brookfield Street had no back doors. A mill wall ran as a common back wall. To get the wee old ladies out in the shooting, the lads had to take the old ladies out the front door. That was some walk down the garden path, that was."

O'Brien interrupted to ask if they wanted a drink. "Fantastic," Deirdre said. "Paddy's. Dermot, a Paddy's?"

"A double."

"Ah, there's Dermot. Up for the riots, are you?"

"We are," O'Brien said.

"Oh Christ, ten times worse," Deirdre said.

"What about the border campaign?"

"Christ, a hundred times worse. Chokin' soldiers to death in front of your own eyes."

"I told yez," the mother's uncle said. "Let's have a drink."

"Do you think we could get into the Falls?" O'Brien said.

"Depends why," Deirdre said.

"Just to have a look. I teach in Dublin."

"Teach where?"

"At University College Dublin."

"Preparin' a paper," the mother's uncle said.

"I'm here only three years," O'Brien said. "I was in

New York. At Columbia. I've got no family. So I decided to come over and view my heritage."

"Ah yes."

"Through the bottom of a glass." He drank his pint like he was playing the trumpet.

Dermot gagged but got the first of his whisky down. The rest went quickly and he put out the glass for more. A tray of sandwiches was under a plastic cover on the back bar. He pointed at them while he drank. The bartender put one on a plate in front of them. It was an Irish sandwich, they give you a third of an American sandwich at best when you order a sandwich, and what they give you is slices of hard-boiled egg and midget tomato on bread thin enough for a Jewish holiday. Dermot waved to the bartender for a stack of them. He held out his glass for another drink. "I'm from New York," he said to O'Brien.

"Are you? Where?"

"Queens."

"Oh, Queens. Of course. How'd you get caught in there? Seeing the relatives here?"

"I don't even know. But I know it's the last time." Dermot gulped most of the new drink and did not gag.

"Did you have to fight yourself?" Donahue said.

"All hands were used," Deirdre said.

"Every lad," the mother's uncle said.

"They miss himself somethin' terrible," she said, slapping the mother's uncle on the back. "But we had to get him evacuated. For Jesus' sake, they were going bloody crazy searchin' for a wee dangerous gunman with a bad leg."

"Ah hah!" the mother's uncle said. He was drinking all over the place. "Give 'em the warks with a Wabley!"

"Liam been in?" she said to the bartender.

"Which Liam?"

"Liam Quigley."

"No."

"Has Pauline looked in, then?"

"Which Pauline?"

"Pauline Duddy."

"No."

"Well, I'll have to find them."

She sat on the barstool facing Dermot, with her back to three men. They were talking about shooting and killing.

"You know." He leaned on the bar and looked at the drink.

"What?"

He drank his drink.

"My fucking head hurts," he said. "Jesus Christ almighty, it's a good thing they didn't break it open. Christ, I got hit a couple of real whacks."

"You were fantastic," she said.

"And what did you say about it?" he said.

She leaned forward and kissed him on the cheek. "And you never said a word of thanks about how I tormented the eejits and got you out."

"I was too worried about myself."

She clapped her hands and laughed, with a cigarette sticking out of her mouth. He took the cigarette out of her mouth and kissed her. It started as the same kind of things she had done, but then right away he was pressing full on her mouth and her eyes closed and her mouth opened, and then she pulled away. Her head was on his chest. He held her left hand and ran his thumb over the top of it. It was cold and rough and red-spotted, but there was feeling coming out of it. He took a drag of her cigarette and held it up to her. She closed her eyes and took a long pull on it. They finished a drink and were into another without talking.

"I've got to find them," she said.

"We got all day or all night, whichever it is now," he said to her.

"No, I've got to."

"What for?"

"Because I've to meet a barrister. I've to be in court in Derry on Wednesday."

"What for?"

"For the usual reasons. Justice. Fairness. Protection of the rights of society."

"You have to testify?"

"In my own behalf."

"What for?"

"Riotin', that's a serious thing here, you know. Major transgression."

"What rioting?" he asked.

"Be so many I can't even recall," she said. "Let's pass that on. Where are you going now that you've found out Belfast is so lovely?"

"I'm going to see relatives in Bundoran."

"Bundoran, is it? Who is it you have there?"

"My name. Davey."

"We've a Davey in Derry. Name of Finbar. Is that any of yours?"

"It could be."

"He lives on Wellington Street. In the Bogside. It'd have to be him, you know. The Davey on Wellington Street is the only Davey I know of. In Derry the big names are Doherty, Quigley, and Harkins."

"Maybe I'll look him up."

"Well, it could be on your way to Bundoran, Derry is. You could go right through it, you know."

"Then maybe I'll look him up."

"Whichever," Deirdre said. "Right now, I've to be goin'." She put the glass down and stood up. He took out money for the bartender.

Outside it was starting to rain. In an old taxicab, rain spilled down the inside of one window which was loose. They went back over the low bridge by the railroad station and came onto a street lined with undamaged shops. The cab let them off at a corner with a pub on it. The rain was heavy. The pub was closed. "Sunday, Sunday," Deirdre said. "Come on, we're just goin' down here a couple of houses." She started running down the side street. Lightning turned the sky yellow behind a white-gray rain and there was a huge thunderclap. They pushed into the doorway of a shop. Deirdre held his hand tight. Thunder, lightning, the millionth of a second, there is not time to be forgiven or beg. You go as you are. A policeman walks in security. He dies in the street

228

with his blood as his penance. Lightning on a street far from home is different. It is a good way to get to Hell.

Again a bolt of lightning exploded through the rain.

"Christ's sake, that was close. It must have hit the end of the street," Dermot said.

"In actual fact, it's beautiful. It is these guns human beings carry around that frighten me. Ugly stupid things. The arrogance of the devil in them. I have life and death over you because I have this bloody gun. That is the sin of sins."

With a crash, the rain became hail. It barraged the street for minutes. They got back in the corner of the entranceway.

"It must be comin' down from sixty thousand feet," she said.

They stood together without talking while the hail became even stronger, turned into sleet, and came back to rain. The deep part of the rainstorm cut them off from everything, the two of them alone in the doorway. She began to hum, a high whine, the wet black hair against her white face.

"When I was a wee girl I used to love rain like this. I'd stand waitin' at the door for it to fill up the streets. We had no drainage, you know. The second it stopped I'd be out with my bicycle riding through the water. Dirty street water and I loved the splash it made."

"We used to sail sticks," he said.

She smiled and kept humming. "I could make the biggest splash with my bike because I used to hold one foot against the front tire and send water scootin' out to the side."

She began humming again. With her wet black hair on her white face and humming her tune in her whine, he did not like it when the rain began to stop. She led him out of the doorway and down to the houses.

She went through the gate of the third house. The front door was open. She called, "Hel-loo," as she came into the dark house. Nobody answered. She snapped on a light in the front room. It was a room almost big enough for an American house. A low couch, pillows for

229

sitting on the floor, and a table with a typewriter and a pile of books and papers. A Che Guevera poster on the wall. A big poster covering the wall from ceiling to the floor almost. The guy and his beard all in black, the rest of the poster bright red.

"What's he for?" Dermot asked.

"Ah dunno. Do you not like it?"

She had her head cocked a little and her eyes alive and her mouth just that little bit open, the way she did when she first came into the saloon.

"He's fine with me," Dermot said. "I'm more worried about you. Get that coat off or we'll both catch pneumonia." He had his coat off, the inside of it damp on his hand. He reached for hers. She was unfastening the toggle buttons. She held her arm out and half turned away from him to help get the coat off. He kissed her through the wet hair on the back of her neck. He kissed her again on the side of the neck. She lifted her face, her eyes closed, he put a hand on her shoulder, the black sweater wet and cold from the rain-soaked coat, and she turned into him and the coat was on the floor and they were in each other's arms kissing. He reeked of whisky, cigarette smoke, coal, and so did she. Beautiful bones under beautiful white skin, beautiful wet black hair. He held her tighter and kissed her more. She stopped and put her chin on his shoulder. He kept kissing her on the neck.

"Actually, I'm uncomfortable wet," she said.

"What makes you think I'm going to leave your clothes on you?"

She made a face like she was horrified. She smiled, kissed him, and stepped away. "I'm more afraid of bronchial pneumonia than bein' ravaged." She went upstairs and he could hear water running in a tub.

"I was just wondering," Dermot called up.

"Wondering what?"

"About the woman. Martin. If the kid had only done what I told him."

"We did our stint," she said.

"I just wish I could've stopped the goddammed kid from getting outside."

"You did your stint, you were fantastic and let's get on to something better," she said.

The door upstairs closed. He went up and sat on the edge of a bed. In the room across the way the walls were covered with drawings kids had made in school. He threw his suit jacket on a chair. He sat until he heard moving in the bathroom. Water was running again. He went out in the hallway by the bathroom door. Inside she was humming in that whine.

She came into the hallway with a towel wrapped around her head like a turban. She was in an old long blue robe. He reached for her and she ducked her head. He was going to pull her into the bedroom. He reached again.

"You're a fookin' strangler!"

"Come here."

"No, no, no. Bloody strangler, that's what you are. Here, here you are. I drew a bath for you, you know."

He started tugging on her arm.

"Oh," she said, "I know what you want to do. You want me to take a bath with you. Is that not what you want?"

The embarrassment was all over his face. When she saw it, her eyes widened and danced.

"Oh, come, that'll be super. We'll bathe together."

In his embarrassment, he backed off without knowing he was doing it. She laughed and her finger came out and poked him in the stomach.

"Do you still believe the Redemptorists?" she said.

He didn't say anything.

"Go on," she said. "You don't turn down hot water for anything. Go ahead. I'm goin' nowhere."

She stepped past him toward the bedroom.

"Worry over nothing," she said. "We've all got good wartime morals here."

Before he got into the bathtub he took a toothbrush from the sink and covered it with toothpaste that tasted like ammonia. He worked on the teeth. The mucilage

231

went away. He lowered himself into the tub. He wanted to get in, get right out, and then be with her. He thought about the blue robe opening from the waist, sliding open across long smooth thighs. The thought went all through him. He settled deeper into the water.

11:

He woke up with the water lukewarm. He pulled the plug and got out. He had a towel around him when he heard the voices downstairs. Two, three different voices. A girl, not Deirdre, laughed. Dermot slapped his hand against the bathroom wall. *Fuck it.* He got dressed quickly and fished through a bureau just inside the bedroom until he found clean socks. He came downstairs. The ones who had come into the saloon on Leeson Street with Deirdre were sitting around. Dermot couldn't remember the names. Deirdre introduced him again. Pauline was drinking wine on the floor. Liam, the smart one, was on the couch on one side of Deirdre. Next to her, on the other side, was a new one. He had one eye closed while he took a long drag on a cigarette. He had a sharp nose with a narrow face running down past it. He raised his head to exhale smoke. His eyes, set deep, darted away when Dermot looked at them. Across the room, at a cluttered table, a black-haired guy smoked while he scribbled on a notepad.

"This is Ronald," Deirdre said, introducing the one sitting next to her. Dermot did not like the way she introduced him.

"Wash Belfast off you?" Ronald said.

Dermot didn't answer him. The one scribbling at the table waved a hand. "I'm Oliver Toolan, and if you'll excuse me, I've got to get to the root of a wee problem here."

233

"He's our fearless solicitor," Deirdre said.

"With quite a bit of work to do," Ronald said. He put his hand on Deirdre's head.

"I didn't know Ronald was an Irish name," Dermot said.

"Must it?" Ronald said.

Dermot didn't answer him.

"Want some?" Pauline said. She held up a bottle of red wine.

"It's too early or too late, I don't know which," Dermot said.

"For our sakes, I hope it's too late for Gerry to be traveling," Ronald said.

"Who?" Dermot asked.

"Gerry Kelly, this is his house," Deirdre said. "He teaches at University. He's away to visit his father for the weekend."

"If he returns tonight he'll be throwing half of us out of his bed, you know," Ronald said.

"Is this the headquarters?" Dermot asked.

"Aye, this is our headquarters," Ronald said.

Dermot sat on the couch and put his head back. It went up against the poster of Che. He snapped forward.

"Do you not like Che Guevara?" Ronald said.

"What do I care."

"You leaped like you were petrified of even his picture," Pauline said. They all laughed.

"How could I like a fuck who was going to blow us up with missiles?"

"America does not have any missiles?" Deirdre said.

"Of course we do. And we should've hit this fuck right on the head with one of them, him and his fag friend Castro."

"Wait a minute, this is new, you know," Ronald said. "Castro now is a homosexual in American lore?"

"Castro's got to be a fag," Dermot said. "Doesn't have a wife, doesn't have any girl friends. Great big fuckin' beard. Fuck, I could read. I never read a story about him and a girl. He was always with this fuck Che. Another fuckin' beard. And the Russians handed them missiles.

234

How do you like that? Communists give missiles to fags."

Ronald was laughing. "I think you're more afraid of the beards than the missiles." Pauline was slapping her hands on her thighs. Deirdre was looking past Ronald at Dermot. She was ready to bite.

"Doesn't the Church tell you to stay away from Communism?" Dermot said.

"There's no such thing as a Church any more," Deirdre said. "There's just a lot of men in black clothes livin' in big stone houses. It was all very good when Christ started it, but like everything else, the thought was dispersed over the years."

"That's your opinion," Dermot said.

"What kind of a church is it that stands by and allows wee children to get killed?" Deirdre said.

"What do you mean by that?" Dermot said.

"We've violence and degradation here for several reasons," she said. "You have here in Northern Ireland a political union between a landed aristocracy and rich industrialists. In order to keep this political union intact, they must have ferment among the workers. Therefore, every thirty years or so, the people in the political union let sectarianism run through the streets of the working class. Each time somebody with minimal intelligence suggests that perhaps one way to remove sectarianism as an issue is to force the Catholic Church to give up its separate schools so the workers can join together, Catholic and Prod, and fight the true enemy, the rich unionists, each time this comes up, the bloody bishops rebel. They have their own political power in their churches and school halls. They'd much rather see the people kill each other than to give up their political power."

"Now that's a lie," Dermot said.

"Is it now?" Deirdre said. "Read the history of your own nation. The Catholic bishops in the North took no stand on slavery because they deferred to the Catholic bishops in Louisiana and Virginia."

"Where do you get that from?"

"From books in libraries," Deirdre said.

235

"Who wrote a book like that?" Dermot said. "A Communist had to write a book like that."

"Now you sound like a policeman," she said.

"A policeman?" Ronald said.

"A policeman protecting people like you from criminals," Dermot said to him.

"Policemen by themselves, one man at a time, are nice enough fellas, I guess, but as a group they're, well, they're policemen, you know," Liam said.

"Actually, the best instruments of oppression on earth," Ronald said.

"Shit. Get mugged and find out," Dermot said.

"Find out what?" Deirdre said. "Find out who they really are for? In Czechoslavakia the students rioted against the Russian troops. Who stopped them? Not the Russians. While the students who fought the Russians threw petrol bombs at their bloody tanks, the policemen, their very own Prague policemen, beat them unmercifully."

"That's in Czechoslavakia. Who knows what they have there," Dermot said.

"Well, then what of Dublin?" Deirdre said. "In Dublin when people in need of housing squatted in some empty buildings who came after them with batons flying? Not the landlords. The Garda. Our own fine Garda. Batoning women holding wee children."

"Fascists," Pauline said.

"Brendan said it so lovely," Deirdre said. " 'I've never seen a situation so dismal that the presence of a policeman couldn't make it worse.' "

"Go ask that kid and his father out in the street this morning," Dermot said to Deirdre.

"You weren't acting as a policeman."

"What the hell do you think I was doing?"

"You were a sensitive human being. There's a vast difference."

"Bullshit," Dermot said. He was irritated. She just couldn't understand what had made him move at the soldier with the gun. "Get mugged and find out what you think about policemen," he said.

The lawyer was leaning back in his chair, stretching his arms. "Let's get on with it now, Deirdre."

"I'm going," Dermot said.

"Going where?" Deirdre said.

"Back to the hotel. Get my hands on the uncle and go home with him."

"It's so late now."

"I don't care, I'm going."

"Stay. We've to be up early for the funeral."

"What funeral?"

"Paddy's funeral. The wee drinkin' man with the flowers."

"I never had a drink with him. Where the hell is the hotel now?"

"What hotel?" Ronald said.

"Where's the International?"

"Oh Lord, man, you can be there in ten minutes. Right down Sandy Row you go. Bus is right on the corner."

The topcoat was in the hall. It still was damp.

"Do you know which way to go?" Deirdre said.

He went out without looking at her.

He was walking on the wet empty street to the corner. There was no bus coming. Trucks and a few cars came by. He began walking past the dark shops toward the center city. Walking and talking to himself inside. The anger nearly forced the words out of him.

Afraid of beards? Dermot told himself. Hey, the beard has nothing to do with what bothers you. It's what's under the beard you hate. When you come up against one of them you see why they go around all the time with their hair down to their ass and a big beard covering their faces. Afraid of them? Huh. One night in nineteen-sixty-eight George Wallace gave a speech at Madison Square Garden. All these beards and fags showed up to picket. They pulled Dermot out of Brooklyn and had him on Eighth Avenue and Thirty-third Street, on the west side of the street. The bastards were behind wood horses there. Motorcycle helmets, beards, Vaseline all over their faces, you'd think they were going inside to

237

box six rounds, Goddam Army jackets, beards, hair sticking out from under motorcycle helmets. They were wearing the kind of eyeglasses, half-glasses, that the horse breeders walk around Belmont Park wearing. They were calling the cops pigs and fascists and they give the "Heil Hitler" and all that and the sergeant out in front kept shaking his head no to the patrolmen. Then the dirty bastards broke out the Viet Cong flags. The sergeant didn't have to say anything. Over the horses all the cops went. The bastards cut and ran and the broads screamed like babies. Anybody standing got a whack with the club. Then here this one guy went. A big tall bastard with a motorcycle helmet and glasses and a Viet Cong flag. He hopped out from behind the barrier and he began running on Eighth Avenue. Dermot went over the barricade after him. Running like hell, he went right out into the traffic on Thirty-fourth Street, hoping Dermot was right out there after him. The guy came running back to the sidewalk on Thirty-fourth Street and he went really flying into the freight doors of the nearest building. The doors figured to be locked, it was a Sunday night. But one of them wasn't. The kid went flying through it. A big brown metal door. Dermot was at the door before it closed. Perfect, because now nobody could see what was going on. The kid was trying to find his way around the packing cases in the freight area. Dermot got to him right away. The bastard turned around and went crazy. He let out a scream and swung the Viet Cong flag. The thing was on a pole made out of cardboard. Dermot just walked right through the swing. The cardboard pole hit him on the shoulder and neck. He was down a little bit, just right for leverage, and instead of throwing the right hand from back behind the shoulder, crazy, he let it go short and nice. His whole side came around with the punch. The bastard fucking went down and he fucking stayed down. Dermot Davey afraid of beards?

Dermot came to the bridge by the railroad station. The hotel was only a couple of empty streets away. He did not go down to the bar. The clerk gave him a room.

238

He said the night porter, who ran the elevator too, would bring something to eat. The night porter brought a plate of tiny wedges of ham on white bread and a glass of milk. He could've eaten five plates of them. He got undressed and into bed. The room was a dungeon.

His empty stomach woke him at ten o'clock. The night's sleep had taken the heat out of his eyes. The end of a morning rain dripped in the shaftway outside the window.

The phone ringing startled him. "Hel-lo, will you have a cup of tea?" Deirdre said. "I'm downstairs here."

"I don't know where I am, let me pull myself together, I'll be right down."

He was stung from the night before. He wondered why she even had bothered to come to the hotel for him. He knew he goddam well liked her body. But he had never touched a Communist in his life. Christ, it was a mortal sin to know one. Vaguely, something drifted through him. *Pro-fessional*. Now Dermot remembered Creel talking the Wallace storefront in Richmond Hill. Dermot rubbed the back of his neck. Maybe the Creel guy would understand her, he thought. I'm running away from her and a professional would walk in and like her. He wished he could think it out on his own without using somebody else as an example, but he did not know how to.

She was at the elevator, smiling, her eyes lively, her hair glistening. He didn't say anything about last night and neither did she. They went down the main street, Royal Avenue, and had breakfast in a place in the Grand Central Hotel called the Copper Penny. The morning paper Dermot bought was the Protestant paper, the Belfast *News Post*. On the first page there was a story about a twenty-one-year-old IRA gunman, Martin Kelly of Leeson Street, Falls Road, being shot while attacking troops of the Queens Second during rioting Saturday night. The terrorist was listed as being in critical condition at Royal Hospital.

"How the hell can they do a thing like this? Twenty-one-year-old gunman?"

"Do it all the time," she said. "Not just this particular

239

newspaper either. The authorities always announce that a wee eleven-year-old boy is a dreaded IRA gunman. If a woman is shot she held a bomb in her hand. The journalists believe the authorities. And the people who read the newspaper account believe what they read. Then you can see why a Protestant bloke on the Shankill thinks all the Catholics are terrorists. Who can blame him?" She looked up at the clock. "I've to be at the funeral," she said.

"What the hell, I'll go with you," Dermot said.

They walked down to City Hall and climbed on a double-decker bus marked FALLS ROAD. A few blocks up, in front of shabby new high apartment projects, children too young to be in school wrestled on the ground in spaces between lines of parked Saracens, the morning sun strong enough now to reflect off the armored turrets over the children. The sidewalks were blackened from petrol bombs and covered with broken glass and paving blocks. The bus came past a wedding-photo shop, the grocery store, and here was Leeson Street. A high-roofed hearse, limousine after it, crept toward them. The street was filled with people walking behind the cars. Deirdre said it would take forty minutes for them to get up to the cemetery. Two blocks up, a burned bus blocked part of the road. Traffic went past it slowly. Past the bus was the gloomy hospital building. Deirdre shrugged. Their bus picked up after the hospital. They got off at the last stop and sat on a ledge of the cemetery wall and smoked cigarettes.

A few minutes later, the hearse and the limousine moved into the cemetery and stopped. Only men were in the procession in the road. Women and children walked on the sidewalks. Traffic from the opposite direction tried to keep going. A bulging woman in her raincoat stepped off the sidewalk. Her mouth had a hard twist to it and she stood in the middle of the Falls Road and stared the traffic to a stop.

Men crowded around the back of the hearse. "Back a bit," a woman called out. All the women around the

240

cars moved away. "Now wee girls. Wee girls. Stand back."
Children moved away.

The coffin came onto the shoulders of men whose
baggy pants were almost over their rundown shoe heels.
Two young boys ducked their shoulders under the casket.
They weren't tall enough for their shoulders to touch
the casket. They each held a hand up so they could
touch the coffin.

"The immediate family have first and last lift," Deirdre
said.

The old priest led the line of men walking behind the
casket. The women and children streamed through the
overgrown grass around the old chipped headstones.

"Still livin'?" a woman from Leeson Street said.

"Still livin'," Deirdre said.

"That's what he gets for sarvin' them for twelve years,"
the woman said.

"Serving what?" Dermot asked her.

"Her fuckin' majesty. He was in the RAF twelve and
a half years, he was."

When she was gone Dermot asked Deirdre, "How
could she say that?"

"Oh, because he was in the RAF."

"How could the guy go out and fight his own then?"

"Who said it was his own? These murderers from
Glasgow? Huh. Catholics are the only ones from Northern
Ireland who ever joined the British service. We had
no conscription in Northern Ireland during World War
Two. The Stormont government fought conscription to
the death. Oh, Jesus. They're loyal to the Queen as long
as it means keepin' Catholics out of work. But ask the
Stormont government to go fight for the Queen, even
for a thing like the fookin' Nazis and, Christ, they had
a fit. No conscription. That's only for Great Britain. So
Catholics enlisted at the ratio of ten-to-one over Protestants. For good reason. Protestants had jobs. Catholics
had no place to go. Once the enlistments began they
became a way of life for Catholics. The poor man here
was in the RAF for a dozen years because it was the
only work he could get. But he certainly was no brother

241

to these scum in the streets. He drew his pay from the RAF. Nothing more."

An old workman guided the family through the weeds to the open grave.

"This is what you get for being a minority," Deirdre said. "It costs forty-five pound to open a Catholic's grave. Haitch Pee, you know. Hire Purchase. Pay so much every week of your life for the ground, you know. Then when you die you still have to pay forty-five pound to have your own ground opened up and your body fitted into your own ground. Protestants are buried for nothing."

"Well, they can only kill us once," another woman said.

"And they never can kill our faith, either!" an older one called out.

The family had their arms around each other's backs as they walked under the casket. The two little boys weaved off balance and bumped into the men while they tried to keep their hands on the bottom of the casket as they walked.

A gold-tipped prayer book in the priest's hands stood out against his black raincoat. The old priest began to shake holy water on the casket and ground.

"Just like he was blessin' guns the other day," Deirdre said.

The children clustered against a headstone near the open grave. Rosary beads came out through the crowd. The limousine driver stood by his car in a long chesterfield coat and smoked. The glove compartment was open, with a yellow can of Simoniz showing. The driver had a rag in his hand.

A gravedigger leaned on the shovel, his chin sitting on his fist. He straightened up and handed his shovel to one of the men who had just set down the coffin. He bent over. There was the sharp sound of the shovel going into the dirt. He threw the shovelful on top of the casket in the grave. The dirt and rocks thumped against the wood. The old priest's voice rose, ". . . dust unto dust . . ."

The man handed the shovel to one of the boys who

242

had walked under the casket. The boy stuck the shovel into the dirt. He sent rocks and dirt banging against the casket.

". . . but the Lord shall raise you again," the priest called out.

The other kid stepped up to do the same thing, the adults making way for him, while the old priest was saying, "You shall rise again."

Then it was over and the people began walking back through the cemetery. Dermot stood with Deirdre, looking across to the hills. The family packed into the Daimler limousine, which was alone on the walkway now. The driver got in. He couldn't get the car to start. As one man came to the car he stooped over and grabbed a handful of grass and wiped his shoes with it. The driver was out lifting up the hood, looking inside. You could see by his eyes that he was looking at a wonderland he'd never seen before. He slammed the hood down and got into the car. He took off the brake and let it start rolling down the hill. While it rolled he was a frenzy at the wheel trying to get the car started. Little faces in tears pressed against the windows for their last looks at the casket in the ground. The car rolled down to the bottom of the walkway, and the driver had to turn it to keep from going into the cemetery fence. The car made the turn and rolled to a stop. It sat there, far at the bottom of the hill, out of sight of everybody. Deirdre looked, lit a cigarette, and started walking toward the cemetery entrance.

"We'll get somebody," Dermot said.

"Let him, it's his business," she said.

They walked out of the cemetery. There was a pub across the road. It was a large, bare pub, jammed with men drinking with caps on. They found two spaces on a long bench against the far wall and sat in silence at a little round table. A waiter got halfway to them and asked what they wanted. They ordered two pints of stout. They were passed along, table to table. They drank a little bit of the stout. The saloon door opened and Pauline and Ronald burst into the place. Deirdre waved

243

to them and jumped up. Dermot followed her. Two bus drivers at the table next to them went for the glasses of stout.

"Why were you not at the cemetery?" Deirdre said to them.

"We were at the church," Pauline said.

"Aye, church," Ronald said.

"I prefer the ground to church," Deirdre said. She hooked her chin onto Dermot's shoulder. "Will you not come to Derry?"

"I don't know, I'll take a shot and stop by the people you told me about."

"Aye."

"Where do I find you?"

She started fitting herself backward into the small crowded car. "City Hotel. Anybody there can put you onto us. Or you can ask anybody where the meeting rooms are for the Derry Socialist Labour Party."

A big old high taxicab rolled along the wet cobblestone street. Dermot waved. When he got to Lansdowne Road he told the taxicab to wait. He knew he wasn't going to spend another night with the aunt. He had any of that he needed in Ozone Park.

He and Johno took a room in the International. Johno went straight to the bar. He found the two guys from the day before. Johno would always find ones like them anywhere. Fuckin' bums, Dermot thought. Fuckin' bums fall onto each other all over the world. Dermot went into the lounge to watch television. Before dinner he went up to the room and called home collect.

"Are you all right?" Phyllis said.

"Sure."

"What's it like?"

"A lot of trouble."

"I know, it's been on all the television. You're no-wheres near it, are you?"

"No."

"That's good."

"It's better than being where there's trouble."

"Uh huh."

244

"What time is it where you are?"

"Five after six."

"Oh. It's only five after one here."

"It's five hours," he said.

"Yeah. Well, Dermot, the car wasn't working right today so I took it to the Gulf station. The man there said there was something the matter with the radiator hose. He kept it."

"Forget about it. Let me talk to the kids."

The oldest one came on first. "Hi, Daddy!" She was gone.

The small one came on with a voice he could barely hear. She was crying.

"Daddy?"

"Yes."

"Kim says you're not going to bring me a present from Irish. She says you're only getting a present for her."

The operator cut in with a three-minute notice. Phyllis had the phone back.

"Oh God, this must cost so much. All right, you'll call again? Everything's fine. Get a good rest and I'll see you when you get back."

When Dermot woke up in the morning, Johno was on top of his bed with his clothes on. "I'm dead," he mumbled. "They gave us whisky all night."

They left in a rented car from in front of the hotel at nine. Dermot drove, following a road map, while Johno kept his head against the window, eyes shut. To leave Belfast for Derry they went up the Crumlin Road, past the men still standing on the street corner you use to get onto Lansdowne Road, and continued until the road runs along a hill looking down on all of Belfast and the long deep, cold-looking loch. The houses on the sides of the road now were the kind guys making big salaries in America live in. The houses ended and they were going through a turn at a long low white building that looked like a stable, or maybe one of those mews things. The black trim and black metal door hinges and handles were shining with new paint. The turn took them around

245

the corner of the stable and brought them onto the main street of a town. The signs said it was Antrim. The place was busy and looked clean. People walked with energy in and out of neat shops which had Union Jacks flying over them. Dermot had coffee and scones. The waitress, a woman of about forty, had good teeth. She and the other people in the place did not have any sadness sunken into their faces, the way everybody on Leeson Street did.

The map showed Derry sitting at the foot of a finger of water coming in from the North Atlantic where it comes against the top of Northern Ireland. Alongside Derry on the west is Donegal, which is part of the Irish Republic. Donegal forms the west coast of the island. The upper tip of Donegal curves with the island. For a few miles, until it reaches the border with Derry, the Donegal coast has the sea coming at it from the west and north. The drive from Antrim to Derry took two hours. At first, coming out of Antrim, the road went alongside fieldstone walls of huge estates. Even when Dermot slowed down at entrance gates, all he could see was a roadway going past ponds and through trees and fields to infinity.

The road sank between cow pastures, then came up into the back of a town. Rows of one-story, dirty white houses with slate roofs wet from the rain and covered with pigeon shit. The end house on one side of the street was plastered GUINNESS FOR GREATNESS. The end houses on the other side of the road had a Gallagher's cigarette sign. On some of the houses on the street the people had painted the window frames a bright yellow. Mostly, the houses were dirty and sat in the coal smoke with kids in front playing games on smaller patches of sidewalk than kids play on in the middle of the city.

Men with wounded faces stood in the doorways. At the end of the row of houses the road turned onto the narrow, dark, gray stone main business street. A bank with a clock and a saloon with a Morton's Red Heart sign and a news agent with a blue Rothman's cigarette poster and a butcher with a whole cow hanging pink and red in the window. On one of the buildings a sign said MAGHERA. The street widened into an empty cobblestone square with a feed warehouse on it. They were onto the other side of the town now. An antiseptic frame building with front steps stood alone on the roadside. The sign over the front said it was the Orange Hall. On the road past the hall there were farmhouses, not shacks. Cows grazed in fields. Men in hip boots and thick suit jackets drove tractors along the side of the road. The men had straight faces that did not show very much damage inside them. A Union Jack flew from a tall flagpole in front of one of the farmhouses.

The road sank between more fields and came out into the back of another town. Half an hour later, they were into empty country. The road widened into a six-lane highway going across a desolate mountain. To the right, the mountain, brown, with glints of green moss on the rocks, rose to a top that was naked of any color but tan rocks. In the middle of the nakedness was a cement building. Out of it rose an antenna—as big an antenna as you've ever seen. The map said it was a United States Military Base. On the other side of the road, on the left, the land dropped away steeply. The steep slope was rocky and dirt-brown. Streams of water that became black, reflecting a sky dark with rain clouds. The water poured through the rocks down the mountainside to the bottom, where a black stream ran through cocoa ground that had stretches of deep green through it. The land rose again, going high up to the left, into the rain clouds. When any light came through between sets of rain clouds it glinted on the sheer rock just underneath the thin covering of dirt and moss. Ahead, on a curve, the traffic stopped. A deliveryman in a cap and smock climbed out of the red three-quarter-sized truck in front of them and stood and stretched. On both sides of the road, cars were lined up. The road was blocked by a herd of sheep. A big herd, hundreds of them. More were coming down from the side of the mountain. The herd was crossing the road and starting down the steepness toward the stream of black water at the bottom. Dermot got out and walked to the front of the line of traffic. Up close, sheep are dirty as hell. The only clean thing about them were purple and red die markings somebody had tossed on them. Their little feet tapped on the highway like thousands of hammers. The sheep coming down the mountainside splashed in water that must have been just under the surface. A black dog chased them. Tail wagging, mouth open, he ran to one side of the herd, barking and pushing the sheep. Then he doubled back and chased one edge of the herd across the road and started them down the steep slope. The dog went back to the man herding the sheep and stood alongside him with his head up. There is nothing like being in charge, whether you're on the side of a mountain or on Forty-second Street.

Half an hour later, a wide river, slate-gray in the dull sky, showed between waves of hills. The hills were green, light yellow, light green alongside the light yellow, then deep green with black hedgelines wavering through the fields. As the car dipped on the road the fields swirled, the colors running together and separating and running together again. A pinwheel spinning or one of those psychedelic things. It looked like the road flattened into a brick street. The view of the river was blocked by the Ulster Fertilizer big gray shed. The first barbed-wire coil showed on the red-brick street. An Army truck went by. The wind whipped the canvas. A soldier with a bare head stood in the back of the truck. His eyes closed in the wind, sandy hair blown straight back. And then here on the right, down on the other side of the river, climbing up from the river, was a gray, age-darkened, smoke-covered city that looked like a torture chamber.

Johno was awake now. "Look at this mother," he said.

You could see walks with parapets and notches for guns, the kind of things kids used to make out of cardboard. Buildings were outside and inside the wall. Here and there you could see archways in the wall with streets running under the arches. The place couldn't have been any different five hundred years ago. Past an empty railroad station and they were at the top of a double-deck bridge going across the river into the city of Derry.

248

A sandbag pillbox with a corrugated-iron roof, a machine gun sticking out of an opening in the sandbags, guarded the entrance to the bridge. At the foot of the pillbox a red sign said: B. CO., 1ST BN. 22D (CHESHIRE) RGMT.

Out on the bridge, four soldiers were patrolling. One listened to a radio strapped to his back, the others held their rifles up. They kept looking straight ahead.

On the other side of the bridge, the city of Derry began with a factory a block long sitting on the riverbank, another factory across the street from it, and off to the left, a narrow street twisting between two gray-blue two-story houses with doorways opening onto clean sidewalks. Union Jacks covered the houses and hung over the street. Dermot asked a cop standing with two soldiers where the City Hotel was. He sent them down a steep street which led to a bus terminal and to the City Hotel, which was on one corner of a square. Behind the hotel was water. Across from its front entrance was a red building, an official-looking building that with its stained-glass window was almost a church. Atop it was a high clock tower, a small copy of the one in London you see pictures of. The building had to be almost a hundred years old. On the other side of the square, facing the hotel and the building with the clock, was the wall. Big stone chunks had rough faces of charcoal-gray black. Black cannon stuck out from gunports on top of the wall. Two archways running through the wall were crowded with traffic. The wall had to be twenty feet high. With the cannon sticking out, the kind of cannon you see in movies about pirates, the wall sat on the place like an old history book.

To get to the hotel, they had to swing around the square and drive along the wharves behind it. An old freighter with more rust than white on the bridge was docked sideways along the wharves. Dermot parked the car at the back of the hotel. Somebody had scrawled across the wall:

SARAH IS A FUCKING HUSSY

12:

The room in the hotel faced the clock tower of the
old brick building. The Guildhall, the bellhop called it. Off
to the right was the water and the wharves along the
water. The bellhop directed them to a street going
through an archway in the wall. He said the Derry
Socialist Labour Party Clubhouse was halfway up the
street inside the wall. The archway really was a small
tunnel. Trucks of almost any size could get through. Inside, two- and three-story wooden buildings stood facing
the dark wet wall. A stone staircase went to the top of
the wall. They climbed up for a look. The top of the
wall was a wide asphalt walkway. Looking along the
walkway, you could see that for long intervals the wall
ran between buildings and was hidden. In other places
it rose out of the streets high and old and bare. Where
Johno and Dermot stood, a sign on the wall said SITE
OF COWARD'S BASTION. BEING MOST OUT OF DANGER, COW-
ARDS RESORTED HERE.

The street inside the wall was steep. They passed an
archway to a street busy with shops. Then up the hill
some more, there was a sign on high wooden garage
doors which said DERRY SOCIALIST LABOUR PARTY. The
garage doors were part of a tea merchant's warehouse.
A small entrance door was cut into one of the large
garage doors. The small door opened into a courtyard
still wet from rain. Cigarette butts floated in dirty puddles. They had to walk through the puddles to a rickety

wooden staircase. "This pussy of yours put you through an obstacle course," Johno said. They came into a large attic with a bumpy wooden floor. Young kids, maybe twenty-five of them, some of them no more than ten or eleven, sat on the floor smoking cigarettes or hunched over a long worktable. Deirdre was at a small table piled with papers in the corner of the room. A mimeograph machine was alongside the table. She was smoking a cigarette and her hair wasn't combed and she was in the same sweatshirt. She came over, rocking and skipping. Her whole body was coming out of her eyes. She took the cigarette out of her mouth when she put herself against Dermot in a hug. She smelled of cigarettes and whisky from last night. Dermot introduced her to Johno. He noticed the wall was covered with big posters of Huey Newton and Bobby Seale.

"What do you call these nigger bastards hanging here?" Johno said.

"The Black Panthers? When they started standing up for their rights in America all the people here read about them. Especially the kids."

"What's nigger derelicts in the Black Panthers got to do with Irishmen fighting?" Johno said.

"What day is today?" Deirdre said to Dermot. Her eyes had hard light to them.

"Tuesday," he said.

"Then will ye fookin' tell him it's fookin' Tuesday so at least he'll know what day it is!"

She leaned over and took the last drag on her cigarette before dropping it onto the floor.

And now the mimeograph machine and the small bare room came together in Dermot's mind with the night in the Wallace storefront on Jamaica Avenue.

"It's a business," Dermot said to Johno.

"What?" Johno said.

"If you never been in it, you wouldn't understand," Dermot said. "It's a business and you never take it personal."

"Well, I take niggers personal," Johno said. "Good and personal."

"How would you like a nice drink?" Deirdre said.

"Jesus, would I," Johno said.

Deirdre stood in the doorway with him and told him how to walk just across the street and through the wall, and the bar, the Castle, would be right there. Johno went down the stairs. "Give the nice niggers a kiss for me," he called back.

"That person sounds just like you sometimes," Deirdre said. "Shitty awful."

"He doesn't understand," Dermot said. "He's never done anything in politics."

"You have?" she said.

"Oh, sure. I worked in a Presidential campaign."

"Whose?"

"Wallace."

"A fookin' Tory! A fookin' Enoch Powell!"

"Who's Powell?"

"He's our fookin' Wallace."

"Yeah, but we were all ready to go one way or the other. Either the Kennedy workers was coming over to us or we'd have gone over to the Kennedy workers. You're in politics in America, you got to survive. That comes first."

"Well, I can understand that. You can't get anything done unless you're there. But why should a fookin' Wallace deserve to fookin' survive?"

"Oh, I don't know about that," Dermot said.

"Well, I fookin' well do," she snapped.

"Hey, it's politics, don't take it personal," Dermot said.

"Who the fook told you to take everything personally in Belfast. Rantin' and fookin' ravin' about a picture on a wall. Jesus Christ!"

"It wasn't the posters I was mad at."

She began to laugh.

"I was mad at the fuckin' people getting in the way of my game."

Now she was laughing. Dermot felt good about it.

"I've a couple of things to do and then I'll get you down to Finbar. I could tell you where it is right now if you want to go down there alone."

252

"No, I'll wait."

She said she had a couple of things to do. She went over to the small table. Dermot sat on a box at the end of the long picnic table. One boy plucked the good string of a broken guitar. Another drummed his hands on the table. A girl picked up a bullhorn and turned it on. The thing screeched. The kids at the end of the table put down the broken guitar. Two of them scrambled for it. One of them got it and sat there plucking the one string. Somebody else turned on the bullhorn.

Dermot took out his cigarettes and held them out. Hands came from every part of the table. Cigarettes came out of the pack as if pumped out by a machine. When the hands stopped reaching he had only half the pack left. They lit the cigarettes and sat there smoking and drumming the table and grabbing the broken guitar and turning on the broken bullhorn.

Next to Dermot was a small boy, about twelve or thirteen, but with the body of a ten-year-old. He rocked back and forth on a wooden chair that creaked loudly. The boy had both hands on the table, pushing himself back, then rocking forward, the hands hitting the table again. His face was flat and the brown eyes were set deep. He spoke in a monotone with almost no facial gestures except for what seemed to be a continual cringe from being either cold or hurt.

"What's doin'?" Dermot said to him.

"I done me stint."

"What'd you do?"

"Puttin' up broadsheets at the Guildhall Square. Broadsheets announcin' a rally. I done it brilliantly."

"You had no school today?"

"Don't go to school."

"You don't go?"

"It's too borin', school."

"Well, how old are you?"

"Thirteen."

"Thirteen? Young to be bored, isn't it?"

"Ah dunno. If they had to educate people when they was young, it would be better. There'd be less of

253

fightin' goin' on. What they should've done is start educatin' sooner. When I was five. I heard I was smarter then."

"Patsy is right," a girl in a raincoat said.

"I know I am," the boy said.

"Tell me how," Dermot said.

"The stories," Patsy said. "All the stories is wrong. We have a book with this story in it about a fella has a horse and he has to go into the Army and they make him leave the horse in a field by his house. The horse, he follows this fella to the Army camp and the fellas there, they take the horse in and feed him and everything comes out fine. That's the way the story ends. Phoo. I like stories that tell the truth. They should make it the way it is in actual life. What should happen in this story is for the fella to go to the Army and the house stays home and nobody feeds him and he starves to death. The fella in the Army comes home one day and he finds the horse dead and the worms crawlin' through the skin."

"That's a nice idea," Dermot said.

"Oh, it's a true story. You want to read things you know is true. Not stories where somethin' comes in and puts everything to normal. Everybody knows it doesn't happen that way. Everybody is happy ever after. Phoo. The way all the picture shows should end, the people should be all together in the house ready to live happy forever and then they should go to sleep and then the house should catch fire. Then all the people is burned alive."

Deirdre came over with broadsheets which said "Unemployed Comrades" and "Capitalist Oppression." Dermot remembered swinging clubs at signs like that in New York. Across the bottom of the signs, in large letters, it said DERRY YOUNG SOCIALISTS.

"I've a few more minutes," she said.

"Then what?" Dermot said.

"I could do with a cup of tea."

"Let me go tell Johno."

"And tell him what?"

"Tell him to make himself comfortable."

"I'll call through the door. But I'm not goin' in there," she said.

"Forget the number, I'll take care of him," Dermot said.

He went out of the tea merchant's warehouse and walked across the street and through the arch in the wall and came into the bar through the side door. Johno was in the smoke and the pale light with his arm around a guy in a neat brown suit. The guy had a thick neck and shoulders and he stood straight up. He had a face made of cut glass.

"Here," Johno called out. "Now we're finally gettin' with our own kind."

He put a hand on Dermot's shoulder to bring him close. He said in a low voice, "This is Eddie Canavan. He's the real. He's not like that fuckin' Communist cunt you got up there. This is the real."

"How are you?" Dermot said.

The Canavan guy took his hand and looked Dermot in the eye. Canavan looked with narrowed eyes. He had high cheekbones that pushed the eyes together anyway. But narrowed into slits, as they were now, the eyes, blue eyes, looked particularly fierce. Canavan had short hair. As they shook hands, Dermot noticed how neat the suit was. Canavan was wearing a blue shirt and brown tie that went with the suit. He was the neatest person Dermot had seen since he came to Ireland. After a quick and hard pump of the hand, Canavan spun and faced the bar, snorting through a squat nose.

"He's in with Joe O'Neill," Johno said.

"Joe O'Neill is in with me," Canavan said. He said it without looking at them.

Johno clapped Canavan on the shoulder. "See? He's the real."

"You up with that Deirdre O'Doherty, are you not?" Canavan said.

Dermot didn't answer.

"That's a whore's get, the lot of them," Canavan said.

"You see?" Johno said. "Communist cocksuckers. I told you."

"They say they're in the IRA," Canavan said. "They're IRA all right. The 'I Ran Away' brigade of the IRA."

"He's in the Provos," Johno said.

"We believe in getting the British out and fook the politics," Canavan said.

"He's my kind," Johno said. "He's no pinko hump. Let's have a drink."

Johno bent over. He whispered. "Show him what you got," he said to Canavan.

Canavan looked straight ahead. He held a glass in his right hand. Dermot noticed the hand was clean. Canavan's left hand pulled aside the front of the jacket. The square grip of an automatic pistol showed from his belt. Canavan went into his pocket. He came out with a roll of Johnson & Johnson adhesive tape. A three-inch roll, the kind hold-up men carry with them to plaster over somebody's mouth during the holdup.

"How do you like him?" Johno said.

"I guess so," Dermot said.

"For Chrissakes, he's the first legitimate man we met here," Johno said.

Pleasure flooded through Canavan's face. He began working his neck around like a fighter waiting for the bell. Canavan went into his pants pocket and came out with a good-sized roll of paper money. He looked at it. "The poor wee people in Aughnacloy thought their money was in safety in the bank," he said.

"The real!" Johno shouted.

Dermot heard quick footsteps coming past the back door of the saloon. He watched the front door. Deirdre came in front of it, looked in, saw Dermot and smiled, but did not come in.

"I'm going to go for a while," Dermot said.

"What the hell do you want to hang out with all the cowards for?" Canavan said.

"Stay around and meet some men," Johno said.

"And some real women, not goddamned Communists," Canavan said.

"I'll see you later at the hotel," Dermot said.

"He's good company, Canavan is, isn't he?" Deirdre said.

"What is he?" Dermot said.

"A bully," she said. "If they ever made things better around here, he'd shrivel up and die. He can't wait for it to get worse and worse."

"Is he the boss of an outfit?"

"The boss of wee small boys who do the fighting," she said. "Trouble is, if the government do not recognize that people need jobs, then everybody will join the Provos. A few men like Canavan will become everybody. Christ, someday you could have everybody who is standin' on corners now goin' around pulling triggers."

"What's stopping them?" Dermot said.

"Us, as little as we are," she said.

Dermot bumped against her. He could feel her body under her coat. They went a few more steps and he put his arms around her and he stopped walking. He held her and had his face in her hair. Stale cigarette smoke, some sort of ink from the posters, and excitement. She laughed and pushed him into walking again. She said she wanted a cup of tea. They went around a corner into the three-quarter-light of a narrow street with shops on it. Men doing nothing lined the sidewalks on each side. The buildings were three-story and then one-story and then two-story and here was a moviehouse that was closed. The cornices of each building, stone or wood, had lions' heads or spouts or some other design that took time to form. They walked toward a café sign. Two waitresses in white uniform dresses had the door open. They stood in the cold air on the sidewalk talking to a guy with black wet hair. The guy walked a few steps away from them to a lamppost. The men standing on the sidewalks all stopped talking and looked at the guy. One of the waitresses held out a watch. A stopwatch, he guessed, because she looked like she was at the race track in the morning.

Deirdre and Dermot came up and stood alongside the waitress. She held the café door with one hand. She balanced on one leg, body bent forward like a dance pose, to see through the men so she could do her timing.

"All right," the waitress said.

"No, no, no," one of the men on the sidewalk said. He pointed to the guy at the lamppost. "Push off the lamppost with yer right hand. Put your hand right on the lamppost and give yerself a shove to start off."

"Dead on," the guy said. He got alongside the metal lamppost and put his right hand against it.

"A wee bit closer," the man said.

"Aye." The guy edged closer to the lamppost.

"Elbow bent," the man said.

"Aye."

"All right," the man said to the waitress. She held the stopwatch out. "Now!"

The guy came off the lamppost and was in the middle of the street in one move. He stopped in a crouch. His right arm came up like he was throwing something. He headed back to the curb. His first two steps were sloppy. He ran with his body all over the place. But when he hit the curb he was tucking in his elbows. He flew through the door of a bookmaking shop, touching nothing. A man at the door to the bookmaking shop held his arm in the air and kept looking into the shop. Now the arm came down. The waitress clicked the watch.

A man from the street came running over to the waitress. She held out the watch.

"No good," the man said.

The guy with the wet hair was back out of the book-making shop.

"Seven," the waitress said to him.

"Fookyesay seven," he said.

"Fookye. Seven."

"Six or better," the other man said. "Has to be six or better or we've all had it." He looked up the street at the pillbox in front of Chada Fashions. "We'll break it off for a bit," he said. When he looked at Deirdre, dislike gathered in his lips.

They walked into the café behind the waitress. The owner stood behind the counter in a gray butcher's apron.

"I got a look at your knickers that time," the owner said.

"Did you, Eamonn, what color are they?"

"Either pinky or off-white."

"Either? I thought you saw."

Well, by that I mean you were jumpin' around so much."

Deirdre and Dermot sat in a booth. "I don't even want to know what that was about," Dermot said.

"Quite simple," she said. "The Army comes at four o'clock every day and parks an armored personnel carrier outside on the street here. The soldiers come bounding out of it, lifting people, searching everybody, pushing us around deliberately. It can't go on any more. We've been attempting to tell them. And while they're busy not listening, here's a young man outside rehearsing every day. The bookmaking shop has a back door to it, you know. Brings you right into the Bogside, you know."

"There's only one hand grenade in Derry," Eamonn, the owner, said. "They won't let it be used unless it's absolutely necessary."

"But in the meantime the lad is out there learning his part," Deirdre said.

"Absolutely," Eamonn said. "I've nothin' to do with it. I'm totally against violence."

"Oh, I'm sure," Deirdre said. "Have you not cleared the operation with Eddie Canavan?"

Eamonn pretended not to hear.

A man in a gray smock came into the shop. A dark mustache twitched as he spoke very rapid rising-and-falling Derry. He became more agitated. Deirdre made room for him in the booth. He sat down and looked at his hands. "Now what in actual fact did they say to you?" she said. He started talking. Dermot leaned over, but could only hear pieces of words. He asked what he was saying. The man in the smock shook his head and said something. "No," Deirdre said, "tell him. It's more important than you think it is."

"Well, I'm Johnny Killeen. I'm a binman, you know."

Dermot looked right at him so he could make out the

words. "I pick up the dustbins. Refuse, you know. There's five of us go out. A lorry-driver binman and four binmen. I'm a binman. The lorry-driver binman is a better job, you know. Pay is one pound four a week more than a binman's. The lorry-driver binman gets the scram, you know. He's the man in charge of the truck, you know. Therefore he gets all the scram. Any bits of copper and brass, ye can sell them and have a little extra. Three times they promised me I was going to be the lorry-driver binman. I've been a binman longer than anybody else on my lorry, you know. I want to be the lad drivin' the lorry. Sit up front and direct the others. They told me I was going to be the lorry-driver binman beginning today. So this mornin', I come down to the garage. The wifey and three wee ones was with me, you know, I was goin' to get in there and drive out right past them, you know. The wee ones were all excited about me drivin' the lorry. But when I do get to the garage this mornin' they say to me, it's all right, we've a man to be the lorry driver. Dead on. Then this Prod lad, Hunter, gets into the seat. They made him the lorry-driver binman. He's hardly worked three years you know, and they put him right in there. The wifey and the three wee ones is standin' there and ex- pectin' to be wavin' to the father. Here comes this Prod lad, Hunter, drivin' the lorry out past them. With the father still a binman, clingin' clingin' to the door like I always done. She rightly would like the money, the wifey. She really wanted the wee children to see me drivin' the lorry out past them."

"Come on," Deirdre said. She stood up. "We'll go across to the corporation."

"Oh, I have to be back on me lorry."

"After the corporation."

They walked to the Guildhall. Deirdre led the way down a hallway and into an office. A man sat at a wooden desk cutting strips of paper with a penknife. Rimless glasses gave an extra pinch to his face.

"Yes," he said. He did not look up.

While Deirdre spoke to him, the man tilted his head and watched the penknife cut the paper in a straight line.

"Well, that's up to Mr. Montgomery," he said through his nose.

"Could you not ring him up and discuss the matter with him?" she said.

"Well, I really don't like doing this sort of thing on the telephone I prefer putting it in writing."

Deirdre took quick drags of a cigarette, the smoke going in the man's face. Her thumb kept flicking against the cigarette. The ashes dropped on the papers on the desk. He reached out and brushed the ashes away.

"Yes, well, but the man here does not have the time. He would like to have an official explanation of this matter. He is quite concerned."

She took two quick drags on the cigarette to develop an ash. The thumb hit the cigarette again and the ash fell on the papers.

The man looked up. She stood and smoked in his face with her scarf dragging on the floor and the ripped coat hem hanging.

"I am worried about our standards," he said. He looked at the guy in the smock. "You are supposedly employed as a binman. Yet you are here in this office rather than working."

"He is supposed to be working as a lorry-driver binman," Deirdre said.

"I said I prefer to put this matter into writing. It is not for us to discuss here."

The penknife began to cut through the paper again.

"Would you please send us a copysheet of what you write?" she said.

"Oh, we really don't do that."

"Well, this time you might. You see, we intend to raise this as an issue in the elections. After the elections we shall have a member of Parliament who can discuss this further in London, you know."

He looked up through his rimless glasses just for a moment. Deirdre's thumb hit the cigarette again. The man breathed in. Slowly his hand brushed the ash away. He went back to the penknife.

"Be careful," Deirdre said to him.

He looked up. "How's that?"

"I wouldn't want you to cut off one of your fingers with the knife."

She dropped the cigarette on the floor. She stepped on it and walked out of the office. "I'll come back tomorrow morning for the copysheet of your correspondence," she said.

"Oh, you can't do that," he called to her.

"Fookye!" she yelled as she walked down the hall.

Johnny Killeen followed her out. On the street he asked her, "Do ye think I could lose me job?"

"They don't do things that way," Deirdre said. "They are most interested in serenity. Your man there would be highly pleased if you were to remain a binman, with no fuss, for the rest of your life."

Killeen shrugged. He walked across the square to an outdoor cigarette machine. He stood at the machine with his hand up to drop in the change. He had the hand up, but it was not moving. He stood there.

"This is our lot," Deirdre said.

"There's nothing you can do about it?" Dermot said.

"We've twenty per cent of Derry Protestant," she said. "The Unionist Party controls one hundred per cent of the jobs within the city corporation. No job is too insignificant for the Unionist Party. Nor is any job too large for them to control. There's a man sitting inside who owns a hundred fifty flats. He collects four pound a week for each. His job inside is to oversee housing. He has prevented the building of any new housing in order to protect his rents. Nobody says a word. It is just another part of the system."

Behind the building, cattle or cows, sounding as if their bodies hurt, made deep calls. Dermot went to the corner of the building and looked down to the wharves on the water. Men with sticks were herding cattle onto a gangplank going up to a freighter with a black hull. The men wore rubber hip boots and slapped the cattle with whittled tree branches. When the last steer started up the metal gangplank, the men started walking up the open area around the wharves. The open area was a couple of blocks long, ending at a gray wooden warehouse. A head looked

out the warehouse door. There was a yell. The big sliding
door was pulled open. Cattle started coming out of the
warehouse at a stupid lope. A couple of young guys with
sticks ran with them, twisting and looking back to make
sure the cattle kept coming out of the warehouse. There
were about fifty cattle in this group, the men half running
alongside with their rubber hip boots flapping and their
sticks waving When one of the cattle began to veer away
from the herd, heading into one of the streets running to a
dead end at the wharves, all one of the men had to do was
to get near him and shout and wave the stick and the
steer, head nodding, these fat bloody eyes seeming to see
nothing, changed direction with his short clumping front
legs and went back with the herd. The metal gangplank
was covered with green slime from the shit of the ones
who had gone up before. The cattle came packing together at the foot of the gangplank, their bodies shud--
dering while they gave thick tongue. The men only had
to yell or wave the sticks or throw in a few slaps to have
the cattle go up to the gangplank. They went up eagerly,
nose to rump. Straight up the gangplank to the deck of
the freighter, then turn and go down a steep gangplank
into the hold. The line of cattle up on the ship had to be
held for a moment. The cattle on the wharf kept pushing
onto the gangplank. They jammed themselves so tightly on
the gangplank that heads were tossing from side to side,
trying to find room.

There was another yell from up at the warehouse. The
next group came running out. Two or three of them got
loose on the side nearest the water. One of the young guys
was on then yelling and waving his stick and the cattle
pushed back into the herd. Another one broke off on the
other side. An old man was too slow in turning around. He
did not get his stick up in time and the steer clopped past
him. Neck skin shaking, head down trying to find a trail,
the steer was heading for the start of the street running
up the far side of Guildhall.

"Run for your life," Deirdre yelled to the steer.

The steer turned away from the opening to the street
and now he was running back from the shed.

"Not that way," Deirdre said.

A man came running out of the shed, hitting and waving his stick. He was running directly at the steer and the steer was running directly at him. When they were about ten yards apart the steer's legs began to chop and his body began to turn. Now he came around, heaving, a vibrating moan coming out of him, a face shaped to be fierce but showing great fear, and he lumbered to the foot of the gangplank and threw his head between the rumps of the last two steers trying to get onto the gangplank. The steer pushed so hard that a man had to wave him back with a stick until there was space for him to go up the gangplank and onto the boat to the slaughterhouse.

"I tried to help him," she said.

Dermot took her hand. Her fingers spread to fit in his. The cattle were up on the freighter now, moaning while they went down into the hold.

"I wish they'd all come running out and then go straight on up the street and never be caught."

"They're too afraid."

"That's what I detest. One lad with a stick in his hand having all that power over anybody. Animal or man."

"What can you do?"

"Jesus, it's even worse with people here. They don't even have to use sticks on them. You saw the poor man. One word and he was half running out of the office. He was frightened that somebody would take up a pen and run a wee line through his name." She sighed. "All you can do is try, I guess."

"Try what?" Dermot asked.

"Try to make them realize that they have legs to stand on. And they should get up off their knees."

The men left the gangplank and were running to surround new steers coming out of the warehouse. Dermot let go of Deirdre's hand and put his arm around her and pulled her into him and kissed her on the side of the neck. She put her hands behind his neck. Her eyes made little darting motions, side to side, but never really moving, tiny jig steps.

"You're a pretty girl."

She put a hand through her hair. "I look like a hag, actually. That's an old trollop, you know."

She said it with softness, without any sharp ridges on her voice. He drew her into him and she put her face into his shoulder. He kissed her on the side of the neck again, where the neck curves into the shoulder, where the softness tells the mouth of more softness, and the feeling was different from anything he knew. So he held her and said nothing.

Her eyes seemed even brighter now. "That's about the prettiest eyes I've ever seen," he said.

Her body came away. "That's just about the last thing we need any more." The words had ridges on them again.

She tucked her hands into her coat and they started walking away from the wharves. He had his hand on her back and he guided her onto the hotel side of the street. At the front of the hotel, he took her left arm and gave half a pull toward the door of the hotel. She pumped her arm back and forth to make him let go. When she got her arm free, she grabbed his arm and jerked him straight ahead. She tugged so hard, he went off balance.

"You're trying to keep the people down," she said. "Every time something important happens and we need people we can't find anybody. We have to suspend the revolution because they're all off havin' a fook."

They went through the wall and up the steep street. They came to a shopping square called the Diamond, then went onto a busy street of shops which were on the ground floor of three- and four-story stone buildings. The windows above the stores were bare, but you could tell people were living there. Next to a pub called the Diamond was a scarred doorway. Deirdre went into it and up one flight of stairs. She pushed in an unlocked door. A man was sitting in a chair staring at television.

She did not talk to the man. "This is my father," she said.

The man was bald and had watery eyes and worn shoulders. When Dermot said some sort of hello to him, he said, "The four sins of earth cryin' out to Heaven for vengeance. Oppression of the poor. Withholding the wages of a workingman. Willfully taking the life of another human being, and sodomy." He kept staring at the television.

Deirdre went through a door behind him. She opened it a little bit and slid through, closing it after her. The door stuck a little. She slammed it. Dermot sat down at a table with oilcloth covering it. Against a wall was a small stove with thick black crusts on the burners and yellow burn marks on the white enamel. Next to the chair the old man sat in was a couch with a ripped covering. The one window in the room faced the side of another building. Deirdre came back out of the door sideways, holding the door only a little bit open, shutting it behind her quickly. She went to the stove and put on a kettle of water.

An older woman came in from the stairs. She was wearing a blue smock. She carried a bag of rolls with powdered tops. Deirdre brought cups of tea over to the table. "My mother," she said. Dermot said hello and the mother gave him a half-smile and moved her chin. Dermot's hands were smeared with ink from touching the broadsheets. He started for the door they had used. "Is it in here?" The mother, who was nearest him, was trying to pull herself out of her chair and stop him with her hands. "No, no, over here," Deirdre said, almost in a yell. She pointed to a door alongside the stove. The bathroom was a closet with a high ceiling. There was a toilet and sink but no bath or shower.

The mother drank her tea in large gulps. She went into the other room, and came out of it, the same way Deirdre did, sliding through a narrow opening and slamming the door quickly. She said she had to go back to work. She walked heavily to the door. Deirdre and Dermot left right after her.

"I'll see you," Dermot said to the man.

"Four sins are cryin' to Heaven for vengeance," he said. "Oppression of the poor. Withholding the wages of a workingman. Willfully taking the life of another human being, and sodomy."

Out on the street Dermot asked if sodomy was considered as bad a crime in Ireland as murder. She began to laugh. Across the street, her mother stood in the window of a bakery with her arms full of bread. "There's mother," she said.

At the archway directly in front of them there was a fence of barbed wire with soldiers watching the people going through an opening at one end of the wire coils. "That's where you go into the Bogside," she said. "Butcher's Gate. They call it that because the blood ran through it."

13:

They squeezed past the soldiers and went through the arch. They came out on top of a hill. There was a cluster of apartment-house towers. They came out of the street at the bottom of the hill. They were fourteen-story buildings. Through the windows you could see scarred hallways. The rest of the ground at the bottom of the hall was a sprawl of one-story huts, coal smoke clinging to the wet slate roofs. The streets in front of the huts were broken up and the paving blocks stacked for barricades. The ground was covered with old bedsprings, broken bottles, and newspapers. A brown sky dripped continually. The little houses spread far to the left. Straight ahead, the houses became two stories high, crammed together on little streets going sharply up a hill. Then it all dissolved into a development of gray houses in wavery, circular lines. The gray houses disappeared over the top of the hill, the brown sky dripping on everything.

At the foot of the hill was a burned truck and piles of paving blocks and barrels and bedsprings. The bare wall at the end house of the first row of huts had a sign painted on it which said YOU ARE NOW ENTERING FREE DERRY.

"All this is what is known as the Bogside," Deirdre said. "This little bit right in front of us here, where the river used to be, that was all the Bogside ever was. Nobody ever called it the Bogside. But when the riotin' started last time, last year, nineteen-sixty-nine, we all started telling the journalists and telly people that this was the Bogside. Christ, but it's a wonderful name, isn't it? It sounds like all of Ireland fighting through all of history. The people got to love the name, you know. In actual fact, the small houses starting right by the Free Derry Corner, that's the start of the Brandywell section. The council houses up on the hill. That's the Creggan Estates. Ye've eighteen thousand people living there. Once they heard the announcers on the news program saying, 'The rebels of the Bogside,' that was the last time anybody wanted to say, 'I live in Creggan.' Maybe the best thing we did in two years of riotin' came up with a name like that. 'Up the Bogside!' "

On the corner, men with wet hair stood in the brown mist. Another group stood on the corner across from them. They kept space cleared around the entrance to a book-making shop. Just enough space so that anybody coming in or going out could fit by turning sideways and shoul-der-bumping through. A ripple went along the men as somebody went into the bookmaking shop. Another rip-ple going in the opposite direction as somebody came out. Everywhere you looked on the street, men walked in the wet half-light of the brown day wearing old suit jackets with the collars turned up.

Deirdre took Dermot up Wellington Street past the book-making shop. She pushed in the door of one of the ce-ment huts. His Uncle Finbar was in the kitchen peeling potatoes. Dermot would have gone up to Finbar anyplace in the world and asked him if they could be related. Fin-bar had black hair and thick eyebrows and long, sad eyes. When Deirdre announced who Dermot was, the man squinted while he figured out who Dermot could be. "Ye be Jimmy's son," he said. "Jimmy didn't tell me he was expectin' anybody."

Dermot didn't answer.

"Did he just send you down?"

"I haven't been to Bundoran yet."

"Bundoran? Just up the road he is."

"Where?"

"Fook's sake, he's in McCann's place."

"Where's that?"

"Brandywell, for fook's sake. Right down the wee road here."

Deirdre pushed him away from the table and began peeling the potatoes. Finbar was in bare feet. He sat on a chair in the front room and began putting on work boots. Two kids, too young for school, sat on a worn couch watching television. A baby in a dirty diaper played on the floor. Nobody noticed them.

"Are you the bloke that's a copper?" Finbar said. "Jesus, they're awful devils, aren't they? They tried to murder the lot of us, you know. We have no police in the Bogside any more. They fookin' well know they'd be shot fookin' dead if they put a foot inside the Bogside. Do you not think that's the way to handle policemen? Christ, but they're awful devils." Finbar's face became red.

"You got all Protestants on the force here, don't you?" Dermot said. "It's no good havin' all one kind policing another kind. New York is different."

"They're the fookin' same the fookin' world over. Ye intimidate the fookin' blacks, do ye not? Same thing with us here. We hadda take a stand you know. There's a couple of 'em be bothering nobody any more."

"Well, I don't know what that settles," Dermot said.

"It settled their fookin' lives, that's what it did."

"Policemen are just fellas doing a job. Same as I do. I can see you taking on the Army. I mean, I had it with these bastards. But what has a poor cop got to do with it?"

"He's got everything to do with it."

"Well, I could be one of the cops who was told to come in here. I would only be doing what I was told to do."

"And we'd only be fookin' killing you then."

They went out into the mist, now almost a drizzle.

The street was filled now with children coming home from school. Two older girls came walking toward them. Two smaller girls followed. The older girls walked by Finbar without saying anything and went into the house. Both of the little ones deliberately stepped into a puddle of water.

"Look at the wee bastards," Finbar said.

270

Women carrying small wax-paper packages came past the crowd in front of the bookmaking shop. Each woman caused one or two men to leave the crowd. Now, a gray-haired woman in a black raincoat came out of the crowd. The little girls in the puddle ran to her.

"Here's the wifey," Finbar said.

"Out shopping?" Dermot said.

"Out fookin' workin'," Finbar said.

When the woman came up to them, Finbar said, "This is Jimmy's son from America."

"Aye," the woman said. She kept going into the house.

Finbar took out a squashed pack of cigarettes. He jammed the pack back into a pocket as Deirdre came out of the house.

"Do ye have a fag?" she asked.

Finbar patted his pockets. Dermot pulled out a pack and held it out.

A few minutes later, Finbar's wife walked out, rolling, as if she were much heavier than she was. She said she had to go back to work. She nodded to Dermot and kept going.

Finbar went inside. He stood looking at the wash hanging and the dirty dishes in the kitchen. The baby was crawling on the floor. The four girls went out in front of the house. A couple of the small kids were out in the back of the house yelling. "Ye think she'd a taken care of the wee baby," Finbar said.

He picked up the baby and carried him inside. The baby started to howl. "Let him rock himself to sleep with the sound of his own voice," Finbar said. Deirdre went in and told him to get out of the house. She started to pick up things.

Finbar and Dermot walked down to the Free Derry Corner. The men on the corner watched every step as Dermot came toward them.

"From New York," Finbar said. "Your fookin' cousin, you know."

"Jesus Christ!" one of them said. He had the collar of a blue plaid jacket around his face. Damp black hair lapped onto the collar. The left eye strayed into the nose, then went back out again.

"I'm J.J.," he said.

"He's my oldest," Finbar said.

"I didn't see you at the house," Dermot said.

"I wasn't there," J.J. said.

"Where were you?" Dermot said.

"Here," J.J. said.

"Where do you work?" Dermot said.

J.J. laughed. "Haven't worked in me fookin' life."

"Come on," Dermot said.

"Ask him when he worked," J.J. said, pointing to his father.

"I worked," Finbar said.

"That's good," Dermot said.

"Worked once in nineteen-forty-three. At Ballykelly. I dug ditches for them to put in the pipes for the fookin' RAF base."

"What'd you do after that?" Dermot said.

"Fook all," one of the men in the crowd said.

"What do ye want to talk about?" J.J. said to Dermot.

"What's your position?" another one of them said.

"I'm standing up," Dermot said.

"What are ye advocatin'?" another in the crowd said.

"A drink," Dermot said.

"Talk about somethin'," another one of them said.

"What's your birthday?" J.J. said.

"October seventeenth."

"What year."

"I was born October seventeenth, nineteen-forty-one."

"Ye born on a Thursday," J.J. said.

"How do you know that?"

"I know. What year was the Statue of Liberty built?" J.J. asked.

"I don't know."

"Eighteen-eighty-six. What year did the War of Independence end?"

"Seventeen-seventy-six."

"Seventeen-eighty-two it ended. What was a great American race horse died in France?"

272

"I don't know, Man o' War? No, they got a big grave for him in Kentucky someplace. Oh, I don't know. Could be any one of them."

"Any one of them? Whirlaway. What about Whirlaway? Don't you think he was a fantastic horse?"

"I guess he was."

While J.J. was rattling on, Dermot looked up at the wall. It was a hundred yards away, up on top of the hill. Two soldiers leaned on their elbows and watched through field glasses.

"Do you not know Tony Bennett?" J.J. said.

"I heard of him, but I mean I don't know him."

"You live in New York. He's from New York."

"It's a very big city."

"You're a policeman, you should know Tony Bennett."

"How do you figure that?"

"Fook's sake, go to any fookin' RUC in Derry City and ask them if they know J.J. from Free Derry Corner. They fookin' well do. Ye be a Yank policeman, would ye not know Tony Bennett?"

"What do I have to know him for?"

"I wrote a song that's dead simple, a perfect song for Tony Bennett."

"And you want me to have him sing it?"

"Notatall. Just have him take a wee minute and listen to it. I had the song recorded in London. But they didn't do it right. The record have only an organ playin'. In actual fact, you need a great big band. A Tony Bennett arrangement."

"Where's the record?"

"In me house."

"Let's get it."

"Oh, I can't go home now. I never go home between dinner and tea."

"Why not?"

"Because I don't."

"Well, what do you do, just stand here?"

"Stand here and be horny. I'm so horny right now I wish I could shag anybody. I'd go home and shag me own mother. I can't. The ole bitch is out workin'."

Deirdre came up to them.

"All right, let's get on with it," Finbar said.

"How long will it take us to get there?" Dermot said.

"Fook's sake, be five minutes."

"I thought it was a trip."

"In the fookin' Brandywell, I told you."

"And that's where?"

"Right fookin' two steps from you is the start of the Brandywell."

"Oh well, then let me go get Johno."

"Jesus Christ, but leave him where he is," Deirdre said.

Finbar started walking.

"The brother's been over here four day now. No, five day. Cousin of ours owns the place. A wee pub, you know. First time in five year he got a chance to go away someplace. Bloody fooker got a few quid together. But he couldn't fookin' afford anybody to stay in his place all the time. So Jimmy said he'd come over from Bundoran, he's with his sister over there, you know. He come over here to help out a couple of days. I tell him, five million fookers left Derry to work in pubs in New York. Jimmy's the first fook I ever heard of comin' from New York and workin' in a pub in Derry."

They walked down the street leading into the Brandywell. A narrow street of smoke and doorways of houses that were huts opening directly against the sidewalk. On the right-hand side was an old green fence from the Brandywell dog-racing track. The street ran out of huts and now it turned into an empty road. On one side was a field running down to the River Foyle. The river was wide and slate-gray and you could see that it moved quickly. The river runs into a lough that goes to the ocean. On the other side of the Foyle, deep-green river moss climbed up from the water and covered rocks and spread into low hills. White houses sat on the deep green. Behind the houses, light-green hills climbed high up, to Donegal.

On the left was a whitewashed saloon. Alongside the white-washed saloon was a hill of dirt covered with garbage.

"Here ye are," Finbar said.

"Wait a minute," Dermot said.

"What's the matter?"

"I just want to wait."

He looked out at the river. The river seemed to be running faster.

"Come on, do ye want to see the fooker or don't ye?"

Dermot watched the river water run faster.

"What's botherin' ye?" Deirdre said.

"Nothing."

"Oh. Well then, we'll have a drink."

Finbar said, "Ye can fookin' well do what ye want to do, I'm goin' inside."

Finbar and Deirdre went for the saloon door and Dermot followed them, and he had wanted it to be a lot of ways but instead he just stepped into a saloon after Finbar and Finbar was calling out, "Oh, Jimmy, look ye what's come!"

Dermot remembered his father as a big man. A small old man was behind the bar, shoulders hunched inside a dark-blue button sweater, smoking a cigarette with yellow-stained fingers. A small old man sitting hunched over on a high stool behind the bar.

He stood up as Dermot came in. Now he was at least of normal height. He had black hair over a sharp, long face. The face had gray in it. Gray running into a heavy black stubble. His eyebrows and his forehead came up. But it took none of the sadness out of the face.

"A drink!" Finbar was against the bar.

"Scotch," Deirdre said.

Dermot did not remember getting from the door to the bar. He was looking directly at the man and he could not think about what he was looking at.

"What do you want?" his father said to Finbar.

"Pint."

The father looked at Dermot. "You?"

"A pint."

The man wrapped yellow-stained fingers around the wooden handle and pulled the pints.

"When did you get here?" he said. He said it to Dermot, but he was looking down at the pints.

275

"Two days ago, three days ago, I don't know. Seems like a week."

"You been in town here that long?"

"No, I just got here today."

"Uh huh."

"Yer fookin' progeny!" Finbar said.

Dermot's father smiled.

"What?" Dermot said.

"Progeny, ye fookin' dope. You're the progeny, here's the great—what the fook do ye say now—prognosis? No. It's somethin' like that."

"Progenitor," Deirdre said.

"No mind, let's have the pint, Jimmy," Finbar said.

Dermot's father put the two pints down. Then he went over to the stool and sat down on it. The yellow-stained fingers brought the cigarette up to his mouth.

Dermot picked up the pint. He felt his hand shaking so badly he put the glass back down.

"Did you see Whitey Ford pitch?" His father's voice came from a long distance away.

"Sure," Dermot said.

"See him much?"

"You know, between television and goin' to a few games."

"Ah, now that was a baseball pitcher," his father said. "He had a head on his shoulders. Did I used to love to see him out there with some big bum of a home-run hitter. Luke Easter. Remember that big dinge? Hated it around the ankles. They all do, but Easter was a special case. Ford used to just stare at the big bum's ankles and he'd, Christ, he'd start doing a jig."

"Easter was with Cleveland," Dermot said.

"Sure he was. A big bum first baseman. Hit the ball eight miles if you let him around on it."

"Hit a lot of homers," Dermot said.

"Seen him one day," the father said, "bases loaded, two out, and here's Easter up. Ford goes zip. Strike—"

"I'll have another," Finbar said. He had drained the glass with a sustained gulp. When the father was at the

276

wooden tap, Dermot picked up the glass in front of him. His hand shook much less now.

"Well," the father said, "one strike, right?"

"On Easter," Dermot said.

"Oh, a terrible bum. First pitch was just at the knees. Just enough to get the bum's feet upset. Now Ford comes right back. Zip. Curve ball outside."

"He must've had five kinds of curve balls," Dermot said.

"That's right, five kinds of curve balls," his father said. "Oh, of course you're right. Curve ball outside. But past the knees again. Strike two."

"Now you're in trouble," Dermot said.

"Now the big dinge starts to wave the bat. He figures Ford wastes one now."

"Into the dirt," Dermot said.

"That's right, into the dirt. Of course into the dirt. And here it comes. Fast ball right down the middle. Belt-high. Right down the pipe. See this big dinge standin' there like he's made of ice."

"He got fooled," Dermot said.

"That's right, he got fooled. Of course he got fooled. He couldn't move. Takes a third strike on two out with the bases loaded. You never heard boos like that in you life—"

"Where was the game, in Cleveland?"

"From Cleveland. I saw it on television."

"They really must've booed him."

"Booed him to death. Poor bum wanted to try and hit the ball. He couldn't. The crowd didn't know what Ford done to him."

They stopped talking. Dermot finished his pint and held it out. The father took the glass and had his hand out for the wooden tap when Dermot said, "Forget the pint. It's too heavy."

"Of course it's too heavy this time of day."

"Give me a Scotch and water."

"That's right, that's nice and light."

Deirdre said she'd have another.

Dermot had the drink in front of him as a prop now. He fingered it, looked at it, and tried to think of a question or a remark that would start the thing. He did not want to talk with the others listening. He was thinking about how he could get them to leave.

"You need some ice," the father said. He went out from behind the bar and walked through a room where there was a dart board in the pale light coming through a skylight. He came back with a small plastic bowl of tiny ice cubes. He put a couple into Dermot's drink.

"Should've seen him a couple of months ago," Finbar said. "Could hardly walk, he could."

"Oh, it's better now," the father said.

"What happened?" Dermot said.

"Dislocated hip. Ripped ligaments and that. Couldn't move a muscle for a long time."

"How long have you been here?" Dermot said.

"Oh, just a couple of months. It doesn't matter."

Two men came into the place and Dermot's father went down to serve them.

"Have you not seen your father in a while?" Deirdre said.

"I don't know, it's been a while," Dermot said.

"Jesus Christ, a long time, isn't it?" Finbar said.

Dermot didn't answer.

"Man has to leave the house, he gets the blame," Finbar said. "Not the cunt drove him out."

Dermot fingered the glass.

"Jesus, when I met my Maureen, they was screamin' to me that the father was the worst animal on the face of the earth," Finbar said. "Night after night, that's all they was sayin' to me. Now, one time I happen to meet the man. He says to me, 'Sit you down, Finbar.' He says to me, 'It's got that I don't care. I don't care.' I talk to him for a wee little while. Turns out he's a good man. Oh, a good man, all right. So who's the bloody cunt? Goddamned wifey. Jesus Christ, but the wind blows and she's angry. My Maureen, Jesus Christ, she still says her father is a shower of bastards."

"Fookin' better off without any mother and father anyway sometimes," Deirdre said. "Ye heard my father makin' his talk about sodomy? When I was sixteen, I had

278

an affair with a girl and he found out about it. This girl I went to school with—"

"I'll have a pint," Finbar said.

"Hey, I didn't come here to work," the father said.

"—a good Catholic education we were getting," Deirdre said. "When my father found out about me and the other girl, he terrorized me. Terrorized me. The fookin' death penalty for makin' fookin' love. The other girl, Jesus, he wanted her burned at the stake. Now you see my father. Sits there all day. He works in the pub downstairs stocking shelves a couple of hours a night. Does nothing else. I feel rightly sorry for him. But I don't like him. And I don't like to talk to him. He sits there and keeps bringing up sodomy. That's his way of getting back at me for having an affair with this girl."

"He's a fookin' fook," Finbar said.

"Who's this?" Dermot's father said. He put the drink down.

"Her father," Finbar said. "And Maureen's mother is a fookin' fook too."

"Ye got to live with yourself, so ye might as well not have any goddamned people livin' it for ye," Deirdre said.

Dermot's father shrugged. Dermot had the glass to his mouth and was drinking with his eyes closed. The other voices were like shouts in his ears.

"Ever see Marciano box?" Dermot's father said to him.

"I was way too young to see him."

"Oh well, it doesn't matter. What do you think of Clay? Did you see him?" Tiny pieces of fear from the conversation around him were in the father's eyes.

"How long has it been since you've seen each other?" Deirdre said again.

Dermot looked at his father and they did not talk.

"Fook that it matters," Deirdre said. "Men leave here every day. They go to England to find work. They don't know how to write and there's no way to call. Nobody has a phone. They stay there for years and never come back. Some of them come back once, twice a year. A lot of them stay there longer than that. Never a word. Postcard once in a while. Christ, there's nothing unusual about anything in life."

Finbar's throat made a low sound as he finished the pint.

"I've got to be going now," Deirdre said. She picked up her cigarettes.

"To where?"

"We've a big meetin' tonight, you know," she said. "There's lots to do."

"What time is the thing?"

"Oh, ah dunno. Half seven, I guess."

"It'll go on for hours," Finbar said.

"I'll make it," Dermot said.

"Ta ta," Deirdre said. She ruffled Dermot's hair and left.

Dermot watched her walk out. Young, body-swinging walk. He was telling himself, somewhere under the numbness and embarrassment, about how she acted much older than he did.

"Ah well," Finbar said.

Dermot fingered his glass again. He stared at it. He was hoping Finbar would leave now. Then he began to think about what he would say if he were alone with his father. He didn't know.

"Wup!" Finbar said.

A tall guy with his mouth hanging open was in the doorway. He was dressed in a City Hotel bellhop's uniform. The bellhop jerked his thumb up.

"Good lad," Finbar said.

Finbar drained the last in his glass and stood up. "This is the time, Jimmy."

"Let's hope," Dermot's father said.

"Ye want to come?" Finbar said to Dermot.

"I think I'll stay for a while."

The yellow-stained fingers wavered as they brought the cigarette to the lips.

"Go with him, you'll see a few good tricks," Dermot's father said to him.

"I was figuring I'd stay and have a few."

"We're all here all day. Go ahead."

The kid in the bellhop's uniform stood in the doorway, the mouth still hanging open.

"What do you have, broads?" Dermot said.

"Oh, Jesus Christ! Birds? We're doin' somethin' important. We're fixin' a fookin' dog," Finbar said.

Outside, Finbar said to Dermot, "Ye've got to promise ye won't admit ye've seen a thing. And ye too," he said to the bellhop.

"Oh, I wouldn't tell me own mother," the bellhop said.

"Fookin' better not."

"Oh, I wouldn't."

They walked down the empty part of the road, with the hill running to the gray river, and then they came into the smoke of the Brandywell. On a corner crowded with men doing nothing in front of a saloon, Finbar led them down an alley covered with smoke. He tapped on a yellow door which had cheap flowered curtains over the glass top of the door. A man opened the door. He sat in the tiny front room with a greyhound held between his knees. The bellhop took a medicine bottle of colorless liquid out of his pocket and handed it to Finbar. The greyhound's black nose came out to sniff the bottle. Finbar said he wanted a spoon. The man holding the dog brought out a tablespoon. He pulled the dog's jaws open. Finbar's hand was shaking while he poured the liquid onto the tablespoon. The man asked Finbar if he was sure about the amount he was giving the dog. "I know everything there is to know," Finbar said. He put the spoon into the dog's mouth and tipped it. The dog's jaws clamped shut and his tongue started running around while he swallowed. The greyhound's eyes narrowed for a moment against the taste of the liquid. He ran a paw over his face.

"All right, I'm off," Finbar said.

"What do I do?" the bellhop said.

"You stay here for a half hour's time to make sure the dog don't vomit it up. Deal's off if the dog vomits."

"Straight story," the man holding the dog said.

"I'll be here," the bellhop said.

"And when ye leave ye'll keep yer mouth fookin' closed," Finbar said.

281

"Oh, I wouldn't tell me own mother."

"Fookin' better not."

Finbar put the bottle in his pocket. They walked back to the Free Derry Corner. "Now I got to go up in the Creggan and give it to another one," he said.

"What is it?"

"Strychnine. It paralyzes their fookin' hind legs. They'll run in slow motion by tonight. That give us two dogs stopped Mickey is over Strabane now. Stoppin' another. Only six dogs in a race, you know. We've three stopped now, you know. Mickey's hound is in fine form. Now if everybody can keep his fookin' mouth shut we're going to fookin' kill a bookmaker tonight."

"You got a lot of guys in it already," Dermot said.

"What can ye do about it? Mickey, he's the bloke with the dog we're going to win with tonight Mickey and me been out walkin' the road for two weeks now. Go out in the mornin' on the roads where the fellas exercise the dogs. We talk to a man with his dog and we strike a bargain. We give 'em a few pounds to stop his dog in the race. If he was a poor man like these two fellas in town, ten pounds stops his dog But Jesus, it's work, you know. Half six in the mornin' we're over to Strabane to speak to a wee man with a dog. Then we hadda get the man to put up the money. If you got some loose pound notes with you, we can get plenty tonight We're all goin' to make it big tonight. We'll kill a fookin' fat bookmaker. Do ye have a cigarette?"

When he had the cigarette, Finbar said, "Jimmy's the one with all the money. Gets the wee small envelope from America every week. He'll make the family fortune for you tonight."

Finbar said they were leaving at half six from his street. He left and Dermot walked up the hill to the Castle He wanted to think.

When he walked into the bar, there was a roar. "Hump!" Johno was bent down with his arm around a tiny woman, stumpy traces of dwarf in her. Her face was seamy and her hair uncombed. Her chin barely

282

hooked over the top of the bar. A bottle of brandy was on the bar in front of the tiny woman and Johno.

"El Humpo! I want you to meet my friend. Tell him your name, honey."

"Attraca," the woman said.

"No, your real name."

"Half Gate."

"Hear that! Half Gate. How's that for a name, hump?"

She whispered something to Johno and he straightened up and began slapping his hand on the bar. He took Dermot by the shoulder and pulled him close. "Do you know what she said? Tell him what you said, dear. Come on, baby."

"Yer man here has to lift me on. Youse could get on top."

Dermot waited until Johno was finished roaring. When it was quiet, he said, "I saw my father."

"Did you?" Johno said. "Where? At the saloon? Let's go down and see Dad. Do you want to come and meet somebody's daddy?" Johno said to the woman.

She shrugged. "Does he not have money?"

Johno laughed until he began saloon coughing. The amount of blood in Johno's eyes was all Dermot had to see. He did not want Johno coming with him.

Dermot felt a heaviness and burning in his eyes. He told Johno he would be at the hotel. He was hungry when he got to the hotel and the dining room was closed until dinner time. He had the waiter bring up sandwiches, the same tray of ham sandwiches as big as a finger and covered with grass, and coffee. He stretched out on the bed and put sandwiches into his mouth and looked out the window at the Guildhall.

He wondered why people had fathers to begin with. Once the baby is born, all the father can do is hurt, Dermot thought. He was wondering what a father does. Does he teach you anything? The nuns do that. Does he tell you what to do with girls? Dermot never heard of a boy's father telling him anything about sex.

He remembered when he was in high school and there

283

was this girl, Beverly Kleinstuber, who used to let all the guys come into the vestibule and fuck her when they took her home. She lived in one of the six-family houses on Woodward Avenue. Beverly never brought anybody upstairs and let them get on the couch with her. She had a brother or somebody sleeping in the living room. Dermot met her at a dance at Sacred Heart in Glendale and he remembered taking her home and he began rubbing against her in the vestibule, a small vestibule with a white tile floor. The tile was cold in the winter night But in the middle of the vestibule floor there was a mat for wiping feet. Dermot decided Beverly Kleinstuber could put her rear end on the mat while he screwed her and she wouldn't catch pneumonia. He hit Beverly with a head-lock and tried to pull her down to the floor. Beverly threw him off. "What are you, crazy?" she said. "At least if we're standing up and somebody comes home . . ." Dermot took a shot at her standing up. He pushed against Beverly so hard that her back went flat against the bank of doorbells. She must have pushed in three or four doorbells. The buzzer started sounding to open the inside door. Dermot could hear grumbling inside one of the first-floor apartments Beverly Kleinstuber smiled at Dermot. "You stupid motherfucker," she said. She opened the inside door and went into the house.

Dermot thought of other things a father does. Does he teach you religion? Huh. The other way around. The father is the first in the family to fall away from the Church. Does the father get you a job? That's a game for rich guys. The average father may get his kid a job and then he may not get his kid a job. Dermot was thinking that you're probably better off getting your own job than taking one the father gets for you. All he can do is hurt, Dermot thought. Teach the boy to box?

He thought about Tomasullo, who had a gas station on South Road in Jamaica One day, Dermot and a friend from the neighborhood, George Ercoli, were walking past it when Tomasullo called them over and asked them if they wanted to make a dime. They were about ten then. They both jumped up. Dermot could hear himself saying,

284

"Yeah! Yeah!" And Tomasullo said, "Good. Now have a fight with each other and I'll pay yez the dime. Just step in there and let me see yez have a fight with each other." Dermot looked at Ercoli and Ercoli looked at Dermot and hit him in the face. They fought, scrambling, missing and whining and crying, and Tomasullo sat on a wooden Coca-Cola box and watched them. He got up and pushed them apart. "Here," Dermot could remember him saying, "watch what you can do if you know." Tomasullo had Ercoli punch with a right hand. Tomasullo showed Dermot how to slap Ercoli's right hand out with the left forearm and then, in the same motion, with Ercoli's right hand way outside, to punch Ercoli in the face with the left. "A out-and-in motion, out-and-in," he said to Dermot. He made Dermot throw a right hand and he was showing Ercoli how to block it and punch off with the block. When he was finished showing the both of them, Tomasullo sat down on the Coca-Cola box again. "All right, the two of yez start fightin'," he said. Both he and Ercoli had tears streaming down their faces. They looked at each other. They couldn't fight. "Yez won't?" Tomasullo said. "Then yez don't get the dime." He got up and went into the gas station. Dermot started to go in after him and ask for the money. "Get outahere or I kick your ass," Tomasullo said.

He closed his eyes and he was thinking about Tomasullo and his father, and he fell asleep. When he woke up, it was almost six o'clock. He took a shower and got dressed and went downstairs.

Finbar was smoking a cigarette in the doorway of a house halfway up the block from where he lived. A minibus was at the curb. An old man was asleep with his forehead on the steering wheel. Dermot's father was in the middle seat, smoking a cigarette. Finbar stepped into the hut and Dermot followed him in. A woman in the kitchen was eating a fried egg. Her husband came through from the back with a fawn-coated greyhound on a thick leash. The wife put down her plate, grabbed a baby, and held it out. The baby tapped the greyhound on its small head.

285

"For luck," the man said.

"Jesus, with all he's been eatin'," she said. "Pound of raw meat, vegetables, and brown bread. The rest of us standin' here with our bones collapsin' of malnutrition and himself there, eatin' like the Bishop." She put her foot out. "If ye don't have luck, ye'll have an arse full of leather when ye get home."

On the sidewalk, the man with the dog was introduced as Mickey O'Kane. Two men standing alongside the minibus bumped into each other trying to open the door for the dog. The dog went in and stood in circles on the seat. Dermot's father patted the dog on the head Mickey O'Kane got in after the dog. Gently, he lifted the dog over the rear seat and into a space at the back of it. The dog stood there excited, tongue hanging out. Mickey patted him and cooed to him and eased him down until he was on his haunches. Men were pushing into the minibus now. All of them called out, "Good lad," to the greyhound. Dermot and Finbar climbed into the back. Dermot's father said hello with a nod of his head. He was taking a deep drag on a cigarette.

Finbar lit a cigarette. "Half six, let's be off now."

"Come on, off with ye," Mickey O'Kane said.

"Shut up, I'm ten-to-one on against the lot of you," the driver said. "Here's Danny comin' now. He gets notions, you know."

"What notions?" Finbar said. "I wouldn't fookin' trust him."

When Danny, a tiny man in a cap, jammed in, it made eight men and a dog in the minibus. The old man driving started it up. Grinding, bucking with little backfires, the minibus started down the street. Fumes began to fill the inside. Finbar tugged at a window. It was stuck. "Somebody open a window," he said.

"Too cold for me," Danny said.

"You can die in your own grave," Finbar said. "The dog needs air. Jesus, his lungs'll flop in the fumes."

A cold wet breeze blew into the minibus. They drove through the streets of cement huts of the Brandywell and out onto a road overlooking the river covered with darkness.

Finbar sat with one arm over the back, petting the greyhound. His breath showed in the cold air while he talked about horse racing with Mickey O'Kane.

"Who does Vincent O'Brien look for when he wants a jockey?" Finbar said. "Piggott, that's who."

Mickey said, "I think Williamson is the best in the world. Put him and Piggott in the same identical race."

Finbar began yelling. "What's the matter with Piggott? He fookin' won the fookin' Irish Derby, the fookin' English Derby, and the fookin' French Derby for fook's sake."

"Close the window, it's blowin' cold on the animal," Mickey O'Kane said.

The bus stopped at a Northern Ireland customs station. Two soldiers glanced over the bus. A uniformed customs guard waved them on. A couple of hundred yards farther down the road the minibus went right through a Republic of Ireland customs station. A man was reading in the customs office.

The bus became filled with fumes again. "Danny, for Jesus' sake, will you not give the animal some air?" Mickey said.

The road ran past empty fields bordered with hedges and trees with winter-green leaves. At the track everybody stood in attendance at the side of the minibus while Mickey O'Kane brought out the dog. A young kid in a white linen jacket walked the dog into the track. He helped the dog into one of a row of green wooden boxes that looked like filing cabinets. There was a slot in the door for the dog to peer out. Barking came from a couple of the other boxes. A man with a roast-beef face came out of an office in a cement hut. He had fat eyes that became agitated when he saw Mickey O'Kane and Finbar. They walked over to a small wooden stand where a girl was putting out plates of sandwiches.

"Want something to eat?" Dermot said.

"I will, I'll have a Harp," Finbar said.

Dermot's father was standing behind them. Finbar

287

moved over to make room for him. Dermot's father stepped up to the counter on the far side. Finbar had to move next to Dermot to make room for the father. They stood there, Dermot with sandwiches and a glass of milk, Finbar drinking Harp beer in the middle, and, on the other side, Dermot's father drinking Harp beer and smoking a cigarette and looking away from the two of them.

"You come here much?" Dermot said to Finbar.

"Oh, now and then, now and then. Every fookin' night it's open."

Dermot's father was smiling. He picked up the bottle of beer.

Dermot waited until the father had his mouth on the beer. Somehow, this made it easier to get the question out.

"Do you bet on dogs much?" he said.

The father took the bottle out of his mouth.

"Flagler," he said.

The father shoved the bottle of beer back into his mouth. The look in his eyes showed that he knew he had just made a mistake. Flagler is a dog track in Florida. He had opened the door to a conversation. Now he closed it as tightly as he could.

At eight o'clock there were, at the most, fifty people at the track. The fat-eyed owner stood in the grass and swore to himself. The people stood under a shedrow that had room for one hundred and fifty. Bookmakers in jackets and ties, cigarettes hanging from their mouths, stood on soda cases and chalked their odds on slates. The fat-eyed man waved his hands. Six boys in linen jackets walked greyhounds for the first race into the weeds covering the infield of the track. A chicken-wire fence ran around the track. The amusement-park sound, the clicking and humming of a ride between rides, meant the rabbit track had started. The rabbit slid past, going around the turn and down to the starting cages. There were so few people that the clack of the cages opening was louder than the yell from the shedrow. The two dogs on the lead ran with lean action. The ones following scrambled. The race was three hundred yards. The finish line was a bright light hung on a wire over the track.

"That's the camera for the photo finish," Finbar said.

"Do they have that much equipment here?" Dermot asked.

"Notatall. It's a hike."

A meat truck stopped outside the admissions gate. A waiter from the City Hotel jumped down. The fat-eyed track owner stood alongside the gate and glared at him. The waiter pretended not to see him. He walked with his head down, went past them through the grass and stopped at the rail on the first turn. When the owner went back into his cement hut, they walked quickly around to the waiter, who took out some money.

"He's a shower of bastards," the waiter said, nodding at the owner's hut.

"He's afraid of us, you know," Finbar said.

"For one race, I never had the dog in better shape," Mickey O'Kane said. "And he's only got two to beat, the others can't fookin' walk."

"You saw them?" Dermot said.

"No, I just know. He done what he had to do."

"Aye," the waiter said.

"One race, that's all you should need," Finbar said. "Right Jimmy?"

Dermot's father nodded.

"Jimmy, for fookin' Jesus' sake."

Dermot's father was paying attention to taking out a cigarette and lighting it.

Dermot said to O'Kane, "Is it good to have a dog trained only for one race? I know from the horse racing that they never like to point a horse for one race. It's a sure way to break him down. The way they do it, if they do right, they get a horse ready for a whole series of races. They don't do that with dogs?"

"Do ye not have dog racin' in New York?" O'Kane asked Dermot.

"No, they got that in Florida," he said. "That's where Flagler is."

Dermot's father was reading the entry card.

"You know," Mickey said, "a good dog like this one here costs twenty pound. He's worth eighty pound now. If he could win a race like this one here, be worth a hundred pound maybe. So you want to win a bet, improve the price of your dog at the same time. We're all poor men. We promised the others ten pound apiece to stop their dog. And my dog here, see him on the program. Number three. He's done seventeen-five. We know we have him so's he can do it in seventeen tonight. Here, look at the three he has to beat. Outclass them, he will."

The name of his dog was Glenshane Rover. In his last four races he was unplaced, the program said. The rest of the small printing under his name was the dog's times. While they were talking, the dogs came out for the second race. To kill time Dermot decided to place a bet. "The fawn bitch?" Finbar said.

"Jesus, no. See the hooky tail? That means the dog is no good on turns." Mickey O'Kane was emphatic. "Hooky tails don't go 'round turns."

Dermot didn't bet. The rabbit skimmed past and the traps opened. The dog Dermot liked broke second. He was a nose off the lead. They went around the first turn. The dog came out of it a half-nose off the leader. The dog with the hooky tail just did miss at the finish. Finbar and Mickey paid no attention to this. They were talking about betting their dog. They walked down to the bookmakers under the shed. Dermot's father stayed at the rail.

"How often do you do this?" Dermot said to the waiter.

"Give a dog something to make him run a wee bit slow? All the time."

"And nobody ever gets wise?"

"Aye, nobody ever gets wise."

"Who gives you the stuff?"

"Bloke lives on the New Road."

"What does he do?"

"He does fook all."

"How do you know he's giving you strychnine?"

"You don't."

"Does it always work?"

"Christ no. It's never worked yet."

"Why bother then?"

"Someday it might work, you know."

The small crowd was standing in front of the book-makers, who kept chalking new odds as they took bets. The first bookmaker wore a hound's-tooth sports jacket. The name on the slate said Charley Mullan. He had Glenshane Rover at 8–5. Danny from the minibus handed him a pound. Mullan reached into a leather bag and brought out a ticket. He gave it to Danny, then changed Glenshane Rover to 7–5.

Finbar spoke to him with the cigarette in his mouth. "Get into the pig," he said. "Oh, he's a frightful shower of bastards, he is. You have big American money. You can hurt him bad."

Dermot took out a five-pound note. "Number three to win," he said.

"Honored to have your business," Charley Mullan said. He handed over the ticket. He did not change the price on his slate.

"Look at the bastard, he's challengin' you," Finbar said.

"What do you mean?"

"He's keeping the price up to try and get you to bet more. See the others?" The bookmaker next to him, Quinn, had Glenshane Rover at 1–1.

"Go ahead, give it to the bloody cunt," Finbar said.

Dermot handed Mullan two pounds. "Honored by your business," Mullan said.

As Dermot stepped away, Finbar came forward with a handful of silver. "The three dog to win."

"Honored by your business," Charley Mullan said.

"Oh, Jimmy!" Finbar called.

Dermot's father walked down from the place where he was standing at the rail.

"Here ye go, Jimmy, give it to this fat bloody cunt."

"I'll take a slight stab," Dermot's father said.

"Oh, Christ, don't just stab. Skewer the bastard."

"It's awfully hard to kill a bookmaker," Dermot's father said.

He smiled and Dermot smiled at the same time.

"Go to it, Jimmy," Finbar said.

Dermot's father took out two five-pound notes. "This is tougher than it looks, you know," he said to Finbar. "I could use a printin' press to stay up with you."

He walked over and handed the two five-pound notes to Mullan, the bookmaker.

"Honored by your business," Charley Mullan said.

"We'll kill him," Finbar said. "Oh, he's a shower of bastards."

They all walked up toward the turn. As Dermot kept going up the rail his father kept moving up the rail too.

"I'm goin' to stand right here," Finbar said finally. "I want to see Charley Mullan's face when he watches the race."

Dermot stopped between Finbar and the finish line. Now, his father moved closer. As long as Finbar stood between the father and Dermot, the father was reasonably relaxed.

"We'll kill him. Oh, he's a shower of bastards," Finbar said.

Mickey O'Kane went far down the track and stood alone.

"He's got all the quid he could borrow or steal for a month ridin' this time," Finbar said.

"What do you have on it?" Dermot asked.

"Whole fookin' dole."

"What if he doesn't win?"

"Notatall. He'll rightly win."

"But what if he doesn't?"

"Dead simple. Mickey has to kill his dog."

When the dogs came out for the race, Glenshane Rover walked easily. All five of the others seemed to have a normal walking motion. No slowness or stiffness in the hind legs. The boys started walking toward the traps. The waiter from the City Hotel took out the cigarettes. His hand shook as he passed them. Finbar's hand shook as he took a drag on the cigarette. "Look at that Charley Mullan," he said. Charley Mullan was brushing chalk from his sleeve. He did not bother to watch the dogs. The traps opened and the dogs lunged out. All six of them. Glenshane Rover was even with the last dog. The other four tore after the rabbit. Glenshane Rover picked up a little coming into the first turn. Only a little.

Dermot tapped the waiter. "Nobody looks poisoned to me," he said.

"Oh, we give it to them too late," the waiter said. "I knew we had to do it earlier. So's it took effect."

Glenshane Rover's running action became confused on the turn. He looked like he was running up an escalator.

The cigarette came out of Finbar's mouth. He turned to an old man standing behind him. "Are you going to Mickey O'Kane's funeral?"

The man's mouth dropped open. "Jesus Christ! When did he die?"

"Not yet, but he's expected."

Up the track, Mickey O'Kane leaned heavily on the fence. He looked like he had shot himself. Charley Mullan was up on his box, rubbing his hands together as he watched the dogs scramble down the stretch. Glenshane Rover still fifth and, it looked, a lifetime or so away from learning to run fast.

When Mickey O'Kane walked up to the bus with the dog, Finbar and Dermot were a step behind. Finbar gave the dog a half-kick, half-shove. Tongue hanging out, tail wagging, the dog looked around the inside of the bus. Finbar put a hand under the dog's belly and threw him over the last seat. Finbar turned around with his hand out. The dog looked up to be petted. Finbar hit the dog on top of the head as hard as he could. The dog let out a yelp. Mickey O'Kane dove into the bus. He slapped the dog in the face.

"Shut up, ye smokin' cunt."

14:

In the darkness in the bus, Dermot's father said to him, "I'm good and tired. The hip knocks me out sometimes."

"What could you do," Dermot said.

"What I'm going to do is, I'm going to go to bed and I'll see you in the morning. We'll sit down."

"All right, fine."

"What I'm going to do, I'm going to bed and I'll see you in the morning. I'm stoppin' right at McCann's. Right over the store. So I'll be in there in the morning. All right, lads, you can let me out."

The bus stopped at the bar and his father got out, and then the bus went through the Brandywell and it was all right with Dermot. He wanted to meet Deirdre.

At the meeting, there were far too many people in the attic. The floor felt like it was floating on liquid. It swayed, seemed to tilt, creaked, and was ready to collapse. People stood pressed against each other or sat on the floor. The smell was wet clothes and no soap. Cigarette smoke was so thick those on the other side of the room seemed far away. Rain drummed on the roof while Liam Quigley, his finger poking the smoky air, talked to them. He spoke with a lot of breath for each group of words. It made the words more forceful. And it gave a rhythm to his speaking that made it very hard for you not to pay attention.

". . . The workingman. All over the earth. Is oppressed by governments. Acting for business interests. I look rightly on the theory. That none of us can be free. Until all of us are free. If Angela Davis is imprisoned unjustly in America. Then we in Derry can never truly be free. No matter how many times we throw out the police. No matter how many times we throw out the Army. Therefore I say to you, We are at the start of a long journey. Do not be afraid. Do not despair. Do not panic. Do not fight out of sheer nervousness or fear. Stand together. We can erode. The oppressive government. With civil disobedience and political activity. The governments are hoping. That we muck about into violence. We understand that violence. Would cost us unnecessarily at this stage. Do not be angered into violence. Do have patience. Do have resolve. Do be canny."

"What is it we do then?" a man in the middle of the room called out.

"The workers will strike," Liam said.

Hands went up all over the room. "What do we do?"

"Anyone can man a picket line," Liam said.

A woman near Dermot called out, "That was a rightly dumb question."

"How would I know?" the man said. "I haven't had a flamin' job in me life."

"Prospect of one'd scare him to death," another woman called out.

A man said, "I worked in Manchester two years ago."

"And what?" somebody said to him.

"I gave it up as a bad job."

"Damien?" Liam said.

"I have a resolution!" Damien was against the wall in the back of the room. "Oppression is a world-wide tactic of capitalism. Therefore, duPont is one of the major oppressors in the world. We must set an example for workingmen everywhere by closing the duPont plant here in Derry. Demand that it be turned over to the workers."

"Well," Liam said, "what do you think of Damien's resolution?"

A man got off the floor. "Will not this take away from me time in the plant?"

"Aye," Liam said. "Not just a wee dispute, you know. A full workers' strike."

"I want me job," the man said.

"Your job?" Damien said. "What of the people in Rhodesia? They suffer because of the very work you do. What of Angela Davis?"

Deirdre was up now. "I stand second to nobody in despising duPont. But we know that duPont pays the highest wages to workers in Derry. We know that duPont hires more workers from the Bogside than any place in Northern Ireland. Therefore, I believe it not to be in our interests to close down duPont."

Another man got up. "No worker in his right mind would strike his job at duPont."

"The workers will strike duPont for the good of all," Damien said. "If the workers cannot see it for themselves, then we will show the workers what is good for them."

Somebody called out, "How would you know what's good for a worker?"

"The last job you had," a woman yelled, "you was elbowin' your way out of the mother."

"Now, that's no example," Liam said. "Lenin never had a job and he was the best friend the workingman ever had."

Deirdre held up her hand. "A strike at duPont would hurt our working people more than it would hurt duPont. I say that if we are to conduct strikes, then we must start with the shirt factories, where the workers are most exploited."

A group of girls cheered.

A heavy-set man in a dark-blue suit jacket and maroon sweater came to the front of the room. Liam introduced him. "This is Michael Heaney. He is the chief of staff for Northern Ireland of the Official Irish Republican Army."

Michael Heaney spoke in a low voice. The people stopped moving so they could hear him. "I just got out of Belfast," he said. "We cannot afford any more of that.

When you fight the British Army, you're fighting trained troops."

Dermot recognized Eamonn, the café owner, when he jumped up. "I totally agree with everything you say. We don't fight an army."

"Civil disobedience can bring the people together," Heaney said. "First you need the people together before you can think of fighting. We can be together, and we can bring down Stormont. The political activity will give us a strong voice in Westminster. And while we do this, we can begin the long-range strategy of taking people over the border for weapons training. But violence should be our last resort. For self-defense."

"We're no animals," the woman shouted.

Eamonn started clapping. The whole room broke into applause.

Deirdre glanced over and saw Dermot. She picked her way through and came next to him.

"What did you do?"

"Went to the dog races."

"How did Mickey O'Kane's pup do?"

"They were beating him with sticks a half hour ago."

"Finbar doing it first," she said. She began laughing. "I wonder why Finbar has not done permanent injury to his shoulder. Hitting the dog so often."

Somebody was shouting and Liam began thumping a table for quiet.

"Gerard Hagerty?"

"Are we not through with the meeting?" Gerard Hagerty said. He had a long chin that he used like a pointer.

"Aye, you have the last statement," Liam said.

Gerard Hagerty's chin waved in the air. "Do you not give out the guns now?"

Liam closed his eyes. A few people groaned. But over half the place came alive.

Heaney stepped forward. "We said there'll be no guns."

"How do you expect us to fight soldiers if you don't give us guns?" Gerard Hagerty said.

"You fight a government with strikes. You don't fight soldiers," Deirdre said.

"That's all very nice," Gerard Hagerty said. "But we're going to have to go at the soldiers, you know. If yez don't give us guns. Then we'll just go to the people who give us guns."

"Gerard," Liam said, "why did you stay here all night sayin' nothing while we made it plain there'd be no guns?"

"I thought you was just talking, you know," Gerard Hagerty said.

He picked up an Army jacket. He put it on. His hand into a pocket. He pulled out a black beret and slapped it on.

"I'm ready to fight and I'm ready to fookin' die for Ireland. Up the Provos!"

"Up the Provos!" somebody else yelled.

Gerard walked out. Old women with mean mouths followed him. One man left. Then another. Then they were leaving by the twos and threes. They looked at Deirdre with disgust as they went past. The young ones were moving around and looking at each other. Deirdre went to the front of the room. Her right fist went up. In a high clear voice, with a little moan to it, she started to sing. "Arise ye prisoners of starvation . . ."

The whole room was standing, clapping in rhythm, singing loudly.

> " 'Tis the final conflict
>   Let each man take his place,
>   The International-alley
>   Shall free the human race."

Dermot was out the door while they were still cheering. He walked down the street and through the wall. As he started across the Guildhall Square, Dermot saw the sky alive with orange from a fire off to the left, up William Street. Orange cinders spiraled into the sky. Alive with color, they blew over the rooftops. He walked to the pillbox by Chada Fashions and looked up William Street. A small crowd stood in the doorway of a fish-and-chips shop and looked up the street trying to see the fire. Every place else on the street was dark. Dermot walked into

William Street and started for the fire. Soldiers leaned against the buildings on both sides of the street. They were in helmets with thick plastic visors. They killed time knocking batons against green metal shields. They did not stop Dermot. He walked up William Street to the corner of Rossville Street. A left turn at the corner takes you into the Bogside. The street with the high flats and Free Derry Corner. A right turn led through an empty lot and the rear of a paint store which was in flames. The fire trucks were out of sight, around on the street, directly in front of the paint store. Firemen from the trucks were in the lot at the rear of the paint store. They lugged a hose and aimed it up at flames reaching into the night from a second-story window. Water came out of the hose in a splurt. It died. Then it came out again, first in an arc and then in a thick white stream. The firemen aimed it at the window. The flames became a red throat around the stream of water.

There was a yell behind Dermot. On Rossville Street, all the way back to the high flats and to Free Derry Corner, kids were shouting and running to see the fire. There were a couple of hundred of them already. They came out onto William Street and cheered as the red throat swallowed the stream of water. Four policemen came up from the paint store and began pushing the crowd back. Dermot went with the kids, back across William Street and into Rossville Street and the Bogside. Two policemen stayed in the middle of William Street watching the fire. They kept looking at the crowd and then up William Street to the soldiers.

A kid came out of the crowd. In a blue polo shirt, bare arms in the cold air, hips swinging. A girl was a little behind him, hands in her raincoat pockets. Deirdre came out of the crowd after the kid. Deirdre's coat was open. The blue sweatshirt did not lump over her hips. Her walk came right through her clothes, the firelight playing on her.

"Be careful, Boxo," she was saying.

"That's no fun," the kid said.

He grinned. He had a front tooth missing. The rest of

299

the teeth, even now at night, were yellow with green tartar at the bottoms. Even when he grinned, there was this sadness in his face.

"I'm not sayin' you can't have fun," Deirdre said.

"What're ye sayin' to me, then?" he said.

"I'm sayin' don't get caught," Deirdre said.

He buried his face into the shoulder of her coat. He kissed her on the coat and then danced back. Wrapped around his right hand was a chain, not too thick to swing but still thick enough to hurt somebody badly.

"Ah, there's my Boxo," Deirdre said.

Boxo laughed. Kids were running around in the darkness and now this big tall kid came out to stand with Boxo.

"Dutsy," Deirdre said to him.

"Eh?"

"Tie your shoelaces or ye'll trip."

He dropped to a knee and tied the frayed laces of pointy black shoes. He scrambled up as Boxo went swaggering up to the corner of William Street. He had a big piece of broken cement behind his back. Boxo came so close to the policemen that they didn't bother to look at him. They looked back at the crowd, then the fire, then at the crowd again. Boxo walked straight into them and he brought the cement from behind his back and, still walking, threw it side-arm. It caught one of the cops in the back of the neck and his hat flew off and he went onto his knees. Dutsy threw a rock at the other cop, who twisted away, and the rock missed. Boxo, Dutsy, and the girl were running back to the crowd with the cop chasing them. A small boy in a suit jacket came running out into the orange firelight throwing a bottle at the cop. Now the cop saw that if he came any farther into Rossville Street he was going to be trapped. The soldiers around the corner on William Street could not see him.

There was a shout and the crowd in the darkness on Rossville Street started running for the cop. Everybody in the crowd had bottles or rocks. The cop started running away as bottles broke around him. The cop who had been knocked down was going backward onto William Street and now he turned and broke into a run. He was gone, and the second cop turned the corner. He stopped dead as a rock hit him square in the back. He started up again and he was gone. The crowd kept going straight, across William Street and into the lot at the rear of the paint store, and the three firemen working the hose on the flames coming out the back window of the paint store heard them coming. One of them turned to look. He held up his hand. A bottle just missed him. Now there was a shower of rocks at the firemen. They had their backs to the crowd and a live hose in their hands and the rocks and bottles came around them and all they could do was drop the hose, the water squirting crazily on the ground. The firemen ran out of the lot and toward their engines, which were out of sight on the street running in front of the paint store.

Deirdre and Dermot walked out into William Street with the crowd. A loud "woe" ran through the kids. To the right, halfway up William Street, running as hard as they could in a tight formation, like a football team coming under a kickoff, came perhaps forty soldiers. The kids ran out of the lot and everybody went back into Rossville Street. The soldiers racing in this V formation came wheeling around the corner into Rossville Street. They came with helmets, plastic face shields, gas masks, untapered white-ash clubs in their right hand. The green metal shields went up. The shields and wire-screen tops for the soldiers to peer through. The crowd of kids had been giving way. Now the kids were running as the soldiers came racing at them.

The tall kid and Boxo were the first to stop. The tall kid wheeled and sent a big piece of rock low. It hit the ground and skipped up against the creased fatigue pants of one of the soldiers. Boxo threw his rock. It went on a line, low, and came skipping up. A soldier's polished boots jumped into the air. Not high enough. The rock kicked off his ankles. Now they all were bouncing rocks at the soldiers' shins. Bottles broke, the glass spattering. The soldiers stopped running, their shields up, clubs waving around their ankles trying to ward off rocks, they began backing up and going around the corner into William Street.

From the high flats and the cement huts back in the Bogside, old men were walking down the streets, knotting handkerchiefs. Dermot was looking at the handkerchiefs when the first pop sounded on William Street. A plume of smoke rose in front of the crowd. A barrage of gas was fired now. Soldiers came around the corner slowly and tried walking through the gas to get at the crowd. Rocks and bottles had their feet dancing. They withdrew back up William Street.

The kids began running out of the darkness and jumping into the gas. A little girl stood in the gas with her hands over her head. She took deep breaths.

"Give us more, it's good for us!"

Boxo was dancing and swaggering in the gas. "More, ye fookers! More!"

Across the street a crowd was in front of a three-story brick building. A sign said it was a whisky and fruit warehouse. The older ones came out with empty bottles. Kids grabbed the bottles and ran up toward the corner so they could be ready to throw them. Kids pushed empty barrels out of the warehouse. They turned the barrels upright and began to bang on them like drums. The light from the fire was brighter now. With not enough water on it, the fire in the paint store was licking through the roof. The flame from the window went high into the sky with a color which had the flatness of lightning.

The crowd was now about three hundred. Growing, too.

"Is this your nonviolence?" Dermot said.

"Aye," Deirdre said. "I don't think it's so bad, do you?"

"Christ, it's a riot."

"Well, is it a riot as bad as Belfast?"

"No. But sure as hell could get there in a hurry."

"Aye. It could build into something. And it will some night soon if the government do not recognize what this is about."

"They turn this place into Belfast, you can forget about me," Dermot said.

"Oh, it will get possibly worse than Belfast," she said. "They're not going to listen to anything we have to say. Governments only listen to dead bodies. The government will keep mucking about and then the gunmen here will take over."

"Then what are you doing with all your meetings and politics?"

"Trying."

"But it's not going to work."

"Aye, that's not going to work."

"So why try?"

"You're supposed to, you know."

A lot of kids were standing out in William Street calling to the soldiers and throwing rocks. The rest of the crowd milled in the street. Gerard Hagerty in his beret was pointing at people and yelling. Finbar was across the street. Deirdre laughed and they walked over to him. A handkerchief was knotted around his neck, a cigarette in his mouth. He watched three girls, the oldest no more than thirteen, break up a piece of pavement. The girls were striking the pavement with pieces from another flagstone. The pavement came apart one piece at a time. Somebody would grab the piece and run into the crowd with it. Finbar shook his head. "Stay easy," he said to Dermot. He walked back into the darkness. The girls kept breaking the pavement.

There was a noise from the corner. The first kids came running back into Rossville Street. Gerard Hagerty came backward through the crowd. The last kids coming into Rossville Street were tearing, mouths open, arms pumping. The football formation of soldiers right after them did not have time to figure out the number of people waiting for them. There was a shout and the whole crowd rushed the soldiers. Now the rocks and bottles had them backing up and half running away. One of the soldiers was going back when he stopped and took a swipe with his club at a very small boy. The soldier missed and his arm dragged him off balance. He put out his hand to keep his whole body from falling. Boxo was out of the crowd and on the soldier. The chain came around once.

The soldier's helmet flew off. The soldier was upright again, short hair wet from sweat, a very young red-cheeked face. His hands went out to catch the chain. Boxo brought the chain half around. Now with the soldier's hands out, Boxo whipped the chain sidearm. The double-up links went over the soldier's arms and caught him full on the side of the face. Boxo took off and came flying back to the crowd as a flock of soldiers, shields up, ran out to help the one being beaten. Dutsy paraded through the crowd, wearing the soldier's helmet. Boxo grabbed it from him and put it on. Boxo walked to the front of the crowd with the helmet on. His right fist went up in the air and he began singing:

> "A nation once again
> A nation once again."

The crowd started singing with him. Men with handkerchiefs knotted around their necks, young boys in rumpled suit jackets, girls in raincoats, women in broken shoes, their seamed faces alive in the light from the fire that the firemen could not get near.

Finbar came back with a sledgehammer on his shoulder. Saying nothing he brought the sledgehammer up over his head and swung it down onto the pavement. Finbar worked automatically, smashing one pavement block, stepping up to another, and smashing it without changing the rhythm of his swing. Hands grabbed the pieces of pavement as quickly as they broke under the sledgehammer. Sweat covered Finbar's face. He stopped and wiped his forehead with his hand. Finbar looked at his hand to see what it was that he had wiped from his face.

Down the street, under a light in front of the high flats, a crowd gathered. Michael Heaney and Liam were walking toward it. Deirdre began running. Dermot had to take long steps to stay with her. In front of the high flats, two boys, fourteen at the most, were standing with a child's wagon filled with milk bottles of gasoline. Wicks of torn cleaning rags were packed tightly in the necks of the bottles.

"What's this now?" Michael said.

"Good enough show without them," Liam said.

Eddie Canavan came out of the darkness on the side of the high flats. Three men were with him. "They're all right," Canavan said.

"El Humpo!" Johno shambled out of the shadows after Canavan.

"They're all right?" Michael said. "One thing leads to another. We're at rocks now. Let's keep it there."

"I hope to Christ one thing leads to another," Canavan said. "Leave them alone here."

Milk bottles clinked. Two boys came up pulling another wagon of petrol bombs.

"Let's get them out of here," Michael said.

"They stay," Canavan said. He tugged on the front of his jacket. His shoulders shook inside the jacket. He wanted to get the suit just right over his shoulders.

The three men stood behind him, staring at Michael and Liam.

Deirdre spoke very softly. "Will you not be the first to throw the petrol bombs at the soldiers? Or do the wee small boys get the honor?"

"Fook off," Canavan said.

"You fook off," Deirdre said.

Johno clapped Canavan on the shoulder. "Come on, let's stop the bullshit with these humps. I've seen better fights than this one here. Let's get a drink until they start doin' some important things."

Canavan smiled. "We're just helpin', you know."

While they were talking, kids came pounding up to the wagons and Michael and Liam were trying to stop them from grabbing petrol bombs, but two or three hands grabbed bottles and got away and Michael and Liam saw it was too late.

Canavan stepped aside as the kids grabbed the bottles. Canavan had his hands out to protect his suit. He walked back into the darkness.

"You comin'?" Johno said.

"I don't know," Dermot said.

"You're a sucker if you stay," Johno said. He left.

Michael and Liam and Deirdre stood in the street. Michael was shaking his head. "The only way to stop the fooker is to shoot him," he said. "Christ, I don't know. Are we gettin' close to that?"

The next time the kids came flying around the corner with the soldiers after them, seven or eight petrol bombs came through the air. The petrol bombs hit the street in a splash of flame which came up waist-high and then went out. The soldiers ran back up William Street. The kids followed them and stood in the darkness on William Street and threw petrol bombs up the block. Soldiers shouted to each other as the flames jumped out of the pavement near them.

Boxo's girl was standing out in William Street. She was singing a rock tune to herself and her hands tugged absently on a lock of hair covering the right side of her face.

"You better not stand there, Kitty," Michael told her. "Petrol bombs. They may shoot now."

Kitty didn't answer.

"They may shoot," Michael said.

Kitty shrugged. She kept looking into the darkness on William Street and singing her rock tune while her fingers tugged at her hair.

Three soldiers raced from behind a building on the other corner of Rossville Street. A small kid was running without seeing them. One of the soldiers chopped at the kid's head with his club. The kid went down. People started to rush at the soldiers. The football-team formation came from the other side and the people had to back up and throw petrol bombs. They could not get at the three soldiers dragging the kid away. A woman screamed and tried to run out after them. She couldn't get through. Petrol bombs hit the street. The woman screamed and collapsed. Michael glanced back and kept walking. "She'll see him in a year," he said.

"He was only nine or ten," Dermot said.

"They give a fook?" Michael said. "Borstal, see him in a year," he said.

A truck came careening out of the Brandywell and

onto Rossville Street. It was a flatbed truck with men standing on the back, waving their arms. The truck made a turn and ran up on the sidewalk and came back into the street and began going in a circle, riding on sidewalks and street. The flatbed was loaded with beer cases. When the truck stopped, men attacked the beer cases. More came running up. Like locusts, they were going through the cases until the floorboards showed. Johnny Killeen in his gray smock from the garbage job came running to the beer truck.

It was a block party at Free Derry Corner. They were talking excitedly, forcing bottlecaps off with rocks, then jamming the foaming tops into their mouths to lose as little as possible. The beer truck was racing around the street. Two guys stood on the back, hands in the air for balance, while the truck started going in circles. One of them fell onto his knees. He grabbed two cases of beer left on the flatbed and clung to them while the truck went around in circles. Up Rossville Street, at the corner, the fire from the paint store waned. But the light from a petrol bomb went through the air. The kids were still at it.

Michael leaned against the hood of a car talking to a couple of young guys wearing James Connolly buttons. One of them, with a round baby face but deep nervous eyes, spoke between drags on his cigarette.

Johnny Killeen was with them. He lurched and held a beer bottle out as if it were a pistol. He pointed it up at the wall. Finbar had the bottlecap off another bottle of beer. His mouth came down on the foam like he was ducking for apples. Finbar handed the bottle to Johnny, who took his empty bottle and threw it in the air. It landed on the start of the incline to the wall. He began drinking the new bottle of beer.

"Anybody want one?" Finbar called out. He had two cases of beer on the street.

Dermot didn't answer. Nobody else said anything. "Well, I'll have one," Deirdre said. Finbar reached down and grabbed a bottle and took it over to her. Johnny Killeen was out in the street with the bottle up. Draining it, he lurched a little and went to Free Derry Corner with the bottle in his hand. He stood under the street-light and held the bottle out and pretended to be shooting at the wall. The back of the gray duster billowed out as the shot came through him and he flopped on his back in the street.

The bar was dark when Dermot got back to the hotel. He had a headache and his legs were wobbly from all the running. When Johnny Killeen was hit, the soldiers sent an armored car down the hill from Butcher's Gate. Michael told everybody to get out of there, the Army would lift anybody near the body. Dermot saw Deirdre get into a car. He ran up Wellington Street. Somebody opened a door and told him to come in. He kept going.

He went up to the room. The room smelled like goats from all the whisky. Two girls were in one bed. Johno was in the other bed, on his back, snoring off a drunk. His shoes were sticking out from under the blankets.

Dermot went downstairs to the sitting room and flopped on a worn couch against the wall. He put his legs over the arm of the couch and fell asleep. The day porter shook him at six-thirty. He went upstairs and banged on the door. One of the girls opened it. She was already dressed. The other one was in the shower. Johno was still stretched out like a traffic victim. Dermot took off his shoes. The girl giggled. He smoothed the bed and got on top of the blanket and used the bedspread as a cover. He never saw the girls leave the room.

15:

The Guildhall clock woke him with its half-hour chiming at nine-thirty. In the shower, he stuck his face up to the nozzle and tried to wash the night away. He reached out for the toothpaste and brush and did his teeth in the shower.

Johno moved his head but didn't open his eyes while Dermot was getting dressed.

"Stay there, I'll be back," Dermot said.

"I'm fuckin' dead," he mumbled.

In the dining room he ate oysterettes while he was waiting for the girl to bring bacon and eggs. He wondered how they all could fight so much. Nobody ever ate. He was in front of the hotel asking the porter for directions to court when the clock started the ten-o'clock toll. He walked through a very early spring day, the sky bright, the air clean, the sidewalks sparkling. The court was on one of the lifeless streets almost into the fountain, the Protestant section. The policemen stood in front of the two-story court building. Four soldiers walked along the far side.

Deirdre was on a bench in the lobby. She was leaning over for the last drag before dropping the cigarette. Liam stood in front of her. Ronald bent over whispering to Deirdre while she finished the cigarette. The eyes in his ferret face darted from side to side.

When she saw Dermot, Deirdre put a finger to her lips. Liam took Dermot's arm.

309

"I was in bed early so I could be fresh for this morning," she said. "You look fit yourself." Liam pressed Dermot's arm.

"I feel good myself," Dermot said.

A cop, pink cheeks sticking out from under his black hat—Christ, Dermot said to himself, the cops in Northern Ireland do look like pigs—had come up behind the bench. Smoke ran out of his mouth and came up around his eyes a little.

A thin woman with sunken cheeks dropped onto the bench alongside Deirdre. The woman clutched the front of an old tan cloth coat.

"Ye have a cigarette?" she said to Deirdre.

Deirdre shook her head yes and went into her coat pockets.

"I'm walkin' around stupid, I swear to God," the woman said.

"Aren't we all?" Deirdre said.

"How long will ye remain here?" the woman said.

"Oh, ah dunno. Hour or so."

"Should I go home and wait?"

"Ah dunno."

"Well, should I?"

Deirdre closed her eyes. Ronald leaned past her to speak to the woman. "This child must walk into a courtroom as a defendant within the next thirty minutes. Will you please let her compose herself?"

"It's all right," Deirdre said. "You'll have to decide. I cannot leave here."

The woman shook her head. "I'm walkin' around stupid, I swear to God."

"That's all right," Deidre said.

"You see, they're in school. Saint John's Convent Primary School. Now, they do not know where I am if they was to come lookin' for me."

"I see," Deidre said.

"I left the wee girl home with the cat."

"Yes," Deirdre said.

"Well, what should I do?"

Oliver Toolan, in lawyer's gray, came out of the courtroom. Feet scraped around the lobby. Two young girls came over and stood with Toolan. A woman carrying a baby and another one trying to hold on to two little boys lumbered after the girls. Deirdre got up and went to Toolan.

"I believe we're about ready to go in," Oliver Toolan said to the circle of people.

"How's the humor inside?" Liam asked quietly.

"Christ, in Heaven, the only thing missing is the hangman. After last night, they don't want to know ye."

"Mother of God, stop talking like that," Deirdre said. "It doesn't mean a thing."

"If six months doesn't mean anything to ye," the lawyer said.

One of the girls was tiny and had huge eyes. The other, a blonde, had on a blue vinyl dress that squeaked like a door. The woman carrying the baby was her mother. She said, "Mister Toolan, do we need more witnesses?"

Toolan smiled. "We've enough of everything except justice."

"I thought you told me this was nothing," Dermot said to Deirdre.

She waved her hand. "And it is, it is." She started walking to the courtroom. "Let's get on with it, Oliver," he said to Toolan.

When the lawyer started for the door, Dermot got next to him. "Is there anything I can do?"

The lawyer smiled. He held the door for Deirdre. The woman in the tan coat called after Deirdre, "What do ye think I should do?"

The courtroom was a small theater. A balcony with two or three rows of benches ran around three sides of the room. People hung over the balcony's wooden railing. There was no jury box downstairs. The spectator rows started back under the balcony and came down one step at a time to the pit in front of the judge. Deirdre and the two girls sat two rows behind the defense table. Everybody looked too white. The pale light coming through a skylight gave the room the look of a scene from something two hundred years ago.

The room was crowded. Liam and Ronald got into a middle row. The women and children were moving around looking for empty seats in the front. Dermot slipped into the first open space, one or two rows from the back. The row on his right was filled with soldiers. Young kids with short haircuts and smooth faces, sitting with a fat officer who was in his fifties. The officer had file envelopes balanced on his knees.

The judge had a long gray face propped up by his hand. He put on rimless glasses and cleared his throat. He put his face almost into the papers in front of him.

"These summonses," he began. He whistled through false teeth when he hit the s's. Not a low whistle. The word "subsection" came out like he was calling a dog.

The prosecutor had a chubby face with a streak of meanness through the eyes and mouth. He stood, hands in the watch pockets of his vest, and began speaking in a voice so low you could hear only a few stray syllables. The judge listened to him closely. In the row behind Dermot, the fat officer was rustling papers. "Now you have it?" he was saying to somebody. "The girl never left your sight."

A soldier stepped out of the row and went down the aisle and sat in the witness stand as if he was going to watch television. The judge said hello to him. The prosecutor waited until the soldier looked toward him before he began questioning. The soldier called out his name, Private Emory Williams, in a strong voice. It had to be his first time ever in court.

You still couldn't hear the prosecutor. The soldier called out, "I was on duty on the night you say. I was in a Saracen car assigned to clear the Rossville Street area. I was on Rossville Street at approximately ten o'clock."

The soldier listened to another question. "Well, we came onto Rossville Street. They was all throwin' rocks and bottles at us. There was this one large crowd in front of the high flats. We approached the crowd to disperse it. As we come up to the crowd, this one certain person remained there throwin' the rocks at us. It was this girl. Wearing a red raincoat. That's how I could follow her so

312

easy. I was climbin' out of the front of the Saracen when she threw a rock what just missed my head. Corporal Woodcock was gettin' out too. He chased after her first. Caught her trying to go into the flats. The arrest was made and there was nothin' else."

Oliver Toolan got up. "Now, as you were the first to apprehend this girl," he said.

"Yes, I was the first to apprehend the girl."

"I thought you just said Corporal Woodcock was."

"Well, I said he was runnin' first to get her."

"Now, on this particular night you came by armored vehicle?"

"Yes."

"And what did you see?"

"As I said, there was this crowd all throwin' rocks."

"Did you see anyone in particular?"

"Yes."

"Would you mind pointing her out?"

He pointed to the blond girl. The three girls started to laugh. Women in the back of the courtroom picked up the laugh. The judge began looking through his papers.

"That is the wrong girl," Oliver Toolan said.

"Well," the judge said, "as far as I can see, the policeman who recorded the arrests has the names mixed up."

Toolan showed the soldier a sheet of paper. The soldier said it was his handwriting.

"The official arrest record," Toolan said to the judge.

"Well, it was this girl," the soldier said, pointing to Deirdre. His voice was strained. "Never left my sight, she did."

"You state on this," Toolan said to the soldier, "that you apprehended this particular girl as she tried to enter the high flats?"

"Yes, that's where they was throwin' things. She never left my sight."

Deirdre followed him to the stand. She had on a dark-blue sweater and slacks. She had run a brush through her hair. Sitting there composed, a long cream neck and the head held very high.

"The evening you had been arrested, where were you prior to the arrest?" Oliver Toolan said to her.

"To a peace meeting at Liam Quigley's house."

"Who were you in company with?"

"Nell Cassin, Frances Doyle, and Father John O'Reilly, C.M."

She spoke to the air, not to Toolan, so the whole room could hear her answers. There was assurance in her voice as she slipped from listening to Toolan's question to answering it immediately.

"And whom did you hear speak at this meeting?"

"John Hume."

"How long did the meeting last?"

"Two hours and forty-five minutes. I know it to be exactly this time because Liam Quigley said he wanted to see the ITN news at ten and Father O'Reilly looked at his watch and said that we had best hurry, it was twenty-five to."

"How did you leave for home?"

"I walked."

"What route did you take?"

"I knew there was trouble down the town. To avoid it, I walked down Southway into the Brandywell and then over the Lecky Road to go up Fahan Street and home. I did this so I would be sure to avoid the areas where there was trouble."

"When did you become aware that there was trouble?"

"I knew there was rock throwing earlier. To make sure I would pass safely to my home for the ITN news, I took this route. Kept me well away from the trouble, you know."

"At what time approximately did you reach the bottom of Fahan Street?"

"About five to ten. I took the short cut through the high flats and the two girls here, they were just standin' there before going inside and go to bed, you know. Soldiers come along chasin' wee children. The soldiers were too slow to catch anybody. By the time they got down to us they was puffin'. They went past us a little. Big Jimmy was standin' out in the street. When you see him, you know, it means the stage of danger has passed. The soldiers gave up chasin' the wee children. On the way back they noticed us and they immediately took us in. For no reason. And this particular soldier here in court today did not arrest me. He did not tell the truth here today. He never did arrest me. He is lying to earn his pay."

"What were you wearing that night?"

"A green jacket."

"Were you wearing any red?"

"No, my color was green that night. Father John O'Reilly, C.M., happened to touch it with his cigarette and put a small brown hole in the sleeve."

Oliver Toolan held up the jacket and brought it to the judge. The judge barely looked at it. The judge was sitting with his chin in his hands. Toolan said the priest was available to make a statement. The judge's eyes went up and he smiled to himself.

The prosecutor stood up with his hands against his fat ribs. You still could not hear his questions, but you could see Deirdre sitting forward to grab the questions as they came to her. She couldn't wait to answer. She answered with one-word yeses or noes. Each time the prosecutor stood there and said nothing and waited for her to say something else. But she was too smart. She answered each question, did not elaborate, and left him there holding his fat ribs. The prosecutor looked up in the air and asked her something and the judge's face broke into a broad smile and the two soldiers at the prosecutor's table, the private and the corporal, laughed out loud. Oliver Toolan was up yelling.

She did not move or change expression. She sat there, with this long cream neck and the head held up high, and the judge told her to answer the question. He waved Toolan to his seat.

Deirdre said, "No." She said it slowly, with great coldness, staring directly at the prosecutor and her eyes made him and the soldiers stop laughing.

Two women got up and said Deirdre had been on the corner at ten that night.

The priest came on as a witness about the meeting

315

and the cigarette hole in the jacket. The prosecutor got up and said loudly, not looking at the priest, "No questions, your worship." The judge's eyes went up and he smiled to himself as the priest got down.

The blonde came up. The blue vinyl dress squeaked as she moved. Her head rocked and her body squirmed each time she answered a question, the dress squeaking loudly. The judge kept his eyes up and a little smile on his mouth.

"The soldier who arrested you," Oliver Toolan said, "did he in fact go past you?"

"Oh, they ran way past us. They couldn't catch anybody. The wee ones ran fast, you know. Then the soldiers came back. Oh, they were mad, you know."

"Have you ever seen the soldier who arrested you?"

"Oh, I know him."

"And how do you know him?"

"I was at a dance and a soldier came up to me and he asked me if he could take me home. I said no, I didn't like him."

"Which soldier was that?"

"That one there." She pointed at the corporal. The back of his neck went red.

"He arrested me because I would not go home with him, he did."

The prosecutor was up and the judge had his face out of his hands. "Don't answer unless you're asked a question," he said sharply.

The corporal had his head turned away from her. His face was flushed.

Deirdre was talking to Oliver Toolan, and the lawyer kept nodding while she talked. He got up and began his summation.

"I wouldn't your worship, rely on the soldier's social record with the girl, of course. But, your honor, he being young and fairly good looking and hurt by the rebuff, being charitable, your worship, this is clearly a case of mistaken identity."

The prosecutor got up with his hands against his fat ribs. He started talking in his dull voice. This time you could get pieces of his sentence. ". . . Private Williams . . . never lost sight of her . . ."

The judge had his chin out of his hands. He was writing in a school composition book.

When the prosecutor finished, the judge said thank you to him. The judge began turning the pages of the notebook and talking to himself out loud. "Now, let me read the notes on the evidence that I've taken. Oh, dear, now let me see, this is simply evaluating two separate sets of evidence. The Lecky Road, came down to Rossville Street . . ."

Still looking down he said, "Well . . . oh dear, I think I'll have to convict. Six months each."

The woman with the baby in her arms was up screaming. The two girls were screaming and covering their faces with their hands. Deirdre got up slowly and started to point her finger at the judge. Ronald took her arm. He had his eyes closed and his face twisted and he held his head against Deirdre's shoulder. Everywhere in the room women were screaming and sobbing. The sound always is the same. In a courtroom, at an accident, on a doorstep when you come with the accident slip. The judge had his chin between his hands. He looked at the soldiers near Dermot and gave a smile and shrug. Dermot caught a black visor out of the corner of his eye. It was a matron in a deep-green uniform. He was into the aisle, blocking it so she couldn't come down after Deirdre. Two other matrons were starting down from the doorway, clomping with wide-legged walks in black shoes with laces. Dermot went down to the pit. A cop tried to block him. Dermot went through him and stood blocking the table. He touched Oliver Toolan's arm. An angry face came around. Dermot had his hand out with money in it. He had to shout the word bail. The lawyer cupped his hands to Dermot's ear. "A cash bond isn't required. That's if you're released."

The judge slapped his hand on the bench. Oliver Toolan began waving the people to sit down. The woman with the child standing and sobbing. A small boy, crying loudly, ran to the table and the blond girl took him by the arm.

Toolan got up and began talking through the noise about an appeal.

The prosecutor was up. "Your worship," he said so loudly everybody could hear him now, "are we to allow these people out on the streets again? We have just come through a night of terror. One terrorist gunman was killed. At great peril to Her Majesty's troops. Are we not entitled to preserve the peacefulness of the community by having convicted people removed from the streets?"

The judge looked through papers and put his chin into his hand again. He looked up at the ceiling. "Oh dear," he said, "first conviction for one, two convictions for another. Oh dear. Four convictions for this girl. Oh dear, I'm afraid that Miss, ah, Miss . . ." he looked at the papers. ". . . Miss McLaughlin is going to have to remain."

"Your worship," Toolan said.

"Oh dear, no, she must go to jail."

The woman with the baby was into the pit and fell on her knees next to her daughter, who was bent over with her face in her hands. The blue vinyl dress creaked as she sobbed.

"What does he mean?" Ronald said.

"Deirdre and Eileen here are released on appeal, and Mary must go to jail," Toolan said flatly.

"Oh," Ronald said. He blew out his breath. Trouble dissolved in the corners of his eyes.

The blond girl in the vinyl dress looked up from her weeping. Her eyes were tearless and her lips curled. She turned to the row of soldiers.

"Black cunts!"

The other girl turned and snarled something. She hadn't been crying either.

Deirdre took the baby out of the woman's arms. "Come on, mother, we'll discuss this outside." The woman on her knees looked up at her. "Come on," Deirdre said. "Mister Toolan has things to do for your daughter and he can't do them here." The woman got up.

Toolan shoved papers into his briefcase. Everybody

318

started up the aisle. The judge smiled and nodded to the matrons. They came around Dermot and tapped the girl on the shoulder. The dress squeaked as she stood up. Stood straight up, her eyes on fire. She walked to a door behind the bench with the matrons. Deirdre carried the baby up the aisle. The mother lumbered after her.

Outside, Oliver Toolan asked Dermot for a cigarette. "Ah, there's your British justice," he said. "It's fine in a textbook, but it doesn't count if you're a member of a minority."

"How could anybody believe the soldier?" Dermot said.

"How could he not believe a member of Her Majesty's armed forces? A man in uniform never would lie."

Deirdre sat on a bench next to Ronald. He was hunched over, his hands between his knees. She bent over to hear him.

"But I'm not going to jail right away," she said. He kept his head down.

"What does the appeal take, a year?" Dermot asked her.

She smiled and shook her head. "Ah, they give rather quick legal service. A month, perhaps two months."

"We'll lose it as sure as we're fookin' here," Toolan said.

Ronald whispered something else. Deirdre bent down. "I know, I know. But it isn't today. It isn't today." Ronald's eyes became easier.

The woman with the baby sat dumbly across from her. "Deirdre." Deirdre had her head down listening to Ronald.

The woman in the tan coat slipped into a space alongside Deirdre. "Could we go see them now?" she said. "Before the lunch, you know."

"Deirdre," the woman holding the baby called again.

Deirdre looked up. She closed her eyes. "Let me think for a wee moment." Ronald whispered something else. She put a hand on his arm.

Oliver Toolan picked up his briefcase. "Let's get out of here and have a cup of tea. So I can think, you know."

Out on the street, everybody, there must have been a dozen people, began walking toward the Diamond. The

woman in the tan coat stood alone. "Deirdre, ye gon'
the wrong way. I'm back here, you know."

Deirdre turned around. Ronald was telling her something. The woman in the tan coat was almost ready to
cry.

Dermot took the woman off to the side. "I'll catch up,"
he said. Deirdre looked relieved. "We'll be at the café,"
she called back to him. He told the woman he had to go
home to New York. She grabbed his arm with both hands.

"She said she was going to take me to the welfare office.
It's just a wee walk. To see about another house for me,
you know. The people where I live say they're goin' to
set us afire at night."

"Can't you go yourself?"

She did not answer. She kept looking at him. Watery
eyes coming out of sunken cheeks.

He started walking with her.

"And what's your name?" he said.

"Oh, I'm walking around stupid, I swear to God. Mrs.
Ann Frances McCausland. I'm not livin' with my husband
in a state of marriage, you know. When I met him, he
was washin' up in a bar. The Great Northern Railway Bar.
Moved over to be a barman at the American base. He
always was chattin' up the girls. He took up with this one
wee girl. At the American base she started a row with a
Yank and my husband took her part. He was fired. Hasn't
worked since. He got mad because I got to fightin' with
the girl. She wanted to be sleepin' all day. She said the
wee children bothered her. We've four, you know. So I
said to her, 'Too bad the wee ones bother you.' He walked
out of the house with her. I hasn't seen him since, you
know."

They went through the arch in the wall and into the
gloom of the Fountain section. On the side of a house facing an alley was a mural of a man in a uniform, the
eyes looking like fried eggs, his hand on a long sword.
Underneath it, the old printing said THE LANDING OF
WILLIAM III AT CARRICKFERGUS, JUNE 14, 1690. After the
alley was a set of houses with boarded windows. She
pushed open the door of the first house. It swung on one

hinge. The door-frame was splintered. Inside, the floor was covered with a linoleum so old and caked with dirt that it stuck to your feet. She stepped into an empty room. A bare bulb hanging from the ceiling on frayed cord was turned on. A girl about three years old stood in the corner of the room, holding a cat against her dirty dress.

"Is she not a good girl?" the woman said. "I told her to stay right here. For all this time she stayed right here."

In the next room there was an electric stove with two burners and a black pot. Dermot asked where they slept. She took him into a room in the back. There was an old bed with a green mattress covered with urine stains. "I put two at the top and two at the bottom. I sort of squeeze in here on the side, you know."

The window was broken and had no board over it. The gray-stone wall was only inches from it. She nodded at the window. "At night, you know, they stand up on the wall drunk and they say, 'You Fenian, you're next.' Sometimes they urinate through the windows. It frightens the wee ones, you know."

"Where's your bathroom?" he said to her.

"Just before five o'clock every night I send the wee ones over to the welfare office, it's just across the street, so's they can use the toilets and clean themselves out for the night. It's the weekends is bad because the welfare offices don't open. I wait in the doorway here with the wee ones. When I see nobody on the street I let them run out to the curb. The one wee boy is afraid to doin' that now. Sunday night, this big man comes runnin' down the street and swats him while he was goin'."

While they were crossing the street to the welfare office, Dermot asked the woman what Deirdre was supposed to do for her.

"Some papers you know. Deirdre have it all in her mind. Meself, I'm walkin' around stupid, I swear to God."

A sign on a gloomy red-brick building said it was the Londonderry County Borough Welfare Office. Dermot held the door for her, but she didn't go in. The little girl clung to her. "Could I stay out here?" she asked. "I'm in a terrible nervous state." He made her come in with him.

321

They walked up one flight. She stopped in front of an office that had a counter as you came in. A man was sitting at a desk by the windows. "He told me he'd be back at four-thirty yesterday afternoon and I waited and he never come," she said. Dermot went up to the counter. She stayed outside in the hall.

The man glanced up. He had a line for a mouth.

"I'm just here from New York. This woman; Mrs. O'Donnell, is my cousin. Somebody was supposed to come back at four-thirty yesterday to see her, but nobody came. Can you do anything about her now?"

The man craned his neck and saw the woman out in the hall. He smiled to himself. Then he cleared his throat to put some authority into it.

"Yes, I see, Mrs. O'Donnell. Uh huh, I've her papers right on the top of my desk, you know."

"She was waiting for you yesterday," Dermot said.

"Aye," he said.

"She wants a place where she can live like a half a human being, and you were supposed to be around to see her yesterday. You never came. That's why we're here now."

"Oh, we've so many requests for houses, you know. We just have no houses, you know. But our decision had been that we do feel Mrs. O'Donnell should have the children placed in an institution, you know. Until such time as, you know."

She had come as far as the doorway. "Gee, not now," she said. "Not after thirteen years. I couldn't give 'em up now."

He held out his hands. "Well, you know."

"I came here to get her a place to live," Dermot said. "Let's keep the conversation on housing."

"Oh, but I have nothing to do with housing," he said.

"What do you mean?"

"Oh, but I don't. That is the province of the housing council. We are merely the welfare department. We investigate and make recommendations. But we do not control the housing council, you know."

"What room is the housing council?"

"Oh, over at the Guildhall, you know."

"Could you call them and save me the trip? We can stand right here and see what we can do for this woman. My cousin. I've seen what she's living in. I don't want her another hour in there. Could you give somebody a call?"

"Well, emergency housing, that's up to Mrs. Simpson, you know."

"Could you call her please?"

"Call Mrs. Simpson?"

"Why not?"

"What good would that do?"

"What do you mean, what good would that do?"

"Well. Everything to Mrs. Simpson must be in writing."

"You can't call her on an emergency?"

"Oh, no, it all must be in writing, you know."

"Write out something and I'll take it over to her."

"Right at this moment I've got to have dinner. And I'm certain Mrs. Simpson will be gone from her office for her dinner by the time you get there."

He got up from the desk and came to the counter.

"Where are the children now?" he asked her.

"Oh, the three are in school. But the other's just outside now."

"Alone?"

"Oh, nobody's with her." She hesitated. "Should I go out with her?"

"Yes, you go with your child."

She went down the staircase. The man left the counter. He opened a door leading into another office and he was gone.

"Hey, you cocksucker!" Dermot yelled.

There was no answer. He slapped the counter hard. He was standing there in an empty office. He walked into the hall and looked around. There was a door a few steps down. He went to open it. It was locked. He rattled the knob and knocked on the door. No sound came from inside. The building seemed empty. Dermot walked outside. She was on the sidewalk with the little girl. He took them across the street and left them in the doorway. He

323

said he'd go up and see Deirdre and find out what to do and be back.

"Can I be able to keep the wee children?" she said. "After thirteen years, I can't be givin' them up, you know."

She stepped into the house and came out holding a can of black shoe polish and a shoe brush. "I try to send them to school neat."

He walked through the somber streets, going away from the Bogside. The street curved and took him in a semicircle that came out of the rows of houses and into the emptiness of the street with the hill of dirt covered with garbage and the whitewashed saloon, McCann's, next to it.

When Dermot walked in, his father was talking to two men who had pints.

"He was there with us," Dermot's father said to the men. They looked at him and laughed.

"How much did ye drop?" one of them said.

"Oh, Christ, forget it," Dermot said.

"The dog must be on the dinner table today," Dermot's father said.

"Won't be the first," the other man said.

"I wonder what a dog tastes like?" Dermot's father said.

"I know they better cook him good and slow, 'cause he's a slow fookin' dog," the first man said.

Dermot stood at the end of the bar. His father was waiting for him to come up and sit with the two men. Dermot stayed at the end. His father walked down to him. The yellow-stained fingers were at the mouth, holding the cigarette. The father rotated his head against the pain of talking. He seemed to be pulling himself together.

"Well," the father said.

"I'll tell you," Dermot said. "I just come from court. These fuckin' people."

"Well, it's their ball park now, you know," the father said.

Dermot didn't say anything.

"Finbar come around this mornin', he was bent in half from last night, and—"

324

"I'll tell you," Dermot said, "I'm thinking of walking down to see her before she goes. I don't know if I'm going to be around to see her again. Poor son of a bitch. I'll go home and she'll be in the slam."

"The girl?"

"The one in here yesterday."

The father nodded.

"Know her?" Dermot said.

"Oh, I've seen her around. I don't know her. Finbar knows her. He told me she brought you to the house."

"Well, she's taking off and maybe I'll walk down and see her before she goes. Maybe I'll do that. Take a walk down there."

One of the two men called for a drink. Dermot's father went up to the middle of the bar to draw a pint.

"I'm going to go," Dermot said.

His father was staring down at the tap. Dermot waved and started for the door.

"Dermot."

It was strange to hear his father call him by name.

He turned around and his father came down to the end of the bar and leaned on his elbows. He had his hands clasped. He looked at his hands.

"You know, once you let one day go, it's a very easy thing to let a hundred days go."

"I know," Dermot said.

16:

At the café, Deirdre was wedged between people, Ronald one of them, in a booth. The juke box loud, dirty-legged children walking around with soda bottles. Eamonn was standing behind the counter. Dermot motioned through the noise to Deirdre, who started pulling herself out of the booth. Ronald's head dropped like a stone. His whispering tugged her down. She was looking at Ronald, not at Dermot. Dermot walked out and went up to the saloon on the corner. The soldiers in the pillbox in front of Chada Fashions gave him the look. Before he had his hand on the saloon door, Eamonn came trotting up, pushed the door in, and followed him to the bar.

"One drink and she'll be right along. She just told me."

"One and I'm gone," Dermot said.

"To where?"

"To New York."

They ordered whisky and water. The bartender poked tongs into a plastic bowl. He came up with a small ice cube. A guy at the bar began to read a newspaper race chart out loud. The barman listened, the ice cube still in the tongs. When he finally put the cube into the drink the ice disappeared.

Dermot took a couple of sips. "I try to do something for her and she sits there with that fuck of a guy," he said.

"Aye. He's a whore's get," Eamonn said.

"I mean," Dermot said.

"It's worse than you could rightly imagine," he said. "Here. Last summer the B Specials is lined up on the wall. They're singin' 'We Are the Billy Boys.' They're goin' to come down on us. Along with the fookin' coppers. We're down behind the barricades waitin' for them. At that very moment, Ronald runs into one of the wee houses on Wellington Street. He barricades himself in the back room. Then he begins screamin' that he will kill himself unless Deirdre comes down from the barricades. He was goin' to cut his throat with a wee razor. We hadda break down the door to stop him."

"Why did you stop the fuck?"

"The lass made us."

They finished their drinks and ordered another. This time the bartender didn't bother with ice.

"I don't even think she likes the fook," he said.

"Well, then what does he have that she puts up with him?"

"Nothing. He's a wet, sticky masturbator."

The drinks went down. Dermot held out his glass for another. "I still can't figure out what she's doing with him," he said.

"Christ, he gets to cryin' and clutchin' her arm. Doesn't have a clue how to get him off her."

"That's sick," Dermot said.

"Aye, it's sick. It's just not Deirdre either. Not a one of them has a man takes care of himself. The stronger the female, the weaker the man around her. Jesus, but it's all mixed up. Thank Christ for the street fightin'. It gives some of the poor fookin' men a chance to be what they should be."

Dermot didn't answer him. He ordered another drink. The saloon door opened and Deirdre came in alone.

"I was goddam near out of here," Dermot said.

"I walked past here before and saw you busy with the glass and I kept going over to the Guildhall. I was in the housing council office. I could look right past the wee man and see out the window to the front of the hotel. So you wouldn't have been able to get to the hotel and then leave it without me knowing it. Hel-lo. I'll have

327

a pint. The wee man was so terrified when I walked in. Christ, but he was thinkin' I was in for revenge for last night. They say, they *say* they'll have the woman in something livable by half three."

"Half three today?"

"Aye, half three today. And you were a good man to go with her. Ah, Jesus, it's all awful."

"No good atall," Eamonn said.

"Whatever you do, you don't have to go to jail," Dermot said.

"Why is that?"

"Well, you're out now. Anything happens, you just run."

"To where? The South?" She said it in disgust.

"Well, I don't know."

"To America?"

"Are not the blacks out rapin' every white woman goin' along the street?"

"Oh, I certainly hope for that," Eamonn said.

"If you want to come to America, you got anything I have." He picked up the glass.

She took his arm and pulled it down. "Look at me," she said. "You're lovely."

"What do you mean by that?" Dermot said.

"Never mind, I have it for myself, my own little secret."

They sat in the silence of the saloon in the afternoon, with the one man rustling the paper loudly and the bartender's shoes squeaking as he rocked back and forth and the sigh of the man swallowing a mouthful of stout.

They sat there a long time. The saloon door opened and Ronald was standing in it. His eyebrows were raised and his mouth half open. His eyes flicked across Dermot's and darted away. When he saw Deirdre get up, he let go of the door and was gone. Dermot paid for the drinks while she drained her pint. Eamonn walked out ahead of them and went quickly up to the café. Ronald was sitting in a red car parked in front of the café. At the car, Deirdre put her arms around Dermot's neck and gave him a quick kiss on the mouth. She threw her cheek against his and held him. He pushed her against the side of the car and kissed her on the neck. He glanced down, his lips still on her neck, at Ronald sitting at the wheel. A small-boy look. He reached down and opened the back door of the car. He put his hand behind Deirdre's back and pushed her in. He got in after her, slammed the door, and sat down with his arm around her shoulders.

"Where are we going?" he said.

Ronald drove without a word, his hands slapping the wheel in agitation, his head jerking as if it were being yanked by a hook in the mouth. They went across the bridge over the cold gray river, the wind putting white flecks on the rushing surface. The pillbox sandbags were dark from rain, the soldiers looked cold, huddled inside their green ponchos, their hands raw red but not moving off their weapons, which were pointed at anything coming at them. The car climbed out of Derry and onto a road running into the sky. Ronald had a hand running through his hair and he was muttering to himself when he came to a section of road under repair. The car crept past. About ten workmen were standing behind a small truck filled with hot asphalt steaming in the wet air. One of the workmen, in a dirty tan topcoat, sunk a shovel into the asphalt. He carried it over to the piece of road dug up for repair. The heads of the crowd of workmen turned as one, following the man with the shovel as he went from the truck to the dug-up road. The heads dropped as they followed the asphalt spilling off the shovel. The heads rose as the man in the topcoat went back for another shovelful. Deirdre rolled down the window. One workman turned to look at her, his chin resting in the aye-it's-tough greeting.

"How come you're all watching him?" Deirdre said.

"It's his turn with the shovel," the workman said.

She grabbed Dermot's hand and they both laughed. The whisky kept the laugh alive. He took out a cigarette and put it in his mouth. He looked at her, pulled the cigarette out, and fell over her with his arms around her. She laughed while he kissed her on the cheek. Ronald looked like he wanted to commit suicide.

They came into a town called Dungiven, as a sudden

thick rain came out of the cold sky. Ronald stopped at a bar. They ran through the water pouring down the sidewalk and into the lounge room. Deirdre slid into a booth across from a guy with a wounded face. Dermot stood shaking the rain from his hair and shoulders. The worn blue carpet smelled of stale beer and last night's puke and piss in the corner. She introduced the guy in the booth as Sean. Sean said hello as if he were saying his daughter just died. The barman, a wet cigarette hanging from his mouth, came in. Sean ordered another pint. Deirdre and Dermot ordered Scotch. Ronald said he wanted a pint. Dermot handed the guy a pound. The barman started to walk away. Ronald called him back. "I think I'll have a wee Scotch," he said.

They sat without talking, and when the barman brought the order Deirdre grabbed her glass and said, "Let's drink it down, we're behind schedule."

Sean took almost the whole pint with one long swallow, he did not seem to need breathing, and then he excused himself to go to the men's room.

"What does he do?" Dermot said to her.

"Ah, he's a good man. He's for the cause. One of the best we've got."

"What is he, though?"

"That boy has a farm. His farm is as hard as this table. But he makes things grow. That boy could make things grow on this table."

"What does he do that's so good?" Dermot asked her.

"He works."

When Sean came back, he looked like he had just seen a bad accident. The rain had stopped as quickly at it had started. They went out to the car and drove for over an hour until the road came into Cookstown. You come down a slope into the town, which runs for a couple of blocks, with shops on both sides of the street. The road runs up a slope and you are out of town. On the front of one of the stores, an insurance agency, there was a British flag flying. Sean pointed to it.

"What do they have the butcher's apron out for?" he said.

330

"What's that?" Dermot said.

"The Union Jack," Sean said. "Butcher's apron. There's been blood wherever they raise it."

Deirdre started to laugh. Sean turned around and stared at her. "Oh, there has been, you know."

Ronald turned onto a side street and came into a cluster of ugly brick garden apartments with cracked sidewalks leading up to the scarred doors. Deirdre jumped out of the car and went to one door. A girl opened it and said something to her. Deirdre jumped back in the car and said something to Ronald and he drove up to the start of the main road, to a two-story white house set back from the street by a small garden. They all got out of the car. Deirdre pushed in the front door and called out.

"Is that Deirdre?" a girl's voice came from the top of the stairs.

"It is."

"Jesus, am I not late again?"

"Aye, late again."

There were some sounds and a guy padded out to the top of the stairs with his pants on, the belt hanging loose, and the rest of his clothes in his hands. He had no chest. If you slapped him on a shoulder it would break. His eyes were beautiful. He did not even try to look at any of them. "Hel-lo," he said. Deirdre waved at him. They went into the living room. It had low, modern furniture. On the walls were these two huge posters, Che Guevara and Mao Tse-tung. They were in black charcoal on white paper. The guy had done Che with wind blowing the long black hair and the beret tipped at an angle which made you feel action. The eyes had the same look a big race horse gives you. Who are you? I am a champion. Sean and Ronald were sitting on low chairs staring at the floor. Dermot asked Deirdre if she wanted to go for a drink. Ronald's head came up. When Deirdre said yes, Dermot said, "Come on, I'll buy you a couple." When he said the word "buy," he looked straight at Ronald, who dropped back onto the couch and stared at the floor.

Deirdre and Dermot walked directly across the road to a pub that had a dirt floor and a bar that was almost shoulder-high. Nobody was in. A door off the bar opened and a woman came out. She poured whisky. There was no sense even asking for ice. She put the bottle on the bar in front of them and went back inside, shutting the door after her. Dermot finished his drink quickly. Only half a taste to it now, which always happens when you're going too strong. Right away he reached for the bottle. Behind the bar, each corner of the mirror had the word WHISKY etched onto it. The saloon door was open. The road outside was empty and silent and the white house on the other side was tidy. Dermot pounded his foot on the dirt floor.

"She lives across the street?" he said.

"Certainly not. She lives at the council houses we went to first. Malachy Carlin lives across the way here. He is a solicitor. He gave her the use of the house while he's off somewhere."

"When she leaves the house is empty?"

"Absolutely empty, because, as a matter of actual fact, we'll be goin' to the meetings too." She laughed and made as if to slap him in the face.

He picked up the drink and looked at the bench against the wall. He put the glass on the bar.

"So I'll throw you right on the floor here."

"Are you not crazy?" she said. She leaned away. "Here." She started to pour him another drink. He took the bottle from her and poured so much into her glass that it splashed. Through the open door, you could hear the car starting across the road. It came around in front of the saloon. Dermot spilled money on the bar. Deirdre began picking out cartwheel shillings and half crowns to leave for the whisky. Ronald was holding the car door open, but Deirdre waved them on. "It's only down the street, we'll walk off the drink."

They walked down the slope to the business streets. There were crowds on either side of the street. Ahead of them, the car pulled to the curb and the candidate got out of the front and got up on the back of a truck. Her voice came out over a microphone. Right away, the crowd on the other side of the street began chanting, "Go home!

332

Go home!" The candidate was calling out, "Mister Sunderland, the Unionist Party candidate, talks of stability. He doesn't want us to riot. He doesn't want us to have jobs or have a roof over our heads either. But that's all right, long as we don't riot." The other side of the road kept up this steady chant, "Go home, Go home, Go home." There were about five hundred on each side of the road. The ones on the girl's side were younger, had longer hair, Their eyes were alive as they listened to the girl over the chanting coming across the street. The traffic kept coming down the road. Across the street, the people seemed to be older and neater, with some color showing in the clothes. One of the shops across the street, the Pearl Assurance Company Ltd., the one flying the flag, had two windows, one saying LIFE—MOTOR and the other saying FIRE INSURANCE. A woman with beauty-parlor gray hair sat in the LIFE—MOTOR window and her knee kept hitting her orange skirt while she clapped and kicked her leg to keep time with the crowd outside her window chanting, "Go home."

There was a break in the traffic and Dermot went through it to the crowd across the street. Women mostly, with neat hair and wearing clean unwrinkled raincoats, they were chanting and cackling at the girl over on the truck. The women wore the only lipstick he had seen in Northern Ireland.

"How come she doesn't have Her Majesty's flag on the platform?" one woman said.

"She'll be under Her Majesty's flag soon enough," one next to her said. "In one of Her Majesty's best prisons."

"Bread and water," somebody said.

A young guy in pressed dungaree jacket and slacks, and with a short haircut, almost crew cut, stuck his head between them. "More than bread and water. The goddamned hangman's noose for her!"

"Yeah! Yeah!" the women yelled.

"Burn her at the stake!" the woman next to Dermot yelled out. She yelled it with her eyes bulging. You could almost hear the anger throbbing at her temples.

"You don't really mean that, do you, lady?" Dermot

333

said. He was talking to her the way a cop would who was trying to calm things down.

She looked at him and she had no control over her eyes. They were rolling around. "Give me the match," she said. Her voice broke loose. "Give me the match, give me the match, give me the match, give me the match. She should burn. She should burn. Burn, burn, burn, burn."

Then they all began to chant, "Go home! Go home!" Dermot waited for a break in the traffic and walked back across the road. The girl talking on the truck really was just a little girl. Long straight hair down the sides of an oval face and a teen-age bad tooth. But her blue eyes were old. She was in a red dress that was as short as you could get it. She finished to loud cheering and clapping from the ones on her side of the street. The ones across the street were shaking their fists.

At the car, Ronald was holding the door. Deirdre slipped into the back. Ronald was bent down to get in after her. Dermot got his shoulder and hip into him and was in beside Deirdre. Ronald came in after Dermot without looking at him. The candidate got in the front seat. Her boy friend came in after her. Sean was sitting in the driver's seat.

"Those people across the street," Dermot said to Deirdre, "do you know what one of these women was saying?"

She put a finger up to his lips.

"Christ, I never heard anything like it."

She hit his arm and kept the finger to his lips. Her eyes went to the girl in the front.

Sean was driving with his head looking all over the car. He turned to the girl next to him in front and he said, "Are the two of you goin' to be stayin' together again tonight?"

"That's nobody's business what I do with my own personal life," she said.

"Christ, though, that's all a lot of them were talkin' about. Did you not hear it?"

"They've nothin' else to talk of," she said. "We'll have to put other things on their minds."

334

"Father McPriest'll keep remindin' them wherever you go," Sean said.

"Tell Father McPriest to fook off," she said.

Sean shook his head. "Oh, wait till the dirt starts."

Nobody said anything.

"Ah, but there'll be dirt."

Again nobody spoke.

"I hear it goin' around everywhere. Oh, dirty this one is going to be."

He stopped at a gas station. The man ambling out rotated his chin in a hello.

"We're off to an election meetin'," Sean called out.

The gas-station man nodded.

"But it's goin' to be a dirty one," Sean said.

The gas-station man nodded twice.

"Oh, the dirt'll really fookin' fly."

The girl next to him snapped, "Sean! Jesus!"

Sean turned to her. "I'm just talking to him, you know."

"Talk no more."

They drove over a narrow, twisting, thicket-lined road. After about half an hour, the girl in the front said, "How did we ever work it out that we speak in Cookstown and then go all this way to Strabane?"

The guy next to her didn't answer, so she turned around and looked at Ronald. He leaned past Dermot and said to Deirdre, "How did this ever happen?"

"I didn't handle the schedulin'," she said.

"Yes, you did," he said. "We had it right out on the desk."

"That wasn't for today."

"Dear child, I remember that we were handling this detail in precise fashion. How it came to this I know not."

"That wasn't for this trip. I did the handbills for Magherafelt," Deirdre said.

"Maghera?" he said.

"No, Magherafelt," she said. "I thought you were working out the details of the particular meetings."

"It most certainly was not. I. Was it you, Wilson?"

The one in the front shook his head. "I was workin' on the manifesto. I had nothin' to do with this."

"Then it was Brian," Ronald said. "Yes, it had to be Brian. I am certain. We said we would handle the Magherafelt, and he was to map out this schedule."

"Well, I'll be talkin' to Brian tonight," the girl in the front said. "We're wastin' fookin' hours drivin' roads."

The ride to Strabane was long and uncomfortable. They came into the back of the town on a gloomy evening, onto a street that was really a rabbit warren of low huts with roofs of broken slates covered with bird shit. The smell of coal smoke was bitter in the wet air. Kids with dirty faces and smeared bare legs hung in every doorway. Men stood on the sidewalks smoking cigarettes. The sky was brown, the clothes were brown. There was no other color on the street. No other color in the clothes, no other color on the window frames. Brown people standing on brown streets under a brown sky.

The house they stopped in front of had children packed in the doorway. A woman looked over their heads, waved hello, and started shooing the kids out of the way. Inside, the walls were wet with dampness. Pajamas that weren't dry yet hung on wash lines strung around a tiny sitting room. The wash lines were tied to a nail holding up a picture of the Sacred Heart and a nail holding up a picture of John F. Kennedy. Dermot turned in circles but there was no space to sit or stand. He squeezed in the space by the kitchen. The woman was at the stove. When she reached for a pot you could see the ripped underarm of her green sweater.

"We got handbills out twice this week, as a matter of actual fact," she said.

"Ah, Jesus, you're a good one, Moira," the girl said.

"Will ye not have a cup of tea?"

"Aye."

The candidate was against the kitchen wall while Moira put on a kettle of water. They were talking. Deirdre stood in the doorway facing Dermot.

"Those people in that last place were good and fuckin' sick," he said to her. He said it without moving his lips.

336

She smiled. "They're afraid."

"Are you goin' to have that here too?"

"No, not here. There's nothin' to be afraid of in this wn. There's no jobs for anybody."

The back door was open. There was a thunderclap and full rainstorm began. The sound of the rain was loud the house because the front door was open too. The oman's husband came out of the toilet outside the tchen door. He came out in a rushing motion through e sheet of rain. The two in the kitchen had to go up gainst each other to make room for the man to pass. e was against the wall, rubbing past them, when a white nd orange and pale-green light exploded into the kitchen. he light was blinding and the thunder deafening. The ghtning had come through the open kitchen door and must have hit the greasy sink. Pots jumped and bounced ut of the sink. One of them rolled out of the kitchen nd spun to a stop at Dermot's feet. He flattened against ne wall. The husband in the kitchen was frozen against ne two women.

"They're tryin' to tell us something," the woman in the weater said.

"The next time I wish they'd do it in Latin. I cannot ranslate fookin' lightning," the candidate said.

They both began laughing and the husband stayed gainst the wall, trembling. Dermot inched his toes away rom the pot.

"That was nice," Deirdre said. She was bending down o pick up the pot. Dermot pushed her away with one and and went down and grabbed the pot. He brought it p so quickly that he nearly hit Deirdre in the face.

"Want some tea?" Deirdre said to him.

He told her no. He went to the front door and watched he rain storm out of a sky that exploded with electricity. The man came up behind him.

"Christ's mother," he said.

The three women were talking in the kitchen as if nothing had happened.

The lightning and rain ended as quickly as they had started. Dermot stepped outside. Even a waterfall had not

337

been able to make the place clean. The street was we
brown. Kids started to trot out of the houses, and soo
slick mud covered the broken pavement. There was tall
ing inside the house and Deirdre came out, calling, "A
right, I'm off," over her shoulder Ronald was a step a
ter her, eyes down on the sidewalk. They all walked dow
the rabbit-warren street onto one street of the busines
district and came out onto the square. There were ston
bank buildings with terraces and turrets and two-stor
buildings with shops on the ground floor. The shop build
ings had slanted roofs. The shops had hand-painted signs
block lettering with the sides shaded, the kind you see i
old neighborhoods in Queens. They walked into the square
past the American Bar, Strabane *Weekly News,* Cath
gart's Clothes, J. P. Colgan Café, Dan Kennedy Chemist
D. J. McLaughlin Clothier. Up at the head of the square
the main road ran out of town on one side and the othe
side was a bus terminal which looked like a small rail
road station. The sign on the bus terminal said ABERCORN
SQUARE STRABANE. In front of the bus terminal there wa
parked a flatbed truck with a high red cab, the cab look
ing powerful enough to ride through a wall. Up on the
flatbed, a guy with great curly red hair and a huge beard
played a guitar and sang into the start of the darkness.
A crowd that was growing stood and watched.

While he sang, people began streaming out of the rabbit warrens and coming into the square. There were perhaps five hundred people in the square now. Deirdre went
up to the truck. A dark-haired guy in a gray button sweater stood with a cigarette in his mouth and one foot on a
stepladder going up to the flatbed.

"He's on the last," he said to Deirdre.

"And then you go," she said.

"Aye, I do me stint."

"You just do the introducin'," she said.

"You're absolutely right," he said.

The singing stopped. The people clapped in the wet
air. The guy went up the ladder.

"Patsy!"

He turned around. "Aye?"

338

"Just the introducin', Patsy."

"Aye."

Patsy climbed onto the flatbed truck. He dropped his cigarette and looked down to crush it with his heel. When he looked up he saw the people in front of him, and more of them coming into the square. His eyes widened and glistened.

The singer called out over the microphone, "The first speaker of the evening will be Mister Patsy Breslin of Omagh."

Patsy put one hand on the microphone. His feet spread apart.

"People of Mid-Ulster! People of Strabane! I don't intend to speak for long."

Patsy took a deep breath. Over the microphone it sounded like a heart attack.

He then started in this measured North Ireland speaking style. "Some people . . . in Mid-Ulster . . . are saying . . . that our candidate . . . did not . . . attend meetings . . . as he had promised to do. People of Strabane. Are you electing . . . our candidate . . . to sit in your kitchens? Or are you . . . electing our candidate . . . to fight . . . for you . . . in Westminster?"

An old gray-haired woman in a yellow raincoat, her legs heavily bandaged, waddled through the crowd smoking a cigarette.

"Do you know . . . what they are trying . . . to do . . . to you?" Patsy roared at her.

The woman took the cigarette out of her mouth and looked up at him.

"I am going . . . to stand here . . . and tell you . . ."

"Jesus!" Deirdre said. She went into her pocket for cigarettes. She leaned against the flatbed and smoked with her eyes closed. Patsy, a roar coming into his voice, kept on. A bald man in a tan corduroy jacket came over, his hand shaking while he took Deirdre's cigarette and gave himself a light.

"Christ, he's fantastic," he said. Then he stood at the ladder, looking up at Patsy, and when Patsy got to one particular rousing part of his speech the guy began clap-

339

ping, and while he clapped you could catch the first whisky sway in his legs.

Patsy's eyes were coming out of his head and his right arm was pumping. Deirdre grabbed him by the pants leg. Patsy lost his cadences. He tried to pick them up again. She tugged the pants leg once more. Patsy's arm dropped and his voice calmed and he came to an end. He started backward down the stepladder. Deirdre went on the last drag of her cigarette. Patsy was on the bottom rung and Deirdre was dropping the cigarette when the guy in the corduroy jacket flew up the stepladder. His foot came on the rung where Patsy had his hands. Patsy had to let go to keep his fingers from being crushed. He tried to get an elbow into the man. The man was past him and up the ladder onto the flatbed. Deirdre kept saying, "Oh, Jesus."

The man strangled the microphone with his hands. He put his mouth against it. He roared, "People of Mid-Ulster! People of Strabane! I am John McGeady of the Magherafelt Official Republican Club!"

There was a commotion in front of the truck. The candidate came walking through, cigarette in her mouth, Wilson at her arm. He held the arm, but he was clinging to it. When she saw the guy up at the microphone, a hand went to her throat.

Up on the truck, he stepped back from the microphone, held his arms straight out, and screamed, "Jesus Christ!"

There was complete silence. He stood there, arms out, head thrown back, eyes closed.

"Jesus Christ Crucified!" When he opened his mouth to scream all you could see was his tongue swollen with drink.

"James Connolly!"

He closed his eyes and held his hands over his heart.

His voice became a whisper. "They murdered James Connolly with a firin' squad."

Now he folded his arms across his chest.

"Mahatma Gandhi!"

In a whisper: "Some lunatic murdered him with a machine gun."

340

Chest heaving, arms flailing, eyes rolling in his head, he roared out, "Che Guevara!

"The Americans murdered Che Guevara. Murdered him for what he was. A Communist. There's a whole generation of them coming up in the world. Thank Jesus Crucified for each Communist he sends us. And remember it was the Americans who killed Che. And they would've killed Jesus Christ if they got the chance!"

The girl had a crooked smile on her face. She said to Deirdre, "Everybody he mentions got killed by a crowd. Now he's fixin' to talk about us. I guess we all better go dash out and get ourselves killed or we'll ruin his wee speech."

John McGeady was rocking on his feet, eyes bloodshot, flecks of foam on the corners of his mouth. His tongue was too thick to work well in his mouth. Half the words were smothered by it. Deirdre was up the ladder. Her hip came out and pushed him aside.

"Thank you, John McGeady of the Magherafelt Official Republican Club."

A couple of people clapped. He went backward waving his thanks. He stood waving while Deirdre took the microphone and called out, "People of Mid-Ulster. People of Strabane."

Then McGeady stepped off the truck with one foot, tried to balance himself and couldn't, and had to half fall, half jump. He fell onto the cobblestones. He gave a red-faced roar: "Mother's cunt!"

The candidate, next to Dermot, had a hand over her mouth to keep the laughing inside. Deirdre kept talking in a quick, clear voice.

" . . . They say to us, the college professors, the monsignors, the politicians, 'Don't talk Socialism to the people, they don't have enough schoolin'.'

"Do you not find it strange that the people advisin' us what to tell you are those who do not live among you? Who do not face your life every day. Who are warm in the cold and dry in the rain. And who have the time to sit in their rectories or business offices and look out on us and decide how we should live.

"You don't see the priest livin' on stewin' meat. You don't find the businessman down here buyin' the tail end.

"We are here tonight to talk of these things. We are political people and this is a political meeting. Political people always are supposed to promise people something for their votes.

"What do we offer you? We offer you pride in yourselves."

She introduced the candidate. The girl came up the ladder and took the microphone. She stood in the gathering darkness with her left hand on her hip and her right hand holding the microphone. Her body was leaning to the right. Her voice seemed to reach inside the crowd and made everything stop.

"We are still slaves in our country," she was saying. "We get up in the morning, those of us who can, and we go to our jobs, and you work all week and at the end you get your pittance. And those who do not have jobs sit home when it is too cold to come out, and when they do happen to leave the house, all there is to do is stand on the corner and wish for the day to end.

"And they say to you, 'Tut tut, if you had any dignity you'd work for nine pounds, not take twelve on the dole.' The people who go and do a day's work never get to share in the fruits of their labor. There is a man sitting in the Mediterranean receiving millions of pounds from your labor. You don't know him and he doesn't know you, but he owns you.

"Last August in Armagh, when the factory burned and was closed down for six weeks, the men had to go on the dole. Nobody came and asked the man on the dole how he did. But the owner of the factory put in a claim for a loss of profit. That is above the cost of the machines and the inside of his factory. His claim was for loss of profit and he got two hundred and fifty thousand pounds. I ask you a simple question. How many workers, if they had worked six weeks in that factory, would have seen any of that two hundred and fifty thousand pounds the owner would have earned? Oh, he earned such money every six weeks. He said it on his claim and the government agreed hat it was right and proper. How many workers ever saw any of that money? How much of that money ever went into housing for the workers?

"No, the man took the money to the Mediterranean with him.

"There are two sources of emigration in Northern Ireland. Out through the banks go the money. Out through the hovels go the people.

"If you want to keep people at home, then keep our money at home. A man here in Strabane with a factory can get a lorry from Belfast and put that wee stick of machinery on the lorry and take it away from Strabane and leave the workers on the corners. And it is your machine he takes away. If any man in Strabane takes that stop sign over there away, six policemen will hit you and put you in jail. But a factory owner can take your job and your country away from you and the police will protect him.

"Well, we own that machinery. We are the people who own Ireland, and it is time we assumed control of what we own. This isn't extreme. This is common sense. Either we start providin' jobs for ourselves or we better start widenin' the street corners.

"They tell us, the government and the industrialists and the church, that we're not supposed to be thinkin' like this. It's all above our heads and the people in charge should be doin' the thinking for us.

"They say we're ignorant. Well, we're not too ignorant to suffer."

Dermot turned around and looked at the crowd. The crowd stood with their feet set apart, hands in their pockets. They had a farmer's stare. An old lady with a hair net on was directly behind Dermot. The man with her had pants cuffs wet from the rain. Frayed ends of shoelaces hung over the sides of his cracked shoes. Thick white hair grew out of his earlobes. Whisky showed in the nose. The two of them stood there, broken by the years, and this little girl on a truck in a wet, depressing town square, with the traffic moving through it, stood and spoke to them and put a light in their eyes which maybe never had been there before.

"You exchange the dignity of your labor—man is no animal—and for it you receive the right to be hungry by Thursday.

"What are we? Are we cattle to be herded to the abattoir? Are we cattle to be herded onto the emigration ship?

"You are humans! You have a heart and soul and brains. You also have feet. Time you stood on them. You also have knees. Time you got off them."

All around the eyes were wet and this haunting voice ran through them.

On the truck, Deirdre stood off to one side smoking a cigarette. Her motions were cool and relaxed. Her head was up, the chin out, the eyes looking out over the crowd as if she were somebody in command of them. She seemed taller than she was. For this little moment she was distant. Standing there and looking out over the crowd, and this little long-haired machine next to her causing the crowd to freeze.

The candidate finished the speech and a big noise came out of the darkness. The crowd pressed around the truck. Deirdre was bent down to jump from the truck. Dermot reached up and she took his hand and came down like a jockey off a horse, with no impact at all, touching the ground instead of hitting it. The speaker climbed down the stepladder frontward, hands were out to help her. The moment she was on the ground she took out a box of cigarettes and walked into a knot of old men wearing caps. The men nodded and grabbed at the cigarettes. One of them began talking to her and she cocked her head and listened to him intently. Deirdre was over with another cluster of old men. She had her cigarettes out and her head bent listening while a man said something to her. His front teeth were missing and he was having trouble putting words together. Deirdre put a hand on his arm and she said, "Ah, now Paddy."

They were all through the crowd now. Sean and Patsy and even McGeady, handing out cigarettes and talking to

344

people. Dermot took out his own cigarettes. Ronald was in front of him, reaching for one. The crowd was starting to clear into the night, flowing around two dogs smelling each other, walking up toward the row houses on the rabbit-warren streets.

Deirdre came over to Ronald and Dermot, and they all walked to the American Bar. It was closed and Deirdre knocked on the frosted-glass door. It opened a crack. A man came out, looked up and down the street, then said, "Come on, come on," and they squeezed past him. The candidate came in at a full run, the boy friend alongside her. They went straight for a small windowless sitting room that was smoky and crowded. Deirdre and Ronald and Dermot went to the bar. Down at the end, Sean and the guitar player were drinking gin. The guitar was on a bench along the wall.

The guitar player said, "Here we go," and the bartender put gin in front of everybody. Just gin in a small glass.

"How'd it go?" the guitar player said.

Dermot rolled his eyes while he drank.

"The wee one gets very special, does she not?" the guitar player said. "She's a poet. Let's have another."

Dermot turned to Deirdre. "I feel like I don't even know you now."

She laughed. They had another drink.

There was more knocking on the glass door. The owner let in a priest, and right after him was a tall guy with neatly combed, wavy hair, dressed in a suit and tie. The priest had the one line of pink on the front of his collar to show he was a monsignor. The tall guy began laughing as he saw everybody.

"Wasn't she great?" he called to Deirdre.

"Aye," she said. She did not turn to look at him.

"Hey! Was that not great?" he called to the guitar player.

"Philim," the guitar player said. He picked up his drink.

"Oh, hel-lo there. Here's the rest of the Organization." He laughed and slapped Sean on the shoulder and held out his hand to Ronald.

345

The Monsignor had silver hair brushed straight back. His face was red with blood pressure.

"How are ye this evenin'?" he said to Deirdre.

She had a cigarette in her mouth. She closed her eyes and opened them.

"Drink, Father?" Dermot said.

"No, thank you very much. Ah, is she about?"

Deirdre pointed back to the sitting room. The Monsignor nodded thanks. The tall guy, Philim, came over to the bar.

"Have a drink, Philim," the guitar player said.

Philim laughed. "Fantastic! Do ye have a cigarette?"

They all got another glass of gin. Philim held his up. "Here's to the finest speaker I ever heard."

Deirdre spoke without looking at him. "Did you listen, Philim?"

"Of course, of course."

"Are ye backin' her?"

"With twenty-five pound. I'm goin' to put twenty-five pound to her campaign."

Deirdre's hand went out. "We'll accept it now."

"Oh, have no worry. I'll be at the headquarters tomorrow first off."

" 'Twould be better right now," Deirdre said.

Dermot pushed his money out and ordered for everybody.

"Is she having something inside?" he said to the bartender.

"Haven't a clue."

Dermot walked to the door of the sitting room and looked in. She was sitting forward, holding a cigarette, her eyes burning into the Monsignor, who was directly across from her. Wilson sat alongside her looking at the ceiling.

"After all," the Monsignor was saying, "the people of Strabane . . ."

She cut in, with hard light deep in her eyes. "The people of Strabane were born cryin' and they'll die cryin'."

She started to sit back. Then she came forward to get as close to the Monsignor's face as possible. The voice came out of her like tooled metal.

"As for the remainder of our differences, perhaps the

Bishop can sleep by himself at night. But I don't. So tell the Bishop that I said fook off."

Dermot got out of there and was back at the bar. "Not for me," he said to Deirdre.

She laughed. "He had it comin' to him, he did."

The Monsignor was standing at the glass door. He raised his chin an inch or so. Philim put down his drink and started to leave. "Do ye have a cigarette?" Dermot fished out one for him. He took it with a great laugh, and he and the Monsignor went out. The candidate and Wilson came out of the sitting room. The girl said she'd be at somebody's house and Sean nodded yes. She barely waved good-by and walked out.

"She's a cold little turkey," Dermot said.

Deirdre shrugged.

"Does she care or is she just doing this?"

"Oh, it doesn't matter whether she cares or not," Deirdre said. "She stands for us in the election, and the people like her and she will win, I hope. And if she wins she will have power and we can have power from being with her. And the power will help us. All we really care about. Doesn't matter whether she cares or not."

Sean went for the car while the others finished their drinks. The guitar player jammed in the back while Sean drove through the rabbit-warren streets and started out of town. He pulled into a driveway at a well-lighted modern house, a lot of glass and dark wood. Sean tapped the horn. Somebody opened the door and waved a hand. They waited there for fifteen minutes. The girl and Wilson came out and got in front. The guitar began singing through the ride in the blackness.

> "Now the sun is sinking low
> Children playing know it's time to go
> High above a spot appears
> Now the sun comes to earth
> Shrouded in a mushroom cloud of death
> Now the sun has disappeared
> All is darkness fear and death."

347

For a strong-looking guy with a lot of whisky in him, he sang with softness and sadness. The candidate started talking. "We are going to be working very hard this time."

"Aye," Ronald said.

"We have a wee, wee election man in Omagh who watches very closely and he says that with a ninety-two-per-cent vote, we still will be losin' six thousand of our voters. Anything in the eighty-per-cent range will make it very tough to accomplish."

"I've worked polls in New York don't vote fifty per cent," Dermot said.

"We have quite a high vote here. And we've a way to make it bit higher than it is. Furthermore, they left our dead on the votin' register."

They all laughed. "You see," she said, schoolteacher in her voice, "all the government jobs are held by Protestants. They keep their own voting registers right up to date. But they don't know the first thing about Catholics. So when a nun dies, we bury Sister Mary Joseph. And the voting-register man strikes Sister Mary Joseph off the lists. That leaves us with the woman's true name; Sister Mary Joseph may be dead, but Margaret Sullivan lives forever on our registers.

"How many of them do you have?" Dermot said.

"As many as we need, I hope," she said.

"How many is that?"

"We'll vote twenty-five hundred of the Lord's best dead."

"Who does that?"

"Nuns with strong legs."

"The nuns cheat?"

"Well, we like to call it impersonatin'. It really isn't very hard, you know. You hand the nun half a dozen wee votin' cards, Anna O'Neill, May McCafferty, and send her to a pollin' place. She just can keep walkin' in, votin', goin' around outside, and comin' back again with a different name card. The election officer can't tell. To him one nun's the same as another. Who can tell a penguin from a seal?"

"It's hardly a sport we're playing, ye know," Deirdre said.

"In most things a person does in life," the one in front said, "you try to be successful. Political life is different. The only word that counts is survival. A person will do certain things to be successful in life. But he will do ennathing to survive."

Deirdre said, "Do ye know of the Russian who was throwing the babies out of the sleigh to the wolves?"

"He was out campaignin' for home secretary," the one in the front said.

Deirdre began singing to herself, in a tuneful moan. Then she began talking, mostly to herself. "This will be a very hard election. We've the Unionists to beat on the one side. And on our own side we have Mister Joseph McCool himself running. And by tomorrow, I bet, the Bishop will have his own personal candidate in the election. Three Catholics fightin' it out. It'll be very hard."

"The Church would rather lose the vote than accept the act of darkness," the guitar player said.

"They are not all that terribly uncomfortable with the Unionists," the candidate said. "And certainly, the Church could care less who wins as long as it isn't this little Communist twit who has the audacity to sleep with somebody and have it public knowledge."

"Who's the Bishop going to put into the race?" the guitar player asked.

"I know right now," she said. "In the interests of charity, we'll wait until we hear it from the man's own lips."

"I know too," Deirdre said.

17:

Omagh is a treeless business street creeping up a steep
hill. At the top, a pillared courthouse looks down the
town's throat.

They came into the town, the streets night-empty, and
went past the small shops, Green Shield Stamps and
Michael Mullen Family Grocer, Swan and Mitchell Ltd.,
Shoes, Blacks Dryers and Washers, past the Belfast Bank,
the Royal Arms Hotel, the Golden Griddle, the Café Rex,
McDermott Chemist, *Mid-Ulster Observer,* and up the hill
to the Melville Hotel and the courthouse steps. Traffic coming down the hill came onto the street from the right of
the courthouse and stopped at an alley running between
the Diamond Bar and a wooden hall with a sign saying
INF. Deirdre and Ronald hurried down the alley. As Dermot got out of the car Sean explained it meant Irish National Foresters, a Catholic social club where you can
drink after curfew. Going down the black alley, Dermot
tripped over beer kegs lined against the saloon wall. Halfway up the alley, Wilson stopped and knocked on the side
door of the saloon. The guitar player and Patsy sat on a
bench against the wall in the lounge. On another bench
McGeady had his head inside the collar of his corduroy
jacket, snoring. Wilson put a five-pound note on the bar
and ordered drinks for everybody. Dermot put money
out, but Wilson waved the bartender away from it. Dermot swallowed the gin and held the glass out for another; this round was on him. The girl wandered in and

took some of Wilson's drink. They spoke very softly to each other.

"Was it not better tonight?" she said.

Wilson said, "Well, it is a bit strange to see grown people hanging on every bloody word you say. When I know and you know that you are just some sort of a freak. A wee girl with a voice that really shouldn't belong to you. Just like a pop star. You still are, in actual fact, what you were the day I met you. And you still should be finishing school, then settling off someplace teaching and raising children."

"Aye," she said.

A few minutes later she said, "But was it still not better?"

"Oh, I suppose for Strabane, you know. But you muck about so much with your rhetoric."

She took out a cigarette. Dermot picked up a yellow box of matches and reached past Wilson to give her a light. Her eyes were uncertain. She thanked him in a small voice.

Dermot had another drink and got out of there. He went down the alley and around to the front door of the INF hall.

Deirdre and Ronald sat in a haze of cigarette smoke. The room was crowded and busy. Deirdre said she would be over to the Melville Hotel for a drink when she could. As Dermot left, Philim Morrison stood at the entrance laughing and shaking hands with a few men. When he saw Dermot, he laughed a loud hello. He laughed even louder when he reached out to shake hands with an old man.

The Melville Hotel smelled like the inside of a beach house first opened for the season. The ground floor had French doors with dirty windows leading into a dining room with dusty paper tablecloths on the wooden tables. An old woman, who looked to be either drunk or retarded, came out from the back. Somehow she got up the flight of stairs to the second floor and showed Dermot to a room directly over the street. The bed was flush against the window. It was covered with a spread as thick as it was smelly. Dermot opened the window alongside the bed to air the place. Then he went down the hall to a vault of a sitting room where the guitar player and McGeady, conscious now, drank gin.

Dermot was on the second drink when the girl and Wilson walked in and sat on the floor. You could hear heavy rain on a skylight someplace. Dermot ordered a pint of stout, but when the old lady put the pint on the small table alongside him, a glass of gin was with it. The guitar player waved at him. His eyes were half shut. Dermot swallowed the gin, motioned to the old lady to bring another, and watched the guitar player drink his. The eyes stayed half shut, but he kept waving for drinks until the candidate gave up, stretching out on the floor. Bowlegged little girl asleep. Wilson stretched out next to her.

The cockeyed old lady came in and threw a blanket over them. McGeady came out of the chair, reaching to pull the blanket from them. "Take it off," he growled at the old lady. She asked him why. "Because it's immoral, the both of them covered." The woman pulled the blanket off Wilson, leaving the girl covered. That seemed to make McGeady feel better. In the middle of the next drink, Dermot's head began to droop. He struggled up and walked out without talking to anybody. The last thing he saw was the guitar player finishing a drink and wiping his hand on his beard.

He went up to his room and flopped on the bed without taking off his clothes. The middle of the bed sagged. There was so much water on the bedspread that it came through his jacket and shirt. He swung up, his rear end going right into the puddle. The streetlight outside the window picked out the rain still dripping from the open window, alongside the bed. He put his jacket and pants over a chair. The floor was wet around the bed. He went over to the door, where the rain had not reached, and sat down and fell asleep with his back against the door.

The noise of trucks shifting gears pulled Dermot awake. The tops of the trucks were even with the hotel window as they started down the hill. The jacket shoulders still were wet. The pants had dried a little. It was after seven o'clock. He looked out the window. Women walked on the sidewalk under the window toward the Catholic church behind the courthouse.

Dermot picked up the jacket and went down into the street. He ordered eggs and coffee at a lunch counter and asked the man if he could put the jacket near his stove. The man hung it over a chair and opened the oven door. When Dermot finished eating, he said he'd come back later for the jacket. He left a few extra shillings. Two doors down, he bought toothpaste and a toothbrush in a news agent's store. The alley between the bar and the INF hall smelled of piss. Dots of blood from a fight were around the beer kegs. Deirdre sat in the office, smoking and going over papers, as if she never had left. The place was crowded. Dermot went into a big bare back room, and brushed his teeth at a sink.

Out the window, across the slate roofs, out where the green hills began, a military helicopter fluttered and spiraled to land. Deirdre walked in while Dermot was watching it. "Lovely. The Army are here to help. The fooks."

"Why did you leave me up there all night?"

"If Lenin had to stay in the Melville Hotel he would have quit the revolution," she said. "I did come up, you know. They said you'd been asleep an hour. I just had some wee time to get to Bridget McAteer's house for a shower."

There was a sucking sound, Ronald with his cigarette. He stood looking at her until she went back to work at the desk.

Dermot stood around, morning-numb, while people walked in and out. Between phone calls, Deirdre asked him if he would go to morning mass.

"What for?" Dermot said.

"We have to watch wee Father McCluskey," she said.

The eight-o'clock mass at Sacred Heart Church had maybe a hundred women, kerchiefs keeping their lined, dry faces in semblance of ovals. Here and there an old man, eyes wet, jaw drooping.

353

After the Gospel, instead of going back and continuing saying mass, the way they always do on weekdays, the priest closed the book, blessed himself, and cleared his throat to begin a Sunday type of sermon. He looked up, then looked down, then cleared his throat again. He started talking about sin in a drone. Catholics are the only people able to make it uninteresting. The hundred women coughed like a thousand. Finally, eyes closed, the priest came up with something.

"The highways and byways of sin in Omagh!"

The amount of coughing dropped.

"Sins of the flesh! On the highways and byways of sin here in Omagh!"

There was complete silence now.

"Sins of the flesh! The Devil's personal sin!"

The priest looked above them, stepping out now. "Teenagers are strolling on the highways and byways of sin. Strolling hand in hand down deserted lanes here in Omagh! Those still unmarried are doing it! You see them of an evening. And even on Sunday afternoons! The Lord's day!"

He closed his eyes and began tapping his hand on the pulpit.

"And I think. . . ." He paused.

"Yes, I think they are. . . ." His head shook with emotion, eyes still tightly closed.

"Yes, I think they are. I think they are. I think they are. . . ."

Everybody was shifting around.

He shouted and slapped the pulpit hard.

"I know they are?"

"Even the widows are doing it!"

Dermot slid down the pew to the side aisle. He was behind a pillar, starting to step across the aisle, when the priest shifted gears casually.

"Now, dear Brethren in Jesus, here in Omagh we are at the very start of a secular exercise, an election of politicians, about which you will hear certain information from us on a regular basis. At this time, I merely would like to say that we are not fooled by any certain candidate who would live in sin in public in disdain for the Holy

354

Mother Church. And who at the same time dares to call *herself . . . herself . . .* a practicing Catholic. Cast about for suitable alternatives. I am certain there shall be one."

He turned to resume the mass. Dermot went out the door. He went down to the lunch counter and got his jacket. When he got back to the office, it was filled with young boys in fishermen's sweaters with sleeves pushed up, carrying stacks of brown franked envelopes and printed sheets to tables in the back room, and young girls with big vaccination marks on their arms. Older women sat at tables. Children ran around the room. Deirdre was talking to them. "While you're sittin' home watchin' TV and mindin' children you can stuff envelopes for us. They used the big hall in this building for dancin' classes Saturday afternoons. The teacher woman complains about us dirtyin' up the hall. Father McCluskey put her on to it. So ye'll best work at home."

Deirdre and the candidate took some papers and walked out of the office. Dermot followed them.

"What did the priest say?" Deirdre asked him.

Dermot told her the priest had said nothing.

"Aye, nothing," she said. "Only I hope you made it plain that the next time he says nothing again he'll have insurrection during the offertory."

They came around the side of the courthouse and almost into a circle of people standing in front of the steps. "Ah, here's me good opponent," the girl said.

Sunderland, the official Unionist Party candidate, stood with his hands clasped behind his back and his eyebrows working up and down rapidly, as if he had trouble focusing his eyes. He wore gray pinstripes and a vest. The other men around him stood with their arms folded. All hair was short, all shoulders squared. A woman came up and stood alongside Sunderland. The wife, it figured. A woman with beauty-parlor gray hair and a subdued glen-plaid suit, handbag held in both hands in front of her, standing with her legs slightly apart, English nature-walk stance. Her mouth might have been scrubbed with a lemon. Her pursed lips seemed to be saying, "Oh, no," as she

355

saw the girl's group, cigarettes in mouths, slacks, wrinkled clothes, round shoulders, long hair, coming toward her. The girl had her chin down and gave Sunderland a dark look as she walked past him. "Thinkin' up your wee election speech?" she said. His eyebrows stuttered in the shock of her talking to him.

They went toward a doorway alongside the steps on the ground floor. As they came to it, the door opened and a great laugh came out of the hallway. Philim Morrison stood there with a group of men, one of them a priest. Philim threw his head back and almost shouted when he saw them coming. He held out his hand in a hello. Deirdre held hers out, palm up.

"Do ye have the twenty-five-pound donation for our wee election?"

He kept laughing. The others with him kept laughing. Philim had a sheet of paper in his hands.

"I see ye've got your wee receipt for your election deposit," the girl said.

Philim kept laughing.

"I thought ye was a great believer in Socialism," Deirdre said. "You were till the end of last night, anyway."

"He runs as a Socialist," the priest growled. "But not your kind of Socialist. He's no Godless International Socialist."

"And what is it that he is?" Deirdre said.

"Philim Morrison runs as a National Socialist," the priest said.

The girl said to Philim, "Is that in fact the name of your official party organization? The National Socialist?"

Philim shook his head yes. Then he and the rest of them went away and Deirdre and the girl looked at each other and laughed. Deirdre stood next to Dermot.

"Are we ever going to get back to Derry?" he said.

"With us tonight. After the last meeting."

"Who's going?"

"Ronald, me, and you."

"Let's leave Ronald here."

She didn't answer him.

Everybody got into cars, three of them, and they drove to a town called Sion Mills. Women sat along a low wall in front of a red-brick Presbyterian church. They turned down a street and drove under trees to a factory. The entrance was a road under trees with a parking lot on one side. At the end of the road was a yellow-brick wall with an arch over it. On it the year 1835 was inscribed. Inside the arch was a courtyard running into a four-story building with the windows painted over. As they parked the cars, a small black car with two men in it pulled alongside. One stayed at the wheel. The other, a tall guy with a blank face and eyeglasses hooked into his mouth came over to them. He was dressed for a country club, in brown plain jacket, yellow shirt, green tie, brown suede shoes. He still smelled cop.

"I'm Inspector Roundtree," he said.

"Ah, yes, I know you, Inspector," the candidate said. She had her small crooked smile.

"Ah, you can't, you know, go anywhere except, in actual fact, the parking lot here."

"Aye. We're law-abidin'," she said.

His knees bent and his head went back in an icy imitation of a laugh. He tapped the end of his glasses against his front teeth. He itched his nose with the end of his glasses. He hooked them back into his mouth. The girl stared at him. "Very good," he said. He took long strides back to the car and drove off.

At one end of the parking lot, a woman came out from under the trees. She had on a white knitted poncho and an orange dress. Blue eye make-up and blue-gray hair. She cocked her head. She pulled a trigger to start her voice.

"Where's Her Majesty's flag?"

Teen-age boys, crew cuts and dungaree suits, tall gawky kids with mean lines to their lips, gathered around her.

"Where's the flag, you varmin?" one of them shouted. "The flag you get your dole under."

"She'll be under Her Majesty's Service soon enough," the woman in the poncho cackled. "Right there, that one there." She pointed at Deirdre. "And the other wee bitch

357

right after her." The woman threw her head back and laughed. "Bread and water."

A bell rang in the factory courtyard. A door in the factory building flew open and people rushed out, tumbling against each other. Over the heads of the people coming out of the door you could see the others jammed on the stairway inside, everybody lined up and straining to leave, just like grammar school. But nobody moving until the final bell. Some of them trotted down the road under the trees. Others stopped and drifted into the lot. Deirdre was standing in the road, calling through a bullhorn. The candidate got up on top of one of the cars in the parking lot.

When a crowd gathered, the girl on top of the car called out through her bullhorn, "People of Sion Mills! Workers of the linen factory!" The voice poked at the people listening to her. It enraged the woman in the poncho. By now, there were other women and young girls around her. And more teen-age boys, and now men came out from the trees and stood with her.

The candidate started talking to the crowd in front of her, perhaps three hundred. "The people not listening to us are the same as the ones who are listening. It's the government who won't give them better housing. As it will not give it to us. They're running out of here to vote for the government that keeps them destitute and in slums. Why run from me? I'm not the person who charges two pounds a week for council housing. I'm not the person who pays you ten-pound wages for a forty-eight-hour week. The factory owner who backs the government does that. I believe there should be a basic minimum wage of twenty pound for a forty-hour week. Does this in fact make me an enemy? Does this make me a dangerous Catholic? Does this make me a Communist? Or does this make me a person who speaks against a Unionist government which has fooled us all, Catholics and Protestants, for fifty years? And which has turned us against each other. Meanwhile, this man owning the factory here sends his linen thread to Belfast and becomes rich, and you go home to your wee houses with nothing. How much of the factory profits go to you? Enough money for you to live on isn't enough money for your kids to live on."

The first stone scaled at her was flat and white and it sliced badly and went far to the right. The next stone was a black rock and it banged off the top of the car at her feet with a loud noise. It brought a growl from the crowd around her. Across the lot, the crowd around the woman shrieked. You could hear the screaming curses. More rocks came. Up on the car, one of her legs came up as a stone hit her on the thigh.

Dermot came through the crowd. He got one foot on the back of the car, came up on the trunk, and got on the car roof. He stood with his right hand out, palm open. One rock came close and he slapped at it and the rock skipped off. The girl poked him. "You'll have to move over so's I can see what I'm about."

Dermot didn't move. The Protestant kids were throwing rocks with a sidearm motion, running up and leaning way back and throwing from just off the hip, the entire body spinning in a follow-through. A few of the rocks came short and the rest of them went wide. The four or five that were on the mark were easy enough to handle and there shouldn't have been any worry. It was only rocks they were throwing. But it was the way they were being thrown that made it different. Young kids throbbing with rage and screaming things while the women with the one in the white poncho cheered and shook their fists.

The group in front of the cars trying to listen to the girl talk was much smaller than the crowd cheering the rock-throwers on. But a couple of young ones picked up rocks and turned around and flung them at the crowd of Protestants. And a girl, barelegged with a factory smock dress under her raincoat, turned and walked toward them, her head bobbing as she shouted things. A girl in a rainjacket and dungarees started out from the other crowd. Deirdre and Patsy grabbed the girl in the smock dress and brought her back. The Protestant girl stopped and went back to her crowd.

But the rocks kept coming, and Dermot took the candidate by the arm and they slid down off the car. The doors were open and they got in. Horn honking, they moved out through the crowd. A rock hit the top of the car. Another one boomed off the side. Dermot was in front with Deirdre. Sean drove. Dungaree suits were loping through the trees trying to get footing to throw, and the car picked up speed and they had to run faster. The car had to go through a loose alley of people. Enough hands coming out to throw rocks to keep it dangerous.

Somebody in the crowd held out a black iron bar and Sean made the car swerve but the bar came at the window, kept coming right at Dermot, and he threw his arm over his face and over across Deirdre. The bar smacked into the windshield and the glass turned to greenish foam and the car skidded, righted, and rushed for the gates. Bits of green-white glass covered Sean's hair like a mantle. Glass was all over the place.

When they got outside the town they stopped. They all got out and brushed thick bits of glass from their clothes. Sean took off his jacket and began swatting it on the seat.

"Just a little glass," the candidate said.

Sean stopped brushing the seat. He looked at the windshield. There was a hole in it. "I hope glass is all it will be," he said.

On the way back to Omagh, the girl said to Wilson, "You were all right, were you not?"

Dermot spun around, but Wilson dropped his eyes and Ronald looked out the window.

Omagh was empty in the early evening. Cars coming down the hill from the courthouse were too loud. The crows circling the courthouse began coming very low, their squawking sounding like shouts on the stone street. At the bottom of the hill, on a street coming out of the Protestant section, three cops in black raincoats stood motionless on a corner.

In front of the INF hall, the candidate got out and went up to Philim Morrison, the priest who had been with him earlier, and a couple of older men. Deirdre walked quickly into the discussion.

"I agree absolutely with what you say," the girl said to

360

the priest. "Neither of us shall attack each other with statements of a personal nature."

"Aye," the priest said. "In that way we can hold the Catholic vote together. It will not be split out of bitterness. Near the end, the candidate adjudged to be losing then can drop out in favor of the one with the better chance of winning."

"Of course," the girl said. She held out her hand. The priest took it. She held out her hand to Morrison. He took it and laughed. They broke up. The candidate went over and sat on the still-empty courthouse steps, a little girl with a bullhorn in her lap and a cigarette in her mouth. People were coming down from the streets behind the courthouse. They gathered in the space in front of the courthouse steps. There were twelve wide steps leading to a front of four pillars and stone lions. Down the hill, out of the street leading to the Protestant section, the gangly kids in dungarees formed in bunches.

Deirdre started up the steps. She turned and looked down at Dermot. "Oh, I forgot, in actual fact, to tell you. Ronald is remaining. So it'll be just you and I going to Derry tonight."

He came up after her. He got her by the arm and started pulling her down. She was laughing. "For Jesus' sake, I've got to make a wee speech."

He walked back to the sidewalk in front of the Melville. Down the street, the Protestant crowd was milling around in front of the Royal Arms Hotel. The Inspector was there, now in uniform. The three cops in the raincoats were coming up the street. The Protestants started up after them. The cops ignored them and kept coming. They stopped in front of the Melville.

"A wee election," one of them said.

"Be over soon, I guess," the one next to him said.

The crowd was getting bigger. Deirdre went up two steps and picked up the bullhorn. "People of Mid-Ulster! People of Omagh!" Philim Morrison, the priest, and two or three others were standing near the cops, listening to her.

"I want to welcome tonight into the election race the very honorable Philim Morrison of Omagh." The men with

361

Morrison clapped and a few others in the crowd followed.

"Actually, I do not welcome him into the race as much as the pub owner who'll finally get paid when the Bishop gives Philim Morrison his bonus for running. However, I like Philim Morrison. I will defend Philim Morrison. I do not think that it is fair for people here to be talkin' about the fact that Philim Morrison lost the farm his father left to him. He lost it backing horses that did not win. I think that is none of our business. I think Philim Morrison . . ."

Standing on the sidewalk, Philim Morrison appeared to be struggling against a stroke. The priest alongside him was thrashing his body in the circle of people around him. One of them bumped and shoved through the crowd. He got to the steps, waving his arm. The candidate saw him. She stood up and came down and leaned over to listen. She shook her head violently and pointed at Deirdre. She shrugged and followed the guy through the crowd to the priest. Dermot got right up next to them.

"You gave your hand . . ." the priest began.

"I said I would not attack Philim Morrison," she said. "I intend to abide by my promise. I shall not mention him."

"But what of this girl's lies?" the priest said, the arm waving like a flag at Deirdre.

The little girl had her eyes half closed. "Oh, you must speak to her yourself," she said. "I gave you my word. If you want hers, then you must get it from her."

She went back through the crowd to the steps.

"Lastly," Deirdre was calling out, "I would like you all to know the name of the political party Philim Morrison represents. It is a party formed by, and named by his good priestly backer. The name of Philim Morrison's party is the National . . . Socialist . . . Party. National Socialist Party."

Deirdre pointed at Philim and the priest and heads turned to look at them.

"The last man who ran as a National Socialist was Hitler!"

The crowd roared and the heads turned and the priest and Philim, heads down, went up the sidewalk toward the INF hall.

Dermot turned around and saw another priest standing in the doorway of the Melville. He drifted down the sidewalk and got next to him.

"What do you think, Father?" Dermot said.

"From America?" he said.

"Yes, I am."

"I've got people there," he said.

"Have you?"

"Cousin in the Bronx."

"The Bronx? Good place, the Bronx."

"They live on Gun Hill Road."

"Gun Hill Road, I know Gun Hill Road."

"There's a wee place there, McChesney's."

"I went to McChesney's all my life," Dermot said.

"Aye," he said. "Nice wee place."

"Are you up here in Sacred Heart?"

"No, I'm from Dungannon," he said.

"What brings you here?" Dermot said.

"Just wanted hear the speakin'."

"The girl?"

"Aye. I believe the girl to be brilliant."

"Do you?"

"Aye. And the wee girl talkin' now is brilliant herself, you know."

Dermot took him by the elbow. "Let's go for a drink."

"Well, I don't want to miss anything."

He said this while he was walking. Inside the Diamond, the priest sat at a table and ordered Bushmill's. The guitar player was standing up plucking the instrument. "I'll have a wee one with you, Father, then I have to go out and do me stint." Dermot said he'd be right back and trotted over to the side of the courthouse steps. Deirdre was finished. Patsy was up with arms flailing the air, screaming about traitors. He mentioned Philim Morrison and the audience clapped. Deirdre came over to Dermot. "When do we go?" he said. She gave him the car keys. "I want to wait for a wee while," she said. He started away. "You're sure about it's just you and me?" She smiled.

He came back into the bar and sat down next to the priest, who was ready for another drink. Dermot got it. They finished the drink and went around to the front of the courthouse. There were about fifteen hundred people listening now. Egan was up, both arms spread to the sky. The guitar player was starting to come up the steps. Egan's foot came out in a semi-kick. The guitar player backed off. Egan screamed something into the night. Dermot took the priest back to the Diamond. This time he stood at the bar. Dermot had stout. The priest stuck to Bushmill's. The door was open and the wet evening air blew in. They went back outside. The guitar player was singing now.

"Want to stand a little closer, Father?" Dermot said.

"Oh, no, I'm sure it's all right here."

"Come on up front so you can hear better."

Dermot put his hand on the priest's shoulder and moved him right to the edge of the steps. Nobody could miss seeing him there. The priest looked at the candidate closely. "She is is a wee little girl, isn't she?" he said.

Dermot walked him right up the steps. Deirdre was up, hand out to greet him. The girl was on the priest, smiling, shaking his hand. The guitar player let out a singing shout and he finished his last number.

"Care to say a couple of words?" Dermot said to the priest.

"Oh notatall, notatall," he said.

"If ye've got sense to come hear her give a talk, then I'll bet you're a fantastic speaker yourself," Deirdre said.

The priest beamed. Deirdre slapped him on the shoulder. She got up and introduced him. "Just a few words," he said to her. His breath made her pull her face back.

The first thing the priest did was try to dig his feet into the batter's box. His chest bulged as he sucked in a deep breath. He jammed his right hand into his jacket pocket. The left hand came out, finger pointing. A perfect imitation of Jack Kennedy until Deirdre put the bullhorn into his left hand.

The voice rolled out of him. "People of Mid-Ulster! People of Omagh!"

Deirdre clapped her hands without making noise. "She is a Catholic!" He pointed at the girl. "But she spoke with a free mind. That's a terrible thing in this country. They want you to agree with them. And always go around thumping your craw. They want . . ."

Deirdre crept along the step to Dermot. "Fantastic!"

"Thank you, and let's go," he said.

"Just a wee little while. I'll come right around to the car."

Dermot walked to the car and Ronald was there looking inside it. He was rubbing the back of his neck. His face seemed pained.

"What's the matter?" Dermot said, It was the first time he'd spoken to him in a day.

"Just lookin' for work to keep me busy," he said. He giggled. "Only thirteen hours so far today. I must fill up the slack time, you know."

Dermot didn't answer him.

"Actually, I'm looking for the keys to the car. I just was on to them at Tobermore. They're all mucking about. I'll have to get Deirdre and drive down straight off."

"Come on for a drink," Dermot said to him.

"I'm best waiting here," he said.

"Come on!"

Ronald slouched into the bar, his head hanging. Dermot stepped out of the way to let him go through. Then he came in after him. Dermot kept his head down and didn't look up. He looked at Ronald's rear end and kept looking at it. He didn't bring the head up, and he kicked him. It was a hard kick, a real hard kick, and Ronald went across the empty lounge to the back of it. He was half paralyzed for a moment and Dermot came right up and gave him another, this one a hell of a kick. It drove Ronald right to the door leading to the alley. He stumbled out the door and Dermot was all over him, shoving him so he would go down toward the office. Deirdre would see him. Ronald started down the alley. Dermot kept his head down. Ronald ran and Dermot ran after him and kicked him again. He didn't look at him. He turned around at the finish of the kick and went out and waited by the car. Deirdre came around from the courthouse running. He held the car door for her.

The wet wind blew through the hole in the windshield. She put her head almost on his chest and pulled her coat together against the cold. As they drove they talked about the election and people in Derry. They did not mention Ronald. When he brought up the word "jail," she closed her eyes. "I don't want to hear it," she said.

"Where are we going now?" he asked her.

"To one more meetin'."

"Then to Derry," he said.

"No, to Donegal. Eamonn has a cottage there and I already rang him up and he said we could use it."

The road came up a hill and into loud noise running through the fields. It grew louder and louder as the car came to a couple of white buildings at a crossroads. Dermot stopped in the middle of the crossroads. A fat guy with hair in bangs was beating an enormous drum. He was bent backward against the size of it. Then he made it sound in a sort of rhythm. He gave three huge booms. Then he began to do rolls on the drum. He made the one last booming sound, then turned around and walked in a one-man parade into the courtyard behind one of the buildings at the crossroads.

"They send messages with it," Deirdre said. "There's certain ways they bang on it and it sends messages out."

"Fuckin' Indians?" Dermot laughed. He got out and walked over to the courtyard. There was terrific noise coming out of it now. Two drummers were in the courtyard, the guy with the bangs and an old man in a brown shirt with suspenders holding up pants that were nearly falling off as he banged away. A crowd of about twenty stood around drinking Guinness out of bottles. The place must have been a stable once, but now cases of Guinness were stacked under the sheds. The two drummers banged the drums with sticks made of long whittled tree branches. The drums had big paintings on them. The guy with the bangs had a drum with ornate printing saying J. WHITESIDE 126 UTILITY. The old man, who was toothless, had a drum decorated with a painting of an immense fat queen with battleship tits. Printing on the drumhead said ABSOLUTE TEMPERANCE OL. As the old man with no teeth banged away on his absolute-temperance drum, one of the men watching held a bottle of stout up to the old man's mouth. The old man stopped banging the drum. He took the bottle in his toothless mouth, gums showing, and the guy holding the bottle tipped it. It was like feeding a baby. The old man had a baseball inside his chicken-skin neck. The baseball bobbed rapidly as he emptied almost half the bottle of Guinness. He began banging again.

The man with the bangs stopped playing. A younger guy took over. A man acting like a fight trainer helped the younger guy into the harness. He pulled on the ropes to tighten the drumhead. The younger guy started playing. Knees bent, pants riding down on his hips, he started to drive the sticks against the drum as fast as they could be moved. His hips swayed and his feet were coming up a bit to break the tensions and everybody stood around and watched him, the way trainers watch a guy hitting the light bag in a gymnasium. The drum was so wide that the young guy's wrists kept hitting the edge of the drum. He had thick bumps on the insides of his wrists.

Dermot walked out of the noise and back to the car. "It seems to be their idea of a sport."

She said nothing.

"Why don't you look next time? It's better to know than to walk around afraid of something you can't see."

"I know what I'm speakin' of," she said. "Nothing is subtle around here."

They came down a long hill running between fields. Everywhere you could hear the big drums booming. Now there were well-dressed, stiff-faced people walking along the side of the road. Off to the right was an Orange Lodge Hall. People were coming out in groups of three and four. The men were all going the other way. The car came down a slope to a small bridge over a shallow river that had mist rising from it. The road went up from the bridge.

A hundred yards or so up the road there was a small store with a night light in the window and a few doors up was a pub with no signs on it.

People were across the street from the pub in an open space that ran along a stone wall. Cars coming up the hill from the bridge rushed along, just missing the people standing at the edge of the meeting area. Then the cars rushed into darkness as the road ran between trees. The cars coming out of the darkness ran past the front of the saloon. The booming of the drums was unnerving as it ran through the hills and fields. The people kept coming along the road. Just a few, and still in the distance. But coming with the sound of the drums in the background. Across the bridge and up the hill came the two small Army trucks, their antennas waving as they came along the bumpy road. The trucks swerved onto a side road several yards from the meeting place. It was getting dark and people were gathering and Patsy wasn't around to start the talking. Deirdre went into the pub looking for him. It was a bare place with a bar that had no mirrors or bottles on shelves. Just a wooden bar and a thin old man behind it and it was packed with men drinking warm stout. Patsy was in the middle of a large circle. As usual only he spoke.

"The first two jabs, will ye not remember them forever?" he was saying.

Somebody said, "What is it he said?" and Deirdre said to him, "When Billy Kelly came out straight off against Sammy McCarthy. The first two jabs."

"Oh, aye," the man said.

Patsy nodded to Deirdre. He drained the glass and reached through them to knock it on the bar. He went outside to start the thing. Deirdre held up a hand and the bartender came over. She ordered two pints.

"The fight I mentioned took place before I could read a newspaper," she said. "But, in actual fact, I have to know every blow that was landed. Billy Kelly was from Derry, you see. He won the British Empire something or other. Defeated Sammy McCarthy in Belfast before Christ was born, as far as I'm concerned. But around here it's their lives, you know."

She put a cigarette in her mouth. Dermot went through his pockets, didn't find any matches. He called the bartender and bought one of the yellow boxes of matches for twopence. He started to light the cigarette for her but a man bumped into him in the crowded room and the match went out.

"Here, I'll do for meself," she said.

She took the matchbox and started for the door. "We'll be ten minutes here and then off to Donegal," she said. She smiled and went out the door, hair swinging.

The barman was standing with his arms folded. He looked down at his watch. "All right, lads," he said. "Time, lads." He began gathering glasses on the bar. The crowd in the room began swallowing and growling. One of them asked him why he was closing. "Because of all the Army and police across the way at the meetin'," he said. "Tonight we best obey the curfew."

"Oh, Jesus Christ," a man said. He had to be over seventy. A cap was pulled over a bony nose specked with blackheads. Watery eyes looked out from under the cap. Dermot walked outside behind him.

Across the road, Patsy was talking. Three words. Stop. Two words. Stop. Three more words. The old man listened for a couple of stops and starts, then he started walking down to the bridge. Dermot went along after him. He stopped and looked at the water. Dark water that looked cold ran fast over a rocky bottom. The mist rose from the water and curled around their feet.

There was a noise, a bolt clicking, and Dermot turned around. In the almost darkness he saw the soldiers, sitting in the two trucks and the jeep several yards down the side road they had turned into. Down the hill, a crowd of kids in dungaree suits and an old man in a dark suit had come along the road until they were within yelling distance of the bridge. They stood in clusters and you could hear their voices calling up, "Dole . . . Vermin . . . Fook the Pope . . ."

The old man was telling Dermot about the good salmon

fishing in the river. Patsy's voice was still coming through the bullhorn when they left the bridge and walked up the hill. The little store with the night light in the window had a display of taffy, cigarettes, plastic hair dryers, and magazines about television stars.

They walked up in front of the saloon. Deirdre was up talking now. Where she was, across the road, there was a half-blue light in the air. To the right, where the road went under the trees, it all became dark. She stood in the deep blue with her voice clear and beautiful and her head high and she talked about prison now, her chin coming straight out.

"I don't give a damn if I go to jail for a million years, we still will bring out people off their knees."

The people clapped and cheered. They spilled into the roadway and a car rushing up from the bridge had to swerve away from them.

The man with the blackheads said he wanted a drink. Deirdre was finishing, but the others weren't here yet, so she wouldn't come down until the guitar player and the candidate took over. She pointed to somebody in the crowd and waved him up onto the back of the truck with her. The old man started down an alley alongside the saloon and Dermot went with him.

"What do you do with yourself around here?" Dermot asked.

"I'm unemployed at the present time. Had been workin'. I was put on redundancy. I was general laborin' at the Michelin plant. I tell you what it is, there's very little industry around here. Most of them here travels, you know."

"Where to?"

"Belfast."

"How far is that?"

"Be forty mile to Belfast."

The old man banged on the back door of the saloon. When nobody answered he dropped onto his stomach, pressed his cheek against the ground, and tried to look through the space between the bottom of the door and the floor. He was still down when Dermot heard noise from the road. He looked down the alley and saw cars pulling into the crowd. Then he heard the voice coming through the bullhorn, and it was the girl's voice, not Deirdre's, and Deirdre was through and they could go to Donegal.

He was just starting up the alley when a car with a loud engine roared up from the bridge. There was an explosion in front of the saloon. It registered slowly. But he knew it was a shot. The car roared up the road under the trees. Screams came from the road. Men were running and shouting.

Dermot was down the alley running to the street. There were more shots out on the road and people were throwing themselves on the ground. A pack of women and men came screaming into the alley. He tried to get through them but they kept running against him and he had to turn sideways and smack at them with his hands to get through. He ran into a small boy and knocked him straight back, and when he tried to step over him he tripped and ripped his knee open as he fell. He got up and half ran, half stumbled, one hand out to keep from falling. He ran into a soldier who was at the entrance to the alley with his rifle at him. Dermot didn't even look at it and started to go past him, but another one came up from the side and slapped his rifle into Dermot's side and he went up against the wall. Soldiers were running and waving and one of the trucks raced past, going up the road into the darkness under the trees. The soldiers in the back of it were standing with their rifles pointed ahead. The soldiers in the road kept chasing everybody away and then the second truck came whining up. It poked its hood into the small crowd of people pushing around where the speaking had been.

Soldiers tumbled out of the rear of the truck and reached down. Patsy's face came up from alongside the truck. He came up with his arms under Deirdre's shoulders, lifting her up onto the back of the truck. Her head was hanging back. As Patsy brought her up to put her onto the truck, the head came forward. There was nothing between the forehead and the chin. Blood pouring onto her black coat. And some white lumps in the blood. They had her stretched out on the back of the truck now. The people got out of the way and the truck pulled back onto the road and it started down toward the bridge, tires whining, with the antenna waving and a soldier jumping on the back, cowboy style, his rifle held up. The soldier pushed Deirdre's legs over so he would have room to sit down.

The candidate, a cigarette in her mouth, eyes straight ahead, walked past the soldiers and slipped into a car. As the car started off, somebody pulled the guitar in through the window. A jeep rocked to a halt in the middle of the street. The driver shouted. The two soldiers, keeping Dermot in the alley, left him. The soldiers ran out to the jeep and swung onto the back. The jeep jumped forward and started after the car with the candidate in it.

There were two groups in the street. The old people stood talking to one another. "Christ," one of them was saying, "they was aiming for herself and they got the goddamned poor wrong one."

"Comin' so goddamned fast, the car was," another man said.

Cold air blowing through the hole in the windshield. There was rain when he got to Magherafelt, where the hospital was, rain coming out of the darkness and streaming down the glass entrance doors. A fat policeman slept on a bench inside the doors. The cop woke up and mumbled that there would be Army surgeons around in the morning. "There are to be an autopsy you know. Searchin' for the type of slug, you know. Dunno if there are much left to search through, you know."

Dermot's car outside was alongside a tree with a puddle spreading from the trunk. He was walking around the puddle when the car began waving and the lights at the entranceway began waving and he felt everything rushing from the back of his head and he put his hands out to stop himself from falling face first into the tree. His palms went against the trees and held him up. He lost a couple of seconds. Then he felt his feet splash in the puddle. His arms were held out stiff. The arms began trembling badly. Dermot hung his head between his arms to try and get rid of the dizziness. In the rain with his head hanging between his arms and the first thirteen years of his life telling him to say a prayer from the Baltimore Catechism.

He did not feel well enough to pick out words.

A few minutes later, when he felt clear, when he could hear and feel the rain, he picked up his head. All he could see was Tara standing on the stoop with her thumbs in her ears and the other fingers clenched in her hair, pulling at it, trying to punish him for not taking her to the puppet show. He got into the car and drove for a while on the black twisting road. His head suddenly became light and he pulled the car into deep grass on the side of the road. He woke up in daylight, damp and shivering. He did not want to drive any more. He stepped into the road and began hitching.

The second ride, a lorry, brought him into Derry. Morning light put streaks of silver into the slate-gray of the river. In the saloon, a man was in the back room, a room with a dart bard. The man read a newspaper in the light coming through a skylight.

"Jesus Christ," the man said.

"Davey around?" Dermot said.

"Jimmy? He had to go away to Bundoran. Go for his mail. Be two hours yet."

The man shook his head as he looked at the paper again. "Christ, it was a fooker."

"Bad night?" Dermot said.

"They be all fookin' bad from now on."

"What time did it start last night?" Dermot asked him.

"Christ, they was out of the house soon as it became dark, you know."

"They heard about it in a hurry, I guess," Dermot said.

"Heard what?"

"The thing last night."

"What did they fookin' have to hear? They was too busy doin' it."

"I mean, the girl got shot last night."

"Which girl is it?"

373

"At the election meeting."

"Oh, that one. She's a fookin' Communist. She's from Derry, you know. I'm sorry she died. Still was a fookin' Communist. We care about freein' Ireland. We're green, not fookin' red."

Dermot spread change on the bar, picked out a sixpence, and went to the phone on the wall. He called the City Hotel.

"El Humpo! Where have you been?" John had a night's sleep in his voice.

"What's doin'?" Dermot said.

"What's doin'? Reading the newspaper and waitin' for you. Listen to this thing. A woman in Letterkenny was too old to take care of her property. The weeds covered her doorway. Nobody could get in or out. Do you know what the judge had them do? He had them tie a goat on her front lawn. How do you like it? Jesus Christ, you ought to read the papers here. Oh, God bless our people."

"I'll be down in a couple of minutes," Dermot said.

At the end of the long narrow smoky street leading to Derry Free Corner, Eddie Canavan was against the wall of a building. He had his hand inside his jacket. Two young boys stood with him, smoking cigarettes. A car came along Rossville Street. Eddie Canavan stepped out and held up his hand. The car slowed. Eddie Canavan slapped the hood of the car. The car stopped. He walked around to the driver's side. Eddie Canavan inspected the car. He kept one hand inside the jacket. The man driving the car stared at the hand.

Canavan nodded and straightened up. The car went on. Eddie Canavan waved to somebody down the narrow street in the Brandywell.

Canavan nodded to Dermot. "Clompin' down now," he said. "Be doin' things the way they should be from now on. This is now a military operation."

He took his hand out from inside his jacket and ran the hand over his hair.

"Here ye be!"

Finbar's son J.J. came out of the crowd on the corner.

Eddie Canavan walked back and stood at the wall with the two very young boys.

"Oh, it got to be fookin' rough last night," J.J. said.

Dermot didn't talk.

"Jesus Christ, where were you? It got good and fookin' rough."

Dermot tried to walk past him.

"Where ye goin'?"

J.J. kept positioning himself directly in front of Dermot. "You said you'd listen to the record for Tony Bennett."

Dermot said nothing. J.J. ran across the street to the bookmaking shop. Dermot started up the hill toward the wall. Footsteps pounded up from behind him. J.J. came alongside Dermot holding out a brown cardboard jacket with a record inside.

"I'm going home," Dermot said.

J.J.'s left eye slid back and forth. "To New York!"

"Yes."

"You said you'd see Tony Bennett for me!"

Dermot went through the arch on the wall and started to turn down Magazine Street, to walk to the hotel without having to pass the old building where Deirdre lived, and J.J. had him by the elbow.

"You said," J.J. said.

Dermot was sleepwalking, and J.J. led him down Butcher Street to an electrical and television shop in the town square. From the shop it was straight down the hill to the arch in the wall and the City Hotel. Dermot was looking down the hill when a loud crash of an organ came out of the stereo. A British voice said, "Lou Gray Music proudly presents an original composition by Mister J.J. Davey. It is entitled 'Jeanie.'" There was another loud crash of the organ.

"Jean-nie . . ."

Dermot barely heard the words. They were being sung to a flat tune. There was a final crash of the organ and the record was over.

J.J. grabbed Dermot's arm. "Did ye not like it?"

"I couldn't make it out so good," Dermot said.

"Christ! I fookin' told you it needs a Tony Bennett arrangement."

"I don't know," Dermot said. "I couldn't make out the tune."

"Oh, I didn't write the music," J.J. said. "I only wrote the words. That's what I mean. It needs Tony Bennett to get a big arrangement. This time just listen for the words." J.J. put the record on again. The organ crashed and Lou Gray's voice came on. When Lou Gray started the song, J.J. began to sing with the record, sing in the same tuneless sound.

> "Jean-nie
> I stand with you
> In the shadow of the wall
> Everything seems new
> My love for you is all
> Jean-nie."

J.J. stood looking at something that was far away and his fingers tapped on the cabinet of the stereo. The organ music on the record of Lou Gray of London crashed. Lou Gray sang the song a second time. J.J. sang with him, sang his song that had no music. J.J. did not hear Dermot tell him that he would be back, that he just was going to walk down to the hotel. Dermot walked out of the shop and went down the hill to the City Hotel, down a hill he would not come up again. J.J. Davey stayed in the shop and looked at things very far away and sang his song that had no music.

epilogue

In May of 1971, the year after, on a bright, soft afternoon, under a sky washed clean, Dermot Davey was walking out of court, coming out of the side entrance, starting up Queens Boulevard to get the Q-19 bus home. Traffic on the boulevard was stopped and, with no noise from cars and busses, the shout stopped Dermot in his tracks.

"El Humpo!"

Johno hung in the doorway of the Pump Room across the street. His stomach was enormous in a tan sweater.

"Come on, hump."

It was two in the afternoon and the bar was empty. Johno was set up for the day. Cigarettes and lighter on top of the cigarettes on one side. Wet bills and change in front of him under the glass. Wooden bowl of peanuts on the other side.

"Let's do some drinkin'," he said.

"I got like four dollars to my name," Dermot said.

"We'll get lucky," Johno said.

They drank beer until five. They had three dollars and change between them. A couple of lawyers came in after court.

"Counselors!" Johno said. The lawyers bought a couple.

Dermot moved over into the corner of the bar so she wouldn't see him when she passed the window on her way into the apartment house. The bar emptied at six-thirty. Johno lumbered to the men's room. On the way back, he stopped to talk to somebody in the dimness up at the

377

other end of the long bar. He stayed there for a couple of minutes. The bartender brought Dermot a bottle of beer. "This is on the gentleman at the other end," he said.

Dermot walked up into the dimness. Johno had his head down, next to a black man. The black man was hunched over the bar. His hand shook as he picked up a drink.

"This is Dick, he got a problem here," Johno said. "He's a good fella and he got a bad problem. Big problem. Giant problem."

"What is it?" Dermot said.

"He goes with the Bailey girl. They got the jury out right now."

Dermot knew the case. Bailey was a black dame in Elmhurst, near where Louis Armstrong lived. She and her husband broke up and they found her little girl strangled. They had her on trial for homicide. Nigger murder, Dermot thought, means nothing to them.

"How the hell they could say she killed that kid," the black guy, Dick, said.

"I wish you luck," Dermot said.

"They told me not to come near across the street," the black guy said. "They let her call me up here on the phone before. Her and the lawyer. They just sittin' upstairs in an office waitin'. They told me don't come near the place. You know, I could make it worse."

"The jury didn't go out to dinner," Johno said. "They must be close to something."

"Christ, I guess so," Dermot said.

Johno came around Dick. He put his hand on Dermot's arm. "Go over there and give us a reading, will you?"

Dermot took his tunic out of the checkroom and went across the street. The courtroom was on the third floor. The attendant standing in the hallway said the assistant district attorney and his detectives were in Luigi's. He was going to call them when the jury came back.

Dermot came back to the Pump Room. He sat at the window and stared down the boulevard toward Luigi's.

"Come on over here," the black man called.

Dermot just waved. "He can't, he's got to watch," he heard Johno telling the black guy.

Dermot was on his third bottle of beer since he'd come back from the court when he saw them, six of them, the three assistant district attorneys walking first, the detectives following them. They walked across Queens Boulevard quickly, their arms swinging. Dermot went out the door after them.

Upstairs, the hallway was empty. The attendant said, "You comin' in, I'm going to lock it."

"I don't want to come in and get stuck," Dermot said. "Just look out and tell me what it is."

The attendant shrugged and closed the door after him. Dermot stood at the window smoking a cigarette and watched the last of the spring evening fade on Queens Boulevard. The red neons over the Pump Room were on.

The courtroom door came open.

"Manslaughter One," the attendant called. The door shut.

Dermot came out of the courthouse alone and on the run. There was a break in the traffic and he ran across Queens Boulevard in full stride, his face becoming red, his mouth open to breathe, his feet coming down sloppily. He came up the steps and into the bar on the run.

"Manslaughter One," he called out.

In the dimness at the end of the bar he could see the black face looking at him. The face looked puzzled.

"Manslaughter One," Dermot said again.

Johno put his arm on the guy's shoulder. "Jesus Christ," Johno said.

The black guy kept looking at Dermot. "They must be crazy," he said.

"Well, that's it," Dermot said.

The guy looked down at his drink. "Manslaughter One."

"Drink up," Johno said.

A few minutes later, the black guy picked up his cigarettes. "I got to go around the corner to the lawyer's office. Thanks for the help."

"Hey, Dick," Johno said.

"What?" Dick said.

Johno dropped his head. Dermot heard him saying, "I

mean, look what the guy went over and did for you. I mean, he had to see somebody over there himself."

Dermot got up from his stool. He walked back to the men's room with his heels making noise so he would not hear Johno talking to the man. He leaned against the door and smoked a cigarette. When he came out, the black guy was gone. Dermot felt better about that.

"El Humpo!"

He picked up Dermot's glass. There were some ten-dollar bills under the glass.

"I told you we'd make a score!"

"I never figured we'd score off some nigger in here," Dermot said.

"Hump!"

Dermot picked up his drink and drained it. The ice came against his teeth and the Scotch tasted good. He put the glass down and picked up some change and walked over to the juke box. While he was at the juke box, he began to think about calling the girl upstairs.

THE BIG BESTSELLERS
ARE AVON BOOKS!

World Without End, Amen Jimmy Breslin	19042	$1.75
The Amazing World of Kreskin Kreskin	19034	$1.50
The Oath Elie Wiesel	19083	$1.75
A Different Woman Jane Howard	19075	$1.95
The Alchemist Les Whitten	19919	$1.75
Rule Britannia Daphne du Maurier	19547	$1.50
Play of Darkness Irving A. Greenfield	19877	$1.50
Facing the Lions Tom Wicker	19307	$1.75
High Empire Clyde M. Brundy	18994	$1.75
The Kingdom L. W. Henderson	18978	$1.75
The Last of the Southern Girls Willie Morris	18614	$1.50
The Wolf and the Dove Kathleen E. Woodiwiss	18457	$1.75
The Priest Ralph McInerny	18192	$1.75
Sweet Savage Love Rosemary Rogers	17988	$1.75
I'm OK—You're OK Thomas A. Harris, M.D.	14662	$1.95
Jonathan Livingston Seagull Richard Bach	14316	$1.50

Where better paperbacks are sold, or directly from the publisher. Include 15¢ per copy for mailing; allow three weeks for delivery.

Avon Books, Mail Order Dept., 250 West 55th Street, New York, N.Y. 10019

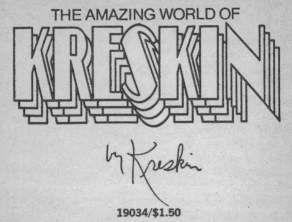